# A REAL
# GOODE TIME

## GOODE GIRLS

# Jasinda Wilder

# A REAL
# GOODE TIME

# ONE

## Torie

"TOR, THIS IS STUPID." MY ROOMMATE, LEIGHTON, WAS sitting on my bed watching me shove random shit into a backpack. "Just ask your sister for a plane ticket. How far do you think you're gonna get on three hundred bucks? Jillie and me can manage your part of the rent, and my cousin said she'll take your room 'til you come back, so that's no problem. So we're fine. But three hundred bucks? If you're lucky, you'll make it to Cleveland, and that's a big "if." You're a beautiful twenty-year-old girl, Torie. And you're gonna hitchhike to Alaska?"

Leighton pretended to talk into her cell phone, "Oh, hi, Mr. Serial Killer. Yes, I'm hitchhiking from New Haven to Alaska all by myself."

I rolled my eyes at her. "Leighton, quit worrying. I'll be fine."

"You're talking as if you're taking an Uber," Leighton replied.

Leighton was somewhat prone to dramatics.

Short, with short platinum blond hair and blue eyes and a curvy figure I'd kill for, Leighton was a bit of an alarmist and a whole lot of pessimist. She had a black belt in two martial arts, and she'd tried several times to get me to go to classes with her, but I didn't like the idea. I just wanted to believe that good karma and good luck would be with me. I'd never been mugged, or worse, walking to my car from the restaurant where I worked. When my car gave up the ghost a few months ago, I started biking everywhere. The trip from work to home is two-plus miles each way, and I've never had cause for concern.

Jillie, my other roommate, arrived at that moment—Jillie was the bridge between Leighton and me. Where Leighton was always ready for the worst, and overprepared for everything, I was a little too easygoing, never prepared for anything, and took things as they came. I was tall and thin with jet-black hair and had basically no curves at all. Jillie wasn't blasé and a procrastinator like me, but she didn't see the worst in everything like Leighton—she was the epitome of a peacemaker, really—and was medium height, medium build, with brunette hair.

"You're really going through with this?" she asked, sitting beside Leighton on my bed.

"I have to," I said. "It's my sister's wedding. I have to be there."

"Yeah, but…just ask them to fly you in. There's no shame in accepting help from your own family." Jillie eyed my backpack. "That's all you're taking?"

I sighed and set my backpack down on the floor and sat beside it. "You don't know what my family is like."

Leighton and Jillie both rolled their eyes at me, in near-unison. "Yes, we do," Leighton said. "We've both met your mom, and all your sisters. And they're nice. They love you. They wouldn't think twice about flying you up for Lexie's wedding."

I shook my head. "You don't understand. They're all successful. Even my younger sister is more successful than me. I'm such a failure. I can't even afford a plane ticket for my own sister's wedding, and it would just kill me to ask them for help."

"You're *twenty*, Tor. That hardly makes you a failure. You're just getting started in life."

I rolled a shoulder, uncomfortable with this line of conversation. "I hate asking for, or accepting, help. Especially from my sisters. I can figure this out on my own…and I will."

"I just don't know that this is the smartest way to try to get to Alaska," Jillie said. "It really is asking for trouble."

"What she really means is this is fucking idiotic and you're going to get raped and murdered. We're going to find out when you're on the evening news, or worse yet, we won't find out at all because you'll just vanish."

"Well, shit, Leighton," I groaned. "Thanks for that."

"You can't just wander out of here and hope good luck and positive thoughts will keep you safe, sweetie," Leighton said. "Walking, hitchhiking, whatever…is stupid. You're going to ALASKA, not New York. If you were like, I'm hitchhiking to New York; I'd be like, go girl. But you're talking about motherfucking ALASKA, clear across the continent, and halfway to the North fucking Pole."

I laughed. "It's not halfway to the North Pole, Ley."

"Yeah-huh, it is. Look at a map. From where we are to Alaska, you're closer to the North Pole than you are the Equator."

"Whatever. I'm doing it." I pawed through my backpack—two pair of jeans tightly rolled, four T-shirts, a sports bra just in case, some shorts for sleeping in, a handful of thongs wadded up into a ball at the bottom, some feminine hygiene products, hairbrush, my phone charger, half my cash rolled up into a rubber band, a pair of sandals, a bath towel, a few pair of socks, some protein bars, a box of mixed nuts in individual snack packs, and my dad's old Leatherman; I didn't own any kind of formal wear, so I'd just borrow something from one of my sisters or Mom when I got there. I would wear my heavy boots and a thick hoodie, and the rest of my cash would be in my pocket, along with my license. I had exactly three hundred and twenty-nine dollars to my name and a brand-new passport; I didn't know you had to have a passport to go to Canada until Mom told me. Luckily, I was able to get a quick turnaround on it. I'd never been anywhere in my life, and having this passport made me realize what a big world we all live in.

I'd done a Google search on Jillie's laptop, and a one-way Greyhound ticket from here in New Haven, Connecticut to Columbus, Ohio leaving Friday—tomorrow—would be two hundred and some dollars. It'd be cheaper if I booked farther out, but I wanted to leave tomorrow. That would get me almost halfway across the continent. Maybe in Columbus I could find some work for cash under the table so I could scrounge another ticket.

For a brief time, I actually thought I could work my way to Alaska…in less than two weeks.

That may have been one of my more stupid ideas.

But I was determined to do this on my own. To prove to myself, and to my sisters and my Mom, that I could do things on my own, and that I wasn't a complete airhead.

Growing up, I'd been the invisible one. Tagging along with Cassie and her dance friends, or worse, with Poppy and weird band of art class dorks. Or sitting at home, alone, while Lexie and Cassie and Mom were at their various lessons, and Charlie was doing cool, successful oldest golden child stuff, and Poppy was in the studio painting. Yes—we had a studio for her. When it was clear Poppy had real talent and a passion for painting, Dad had built her a "studio" in the backyard. Little more than a garden shed with windows, it was her pride and joy, her favorite place.

Everyone was always away at school, or at lessons, or with friends, or busy at home with their hobbies and their passions.

I had none of that, and no special friends. I was always just...there, at home.

Then, one by one, everyone left home. Charlie for college and life on her own, Cassie for Julliard, Lexie for U-Conn, Poppy for Columbia University, and then finally even Mom left for Alaska. Leaving me alone in New Haven to fend for myself.

I wasn't bitter about it, really I wasn't.

I finally looked over at my roommates. My best friends. "Guys, look. I…I can't ask them for help and I won't. I know this is a little nuts. I do. It's not like I'm some naive little girl hoping to find Prince Charming on a magical road trip adventure. I'm not that girl. I have major creep radar, and I don't trust anyone. I'm not getting in a car with anyone I don't have a good feeling about. I'll be okay. I just…I *have* to do this on my own. I know you don't really understand, but I hope you can respect my decision."

Jillie slid down to sit on the floor across from me. "Of course we understand, Torie. I don't talk to my family, and Leighton doesn't have one for all intents and purposes, so we *get* being independent. But there's a difference between independence and foolishness. We're your best friends, Tor. We love you. We just want you to be safe."

"I will be."

Leighton joined us on the floor. "You just have to call us every day, okay? Promise. You call one or the other of us every single day, no matter what. If you miss a single check-in, we're calling the police."

"Since I'm going across state lines, I think you'd have to call the FBI, and I don't think they start looking until someone is missing for, like, forty-eight or seventy-two hours." I zipped up my backpack. "But, yeah, I promise I'll check in every day."

"What time?" Jillie asked.

I shrugged. "I dunno. Whenever I stop for the day?"

Leighton shook her head. "It has to be at the same time every day. Like, nine p.m. Eastern. We're both usually home by then."

I nodded. "Okay, nine it is. I'll group FaceTime you."

"Memorize our numbers," Leighton said. "So if your phone dies, you can borrow someone's phone."

I snorted. "Who memorizes phone numbers anymore?"

"You do, now."

I laughed. "I don't think I even know my own number by heart, if you want to know the truth."

Jillie wasn't laughing. "You're always forgetting to charge your phone. And what if you're, like, not near a charger? You're doing this with three hundred and thirty dollars, Torie. You gonna get a hotel room? Not likely."

"Stop trying to freak me out with details." I tried to make it a joke, but it fell flat.

"Details like where you sleep at night and, oh, random shit like not being *raped and murdered?*"

"Would you stop with the raped and murdered shit, Ley? For real." I tossed the backpack to the foot of my bed and flopped onto my back. "I'm going to make it to Ketchikan in one piece, and on time, for my sister's wedding. It's going to be fine. I'll be fine."

"You sound like you're trying to convince yourself more than us," Jillie said.

"Maybe a little bit."

Leighton lay down beside me, Jillie on the other side. Leighton dug in her jeans pocket, brought out a small Ziploc bag with a single fat green nugget of pot inside. "We're just as broke as you are, so we can't give you money, but we went in together to get you this."

I took the bag and unzipped a corner. Sniffed. "Ohh, wow. No way! This is from Steelie, isn't it?"

"Yeah." Leighton's voice was tight.

"Ley. What'd you do?"

She pulled out a small glass pipe and a different baggie, pinched a tiny bit off and rolled it between her forefinger and thumb to grind it into the bowl. "Nothing."

"Ley."

"What?"

"Steelie's prices are insane," I said. "No way you two broke-ass bitches could afford this."

Steelie was our neighbor who lived one house over. He grew and sold some of the best pot in the whole New Haven area. One smell and you knew it was his crop. Sticky, potent, fragrant. And expensive as hell. One nugget of this size from Steelie was worth at least thirty bucks. And when you're living life on the edge of broke, that's too much for an extra like pot. We usually got ours from Mario, a dishwasher at the bar where Jillie worked, and it was...well...of far inferior quality, and thus *much* cheaper.

Leighton just shrugged again. "I cleaned his house. That's it."

"Promise?" I looked at her sideways.

Leighton had been on her own since she was sixteen and had, in the past, been known to do some shady shit to get by, accounting for her general outlook on life.

She nodded, meeting my eyes—I saw honesty there. "I'm telling the truth. I cleaned his house and let me tell you, he got the deal. I did *way* more than thirty bucks worth of work just on his bathroom. The dude grows good herb, but he's a fucking slob."

"You didn't have to do that," I said. "But thank you."

She handed me the bowl and a lighter. "I got that nugget, and an extra pinch, which is what's in there." She grinned at me. "Call it a going away present."

"I'm coming back," I said. "It's not goodbye."

Leighton shook her head. "No, this is goodbye. I can feel it in my nuggets."

I laughed—one of our favorite movies to watch stoned was *Surf's Up*, an animated movie about a surfing penguin, and she'd just quoted one of our favorite lines.

"I'm coming back," I insisted. "Soon as the wedding is over."

"Light it up, Tor," Jillie said, and I did, taking a long hit then handing it to Leighton. "I agree with Ley. This feels like goodbye."

"It's *not* goodbye," I said, after exhaling a thick cloud of smoke.

"Your whole family is there," Leighton said, holding the smoke in. She exhaled, speaking around the plume of smoke. "Why would you come back here when everyone you know and love is there?"

"You guys are here," I said.

Jillie took the pipe from Leighton, hit it, and handed it to me. "That's sweet, babe, but we're your roommates. They're your family."

"You're like family, though."

"Just…" Leighton sighed. "Just remember that we love you and we'll miss you, but we know you're staying in Ketchikan, so when you have that argument with yourself, remind yourself that we already know you're staying, so don't worry about us."

I frowned at her. "I think that made sense. Maybe."

"Shut up, you know what I mean." She laughed. "Shit, Steelie's stuff is *potent*."

"That's why he named it Sledgehammer," Jillie said. "But I know what Leighton means, Tor. Just keep in mind that you have our blessing to move to Ketchikan to be with your family."

"I don't *want* to move to fucking Alaska," I said, sighing. "They all left me here, so I'm staying here."

Leighton and Jillie exchanged glances over me.

"What?" I demanded.

"I just don't think you've ever admitted that in so many words," Leighton said.

There was enough left for one more hit each, and then Leighton put her pipe away and we all lay on the floor, floating pleasantly.

"Admit what?" I asked, after a comically long delay.

Jillie snorted a laugh. "That you're bitter about being left here."

"Oh." I blinked. "Ohhh. Wow. Yeah, you're right. I guess maybe that's why I'm being such a pain in the ass about this trip up there."

"At least you can admit you're being a pain in the ass about it," Leighton said.

"It would be much easier if my stupid pride would let me just call Lex for a plane ticket. Shit, I think her fiancé has his own jet. He could pick me up in style. But *nooo*, I have to be all miss independent and shit."

I groaned. "I don't know how to make it make sense to you guys…or even to myself. I just…I have to do it on my own."

"I guess just look at it as, like, a spirit journey or something," Jillie suggested.

"I'm not Native American," I pointed out.

"Maybe it's a gap year then," Leighton said.

"What? A gap year from *not* going to college?"

"Okay, well, whatever. You're doing it the stupid way, and we've done everything we can as your friends to get you to be smart about this. But I ran away from home at sixteen and I made it all right. Jillie was homeless for a whole year, and she's okay. So I suppose you'll probably be fine. Just check in every night at nine, no excuses."

"I promise," I said.

"Have you told Max?" Jillie asked, a few minutes later.

I groaned. "Shit. No, I haven't."

"Are you going to?"

"I dunno, I probably should, but I haven't seen him for a couple of weeks," I said.

"Are you ever going to sleep with him?" Leighton said.

"No, but I bet he wishes I would."

Jillie rolled to lay on her side, head propped on her hand. "Why won't you?"

I shrugged. "It was never going to be Max. I've known him since second grade. I know we, like, mess around, but it's…I want to say platonic, but that's not quite right. It's fun. It's messing around. But I'm not sleeping with him. If I was going to, I would have done it a long time ago."

"That's a weird situation, I have to say." Leighton rolled onto her belly and stared at me. "So, random question."

I laughed, because her random questions when stoned were usually good ones. "Okay, shoot."

"So, would you ever say you and Max were dating?"

"No. No way."

"And you never will?"

"Nope."

She smirked at me. "So if I were to admit that I think he's cute, and that I have little crush on him… what would you say?"

"Ley, are you serious?"

"You're leaving." She shrugged. "I'd never do anything with him if you said it would bother you. I just think he's cute."

"He *is* cute," I said. I considered her questions. "But he's my best friend. Not in the same way you guys are my best friends. It's different. He's my *oldest* friend, I guess that's more accurate. But…if you were to date him, you'd sleep with him. And that would be kind of weird."

"Why?"

"Because we'd both have intimate knowledge of his penis," I said.

"You said you've never slept with him," Jillie pointed out.

"No, I haven't. But we mess around. All but sex, basically. Usually just…hands. And sometimes mouths. That's it."

"You've gone down on him?" Leighton asked, sitting up to face me.

"I'm not talking about this with you," I said.

But my blush gave me away. My pasty-white skin turned bright pink when I was embarrassed or turned on.

"You have!" Leighton shrieked. "Okay, so I can see how it would be a little weird for both of you to have had the same guy's penis in your mouths."

"Ohmygod, gross," I said. "Don't say it like that."

She cackled. "What? You can do it, but not talk about it?"

I laughed, covering my face with both hands. "It's weird. Max and I never talk about what we do together, physically. It's always been, like, not secret, but…just…a thing we do that we don't talk about or reference. And it's always at his apartment, always at night. And I always come home right after."

Leighton chuckled. "You need to get laid, girlfriend."

"I've waited this long for it to be right," I said, "I may as well keep holding out until the right guy comes along."

"But what's right, Torie? How will you know? Some magical sensation in your hoo-ha?" Leighton snorted. "And trust me, your first time ain't something to write home about."

"I'd be an adult," I said, approaching this delicately, "and it'd be…voluntary."

"Not a child and against your will?" she muttered. "Like poor little ol' me?"

"Not how I meant it, but…yeah, basically."

She was quiet a long time. "Well, Tor, for your sake, I do hope your first time ends up being worth the wait. I really do."

"And, for my part," Jillie added, "I agree with you, Torie—you've waited this long, so keep waiting for the right guy at the right time. For it to be worth it. Just don't give it away cheap."

I sighed. "That's the plan."

"But first," Leighton said, "get to Alaska without getting raped and murdered."

"Yeah, that too," I said.

Friday afternoon, 4:00 p.m., after a midday shift.

Mr. Sokoli, my boss, had given me the okay to take time off—I'd told him I'd be gone something like three weeks, and that I'd call him if I needed more time. I'd worked for him part-time and full-time since I turned fourteen, so I had a guaranteed job at his restaurant pretty much whenever I wanted.

I'd checked the bus times last night, so I knew I had plenty of time to walk to the Greyhound station from the restaurant and buy a ticket as far as half of my cash would take me.

I said goodbye to everyone at the restaurant and I set out. It started out pleasantly enough—cool and overcast, but a good day for walking. I had earbuds for my phone, but I didn't use them. I wanted to preserve the battery life of my phone, as it was old and prone to dying pretty quickly.

It was six miles to the bus station, and I figured I'd need an hour and a half or two to get there. As I was nearing an hour in—too far to turn back but barely halfway there, the overcast sky began to darken from a slate gray to a heavy, threatening, sullen coal color.

The wind picked up.

The cool day turned almost cold.

I felt a droplet of rain on my head. "No." I stopped, and stared up at the sullen, blackening sky. "No, don't you dare."

*Drip-drip. Dripdripdrip.*

*SPLAT.*

*SPLATSPLATSPLATSPLAT.*

I whimpered. "You bitch," I said, staring up into the rain, which turned into steady fat drops. "You absolute and utter bitch."

I was in the middle of suburbia with nowhere to duck in and wait out the rain.

I slogged on, tugging my hood up.

What only moments before had been a steady rain was quickly worsening into a downpour. My boots began to squelch. My hair started to feel damp even under my hood. The wind blew buckets of cold rain sideways, splattering and battering me. Within a hundred yards I was as soaked as could be.

Within half a mile, I couldn't get any wetter if I jumped into a pool.

I was shivering, angry, and cursing my luck.

Even if I called Lex right now and begged for help, I'd have to turn around and walk back home, and this rain did not look like it was going to let up anytime soon. So, I was screwed. I may as well carry on with the plan, and just get used to being wet.

I still had another couple of miles to go, and then I had a bus ride in wet clothes to look forward to. My backpack was probably soaked, along with everything in it, so I'd have no dry clothes to change into.

What a stellar start to the trip this was turning out to be.

A car flew past, spraying me.

I finally turned onto a main road and every few seconds another car sped past, flinging muddy water onto me. So now I was muddy, dirty, *and* wet.

Super.

It's hard to not to be depressed in a situation like this—wet, alone, cold.

I was wallowing in poor-me thoughts, bemoaning my shit luck, my shit life, my shit self.

*Splash*—another vehicle bashed through a giant puddle; this time it was a semi, and if I'd thought I was soaked to the bone before, I was even wetter now.

"FUCK YOU!" I screamed at the semi.

Immediately behind the semi was a giant red jeep—an older one, with a lift kit and huge mud tires and a flapping soft top.

Instead of barreling past me and splashing me, the Jeep slowed, went another twenty yards or so, and then rolled to a stop.

My heart leapt, skittered—I desperately wanted to hitch a ride, but for all my blasé assurances to Jillie and Leighton that I'd be fine, the idea of getting into a car with a stranger made my knees quivery and my palms tingly. Leighton's parting words this morning rang in my head: *"Remember, priority number one is don't get raped and murdered!"*

I approached the red Jeep with trepidation. The emergency flashers were on, and the driver's side door flew open. A long, lean leg and hip emerged, followed by the rest of a hard male body in a mechanic's coverall, the upper portion knotted around his waist, leaving a plain black T-shirt on his upper body. He jogged around to the passenger side and yanked open the door as I approached.

"Hop in!" he said, with a distinct southern twang to his voice. "Ain't a fit day for man or beast, let alone a pretty lady like you."

The most mesmerizing puppy dog brown eyes I'd ever seen in my life looked me over, met my eyes. His smile was wide and genuine, with an amused quirk to his lips. Sharp features, hawk nose, chiseled, granite jaw, expressive lips, a two- or three-day stubble. Jet-black hair, messy, sexy in a don't-give-a-shit-what-I-look-like way. Just-fucked hair begging to have my hands run through it.

Those eyes, though.

Amused. Intelligent. One long look into his eyes told me he'd be funny and sharp-witted, quick with a comeback.

Shit.

My savior had to be the single hottest male I'd ever laid eyes on. Of course.

I climbed up into the Jeep, slid onto a cushy black leather bucket seat, tossed my backpack into the foot well, and reached for the seat belt…only to discover it was a complicated five-point racing harness.

My savior closed the door after me and jogged around the hood, hopped up into the driver's seat, clicked his five-point harness into place, shoved the clutch down with his foot and smacked the shifter into first.

He grinned at me, extending his right hand to shake mine. "Name's Rhys." He pronounced it *Reez*, with the final sound somewhere between a soft S and a hard Z.

Holy moly. That grin. Those eyes.

This was bad.

My belly was flipping, my knees pressed together, and my hoo-ha was taking notice of the way the black T-shirt was molded to his lean, lithe, iron-hard body.

"Hi." I swallowed. "I'm Torie. Thanks for stopping."

"Pleasure," he said. "So. Where to?"

I laughed. "Alaska?"

# TWO

## Rhys

GOD ALMIGHTY, THE GIRL WAS THE SINGLE WETTEST human I'd ever laid eyes on that wasn't in a swimming pool. She was wearing a thick black North Face hoodie, tight, faded jeans, and Timberland boots, and she was absolutely dripping wet. To call her a drowned rat would be generous to drowned rats. In fact, I'd seen folks come out of pools less wet than this chick.

Despite this, with her soaked hood drawn forward, black hair pasted to her cheeks, she was the most stunning girl I'd ever seen. I'd used the pretty lady line out of what you might call habitual southern charm, having not really gotten a good look at her. I mean, I'd noticed her tight backside as she'd climbed into the Jeep, and there was no mistaking the taut sway of an ass like hers for anything but that of a hot young thing.

She was tall, only a few inches shy of my six feet. She was slender, but not frail. Couldn't tell much more about her body due to the heavy sweatshirt she was wearing, but her eyes spoke of equal parts sadness and humor, and I had trouble looking away in order to check over my left shoulder.

"Alaska, huh?" I chuckled. "Not sure I can go quite that far."

She shrugged. "Nearest Greyhound station would be fine."

I knew where that was, so I headed in that direction. "You're serious? Alaska?"

She nodded, and pushed her hood back. Her hair was crazy long, black as mine. It'd be thick and glossy, if it were dry. She pushed it away from her face, and her hands came away dripping. "Yeah, seriously, Alaska. My mom and a couple of my sisters live up there, and my one sister is getting married, so I gotta get to Alaska."

"A bus'd take…shit, days. Not even sure a bus goes directly there." I rubbed my jaw. "Better to just fly, I'd think."

"Flying is not exactly in the budget," she said.

"Your sisters or your mom can't help?"

The annoyed huff she gave me was an indicator that I'd just stepped into something smelly. "I'm sure they would, if I asked. But I won't ask."

I nodded. "That I get. Gotta make it on your own two feet, I guess, huh?"

She eyed me sideways. "Yeah. Something like that."

"So…you really want me to take you to the bus station?" I asked.

"Yeah, why?"

I tapped the round analog clock in the dashboard—5:26. "Pretty sure departing buses will have left already."

"I checked before I left work and there's one at six thirty."

I shrugged. "I mean, there might be."

Six thirty in the morning, I thought, but didn't say.

She didn't respond, so I left it. One time I'd looked into taking a bus to see my folks in Lexington, Kentucky, and I knew most buses traveling west left in the morning.

But, if she wanted to go to the bus station, I'd take her to the bus station.

We got there in about fifteen minutes, and I parked as close to the doors as I could get, noting the lack of buses. She eyed the parking lot.

"Not too many people here," she said.

I didn't want to insult her, so I said nothing; she seemed like she was having a rough enough time without me adding snarky comments. She glanced at me. "Well, Rhys, thanks for picking me up."

"Pleasure," I said. "Good luck getting to Alaska."

"Yeah, I'll need it."

She took a breath, shoved open the door and hopped down, closed it, and walked over to the front doors. I was about to take off when I noticed she'd left her backpack in the foot well. Plus, I knew she wasn't going anywhere tonight.

I couldn't leave her here. Sleeping in a bus station sucks.

Crap.

So, I waited.

A few minutes later, she yanked the doors open and exited the bus station, standing in the rain, head down, shoulders shaking.

Dammit, she was crying.

She hadn't noticed I was still here.

I put the Jeep in Neutral and yanked on the parking brake, leaned across the passenger seat to unzip the passenger window. "Hey! Torie!" I shouted, and then zipped it back up.

Her head whipped up, and she saw me. The shaking of her shoulders paused, and she came over and got back in the Jeep.

The Jeep was suddenly full of her, again. Wet girl, and sniffles. "You waited."

"You weren't going anywhere," I said. "Buses to points more'n a couple hours from here leave in the morning." I pointed at her backpack. "Plus, you forgot your bag."

"Yeah, I noticed that as I stood at the counter wondering what the fuck I was gonna do." She groaned. "The bus left at six thirty in the *morning*, not in the evening." She laughed, bitterly. "I guess that's what I get for checking bus times when I'm stoned." Her head thunked back against the leather seat. "Now what do I do? Go back home and try again tomorrow?"

"You could."

"I'd have to start walking at like, four in the morning to make a six-thirty bus."

I winced. "Oof. That'd suck." I gestured at the rain. "Especially since this shit is supposed to go on till, like, Wednesday."

"Fuck." She whacked her head back against the seat again. "I *have* to get to Alaska. My sister's wedding is in two weeks. I have three hundred and twenty-nine dollars to my name, and I've only got that much because my roommates said they'd cover my share of rent this month. I have no car, and I won't ask for help from my family."

I've always had an issue with my mouth running ahead of my brain. Case in point:

"I don't live too far from here. Stay with me. I'll drive you over in the morning." I realized she might think I was coming onto her and, I mean, she wouldn't have been entirely wrong. But still. "I have a pull-out couch. I don't mean anything...forward."

She turned away. "I...I couldn't impose on you like that."

"Not imposing if I offer," I said. "I live alone. I have the hide-a-bed couch. You'd be close to the bus station and you'd have a guaranteed ride." I grinned. "Plus, I make a mean pot of coffee."

She laughed. "Is it weird if your offer of coffee is what changes my mind?"

"Nah," I said, laughing with her. "I go to bed dreaming of coffee in the morning."

She was staring at me. Searching, looking for something in me. To see if I was safe, maybe. "I have an older sister. I hope someone will help her out if she ever needs it. That's it."

"My roommates would not approve."

"What about your family?"

"Well, what they don't know won't hurt them."

"What about your roommates?"

"Yeah, well, I promised to check in with them every night at nine."

"I'll talk to 'em, if it'll put 'em at ease."

She nodded. "Yeah, maybe. If you let Leighton interrogate you, though, you may end up regretting that offer."

I was already half regretting offering to let her stay at my place. She needed the help and I didn't regret offering. I just knew it'd be hell on my libido being a gentleman, and something told me she wasn't in a place where she'd want me making a move on her.

I wanted to, though. And that was even before sleeping under the same roof. And shit, I'd offer her my shower, because that's the nice thing to do.

I'm an idiot.

I was already halfway home by this point, and I couldn't take the offer back, so I'd just have to do my best to be decent, keep my hands to myself, and not let my dick run away from my manners like my mouth does my brain.

Problem is, my dick and my mouth have similar issues, and this chick was proving to be havoc on my impulse control.

We were at my place in less than ten minutes, and I pulled to a stop outside the building. I could tell she was confused: I lived in a tiny loft apartment tucked into the top back corner of a small warehouse. I owned the warehouse, which was where I ran my business. But from the outside, it just looked like a generic square of metal in an otherwise industrial area.

"You…live in a warehouse?"

"Sort of," I said. "C'mon, I'll show you."

She grabbed her backpack this time and followed me out of the Jeep and through the rain to the huge garage door. I grabbed the handle and pushed in, flicked on the overhead lights, and gestured at the shop. "So this is what I do."

She stood up, backpack dangling from one shoulder. A gorgeous black '74 Nova SS, raked, with wide back tires sat menacing and sleek on the floor, hood up. My work light hung from the open hood, my rolling toolbox nearby, wrenches and sockets scattered on the top.

"You're a mechanic?"

"Among other things, yes."

She eyed me. "You can't be old enough to have your own shop, and do work like that."

I laughed. "I've been working on cars since I was a kid, and I had some money saved for a down payment. I don't do bodywork, I just do engines. Tuning, rebuilding, maintaining, that kinda thing. And, honestly, I don't usually do muscle, I'm more of a trucks and 4x4s guy. Do most of my work on big block V-8s and old diesels and in-line sixes and shit." I gestured at the Nova. "But the owner of this baby heard of me through a friend and he wanted his 440 tuned for some extra horses, and I'm not gonna turn down work I'm more'n capable of doing."

She took in the shop—a hydraulic lift, an engine hoist, several different rolling toolboxes, an air compressor and impact drill, and the various equipment and machinery required for engine work. In the back corner sat my pet project: a 1949 Ford F-1, currently half disassembled. It was, ostensibly, baby blue, but was dirty and old and had a lot of surface rust. Once I rebuilt the engine, transmission, and exhaust system, I'd have it sandblasted and repainted and then I'd replace the front bench and she'd be good to go.

Basically, I had a shitload of work to do on it.

"How old are you?" Torie asked.

"Twenty-six."

She shook her head. "And you have your own business?"

"My dad was a mechanic at a gas station, and my ma was a waitress, so I spent most of my childhood in that gas station shop helping Dad. We didn't have much, so if I wanted anything, I had to work for it. Trouble is, even in the boonies of Kentucky, most folks won't hire a nine-year-old. So I started figuring out ways to earn money on my own."

"Like?"

I laughed, self-conscious. "Well…when I was

nine, I found a five dollar bill on the ground. Being nine, I wanted the one thing a nine-year-old boy would think to buy: candy. The most candy I could get for five bucks from the dollar store was an old bag of assorted Halloween candy. I put the candy in my backpack and sold it for fifty cents apiece. It was a fifty-piece bag, so I made twenty-five bucks. I went out and bought two more bags, sold the candy for seventy-five cents apiece, and made almost seventy-five bucks. Bought three bags, and sold the candy for a buck a piece." I chuckled. "I was a ruthless little shit, now that I think about it."

"So you found a five-dollar bill and turned it into more than a hundred dollars by reselling candy?" She sounded impressed. Which I admit did feel pretty good.

"Yeah…until I got shut down by the principal. She said if she caught me selling anything else on school property, I'd get suspended."

Torie laughed. "Let me guess…you found a loophole?"

I shrugged. "Sort of. By that point, my client base was sort of tapped out. I mean, little kids can only scrounge up so much loose change, and I'd gotten greedy, charging a dollar apiece. I spent some time collecting bottles and cans around town, and even tried setting up a system where I would pay neighborhood kids to collect for me, but that was too much to keep track of: who I owed, how much, and how much to pay them and still make a profit."

She snorted. "You're a real natural-born entrepreneur, huh?"

"I mean, we were dirt poor. I was stuck wearing my dad's old six-sizes-too-big boots and my sister's old jeans cut off into shorts. So yeah, if I wanted to buy lunch at school, I had to find money, because god knew my parents could barely afford rent with them both working two jobs. They often had to decide between keeping the lights on and buying food every month." Out of habit, or instinct, I'd wandered over to the Nova and started tinkering with it; Torie followed, leaning against the side of the hood and watching.

She was watching me mess with the radiator, and circled around to the toolbox, rummaged through the sockets with what seemed like a knowledgeable eye, and handed me the correct size socket.

I eyed her. "You've worked on cars."

She shrugged. "Sort of. My dad liked to tinker in the garage on the weekends. He had an old…oh what the hell was it? Two letter name. English, I think."

"MG?" I suggested.

"Yeah, that's it. It was little two-door convertible he bought for cheap from a neighbor. I'm not sure

what he was doing on it, honestly. He'd go out there
early Saturday morning after breakfast and I'd go with
him, and he drink coffee and putz with the car, and
I'd hand him wrenches and sockets, and sometimes if
there was a spot too small for his big old sausage fingers to get to, he'd have me try. I got to know which
size bolt was which, and I made it my job to keep his
tools organized, because on his own he would just
lose everything." She laughed at what was clearly a
fond memory. "That was my special time with Dad,
those Saturdays and Sundays in the garage."

"Did he ever finish it?"

She grinned. "I don't think he was really doing
anything important to it. Replacing hoses or something. Just…tinkering. It ran, and it always did run.
We'd spend a few hours tinkering, and then we'd go
for a drive. 'To test it out,' he would always say. Maybe
he was just making sure what he'd done worked, or
something."

"Sounds like a lot of fun, honestly."

She nodded. "It was. Probably among my favorite memories." There was a wistfulness to her voice.

"I, uh. Don't want to bring up anything bad since
you've already had a bad day, but…it sounds like
you're talking in past tense, here."

She smiled at me. "Yeah, he died a few years ago."

I winced. "Sorry to hear that."

"Thanks. It was sudden. Pretty rough on all of us, but Mom most of all."

"I bet. You guys were all close, I take it?"

She shrugged again. "I mean, early on, yeah, I'd say so. By the time I got to high school, things were a little…strained, I guess. He wasn't healthy, and it was a sore spot for Mom. Then he died, and she ended up moving to Alaska to start over and it seems like all my sisters are gradually ending up there. And now I have to go up there for this wedding, and I'm scared I'm gonna get stuck up there too."

"You don't want to?"

She shook her head. "No. What the hell is there for me in fucking Alaska? My friends are here. My job, such as it is, is here."

"Why do you say 'such as it is'?" I asked.

I was struggling to get a bolt started in a small space; she moved in beside me, and slid her small hand in the engine bay, threaded the bolt, fitted a ratcheting wrench to the bolt, and tightened it. She smelled like wet hair, wet clothes, and something else indefinable but feminine and intoxicating.

Another shrug, laconic. "Waiting tables is not the best job. I barely make ends meet, and it's a dead end. But th-that's a different conversation." She shivered, teeth chattering.

I huffed. "Shit, I'm an asshole, keeping you out

here talking while you're dripping wet. God, I'm sorry. Let's go upstairs. You can take a shower and borrow some sweats from me while your stuff dries out."

A look of longing crossed her face when I mentioned a shower. "God, a hot shower would be amazing."

I led her to the stairs in the back that led up to a small loft apartment occupying a few hundred square feet over the back end of the warehouse; it had originally been an office, but some enterprising soul in years past had added a small shower, a sliver of a closet, and a separate entrance and exit at the side, as well as a kitchenette. It was all open, even the bathroom was not completely closed off. It was a space clearly meant for one person only, which worked for me.

I'd left a hunk of meat roasting in a Crock-Pot this morning, and so the whole loft smelled wonderfully of a hot dinner.

"Holy shit," Torie moaned, "that smells amazing."

"We pretty much lived on Crock-Pot roasts. She got a Crock-Pot at a thrift store for, like, ten bucks, buy an about-to-expire shoulder roast from the grocery story, she'd put it in there in the morning before she left for work and by the time Dad was done working and I was home from school, it'd be done. I can't cook for shit, but I know how to crockpot the hell out of a roast."

She inhaled deeply, eyes closed. "My mom used to do roasts every Sunday, but she did them in the oven in some sort of special pan. I always looked forward to Sunday roasts."

"Well, there's six pounds of roast beef shoulder in there, so I hope you're hungry." I brought her to the bathroom, which, as I've said, was only nominally partitioned off from the rest of the loft—the toilet was in its own little closet, but the shower was glassed in, and the sink, mirror, and cabinets were all open to the loft. "I'll, um…I'll grab you some of my clothes and then head downstairs so you can shower. As you can see, there ain't a lot of privacy."

She just nodded, setting her bag down on the bathroom floor. I grabbed a pair of sweatpants I'd had since high school which were the smallest I owned, and a T-shirt I'd had since middle school, which I kept for sentimental reasons since it didn't fit me.

"These ought to do the job," I said, setting the clothes on the closed toilet lid. "The hot water tank is industrial size from downstairs, so you can stay in there as long as you want, you won't run out of hot water. But watch out, that shit gets scalding hot in a hurry. I only have guy shit in there, three-in-one body wash and shampoo and all that."

"No girlfriend keeping her shampoo here?"

Fishing, I see. "Nah, no girlfriend or nothin'."

She shrugged, smiled. "Well, clean is clean, and beggars can't be choosers."

"Right." I shuffled away, trying like hell to not wish I could see what she looked like out of those baggy wet clothes. "Well, I, um…I can hear the water from downstairs, so I'll wait till I hear it shut off, give you a few more minutes, and then come up. And I'll knock before walking in. So you're comfortable."

Her smile of appreciation and gratitude was a sight to behold—it took her from drowned rat but sexy to just plain stunning. "You're awful polite, Rhys. I can't thank you enough."

"Well. You're in the home of a dude you just met. Don't want you to think I'm…creepy or nothin'."

"I won't be too long," she said. "I'm a short shower kinda girl."

"Take your time. Warm up." I turned away, and then a thought occurred to me and I turned back to Torie—and froze, mouth dropping open and then clacking shut as I saw her, whatever it was I'd been about to say utterly forgotten.

Torie had stripped her sweatshirt off, and was holding it out—it was dripping a steady stream of water. Damn, damn, and double damn—her T-shirt underneath was a plain heather gray V-neck, and it was soaked through. Absolutely sheer. She wasn't wearing a bra.

Call me an asshole, but I took a long, blatant look. I mean, it was impossible not to. Her nipples were peaked and hard, poking the fabric, and her breasts were outlined by see-through wet gray cotton. While technically not very large, her breasts were plump, sloping downward with pert nipples pointed upward; they were just begging to be cupped and lifted into my mouth…

Her eyes met mine, and I flinched. "I…um."

Her arms went across her chest. "Sorry, I didn't realize I'd be so, uh…"

"No, I'm sorry. I was just going to tell you something and then I forgot was it was. I'm—I'll go."

I turned on a dime and ran down the stairs to the garage to my Ford project. I slumped onto the floor, lay back on the creeper, and rolled under the truck, grabbing the nearby wrench and viciously attacking the bolts holding the exhaust pipe to the underbody.

"The fuck is wrong with me?" I snarled to myself, under my breath. "Picking up random chicks off the side of the road? I must be sick in the damn head."

I lost track of everything as I worked to rip the old exhaust system out. Didn't hear the water, or the lack thereof, I was too busy skinning my knuckles and swearing as I fought with the last stubborn piece of shit bolt, which was rusted on and refused to budge, even with a long-handled socket. I didn't want to have to grind the bastard off, as the plan was to restore the truck to as close to bone-stock factory original as possible.

"Rhys?" a soft, quiet voice.

I tend to get lost and forget everything when my I've got my head and hands in a truck, and this was no different. I'd forgotten all about Torie, and so when I heard her voice, I flinched hard enough to crack my head on the underbody, drawing blood for sure and eliciting a long series of snarled curses from me as I slid the creeper out from under the truck.

I sat up on the creeper and touched my forehead where I'd whanged it—no blood, but a decent lump.

Torie was holding back a grin. "That was like out of a movie." She crouched and peered at my head. "Just a little boo-boo. I'm sorry for startling you."

I shook my head. "Nah, I get distracted when I'm under a truck. Tend to block out the world."

"I'll say." She poked at my forehead gently, squatting on her heels. "I've been out of the shower for an hour."

I glanced over at the schoolhouse-type analog clock on the wall above the door. "No shit."

How the hell did she manage to smell feminine and sexy when she'd used *my* shampoo? Freshly showered woman is probably the most arousing scent on the planet, if you ask me.

Then I got a look at her—the sweatpants hung loose on her hips, highlighting the sharp V where her hips and belly angled in toward her sex, the waistband slung low enough to make me wonder if I'd get a glimpse of something more if she moved the wrong way. Despite having a tight, slender waist, her hips and ass filled out the old, stretchy cotton until the sweat pants fit her like a second skin, to the knees at least; she had the cinched cuffs tugged up to her knee, leaving her shins and feet bare. The shirt...shit, I shouldn't have given her that damn shirt to wear. My poor dick couldn't handle it. It was, stupidly on my part, a white shirt. A very old white shirt. Threadbare. It had holes in it, near the underarms and over the belly and chest. It sported the name and logo of my middle school in peeling letters.

If her tits had been on full display in her wet gray shirt, they were only slightly more concealed in that one, and the holes gave me tantalizing hints of skin and, on occasion, on the right side of her chest, I think there were even glimpses of the darker brown of her areola.

Shit, shit. She was just too damned perfect. She made my head feel tight and woozy, my chest thump, and my cock go ramrod stiff behind my coveralls. Thankfully, I had the upper part of the coveralls tied around my waist so the sleeves hung over my groin, hiding the evidence of my monster hard-on.

From one look at this girl, fully clothed, I had an erection so painful I had to hold back a wince.

Shit. This had been a mistake for sure. I was behind schedule on the Nova—I'd promised the owner I'd be done today, and I still had several hours of work left. I had salvage work to do, plus several hours of finishing work at the build site for Jeremy. Not to mention the online realtor class I was taking. Point being, I did *not* have time to waste on a random girl needing to get to Alaska.

Random *hot* girl. With amazing tits, sexy hips, and a bangin' ass.

Not to mention the vivid, light brown, almost khaki-colored eyes that drew me in like flies to honey.

Thick black hair, straight and glossy as a raven's wing, hanging well past mid-back, nearly to her butt. Loose, brushed, a wild jet fall of glory I wanted to sink my fingers into.

I reminded myself I didn't even know her last name and she was a damsel in distress. Not a hookup from the local bar.

She looked young—younger than me. Over eighteen, I fucking hoped. But probably not old enough to even go to a bar.

God, I'm an idiot.

"You just gonna stare at me, or do you have something to say?" she asked, her voice wry and amused.

I blinked, shook my head, turned away, tossing the wrench onto a nearby tool chest. "Sorry." I wanted to provide some kind of explanation for my asinine behavior, but I had none.

She was leaning against the bare steel column holding up the loft area. "Just wondering, if you have a lift, why you're not using it." She pointed at the hydraulic lift, capable of lifting several tons well overhead.

I kicked the whitewall tire of the truck. "This is a personal project, so I don't wanna tie up the lift in case I need it for a client."

"Oh. Makes sense." She walked around the truck, glanced into the open engine bay, into the cab. "What's your plan with this?"

"A full restoration, eventually. It's got a nice straight body, no rot, and just a little corrosion here and there, a few edges and corners to fix up. The engine is seized and the tranny is fucked, though, so I'm replacing both."

"What are you putting into it?"

I gestured at a motor sitting in a wooden crate. "A three-fifty-one V-8 from a seventy-seven Bronco I salvaged, with a rebuilt three-on-the-tree from another old Ford."

"You do a lot of salvaging?"

I swept a hand at the parts I had piled all over

the garage. "It's the other half of my business, and salvaging is actually where I really started in the automotive business. Soon as I could drive, I bought a beat-to-shit old wrecker, got it running, and started salvaging. I'd drive hours to get old wrecks off of lawns, out of backyards, from impound lots, wherever I could find 'em. Dad got his boss to let me use their shop after-hours, so I could strip the wrecks of usable parts, which I'd sell piecemeal to local garages, auto body shops, and dudes looking for parts for their pet projects." I tapped the motor on the truck in front of me. "I think I learned more about engines from taking them apart as I did from helping Dad fix them." I pointed at the back wall of the shop. "Out back is my salvage yard—I've got about fifty different vehicles out there that I need to strip, and I'm actually still running that old wrecker I got in high school. It's more replaced parts than original at this point, but she still runs."

She inhaled deeply. "The smell of this place brings back a lot of memories."

I grinned. "Best smell on earth, you ask me." I thought about the scent of freshly showered woman, which was higher on the totem pole than even an auto garage, but I wasn't about to say that to this chick. "Grease and metal and oil and...I don't even know what else, but it's the smell of home, to me."

At that moment, I heard the unmistakable sound of a stomach growling—Torie's.

I scoffed in annoyance at myself. "God, here I go again, running my idiot mouth while you're probably about to pass out from hunger."

"I am pretty hungry," she admitted. "But I...I don't want to—"

"Where I grew up," I cut in, "hospitality was a way of life. We didn't have much, but if we ever had a guest, we treated them like royalty with all we had. So you ain't imposing or asking or being needy—I'm insisting." I moved for the stairs. "Now come on and eat, before you faint."

I made sure to precede her up the stairs, or I'd spend the whole walk up staring at her ass, and she didn't need me ogling her backside, too. Again.

I pulled the roast out of the Crock-Pot, set it on a platter, and set about slicing it the way I'd watched Dad do countless times. I plated up two heaping portions, and set the plates on my little round table, which was about halfway between the kitchenette and the living room area.

"I don't do much by way of sides," I explained. "I tend to just eat the meat and not much else. Don't have the patience or the time for the other shit."

She just did that sultry, negligent roll of her shoulder. "I'm not picky. Just grateful to be somewhere warm and dry."

"You want somethin' to drink?" I asked.

"Whatever you've got."

I rubbed the back of my neck. "Well, being a bachelor, I've got tap water and beer."

She just grinned at me. "Beer is good."

I arched an eyebrow. "Hate to sound…I dunno, like a fartsy old guy, but…are you legal drinking age?"

"Twenty," she answered. "Twenty-one in a month and a half." A wry grin. "So, close enough, I'd say."

Phew. Well over eighteen, and almost legal to drink, so I didn't have to feel shitty about having a hard-on for a seventeen-year-old. And, really, she was only six years younger than me. Shit, my ma was eight years younger than Dad, and they'd been together going on thirty years.

She smirked at me. "You were worried I was a runaway, weren't you?"

I shrugged, shook my head as I got us both a beer, uncapped them and handed her one. "I mean, it crossed my mind, but I knew you were probably at least eighteen."

"Thank you," she said, smirking at me. "I won't tell, I swear." She tilted her head to one side, severing a piece of roast off with her fork, stabbing it, and popping it into her mouth. "I look that young, to you?"

*It's a trap*—the Star Wars quote ran through my head in Admiral Ackbar's voice. "Uh…well? I'm not that great at knowing how old someone is by looking at them. All I know is, you're gorgeous."

Her ivory skin went pink as she blushed. "Thanks?"

I hadn't meant to say that out loud, but it was true, and it was an understatement. Now that she was clean and dry and her hair was brushed, the raw, stunning, artful perfection of her face was highlighted. Her cheekbones framed her deep, pale brown eyes; the sharp point of her chin enhanced the delicate angles of her jaw, the sculpted cupid's bow of her upper lip was perfection. God, she was so much more than merely gorgeous.

I ducked my head to pull my gaze away from her, digging into my food.

A strange not-awkward silence ensued as we both ate. She devoured all I'd given her in a matter of minutes and gave a longing look at the platter between us—I didn't wait for her to ask, I just slid a few more pieces onto her plate, and onto mine, and we kept eating.

She glanced at me, now and again. "Do you see yourself always working on cars?"

"I don't know. I'm working on getting my realtor license. If I can make more selling houses, maybe I could do less salvaging. I'd like to be able to do engine work full time, but I just don't have enough clientele for that, yet. All my business is word of mouth, and I'm doing all right considering I'm only twenty-six, but…I guess I'm just impatient."

"Well, I'm almost twenty-one and I don't have a damn clue what to do with my life. I know it's *not* waiting tables, but I don't have any idea what it *is.*"

"There's nothing wrong with waiting tables," I said.

"Hell no," she said, around a mouthful. "I know that. I've worked for Mr. Sokoli since I was fourteen. It's a good job and I'm good at it. But it's just not something I want to do forever."

"So?" I said, waving with my fork. "You've got time to figure it out."

"Not really. I mean, I know I don't want to go to college. I tried that for half a year and I fucking hated it."

"There's lots of stuff you can do without a degree." He gestured. "I don't have one."

"Yeah, but…you have the skills and experience. I just…" She sighed. "You'd have to know my family to understand. My oldest sister, Charlie, is super successful. She went to fucking Yale on a full academic scholarship, where she got not *one*, but *two* degrees."

"Yikes," I said. "I barely graduated high school. Book learning and classrooms just wasn't my thing."

"Same," she said. "Then there's Cassie. She went to Julliard for dance, and was lead dancer for one of the most prestigious dance companies in the world, and lived in *Paris*."

I arched my eyebrow. "Damn."

"You begin to understand," she said, droll. "But wait, there's more. Lexie, my sister who's getting married, did the whole college thing, went to the University of Connecticut and then Sarah Lawrence for women's studies or something like that. But overall, not totally out of the ordinary, right? Just a normal girl going to college. Only, she recently did some kind of dumb shit and got herself kicked out of Sarah Lawrence—what, I don't know—and she and Charlie went on some super cool road trip. Lexie met Myles North, and yes, I mean *the* Myles North, and now Lexie is getting married to one of the most famous humans on the planet. But wait, there's even more—he got her to play the guitar and sing for him, and they discovered she's like insanely talented. He recorded her and that video broke world records for most views in twenty-four hours."

I dropped my fork. "Wait. You gotta be shittin' me. Your sister is *that* Lexie? The Lexie from Myles and Lexie?"

I nodded. "Yes. That Lexie is my sister."

I rocked back in my chair. "Okay, that'd be a little intimidating. She's crazy talented."

And crazy hot, but I didn't say that. Mainly because the girl across the table from me was, in my opinion, even hotter—and not just because she was here in person, in my home, and was not getting married to a rich and famous dude with magazine perfect looks and bonkers musical talent.

"Yes, it's a little intimidating, and it makes me feel inferior."

"Well, she's her, and you're you. You gotta live *your* life."

Torie rolled her eyes at me. "Thank you for that stunning insight, Rhys."

I laughed. "A little inane, huh?"

She held her thumb and forefinger an inch apart. "Just a little." She stood up, took my plate and hers to the sink—scrubbed the forks and the plates clean with my sponge and soap, and set them in my drying rack.

"You shoulda let me do that," I said.

"I appreciate the hospitality, but I like to be useful. With four sisters who are all way more talented and successful than me, being useful is about all I've got."

I frowned. "Wait. Charlie, the oldest, went to Yale, Cassie the next oldest is a dancer, Lexie is marrying *the* Myles North…that's three sisters."

"Can't forget about Poppy, my younger sister. She's eighteen, and poised to become the next, like, Georgia O'Keefe. My dad built her her own art studio in the backyard, she's that talented. She graduated high school just before her seventeenth birthday because she's crazy smart and has zero chill, and got accepted to Columbia University's visual arts program, where she's in a private study program with one of the most famous art instructors in the world, because she's got this, quote, 'brilliant and unique voice as a painter.' Apparently, she's, like, a genius with brushwork and lighting, and can replicate some of the best works by the greats of the Renaissance. But her real passion is this artwork she does with her own black and white photography and magazine cutouts and paint…I don't know exactly how she does it. Anyway, it's taking the art world by storm, I guess. Plus, she's always been the prettiest of all of us."

I arched an eyebrow. "I dunno, Torie. I'm sitting here looking at you and thinkin' I'm not sure how anyone could be prettier than you."

She blushed again, fidgeting and squirming uncomfortably. "Oh, shut up. You've seen the video of Lexie. I'm the plain sister, no question about it."

"There is absolutely nothing plain about you, Torie."

She got up, headed for the bathroom, snagged her phone off the top of the toilet tank, and brought it to me, bringing up a photograph. It was of her whole family, her mom and four sisters and Torie, and had obviously been taken within a year or two.

"This was two, almost two and a half years ago,

before Mom moved to Ketchikan. So Poppy is only sixteen here." She tapped the sister in question on the screen. "She hit puberty just shy of her tenth birthday, had bigger tits than me by thirteen, and was fully developed, done growing, and was basically, physically fully an adult by the time this photo was taken. Her junior year, the year after this photo, she actually got our high school English teacher fired because he kept hitting on her. Claimed he thought she was a teacher. She's been proposed to four times by adult men, propositioned countless times, has had multiple offers from every reputable modeling agency in the world despite not being the classic model body type and, oh yeah, some big name Hollywood producer offered her a starring role in a major summer blockbuster. She almost took the offer, but she had to be topless, and Mom flipped her wig."

I believed every word. In the photo were six women: their mom, and the five girls. And, by god, each of them was unbelievably beautiful. All of them had their mother's dark hair except one sister with platinum blond hair, but she had their mother's facial features. It was ridiculous, honestly. Even the mom was—at the risk of sounding like I'm into older women, which I'm not—sexy as hell, fit, ageless, yet obviously a mature woman. Of all the girls in the photo, Torie most closely resembled her mother, being tall, slender, with thinner hips and a smaller bust than the sisters.

Damn.

Poppy was everything Torie had claimed. If I didn't know she was only sixteen in the photo, I'd have taken her for eighteen, at least. She had the face and body the younger Kardashian sisters had paid a fortune in surgery to attain. Poppy was the kind of beautiful that started wars—the face that launched a thousand ships. She was angled behind Torie in the photo, so her figure was mostly hidden, but it was obvious that she was…blessed with an excess of beauty in the figure department.

"She's only gotten more beautiful since this photo," Torie said, sounding annoyed and amused.

"Crazy."

"Doesn't seem right, does it?"

I hunted for something to say that wouldn't be creepy. "I mean, yeah, she's really pretty."

Torie snorted. "It's okay."

I laughed. "Okay, fine. Yeah, she's pretty unbelievable." I met her eyes. "But she's not you. And I'm not attracted to her. Not like you mean it. And not like I am to you."

She swallowed hard. "Easy there, tiger. Don't play all your cards at once, huh?"

I shrugged. "I'm not playing cards, or games. Just

putting the truth out there. I think you're damn sexy. Yeah, your sisters are all beautiful, and yeah, Poppy is definitely…somethin' else. But Torie, so are you. I'm not playing, or blowing smoke at you."

"Isn't the phrase 'blow smoke up your ass?'"

I snorted. "Yeah, but most ladies I've met don't appreciate crass turns of phrase like that, so I changed it."

She smirked. "Well, I appreciate the gallantry, but I'm not sure I'd call myself a proper lady." A laugh. "And it wasn't for lack of Mom trying like hell. She raised us to be ladies, but we all had other ideas." A thoughtful glance at the ceiling. "Well, Cassie, Lexie, and me, at least. Charlie has always been the proper one, and Poppy is just…Poppy. Charlie always seemed to feel like it was her responsibility to be the proper and responsible one."

I eyed her. "You're a rule breaker?"

She shrugged, lifted the beer she was casually holding. "Sure. I mean, this obviously isn't my first drink, right?"

"That doesn't make you a rule breaker, more of a totally normal young person. I mean, shit, I was drinking fairly regularly by the time I was eleven. But then, I grew up redneck white trailer trash."

"You shouldn't say that about yourself."

I laughed. "I say it with pride. It's where I came

from and who I am, and I ain't ashamed of it. But there are certain stereotypes that are just true. I had access to all kinds of alcohol at a young age, and I was left unsupervised, like, pretty much my whole life. I did what I wanted, and no one said boo about it."

"How old were you when you had sex the first time?" she asked.

I was surprised by the forwardness of the question. I laughed and rubbed the back of my head. "Ah, like…fourteen, almost fifteen."

She made a face, but I knew it was meant to cover somewhat judgmental surprise. "Fourteen, huh?"

I shrugged. "Shania Lautner. She lived in the trailer next to ours. She was sixteen, I was fourteen. Her parents were a mess, mine were always working, so we were both home alone a lot. Well, her folks were always drunk and fighting so she was never in there if she could help it. She came over a lot, and we'd watch TV, drink my dad's beer, and sometimes steal her dad's shitty whiskey if he was passed out. And one day, she looked at me, shut the TV off, and took her top off." I laughed, remembering. "I was shocked as hell. I mean, don't get me wrong, I was a horny fourteen-year-old with a hot sixteen-year-old neighbor, and those bathroom windows weren't exactly frosted too well, so I'd gotten some looks at her, I'm ashamed to say. But oh boy, seeing her take it off in front of me like that? Coulda knocked me over with a feather."

She laughed. "Lucky you, huh?"

"I guess so, yeah. She and I...well, I wouldn't call it dating. We were just kids and it was mostly just sex. But it was some good times. Then she started dating Kyle Kuhn, who was nineteen and had a cool Trans Am, and that was it for me and Shania."

"Just like that?" she asked.

I waved a hand. "Eh, I knew it was coming. She told me as much. After, one time. She was like, 'you know, one of these days I'm gonna have to find a boyfriend who can get me the hell out of here, and I hope there won't be no hard feelings.'" I sighed, because I really did have fond memories of Shania. "She told me before she started dating him. Gave me a real nice last hurrah, and told me she had to stop coming over to see me, because she was gonna start seeing Kyle, and she was gonna get him to move to Lexington with her so she could get the hell out of our shitty podunk little trailer park and shitty podunk little backwoods town."

Torie was intently watching me. "And? Did she?"

I winced, shook my head. "Nah. He knocked her up, and now they've got four kids and she's cutting hair at a Fantastic Sam's or something like that, living in a different trailer with him in the town we grew up in."

"Oof. That sucks."

I nodded. "The way shit works for a lot of folks. Shania's mom had her when she was sixteen, and Shania had her first kid at just barely seventeen— sometimes, you just get stuck."

"But not you."

I laughed, not a little bitterly. "Yeah, not me. I kept my ass unattached and saved every penny I could. The day I got my diploma, I had my truck packed and I was gone. Didn't even bother walking in the commencement. Got the diploma from Principal Hyde, and I left from school that very day. I'd already said goodbye to Ma and Dad, and they knew I wasn't coming back."

"How'd you end up in New Haven?" she asked.

"You got a lot of questions, don't you?" I said, wryly.

She pulled a face. "Sorry. I get nosy. You don't have to answer."

I waved. "Nah, ain't got any real secrets. I left town with no clue where I was going, just figured I had to get away. I'd planned on going west; I guess I was thinking California because that's basically as far from Kentucky as you can get. But I took a wrong freeway exit and ended up going north. So I said fuck it, I'll go north. I was sort of homeless for a while, lived in my truck. I'd stop at a local mechanic in a random town or city and beg for busy work. Those guys always got brake jobs and oil changes and shitty boring tedious things like that when they'd rather be doing the big-dollar stuff. So I'd do those shitty jobs for cash, and take little enough that they'd make a profit on the job. That work put cash in my pocket and taught me more of my trade. I'd stay in town a few days, then keep heading north."

"Wow. And you were, what? Eighteen?"

"Seventeen, couple months shy of eighteen." I gestured at the shop below us. "I ended up here sort of by mistake. I was driving around looking for somewhere to park so I could sleep. Happened by this building—it was opened up and had a For Sale sign. The owner was just about to close up, and I asked him how much he wanted. I had quite a bit of cash saved up, because my goal all along was to open my own shop. He named a price, and I haggled him down. We came to an agreement, and I managed to talk a banker into giving me a loan, with almost all my cash as a down payment. Shouldn't have gotten that loan, honestly, being seventeen, no credit, just a duffel bag full of cash I'd spent ten years saving."

"It's impressive as hell, Rhys, is what it is."

I shook my head. "Nah. Just making ends meet, keeping food in my belly."

She blew a raspberry. "Quit being modest, Rhys.

You're twenty-six and running a successful garage. It's an impressive accomplishment." She gestured at her backpack and the pile of sopping wet clothes. "That's just about everything I own. I have no education beyond high school, no real skills other than waiting tables, and not even a hobby I'm passionate about."

I sighed. "If you ask me, I think you're being too hard on yourself. Just because your sisters have figured their shit out doesn't mean you're behind because you haven't decided at twenty what you want to do with the rest of your life. You're twenty and you've been living on your own and taking care of yourself. That on its own is no mean feat. Most twenty-year-olds I've met ain't got a clue about taking care of themselves. You and me, we're a rare breed, Torie."

She yawned, stretched, and I had force my eyes away from what the stretch did to press her tits against her shirt. "God, what a day," she mumbled.

I pointed at the corner of my loft where my bedroom was. "Take the bed. I'll head back downstairs and work for a while so you can get to sleep."

She shook her head. "I appreciate your kindness and generosity more than I can say, Rhys, but I draw the line at taking your bed. The pull-out is absolutely fine."

My drive to impress her, to do good things for her was shouting at me to press the issue, but I saw something in her eyes, an independent streak that I recognized as like my own. If I was in her position, I wouldn't take the bed.

"I really don't mind," I said. "My sister visited me a few months ago, and I gave her the bed, and I slept on the pull-out. Slept like a baby." Sue me—I had to try.

"If you slept like a baby on it, then so will I."

The conversation had been easy, and I hadn't even noticed when we'd moved to sit on the couch. We were close—not quite touching, but sitting with less distance between us than near-total strangers would normally have. She leaned forward, and I thought for a split second that she was going to kiss me; my heart started pounding and my dick sat up and took notice.

Instead, however, she slid her arms around my neck in a hug. God, she smelled good. Felt good leaning against me. Soft, warm. I hugged her back.

"Thank you, Rhys," she whispered. "I'd still be out in the rain if it wasn't for you."

"Yeah, I—no problem. It's my pleasure to be able to help you out." I had to let go. Didn't want to, but if I didn't let go, my idiot dick would start thinking something was going to happen, and I'd never sleep.

When I let go, so did she, and there was a split second, a brief moment when we were within kissing distance, and I felt an electric sizzle like static jumping from my lips to hers.

A heartbeat…

And the moment passed.

I stood up. "I, uh...I'll hunt down some extra sheets, blankets, and pillows. I think there's some in my closet."

She licked her lips, watching me with an expression on her face, one I couldn't hope to fathom. "Yeah, I'll open this up," she said, gesturing to the pull-out.

It wasn't an awkward moment. It was...tense. Thick with chemical reactions.

I dug the extra sheets and blankets from the top of my closet, brought them to the couch, and I flung the fitted sheet toward one corner, and Torie, already on that side of the bed, took it and fitted it onto the corner of the mattress. Working together, we finished the job as if we'd been making a bed together forever.

It was a stupid little thing, but something about the ease with which Torie and I moved in synch stuck in the back of my head as being...shit. Something? I had no words for it, but it was just a tickly, niggling, fuzzy little feeling of...rightness.

Too bad she was going to Alaska, and I'd never see her again.

"I'm uh...gonna go." I spotted her wet things on the bathroom floor. "I'll toss your stuff through the washer and dryer."

She grabbed her backpack, pulled things out of it—hairbrush, cell phone charger block and cord, and a handful of other items.

I also spotted a Ziploc bag with something green in it—she was quick and crafty about the way she moved it so I wouldn't see it, but I did.

"Rule breaker, huh?" I said, grinning.

She seemed embarrassed. "Yeah." A shrug.

"Hey, no judgment here."

She lifted the bag and held in up, displaying it. "You ever smoke pot?"

I shook my head. "Nah. Was offered it a few times, but I was too scared of getting hooked on pot and ending up a meth-head like so many people I knew, so I just never had the balls to try it. I knew my only shot at getting out of the trailer park was keeping clean, saving my cash, staying out of trouble, and leaving the very second I had my diploma. I'm a follow-the-plan kinda guy, anyway. Not really rules, just…I figure out where I want to be, make a plan to get there, and I don't deviate from the plan."

She withdrew the small bag. Eyed me. "Now that you're out, and on your own…interested in trying?"

I hesitated. I didn't want to seem like a straight-laced nerd. I wasn't. But old resistances died hard. But like she said, I was on my own, running my own business. Why not?

"Sure?"

She shrugged. "No pressure. Just offering."

"Would you smoke right now, if you were at home?"

She nodded. "It's been a hell of a day. One little hit will take the edge off my stress and let me actually fall asleep. Otherwise I'll be up for hours, no matter how tired I am."

I snorted. "That I get. It's hard as hell for me to fall asleep. My brain is just always going."

She fished in the outside pocket of her backpack, and pulled out what looked like a ceramic cigarette, and a clear red plastic lighter. She opened the bag, reached in, pinched off a tiny bit, thumbed it into the tip of the…whatever that thing was called. It wasn't a pipe as I'd think of it, and damn if I had a clue about paraphernalia terminology. She closed the baggie most of the way, pressed the air out, zipped it the rest of the way closed.

"Outside?" she asked.

I nodded, gestured at the door near the kitchenette. "That goes to a separate entrance."

We went out and sat side by side on the top step, and again, we were just slightly too close. And this time, her thigh was touching mine. Like I was fourteen again with Shania, my heart was palpitating. Before we slept together the first time, every time

I was around Shania, my heart would hammer and my palms would sweat, and my kneecaps would feel numb. Odd, that last one, I know. I'd have involuntary hard-ons around her that would last for fucking hours, until I could get alone and alleviate things for myself.

Those feelings went away after Shania and I screwed, and I haven't felt them since.

Until now.

With Torie.

Heart? Hammering like a damn kettledrum. Palms? Damp and clammy. Kneecaps? What kneecaps?—they were totally numb.

Involuntary hard-on? Had one since…shit, since I saw her in that wet fuckin' T-shirt.

This was shaping up to be…potentially problematic since, again, she was bound to exit my life permanently, and soon.

More's the pity for my dick, since I was feeling fairly desperate to see her without a shirt on…if not get my hands on her.

I doubted it would happen before she vanished to the far north, but a guy could dream, right?

Although maybe fantasize was a better word…

# THREE

## Torie

STUPID MAN, WITH HIS STUPID SEXY STUBBLE.

And his ridiculously huge, grease-stained hands, which were always fidgeting. He had so many scars on his hands—from skinning them and burning them on hot engine parts and smacking them on sharp nuts and hard edges. Strong, nimble hands. *Huge* hands, especially considering he wasn't a huge guy.

Dad had been a big guy—six-four, and toward the end of his life weighed probably near three hundred pounds and, sadly, for his health, it hadn't exactly been all muscle. I remember being a little girl and being fascinated by how enormous his hands were. He could engulf my entire hand in his, and if I made fists, he could fit both in one hand.

Rhys's hands were bigger than Dad's had been.

I watched his hands, now, as he plucked at a loose thread on the knee of his coverall, the grease in the wrinkles and folds, and under his nails. Even if he washed his hands, I knew they'd still look slightly grease stained, as if the grease and oil was just embedded in the molecules of his skin itself.

His eyes, god his eyes. Puppy dog brown.

Growing up, we'd had a beagle, Mr. Dillingsworth, named by six-year-old Charlie. We all called him Dilly. He had the biggest, brownest, most mournful and expressive brown eyes I'd ever seen. One look into his eyes and you'd just melt and want to hug him and snuggle his big floppy ears, and give him all the treats. Of course, the amount of treats he'd gotten from being so darned cute had probably contributed to his demise at the not-very-old age of twelve. But still, Dilly's eyes had just been these huge brown pools of warmth and love and exuberant puppy affection.

Rhys's eyes reminded me of Dilly's, only less mournful and more...everything else male and intoxicating. Intelligent, amused, kind. So many things, and all of them had this way of just sucking me in. Drawing me in and refusing to let go.

We'd been just sitting on the step for who knew

how long, not talking, not quite touching except for the outside of my thigh on his. I had my one-hitter and lighter in my hand, wondering if this was me being a bad influence on this otherwise amazingly *good* man.

I handed him the paraphernalia. "You first. Only if you want to, though. I won't, like, think less of you for saying no, okay?"

He sniffed the tip of the one-hitter. "Wow. Smells…pretty cool actually." He glanced me. "First timer, here. Just…light it and inhale, huh?"

"Draw it into your mouth first, and then breathe in. Otherwise it'll shotgun into your lungs and you'll start hacking." I tapped the ceramic tube. "That's very, *very* potent stuff, so one hit is all you need."

"Am I going to, like, see shit?"

I laughed. "Marijuana is not a hallucinogen, so no, you won't see anything. You'll just feel…floaty. Loose. Happy, probably. Maybe a little paranoid."

He sighed. "Well, I guess we'll see, huh?"

I touched his hand to stop him. "Rhys—"

He smiled at me gently. "I appreciate that you're concerned about not pressuring me. But hon, I made it through middle school and high school without giving into a shitload of peer pressure. Like, Shania smoked cigarettes, my best friend Dougy was a pot-head, everyone I knew drank like fuckin' fish, and several dudes I knew well got into meth and crack. I was the goody-goody in my town. Didn't get drunk pretty much ever, didn't smoke, didn't do drugs. Didn't skip school, didn't go to none of the parties in Old Man Fenner's back forty."

"Old man's who's what?" I asked.

"Old Man Fenner's back forty," he repeated. "James Fenner, he was—still is, far as I know—one of the most successful farmers in the area. Owned like two hundred, two hundred 'n fifty acres of the most prime farm land, had it fenced off into chunks of forty acres, most of it south of the county road, with like, two chunks of forty north of it. The chunk of forty that was north of the county road was way back, out of sight of the road and the town, and it was the party spot for the kids in town. Any given night after sunset, there'd be trucks parked all over the field, kids sitting in trees, maybe a bonfire going."

"Didn't Old Man Fenner do anything about it? Seems like a liability."

"Oh, he knew," Rhys said, "but it was an unspoken rule that you cleaned up after yourself. You didn't leave cans or bottles or trash, you put out your fire, and you didn't do donuts and tear shit up. If you didn't fuck up the field, he wouldn't come checking, and nobody ever broke those rules. The adults all knew, because the back forty had been the party spot for decades. Generations of people from my town had their first drink in that field, their first kiss, and for a lot of us, lost our virginity there. The deal was, you didn't drive around town acting a fool and being vandals and jackasses and hooligans. You got your kicks out in the field, far from the houses, where no one would get hurt and shit wouldn't get broken. The sheriff and deputies left us alone as long as we kept a lid on it. And we, in turn, had a place to go be kids."

I frowned at him. "You say 'we,' but you said you didn't go to the parties."

He grinned, somewhere between amused and sheepish. "Well, I did go sometimes. But there'd be at least a handful of kids in that field every night, and probably a few dozen on the weekends. It was pretty much the only thing for anyone between the ages of fifteen and twenty-one to do in town, so it's what you did. So yeah, I went. But not every night or every weekend, and I usually only had a couple drinks. I almost never drank to get hammered, but for a lot of the kids I grew up with that was the only goal, and as frequently as possible."

I nodded. "So you've always just naturally been a man of moderation."

"More or less, yeah," he agreed.

I indicated the paraphernalia in his hand. "Well, be moderate in taking a little puff. See what you think."

Rhys laughed. "Enough talk, huh?"

He put the pipe to his lips, flipped his thumb over the wheel of the lighter; the flame erupted to life with a soft *whump*, and he touched the flame the tip of the tube. There was a soft crackling, and he drew his cheeks in concave and inhaled. Except he did it wrong, and the pipe was still in his lips when he inhaled and got another bolt of the smoke. Immediately, his lungs reacted, forcing him to cough, but coughing only meant he sucked more smoke in, and then he was hacking and his eyes were watering.

I watched him with amusement. "You were supposed to pull it away from your mouth *before* you inhaled," I said, my voice wry.

He laughed as the hacking spell tapered off. "Yeah, no kidding."

I took the fake ceramic cigarette from him and took a hit with familiar ease. Inhaled, held it, and exhaled the smoke out of my mouth, inhaling it again through my nostrils before spewing it out again— showing off a little, I admit.

"How you feeling, Rhys?" I asked.

"Um, fine, so far?" he said.

I nodded. "Give it a few minutes." We sat in silence for a while. "You said you have a sister?" I asked.

"SEER-sha."

I blinked at him. "Say what?"

"It's an Irish name. S-A-O-I-R-S-E, pronounced SEER-sha." He laughed, sounding somewhat self-conscious. "My mom has always been a little obsessed with Ireland. She's first-generation American, her parents moved here from Ireland when they were first married, ended up in the town where I grew up, outside Lexington, Kentucky, had Mom. Mom met Dad and had Saoirse at eighteen, and thus the cycle began. Except Saoirse was pretty much my idol and example growing up—she's three years older than me. She kept her nose clean, stayed off drugs and alcohol, did good in school, worked her ass off during the school year and had two jobs in the summer to save up enough money for a car, and then enough money to move the day she graduated. And she did exactly that, just like I did—the day she got her diploma, she left town and didn't look back. She's living in Dallas, Texas, and she's…" He rolled a shoulder uncomfortably. "Ah hell, she ain't embarrassed about it, so I shouldn't be. She's stripping to pay her way through med school."

I widened my eyes, and hunted for something to say. "Med school. Wow. Good for her."

He laughed. "Don't hold back on me, now, Torie. You can say what you're thinking."

"I guess maybe it seems a little ironic that she kept herself out of trouble to leave your hometown, only to end up a stripper."

He chuckled. "I guess there is a certain irony in it. But the club she works at sponsors this competition or something where the dancers get scholarships, and I guess she's pretty good because she's getting a scholarship, plus she got good grades and is getting more money in loans and grants and scholarships from the federal government, so she's gettin' through med school with pretty minimal debt. And I guess, to her, that's worth being a stripper." He laughed. "And, truth is, when I said she stayed out of trouble, I meant the chemical and pregnancy kind. She was kind of, um…fast and loose, you might say. Not exactly concerned with her reputation, and I guarantee you, tell anyone we grew up with that Saoirse is stripping her way through college, not a one would be in the least surprised. She's smart as hell, she's just not overly concerned with virtue or modesty. Part of the reason I avoided the back forty parties was because I stood a good chance of seeing my sister parading around topless. She just didn't much care about folks seeing her topless, if not naked."

I nodded, shrugged. "I'm…well, not prudish or overly modest, but not extroverted like Lexie, or not giving a shit like Cassie."

"Takes all kinds to make the world go round, so no shame in being who you are." He shrugged. "It is a little weird to me that my sister is a stripper but, like I said, she ain't embarrassed by it, and hell, she's almost proud of it. Some girls wait tables and pour drinks to get through college, she takes her clothes off. In the end, she's doin' what works for her, and I ain't about to judge her for it."

"Are you close to her?"

He tilted his head side to side. "Kind of. We talk pretty regular, every week or two. Text each other now and then, keep up with each other. She's in Texas and I'm here, so I wouldn't say we're, like, besties, but I love her and if she needs me, I'm here for her."

He was smirking. His eyes were glassy.

"How you feeling now?" I asked

He laughed. Nodded. "Pretty good. Just sorta… *whoosh*." He rocketed his hand in an upward arc. Laughed again. "Whatever the hell that means."

I chuckled. "It means you, sir, are stoned."

He nodded. "I guess I was expecting something more…nefarious. This is just…mellow."

"Right? There's a reason you never hear about a stoner getting in bar fights."

I peered at the tip of the one-hitter, saw there was a bit of green left, so I finished it off with another partial hit. Tapped the ash loose, put the lighter and pipe in the pocket of Rhys's sweatpants.

You wouldn't think ratty old sweatpants and a threadbare T-shirt could make a girl feel sexy, but somehow…these did. The sweats fit like my tightest pair of yoga pants, form-fitting on my ass, hips, and thighs, and I hadn't bothered with underwear since I was planning on taking Rhys up on his offer of laundering my clothes. No underwear, no bra—not that I ever wore a bra, anyway. I hated the damn things and wore them as infrequently as possible.

So, like, never.

The shirt fit about the same as the pants: tight, and it was see-through, and my areola were playing peekaboo—or should I say, peek-a-boob? I know he noticed—I'd caught him staring.

And liked it.

I had a weird, out of character, impulse to peel the shirt off and see what he did. I restrained the impulse, thank god, but it'd been a close one.

Max was the only guy who'd seen me naked since I was a little girl, and we tended to do our messing around in the dark with all the lights off, so I wasn't sure he could even pick out my naked body in a lineup.

So why the hell was I even thinking about taking my shirt off for Rhys?

More to the point, why was I wondering what those huge rough hands would feel like? Why was I wondering if the grease would rub off on me?

Why, god, why, was I picturing his hands, black with engine grease, slicking all over my body in intimate ways Max had never dared touch me? I had a distinct vision of my naked body covered in hand-prints of grease and oil.

Gahhh. I wished I could blame it on the pot, but I'd been dealing with these images in my head since I took my sweatshirt off and Rhys's eyes went straight to my breasts outlined beneath my wet T-shirt.

Also, you don't hallucinate on pot, and I had no excuse other than plain old-fashioned horniness and sexual attraction.

Rhys was shifting, wiggling. "I gotta do... something."

I laughed. "Figures you'd get even more moti-vated to do shit while stoned."

He laughed. "I'm a go-go-go type of guy. As a kid, I was always moving. Even now, if I gotta sit still for some reason, my knee will start to bounce. Even mellowed out, I just gotta be doing something."

I felt a yawn starting—it bubbled in the back of my throat, expanded to my chest, blossomed in my belly, and then burst up through me, forcing me into a decadent, muscle-quivering stretch; spine arched, head tipped back, arms lifted up over my head...

Shaking myself out of the yawn, I glanced over just in time to see Rhys watching me, eyes wide, mouth slightly ajar.

The sheer, blatant attraction on his face was like

a fishing hook setting in my gut, digging in, latching onto my own attraction to him.

His eyes were fixed firmly on my little chesticles, such as they were. Even when I looked right at him, his gaze stayed there.

I arched an eyebrow. "Take picture—it'll last longer."

He blinked. "Oh. Um. Wait…really? Can I?"

I blinked back at him. "Ha, no, you can't take a picture."

He blinked again, even more slowly. "Oh. Okay. Damn. It'd be a hot picture."

I gave him a look that was equal parts puzzled frown and flattered grin. "I'm wearing your old sweatpants and raggedy T-shirt." I plucked at them. "Why do you even still have this, anyway? It barely fits me, there's no way it'd fit your giant shoulders."

He chuckled. "My shoulders are hardly giant, but thanks for the compliment." Rhys rolled a shoulder. "I guess I'm a little sentimental. I mean, don't get me wrong, I hated middle school, and I hated high school, and I couldn't wait to leave town, but it's still the town where I grew up. I didn't bring anything with me when I left except clothes and money and a handful of auto mechanic manuals and some tools. That shirt just sort of represents…home." A sigh, gruff and annoyed. "It's complicated. It ain't home anymore, but yet in a way it'll always be home even if I never go back. Which I won't."

I yawned again. "Yeah, I think if I ever leave this area, that's how I'll feel."

He blinked slowly at me. "Shirt looks helluva lot better on you than it did on me."

I snorted. "You need glasses."

He crinkled his brow. "No, I have perfect eyesight. Had it tested. Better than normal, actually—I've got twenty-ten."

"What's that?"

"Twenty-twenty is normal eyesight where you can see something twenty feet away with perfect clarity. I can see perfectly clearly at twenty feet what someone with twenty-twenty can at ten feet." He laughed. "According to the eye doctor, I shoulda been a pilot or a sniper or something. But I just like working on engines."

I cackled. "Dude, you are so stoned. What does your better than perfect vision have to do with how I look in your shirt?"

He seemed to be puzzling that through. "Oh. Well, it means I can see very well how sexy you are in my shirt, so I don't need glasses. Your boobs look fantastic in it. The little holes make me crazy, like I just wanna see more."

I blushed, covered my chest by crossing my arms. "I…"

He put his face in his hands. "Wow. That was some really unfiltered bullshit, wasn't it? Sorry." A bob of his head to one side. "I mean, it's true, but I didn't mean to be forward, or to embarrass you."

I was blushing so hard it hurt. "I'm just…not shy, I just…" I struggled for words. "I don't normally wear a bra, because my boobies are small enough I don't need the support, and I don't work out so I don't need to contain them, and I don't really give a shit if my nipples poking into my shirt makes people uncomfortable. But I'm not, like, looking for attention." I groaned, putting my face in my hands. Now we were sitting in matching positions. "Wow, I'm not sure why I said that either. We've both got stoned diarrhea of the mouth, I guess."

Another jaw-cracking yawn, another back-arching stretch, another sideways stare from Rhys. And then he thumped his forehead. "I have a really bad habit of not thinking about what you need, don't I? You've got to be exhausted. You've yawned like, three times in the last twenty minutes."

"I am pretty tired. But, could I throw my stuff into your dryer?"

"Shit. I forgot that too. The thing with the pot sort of distracted me." He stood up. "I'll do it. You go crash. I'll wait until your stuff is in the dryer. That way you can fall asleep without me puttering around."

The thought of Rhys puttering around while I tried to sleep was equal parts inviting and worrying. His presence did weird things to me. Made me feel wired, yet soothed me. Made me agonizingly aware of him, and myself, yet utterly comfortable. Turned on and sexually fraught, but comfortable just…existing near him.

It was a lot to feel from having known him for a handful of hours.

We went back inside, and I handed Rhys my bundle of wet clothes—which was everything, since my backpack had gotten soaked through. I'd tried to bundle it in such a way that my underwear was inside and he'd just have to toss the whole pile in but, of course, as I handed over pile, what should fall out but a lacy pink thong and my favorite stretchy gray romper underwear thing, which I often wore as loungewear—it wasn't something I'd wear out, as it was definitely meant as underwear, and was clearly what you might call an "intimate" garment.

I looked at my undergarments now sitting on the floor, and Rhys looked at them, and I could see him wondering if he should pick them up, or if I should…

I picked them up, held them. "I, uhhh. Maybe just show me where the laundry is?"

He smiled, not quite a smirk, not quite a kind dismissal of my further embarrassment, but somewhere in between. "It's just underwear, you know. We all wear it." He frowned. "Except, I don't, always. These coveralls tend to fit weird, and they're more comfortable like this, but commando. I wear underwear with jeans, though. 'Cause of the zippers."

I felt my cheeks heat again. "You're…not wearing underwear."

"Nope. Free-ballin' it."

I laughed, and took my laundry. "Well, it's still weird for you to be handling my unmentionables. We just met. Just show me to the washer."

He led the way back downstairs to the garage— an industrial-sized, Laundromat-style washer and dryer were up against the back wall; I tossed my stuff into the washer, he added detergent, closed the front-loader washer, adjusted the settings, and pushed the empty quarter tray in to start it.

"It's a thong, not a dildo," he said, once the washer was filling with water. "No reason for it to be weird."

I choked on a gasp of embarrassed indignance. "I don't have a dildo."

Another shrug. "Be fine if you did—you're an adult. May even be a little weird if you didn't. Girl's gotta do what a girl's gotta do."

"This girl doesn't do dildos."

I didn't mention that I did do vibrators, and

clitoral stimulators, and that I had one of each in my toiletries bag, which, thank sweet baby Jesus, was waterproof-treated leather and thus had survived being soaked and was, more importantly, opaque, and so he couldn't see what was in it.

He, however, being stoned out of his head because the pot was exactly that strong, kept talking. "No? Do you masturbate?"

"Rhys, I think that's a little personal for having just met."

He blinked at me again, and I saw the normal Rhys poking through in his eyes. "Sheeeit. Maybe this stuff isn't so good for me. I don't seem to have a filter at all, huh? I'm sorry. I'm not normally so unfiltered about what's going through my mind."

I was feeling that second hit, now. Less offended, and maybe a little more...turned on by his curiosity. And it was definitely *just* the pot, and not at all anything to do with my own chemical reactions to Rhys.

We headed back upstairs, him leading again.

"So...you're curious about my personal sexual habits?" I asked, a step down from him.

"I mean, yeah." He smirked over his shoulder at me. "Aren't you curious about mine?"

"I can honestly say that I have not thought about your masturbatory habits." I huffed. And I *hadn't* given them a second thought. "But now, yeah, I am a little curious."

We were in his loft, now, standing near his bedroom area. His bed was the coolest thing I'd ever seen: the footboard was a vintage Ford truck bed gate, the latch cables fastened to the frame, and the headboard was made from the backrest from a bench seat, with the grille from the same Ford pickup mounted on the wall above it. It was a queen-size bed, neatly made. Beside it was a small nightstand made from the springs of a suspension system that had a glass top.

I gestured at the bed and nightstand. "You find that on Etsy?"

"Nah, made it myself. Saw some similar designs on Pinterest, and figured I could do something fairly similar myself."

I was impressed. "That stuff is really cool. You could probably make money just doing that."

He nodded. "Been thinking about it. But between salvaging, my tuning and engine repair clients, my real estate agent classes, and my own restoration projects, I haven't really had time to work on that."

"You do like to stay busy, don't you?" I asked.

He nodded. "Yeah." He looked around the room. "Well, you know where everything is."

I laughed, gesturing at the open loft. "Yeah, it's pretty obvious."

He rubbed the back of his neck. "Well, I'm gonna putz around downstairs until your laundry is ready to go in the dryer." He grinned at me. "I'll do my best to not handle your panties."

I faked an overly dramatic gagging sound. "God, eeew, don't say that word. Fucking gross."

"What, panties?"

I shook my head back and forth, pretending to be retching. "Stop! Stop saying that word! It's forbidden!"

He laughed. "Okay. I won't say…*panties*…again." He cackled as I retched again. "So it's just underwear, huh?"

"Some words are not meant to be uttered, and should be abolished. Like that one."

"What others?"

"Moist." I retched again. "The C-word, most of all. I hate that word. Unless you're Australian, then it's different."

"The C-word?" He mused. "Oh. Cunt."

"Don't fucking *say* it! God, Rhys."

He blew a raspberry. "Jeez, how are you even functioning on two hits? I'm clearly a disaster on *one*."

I laughed. "Oh, I'm just buzzed. Maybe sometime I can get you well and truly stoned out of your gourd. That would be hysterical, if this is any indication."

"I dunno. This is pretty nice, except for the fact that I keep saying offensive shit to you."

I laughed. "Pro tip about me, I don't really get offended, or at least not easily."

"Oh good. I like you. I wouldn't want to actually offend you."

I blinked at his casual admission to liking me. Maybe he just meant it as liking me as one person platonically likes another, in a just-friends sort of way.

That's probably all he meant.

"You never answered the question about masturbating."

I laughed. "There was a question?"

"Yeah—do you?"

I laughed even harder. "If you're trying to not offend me, asking me if I masturbate is a bad place to start."

"True, but I did just admit I like you. And I do. And not just as friends. But I do want to be your friend. Only not *just* friends, because boobs."

I pushed him toward the door. "Good night, Rhys. Thank you, more than I can say, for rescuing me today."

He laughed as he walked away. "I've never been this talkative or inappropriate in my life. Not sure what's come over me."

"Apparently getting stoned seriously loosens your filter."

I sat on the pull-out as he paused at the door,

holding it open, one foot on the first step, looking at me. As if memorizing the way I looked, sitting in his loft.

I held that thought at bay, giving him a level look, hoping he didn't see the curiosity and attraction pulsating through me. I was leaving tomorrow and didn't need the complication of liking a really hot, nice, successful guy with huge strong grease-stained hands and stubble that I wanted to run my fingers over and feel scratching against my skin—

GAHH, no. No, Torie. Bad girl.

Don't sleep with the first hot guy who gives you attention. That was the gist of what Lexie had said one time.

And it was good advice.

But if Lexie were me in this situation—single Lexie, not about to be married Lexie—she'd be all over this guy.

I was tempted to call her.

Maybe she could talk me down from this ledge.

Because I was on a hell of a ledge—and about to slip off. And if I slipped off, it'd be into bed with Rhys. Which, I reminded myself, was a very unwise idea. I did not need a distraction right now. I had to get to Alaska.

I had no business giving my virginity to a man I'd literally just met. No matter how hot, sexy, ripped, funny, successful, or kind he might be.

I mean, sure, a guy that was nice and kind and genuine, as well as gorgeous and sexy, was about as common as unicorns, and Rhys seemed to be all that and more.

And those were perfectly good reasons to have sex with him, right?

Wrong.

The fact that I wanted to climb on his lap and lick his stubble and get his hands on my body...*that* was reason to have sex with him.

But it wouldn't *mean* anything. I'd be going to Alaska and he'd be staying here, and it'd be a one-night stand. A hookup. And I'd been promising myself since I was sixteen that my first time would not be a hookup...which is why I'm still a virgin at almost twenty-one.

So far, no one has captured my attention, let alone my physical desire.

But Rhys...

The man had both, and it was a problem, because it was the worst possible timing.

Deep down, I knew Leighton and Jillie were probably right about me not coming back to Connecticut. I wasn't ready to admit it just yet, but I could feel the truth of it percolating deep down, where you just *know* things that you can't quite formulate into words, or even coherent thoughts.

I lay back on the pull-out, on top of the blankets, and stared at the ceiling.

My thoughts, dizzied by the smoke, circled and floated and wafted as I drifted toward sleep—and when I did fall asleep, my dreams were all of Rhys.

And they were all…decidedly naughty.

And I enjoyed every single one.

Even the one where he was seconds from putting himself inside me and I told him I was a virgin, and things got awkward. I woke up from that one, panicking, knowing I couldn't let anything happen between us because having to admit to him that I was a virgin would be mortifying beyond belief.

So…nope. Nothing was happening here.

I'd go to Alaska as planned, and would arrive in Alaska a virgin. Rhys would *not* be deflowering me.

I made myself a vow, promising myself I wouldn't let him or anyone else have my virginity right now. I just needed to get to Alaska. That's all I had to do.

Simple, right?

# FOUR

## Rhys

I GOT NO SLEEP THAT NIGHT. I LAY AWAKE ON THE BED, listening to the soft breathing and occasional snorts and snores from Torie. Again and again, my idiot sex-obsessed brain conjured up images of Torie.

The moment she took off her sweatshirt, in particular, was etched indelibly on my brain. Every inch of her upper torso had been all but visible beneath her wet T-shirt.

Being a heterosexual male without a significant other, or regular access to sex, I had, of course, spent maybe more time than necessary online looking at photos and videos of nude and partially nude women…and, ironically, a wet T-shirt was one of my favorite things. And good *god* did Torie fulfill that particular fantasy for me. I mean *shit*, the way her tits sloped downward before tilting up and the plump thick long nipples? Small in size, perhaps, but perfect in shape. And I've always just personally liked smaller breasts. Call me weird if you want, but it's my thing.

And hers are…just fuckin' perfect.

In non-tit related news, I'd smoked pot.

It was fun, and I'd probably be willing to try it again, but it's not something I could see myself getting obsessed with, or addicted to. It was nice to be able to turn my brain off, though, that was for sure.

Except it had also turned off my filters, and I'd said some shit I probably shouldn't have.

For example, that I really wanted to see Torie naked.

I bet the rest of her body was just as perfect— slim, slender, tight. Her ass in those sweatpants was… crazy making. Taut and round and high, with mile-long legs and hips just curvy enough to make my dick hard every time I saw her from behind. If I could get just one look at her in the full nude, I'd probably come in my pants…like I had the first time Shania had touched me.

I hadn't shared that particular detail. I'd been fourteen and had basically just discovered masturbation, which meant I was jerking off furiously every chance I got, and could summon the ability to ejaculate from the simplest of visual stimuli—like Shania on the roof of her trailer in a bikini, sunbathing. Or the partial glimpse I'd occasionally get of her through the bathroom window as she took a shower. I could see just enough to make out the outline of her tits, but couldn't see her clearly, and it was enough to drive me fuckin' nuts. Then, one day she'd shut off the TV, looked at me for a second, and had peeled off her shirt. She'd been wearing a bra, and I remember it in detail. White, lacy, pushup—which even at sixteen she hadn't really needed, I realize looking back—it had clearly been a hand-me-down, stained, with sagging underwire and a safety pin holding one strap in place. She'd kept her eyes on me, looked me dead in the eyes as she reached behind herself and unhooked that old bra, and I'd gotten my first live and in person look at teenage female breasts on a girl who wasn't my sister.

My cock had gone ramrod stiff in a split second, and the moment she'd put her hand down my pants, I'd shot my load. Embarrassing as hell. Shania had been sweet about it, though, and hadn't made me feel bad. Instead, she'd let me play with her boobs until I was ready again, and that had been the real start of things.

God, why was I thinking about Shania?

Probably because I hadn't felt about anyone the way I had about her. Until I met Torie.

And my feelings for Torie, as early as it was to be thinking about feelings, were those of an adult, not a horny teenage boy with his first crush. What had me wigging out was how strong my feelings were, both my physical reactions and emotional connection.

I wanted to see all of Torie in the worst fucking way, wanted to touch her, kiss her, make her scream my name. Get her on her hands and knees in my bed and fuck her from behind until we were both unable to come anymore.

I wanted her mouth on my cock and her pussy under my tongue.

I sat up on the bed and scrubbed my face, groaning in annoyance at myself.

It wasn't going to happen.

She was going to Alaska.

In all likelihood, I would never see her again.

So I just needed to get her out of my system, and stop thinking about her.

My cock did not agree. It was hard as a rock, and I'd been fighting this damned erection for hours. Trying to ignore it, to get it to subside. But every time I thought about Torie, I'd see her in that wet T-shirt with her fat little nipples poking against the sheer cotton and my cock would go aching and huge all over again.

I had to get some kind of relief.

Problem was, she was in the living room. My bathroom was in plain view of the pull-out couch, and if she woke up, she'd see me. There was nowhere in this loft I could go. And I was tired and exhausted—I'd been up since five the previous morning, and I didn't want to get up and go down into the garage and deal with myself down there.

Gahh.

I tried again—closed my eyes, and focused on breathing slowly, steadily. Clear my mind. Picture a blank black nothingness in front of my eyes, blackness subsuming my view, blackness soft as velvet pulling me down…

*Torie was in bed with me, her tongue sliding down my abdomen, toward my throbbing cock. Her long black hair was loose and wild, a river of black cascading over her shoulder and onto my chest as she licked and kissed her way south to my pulsating, painfully hard cock.*

*Her breasts rested on my thighs, her hard nipples dragging over my bunched quads, her hands grazing up my hips, nails raking down my chest and tickling my abs and finally wrapping around me…*

I woke up seconds from making a mess in my shorts.

"Fuck," I snarled.

This one wasn't going away. Not with the dregs of that dream rattling around in my skull. It was too early to get up, but I knew I would never get back to sleep.

I grabbed my phone and tiptoed downstairs to the "office," which was little more than an old truck hood resting on a pair of dented, ancient, three-drawer filing cabinets, with a desk chair I'd rescued from a curb on garbage day.

I sat down at the desk, the lights in the garage turned off. I had a roll of TP at hand, a little tube of lotion I kept on hand—I got gnarly calluses, okay? They'd get torn open and painful if I didn't lotion them once in a while. I didn't go around rubbing lotion on my hands all day.

I switched on my aging desktop computer, pulled up one of my favorite sites, and scrolled through images and gifs and video clips, looking for something that caught my interest.

And what do you know? The thing that did catch my interest was an upload of a homemade video of a girl in a wet T-shirt. With long black hair. And tits that looked remarkably like Torie's.

Shit.

I watched the whole video, which started with the girl and her wet shirt, and ended up with some pretty obviously scripted sex.

I went back to the beginning, the part I really liked: her, in her wet shirt, looking sultry as she peeled it off.

My imagination went haywire, and it was Torie I was seeing.

Looking at me like that.

Baring those beautiful tits for me, approaching me.

I saw her as she'd been in my dream, eyes gazing up at me over my body as she slid down, down...

I had my shorts down past my thighs, cock in hand, squeezing, sliding.

I shouldn't have Torie in mind as I did this, but...I did.

The video lost its hold on me, my own mental image of Torie in her wet shirt was all I really needed to get me to the edge.

I gritted my teeth and hissed low as I neared climax.

The blood pounded in my ears, heart hammering loudly.

"Fuck..." I growled, as the surge hit me in a hot wave, crashing through me.

I exploded into a handful of TP.

As my pulse slowed and I was able to hear properly again, I happened to glance to the side. To the doorway which led upstairs.

Torie.

Halfway out the door, hair loose around her shoulders, wafting in staticky black waves and kinks, eyes sleepy but shocked—fixed on me. On my still-hard cock, held in my fist, cum now leaking out of the tip and spilling over my fingers.

She was less than fifteen feet away, and my computer was angled so she could clearly see the paused image of the girl with her shirt off and in hand, tits bared.

She'd just watched me jerk off...and there was no way she could miss the resemblance between the girl on my computer screen and herself.

I flapped my mouth open and closed, but my brain was blank.

She looked at me—at my eyes, then down to my cock where her eyes lingered for...a very long, tense, odd, chemically combustible moment. To the phone, on the desk.

Her mouth flapped, like mine had. "Sorry, I—"

"No, I'm sorry, I—" I said it at the same time, over top of her words.

She whirled around, her face in her hands. "I'm just...I'm gonna..."

And she was gone, running up the stairs.

Shit, shit, shit.

I cleaned up, clicked out of the website, yanked

up the gym shorts I slept in, and went to the stairs. I couldn't bring myself past the threshold into the loft. What was I supposed to say? *Sorry you caught me masturbating to a girl who looked a hell of a lot like you?*

I just had to deal with it. No sense putting it off.

I entered the loft, went to the kitchen sink and washed my hands. Set about making coffee. Torie was making up the pull-out.

The tension in the loft was so thick and hot you could scoop it out of the air with a spoon.

I felt her behind me as I started the burr grinder; she waited until I shut the grinder off and dumped the grounds into the filter basket, poured water from the Brita into the reservoir, and started the machine.

I pivoted, put my butt against the counter, facing Torie, who was a few feet away, a hair tie in her teeth, braiding her hair. She paused, took the hair tie and slid it over her wrist, and continued braiding.

"Torie, I—"

She cut in. "Rhys, this is your home. You don't need to apologize or explain." She wouldn't quite look at me. "I thought you'd be still asleep, so I was going to check and see if my clothes were dry."

I had no idea what to say, or how to broach the elephant in the room. Of if I even should.

The coffeemaker gurgled, splurted, chuffed into the tense, awkward silence.

Her eyes met mine. "I, um…is that, like, your thing? Skinny girls with black hair in wet T-shirts?"

"No…not till yesterday."

She blushed, her pale skin going pink over her cheeks. "Wait…were you—were you thinking about…*me*?"

I swallowed, not able to look right at her. "Um. Yeah. I was trying not to, thus the video."

"Trying not to?"

I shrugged. "I guess…it felt like maybe it'd be disrespectful or something. To you. To do…that…thinking about…you."

She shrugged, and I was starting to decipher her language of shrugs. She had a shrug that meant, *I can't be bothered to formulate a response because none is technically required but social mores say I have to at least indicate I heard you*; she had a shrug that meant, *I really don't care one way or another, whatever*; she had a shrug that was something like *there are a shitload of possible responses to that, so here's a shrug, you pick what it means, I don't care*; she had a shrug that was meant as *yeah, sure, why not*; and then there was a shrug along the lines of *it would be rude to agree with you verbally, so I'm not agreeing with you but nor am I disagreeing*. There were others with more nuanced meanings which I had yet to sort out, but those were the basic essentials as I had translated them thus far. The one she'd just given me meant something like, *I have absolutely no fucking clue how to respond to that.*

Her eyes lifted, and our gazes met for a split second of sexual tension and molasses-thick awkwardness. "I don't feel disrespected." A brief but powerful pause, her eyes meeting mine. "Flattered, if anything. I...I would never have imagined a guy as...as hot and successful as you would want to...to jerk off to *me.*"

"I'd like to do a hell of a lot more than jerk off," I heard myself say, and not exactly under my breath.

Her blush turned from pink to red, and she shifted, her eyes dropping. "Rhys, I—I can't. I can't start anything. I have to get to my sister's wedding." Her eyes widened. "Shit! What time is it?"

I turned to glance at the clock on my range. "Six forty-five." Understanding dawned. *"Fuck.* Your bus left fifteen minutes ago."

She slumped backward against the counter beside me, her face in her hands. "God...*dammit.* Again. Why am I such a fuckup?"

"I'm sorry, Torie. It's my fault. I'm normally up way earlier than this even without an alarm, but I just...I had trouble falling asleep last night, and I..." I let out sound that was more growl than sigh. "Fuck that—I'm not going to make excuses. I told you I'd get you on that bus, and I didn't."

"It's Saturday. There are no more busses till

Monday now, probably." She groaned. "It's not your fault. You're not responsible for me. I should be responsible for myself." She looked at me, and it was clear she was battling tears of frustration. "I'm sorry you had trouble sleeping. It's probably weird having someone else in the loft."

"It wasn't that."

She frowned. "But you said you had trouble falling asleep."

"Yeah, just not because of the bed." I chewed on my upper lip, considering what to say. "I had…things on my mind."

Her eyes flicked to me—to my hands, as if remembering what she'd seen. "Things on your mind, huh?"

"Yeah. I've got an overactive mind. It's always going, you know?"

She wanted to say something, I could tell, but she made a face like *nope, not going there,* and looked away. "So I have to figure out what to do now. I can't just stay with you all weekend."

"Sure you can," I said, before I could stop myself. "We could work on the Nova together. I could use the help getting it done. Plus, later, I have to get to the build site and finish up some stuff."

She gave me a quizzical look. "Build site?"

"Oh, yeah, I work for a home builder on the

weekends. I do finishing stuff, small jobs. Put in electrical outlet plates and light switch covers, install cabinet and drawer pulls, basically just button things up so it can be turned over to the owners or the listing agents." A thought occurred to me, then, and I snapped my fingers. "Actually, Jeremy, my boss who owns the company, he's always looking for people to help clean up once the bulk of the build is done, and we're at that stage now. I have about six or so hours of work to do, and there's about that much to do in cleaning. Vacuum rugs, sweep up sawdust and shit, mop, wipe down walls and counters, all that shit. He'd pay you fifteen an hour cash to get it sparkly for the new owners. You interested?"

She blinked. "Wait, what? Like, a job?"

I tipped my head to one side. "Not really a job, just an afternoon or so of work for cash under the table. Whatever we don't finish today, we go back and finish tomorrow. He just wants to turn over keys Monday. You need the money, and he needs someone reliable and hardworking to get it done."

She eyed me, smirking. "How do you know I'm hardworking and reliable? I smoke pot and I missed my bus not once, but twice."

I laughed. "I'm pretty good at getting a sense for people. And I overslept too, so it's just as much on me. And I mean, you wouldn't be able to support yourself at twenty years old waiting tables if you weren't hardworking and reliable. Trust me, I know. My mom waited tables for most of my life, so I know exactly how hard it is to make ends meet as a server."

She grinned. "Well, I appreciate the vote of confidence. And yeah, I'd love a chance to make some cash."

I waffled on another thought, and then blurted it out. "I also could really use an extra pair of hands getting this Nova done. I could slide you some cash for that, too."

She shook her head. "Working on the car I'll do for free, for the nostalgia of getting engine grease on my hands again. And for the hospitality."

"Sounds like a plan to me. If all goes well, we'll have the Nova done by noon, I'll cash out that account, and we'll head over to start work at the Setters Road house."

"Coffee first?" She sounded so eager, so excited for coffee that I laughed, and grabbed a mug, poured her a hit of thick black caffeine. "Hope you like your coffee black and strong, because I don't have milk or sugar."

"Would you think less of me if I did like it milky and sweet?"

"A little bit, yes," I said, laughing.

Her skin looked milky and sweet is what I was

thinking—her pulse was throbbing in the delicate vein of her throat, and I wanted to put my mouth there, feel her pulse under my tongue as I tasted her skin.

I blinked and looked away. I'd never found a throat sexy before, but hers was elegant and delicate and…sexy, and it was wreaking havoc on me.

I turned away, poured myself some coffee, and we stood in the kitchen in companionable silence.

She spoke again. "I had trouble falling asleep last night, too," she murmured.

"Oh?" My mouth was dry, the aftertaste of my coffee souring on my tongue.

She held the mug in both hands in front of her mouth, eyes on mine over the rim, her voice muffled behind the ceramic mug. "Yeah. I have an overactive imagination, too. Had…things on my mind."

"Things on your mind," I echoed. And then it dawned on me what she was getting at—repeating my words about why I couldn't sleep, which had led to the little scene this morning, downstairs.

"Yeah. You asked about…certain habits of mine." She chewed on the inside of her cheek, a shoulder lifting, lowering, demure. "Sometimes, that's the only way I can fall asleep. I get…tense, and worked up, and my brain keeps feeding me these images and ridiculous scenarios, you know? Things that will clearly never happen, and I can't shut my brain off, can't stop the scenarios—the fantasies, I guess you could call them—from running through my head, until I'm so frustrated and worked up…" Her eyes dropped. "You know."

I swallowed hard. "And you…had trouble falling asleep last night?"

"Uh-huh." She laughed, embarrassed, blushing, the mug now fully obscuring her face. "God, why am I telling you this?"

"Well, it can't top the fact that you *saw* me."

"I didn't mean to. And I know I should have gone back upstairs, but I was so…not expecting to see… *that*, that I just…froze."

I held her gaze. "It happens, Torie. I ain't mad about it."

She looked back, a moment of boldness. "And, if you want the truth, I didn't…mind what I saw."

"Even though I was watching porn? And the girl in the video looked like you?"

"I did notice a resemblance." God, this moment was tricky. The sexual tension was through the roof. "I watch porn sometimes, too."

Well…that was hot. And unexpected.

"You ever watch *with* anyone?"

A long hesitation. She looked away. "*God* no. No way." As if the very thought was utterly alien.

"Me either. I always thought it would be fun, though. With the right person."

"Yeah, I can see how that would be...fun—hot... with the right person."

The undertones were clear as day. She saw and felt them as much as I did—I saw as much in her eyes, the way she shifted, would meet my eyes, and then look away.

But then, she'd just said she couldn't start anything. Not unexpected. But part of me wished I was asshole enough to push for a little messing around before she had to go. Take what I could get.

I couldn't, though. I'm not that guy. I wanted more than to just mess around with this girl. And if I couldn't get everything with her, it was best for her and me both if we just didn't even dip our toes in that pond.

I cleared my throat. "I, um. I'll get your things. So you can change. Be right back."

I bolted before my libido ran away with my sense. Her clothes were in the dryer, and I dumped them into a plastic laundry basket. Brought them up to her. "Here. I'm gonna go get started on the Nova. Join me whenever. I'm not much of a breakfast person, but help yourself to whatever, if you're hungry."

"Not a breakfast person, either." She took the laundry basket from me. "Thanks for this."

"No problem."

I turned away before I flat out asked her if I could watch her change. Fucking creep.

I headed downstairs, for the Nova, grabbed a socket wrench and flipped it in my palm, peered into the open engine bay and figured out what was left to do on the installation of the rebuilt 440.

Once I had my game plan for the rest of the work mentally sorted out, I got to work. I was just getting started on the wiring harness when I happened to glance up to where the laundry machines were—and saw that an article of Torie's clothes had fallen on the concrete floor at the base of the dryer.

A bright red thong. Barely a handful of silk strings and a scrap of crimson lace.

Shit.

I left the wiring harness and snagged the underwear off the floor, headed back upstairs to give it back to her. I didn't sniff it, because that would be creepy. It was just clean laundry. Nothing weird.

I tapped a knuckle on the door and pushed in, speaking as I entered. "Sorry, I just realized this fell out of the basket—"

Torie—standing in the middle of the loft, a pair of jeans up around her waist but not yet fastened, opened to show an upside down triangle of bright yellow. She was topless. Her shirt was in her hands, and she was about to lift it up and put it on—frozen, now, the shirt crumpled in her fists at her waist.

I blinked, my eyes helplessly taking in her bare tits, which were just as magnificent as I'd imagined.

A beat.

"Um. Hi." Her voice, soft, hesitant, shook me out of my tit-hypnotized stupor.

"Wow. I…sorry." I held up her thong and let it dangle from my finger. "This…um, didn't make it into the basket."

Less than six feet separated us. I took a step forward, extending the thong to her.

She stepped forward to meet me, took it from me. Our eyes locked, momentarily. She held my gaze.

I couldn't help the way my eyes involuntarily dropped from hers to her chest, taking another long, hungry look. And then, with an effort of will, I shut my eyes, gritted my teeth, and turned away. "I'm sorry," I said. "I should have waited for you to tell me to come in."

A soft rustle of cloth. "I'm wearing a shirt, now," she murmured.

I turned back around. "I'm sorry, Torie."

She shook her head, shrugged, but her pink cheeks told a different story. "Well, now we've both walked in on each other. Call it even?"

"Yeah…even," I said, my voice faint.

She held the thong up. "I was actually looking for this. Thought I'd packed it and wanted to wear it. Explains why I couldn't find it and had to settle for the yellow one."

She'd buttoned her jeans, too, but I had a pretty solid mental image of the not-quite-sheer lace of the yellow underwear.

"The yellow looked plenty good to me," I heard my own idiot voice say, and then I apparently doubled down on stupidity. "But I've always been partial to that shade of red. It bet it would look super hot on you."

"Yeah, it's my favorite thong. Looks good, feels good."

"Glad it wasn't lost, then."

"Me too."

Okay, time to go. This was getting weird.

"I'm…" I somehow had my coffee mug in hand. Not sure when or where I'd grabbed it, and I didn't remember taking it downstairs. Was I losing my mind? "I'm gonna get more coffee."

I turned away, blinking to clear my mind of the vision of Torie, topless, as glorious and gorgeous as I'd fantasized her to be. More—she was breathtaking. Porcelain skin, long, elegant arms, delicate ribcage supporting those mouthwatering breasts, a waist curving in to strong hips. Flat, taut stomach, a hint of abdominal definition. Jesus, she was perfect. Those tits, god, those tits. Plump at the base, peaked and pointed at the tips. I loved how they curved slightly upward. Her nipples made my brain explode and my cock throb—so plump, so fat, so long. Begging to be kissed and licked and teased.

I poured coffee, trying to banish the memory so I could look her in the eye without popping a boner—too late, I already had one.

But I was so distracted, I overfilled the mug—scorching hot coffee scalded my hand, and I shook it, snarling a stream of curses as I fished ice from the freezer and ran it along the web of my thumb where the skin was burned.

"God, I'm an idiot," I said.

"You okay?"

I nodded. "Yeah, fine. I'm not normally a klutz like this, I swear."

She sounded like she was holding back laughter. "No? Something's got you off your game, huh?"

"Something…or some*one*." I tossed the ice into the sink and grabbed my coffee. Headed for the stairs. "Sorry one more time for walking in on you, Torie."

She shrugged. "It happens."

Something in her eyes was not as nonchalant as her voice and words. I didn't push it, though.

She followed me down to the garage, her own

coffee mug in hand. I pointed at the wiring harness I'd begun reinstalling. "That's our first job."

And so the morning went—she was a lot more knowledgeable than I think even she realized. Any tool I needed, she was ready with it. She knew what I needed almost before I did. And there were many times that morning that her slender, long-fingered hand could reach places to thread a bolt that I couldn't get to. She was nimble, and had this adorable, sexy way of reaching down into the engine bay, bent over and turned sideways, and she'd turn her head up, and her eyes would go glassy as she focused on working by feel, and her tongue would lick at the corner of her mouth as she threaded the bolt by touch.

In less than half the time it would have taken me working alone, the job was done. I used a handful of rags to clean and polish the engine, making sure the headers and the chrome top of the Edelbrock air cleaner gleamed, made sure the wires were neatly leading where they had to go, checked over all the obvious things once more, and then stood back, nodding.

"There she is, looks good." I grinned at Torie. "Keys are in it—you want to do the honors?"

She looked eager, giddy. "Hell yeah!" She slid behind the wheel, and a moment later that big old 440 turned over and caught with a throaty snarl, the fat exhaust pipes turning the snarl into thunder as she revved it up.

I saw the thrill on her face—the feeling you only get when a big motor sings like that. "Wanna go for a spin?"

Her eyes widened. "Um. I mean, yeah? But it's a client's car."

I winked. "Gotta put it through some paces, make sure there's no rattles or hiccups at higher RPM."

"Sure you do," she said, with a droll grin.

"I do! I always go for a test drive, listen to the motor, make sure everything is right."

She shrugged. "I mean, I'd love to go for a spin. But you better drive."

I slid into the passenger seat. "You have a license?"

"Yeah."

"You know how to drive a stick?"

"Yeah—my dad taught me how to drive on the MG, which was a manual. Said knowing how to drive stick was a dying art and I should know."

"It is a dying art, these days. There's a joke that says having a manual transmission almost makes your car theftproof because most younger car thieves can't drive a stick." I gestured at the bay door, which I'd opened several hours ago to let in sunlight. "Nice and slow, Torie. Take her around the block and then we'll switch."

She eyed me. "You're sure? I don't want anything to happen. I'd feel awful."

"Just be careful." I grinned. "Now come on. Listen to that purr...this old beast is begging to be driven."

She pushed the clutch in, snugged the shifter into first, glanced at me with a heady, eager grin that shot straight to my gut...and then slid us slowly out of the garage. A few turns took us out of the industrial complex and onto a side street, and then to the main road. It was a Saturday morning, and the industrial area was deserted. When we got to the main road, she pulled a slow right and I held out a hand for her to stop.

She braked, glanced at me. "Ready to take over?"

I shook my head. "You should know, first, that I have an understanding with the officer who patrols this area. He knows I do burnouts to test my work, and as long as I'm not driving recklessly or pulling burnouts during business hours, he doesn't pay me any mind."

She grinned, a wobbly one as she started to understand what I was getting at. "Rhys, I'm not—"

"Ever do a burnout in a muscle car?"

"No, and I—"

"I tuned her a little in the rebuild. She's running three hundred and seventy-five horses and four hundred and ninety pound-feet of torque. A real bitch of a beast. She'll put your hair back without even trying hard." I grinned at her. "Give it a shot. Hold the clutch in and rev 'er up to redline. Once it hits redline, pop the clutch and hold on tight."

She looked nervous. "What if I—"

"You won't. It's easy. We're on a four-lane road, deserted, at ten on a Saturday morning. No one for miles, babe. You start to get twisted around a little, just pull off the accelerator and straighten her out."

"You're sure?"

"Everyone oughta know the thrill of popping the clutch on four hundred horses at redline. There's nothing like it." I buckled up, and she did the same. The engine was idling, and we were, naturally, in the far right lane. "Pull over so you're in the middle of the road. Go when you're ready."

She nudged the Nova over to the center, pressed the clutch in, took a deep breath, and then slowly depressed the accelerator. As the engine revved higher and higher, the roar turned into a deafening howl, and then it was at redline. I saw her clench her jaw, eyes wide, and then she let the clutch out all at once—rubber screamed and white smoke billowed as the rear tires spun, and we skidded and bounced and almost floated sideways, and then the tires caught and an invisible hand slammed us back into the seats as we rocketed forward. She was screaming with nervous, excited energy, the thrill of wild acceleration drawing a peal of childlike laughter, wonder and glee lighting up her face. She hit sixty in under five seconds, easily, and then I felt her slack off the pedal and we slowed to street legal speeds.

She glanced at me, her eyes wild. "Holy *shit.*"

"Right?"

"That was *insane*. It was like driving a bolt of lightning."

I laughed. "Ohh man, you oughta feel what it's like driving something tuned to get five hundred horses. I drove this guy's Road Runner once, and he had a monster of an engine in there. It got like five or five-fifty, and over six hundred pound-feet of torque. Fuckin' scary, man. You don't *drive* a car like that so much as try to just keep it straight and hope you don't crash it."

"No thanks. That was wild enough for me." She took us around the corner, still laughing. "Thank you, Rhys. That was the most fun I've had in a car in my life."

"I can think of some other fun things we could do," I mumbled under my breath.

She eyed me. "Rhys...I..."

I sighed. "Yeah, I know. You can't. A guy can fantasize, though."

"Is that a fantasy for you? In a car?"

I laughed. "Nah. Just before she left town, my sister gave me some advice. She told me to remember three important things: one, just because she's not saying no doesn't mean it's yes; two, never make important decisions drunk, and three, sex in a car is never as hot as it seems like it should be."

"Wise advice, huh?" Torie laughed.

"Coming from an eighteen-year-old, yeah." I rolled a shoulder. "So, perhaps surprisingly, no, I've never had sex in a car." I glanced at her. "You?"

She coughed, as if choking on something. Looked beet red for a moment. Shrugged. "Ahh, no. Nope. Never had sex in a car."

There was more to her answer, but she clicked her teeth shut and studiously focused on another right turn, which brought us to the homestretch back to the industrial complex where my garage was.

She eyed me. "You want to take the wheel, do whatever tests you need to do?"

I laughed, shook my head. "Nah, you took care of it. I heard it go through all the gears. No rattles, bumps, knocks, squeaks, or hitches. Everything is good to go. I just gotta call the owner and tell him it's ready."

She remembered the directions to get to my garage, which impressed me because it took me a couple of weeks before I could go straight there without a wrong turn or two. She parked it at an angle out front of the garage, put it in neutral, set the brake, and pulled the keys, handing them to me.

"You sure know how to show a girl a good time, Rhys," she said, grinning at me. "Good coffee, greasy hands, and a burnout. Good way to start the morning."

And I got to see her tits, I thought but didn't say. It had been a genuine accident, but not one I regretted in the slightest.

On the contrary.

I called the Nova's owner, told him it was ready, and he promised to come over within the hour—he was excited, because I'd told him it would be Monday at the earliest. One of the best lessons I ever learned from my dad—the only good lesson, aside from a love for cars—was to under-promise and over-deliver, so I always quoted a little high and long and tried to get the job done for less and sooner, which always made my clients happy.

While we were waiting, I cleaned up the tools and put them all away, as my next job wasn't going to be arriving until I let the owner know I was ready. When I went up to wash my hands, Torie had made my bed, done all my dishes, emptied the garbage, wiped down the counters, and had made us both sandwiches as, by this time, it was past noon.

"You shouldn't have done any of this," I said. "For real. No need. But thanks, I'm starving."

She just smiled at me, pulled the little pipe out of her jeans pocket. "A little toke and I'm off and away, power-cleaning. It's what I do every morning at home. It's my happy place." She gestured around. "I couldn't find a radio up here, so I had to clean without music, which was sucky, because I'm trying to conserve my phone's battery. The poor thing is from twenty-ten and it's only got so much life left in it."

I sat down at the table with her, and we ate in companionable silence. "Well, thank you. I don't think my loft has been this clean in a long time. I try to keep it clean-ish, but I don't always have time to get very detailed."

She smirked. "It's pretty much what I would have imagined a typical bachelor pad to be." A shrug. "I also wanted to prove that you wouldn't regret having your boss pay me to help today. I do really need the money."

"Didn't need to prove nothin'," I said. "But I do appreciate it. Just don't think you ever gotta prove anything or try to earn nothin' with me. I helped you out because you're a person who needed helping. I've been in that position before, and the helping hands I've received when I needed it most kept my faith in humanity alive. I was down to my last five bucks, once. No gas, no food. Nowhere to go. My tools had been stolen, my tire went flat, and I was on the side of the road in the middle of nowhere. This old fella came along in a gorgeous '55 Studebaker pickup. Saw my flat, pulled over. I didn't have a spare, so he drove me to town. Got me to tell him my story along the way, and by the time he brought me back to my wrecker later that day I had a tool-box full of old tools he didn't need anymore, a new tire for my truck, a full belly, and a job waiting at the next town, because his nephew ran an auto body shop and needed a hand for a few weeks."

She had stopped chewing and was listening closely.

"There are good people in the world, folks willing to do good things for no reason but that it feels good to do good." I shrugged. "After that old fella helped me out, I swore then that I'd always try to do the same when the opportunity came around. So... point is, Torie, I know there's some...stuff between us. But you don't and won't ever owe me shit, okay? Meaning, I don't expect anything. Not asking for anything. You said you can't start nothin', and while I admit I got what you might call more than a little spark of attraction for you, I won't push it, since you said you can't start nothin'. So...yeah."

She swallowed a bite with a loud gulp, set half of the sandwich down, and let out a breath. "Thank you, Rhys. That means a lot, actually. More than you may realize."

My phone buzzed then, the Nova owner letting me know he was here and ready to settle up.

Torie waved at me. "Go. Clients wait for no one."

I laughed as I headed for the door. "Well, he'd have to, since I've got his keys."

My heart was in my throat for some reason. Something to do with the unexpected seriousness of emotion I saw in Torie, when I'd said what I did. There was something there.

For her, and between us—and the two weren't the same thing. It was confusing and, as I headed down to the garage, I wondered what it meant.

# FIVE

## Torie

FORTUNATELY FOR MY OVERTHINKING BRAIN, CONFUSED heart, and not at all confused body, we were busy for the rest of the day. The build site was a good thirty minutes away, and when we got there I was introduced to Jeremy, the boss, and several other contractors; I was given some work gloves, a rolling garbage can full of cleaning supplies, and put to work with the promise of, as Rhys had said, fifteen dollars an hour cash.

For cleaning a build site? Damn, I was in the wrong business. It wasn't backbreaking labor by any means, but there was a *lot* of work to do just cleaning up after the business of building a home. I was everywhere and so was Rhys, who had donned a tool belt at some point, and damn if that didn't do something wicked to my loins. Did I know I had a fetish for a man in a tool belt? I don't think I did know that until I saw Rhys in tan Dickies cut off at the knees, with battered, paint- and grease- and caulk-spattered steel toe work boots, and a sleeveless neon green T-shirt sporting the logo of a local paint company. And, don't forget the backward University of Kentucky ball cap, the week-old black scruff darkening his hard jawline…and the tool belt.

Hard, defined arms.

Lean, rounded shoulders.

He wore safety glasses upside down on his backward cap, except when he was wearing them.

He seemed to be responsible for catching whatever was missed. I saw him putting in crown molding, baseboard trim, installing a light fixture in a closet, putting on about a dozen light switch plates and blank plates and socket plates. There was a faucet in a bathroom nobody had gotten to that he installed, a window with unpainted trim on the inside…a little of everything, and he did everything with conscientious care and professionalism.

Why was *that* a turn-on?

Why was EVERYTHING ABOUT HIM a turn-on?

The biggest turn-on of them all? That was when he'd made it absolutely clear that he was going to respect my wishes to not get involved with anyone

Which was a mixed-up thing for me, because I badly, desperately wanted to get involved with him. My core was aching for relief every moment I was around him. My skin ached to be touched by him. My lips tingled, begging for his kiss. Every single part of me was desperate to feel whatever Rhys could make me feel…which I was certain would be more than I could ever comprehend.

My heart and my head were clueless as to what I wanted.

This was so confusing, and unexpected. Two days ago I didn't even know Rhys.

My body was screaming *HAVE SEX WITH HIM! HE DESERVES YOUR VIRGINITY! YOU WON'T FIND ANYONE BETTER!*

My heart was pretty sure that'd be a terrible idea because our paths were surely not destined to go the same way beyond tomorrow, Monday at the latest. And if I gave in to what my foolish body wanted, I'd get *involved* with Rhys—and that could not possibly go anywhere good. I had to remind myself that I had somewhere to be in less than two weeks.

And my brain was trying to mediate between my scared heart and my sex-starved body—

*I WANT HIM. I NEED HIM. PLEASE, PLEASE CAN I HAVE HIM?*

**No, silly libido. You can't have him. That's a terrible idea. He's too good. Too perfect. Nobody is that good, that perfect, and that means you can't have him because you don't get to have nice things. Or nice people.**

My brain, my heart and my body were all talking at once:

*We can't have Rhys, and what about Leighton and Jillie? It's just not PRACTICAL to get involved with Rhys right now, because we're not a one-night stand, hookup kind of girl and we're not in a place in our life that makes sense to get involved with a sexy, amazing, funny, successful, insanely hot guy…who likes us…and jerked off thinking about us…jerked off his giant, thick, hard cock. His HUGE, enormous cock …and he was thinking about ME… touching himself and imagining ME…and he saw my tits and I didn't die of embarrassment like I imagined I would if I guy I liked walked in on me. No, I did almost die, but from wishing he would just make a move and touch me, because the fingers I used on myself last night hadn't done crap to alleviate my need…*

My body had a loud, insistent voice, my heart had issues with trust, and my brain was all over the place.

I know I did everything I was supposed to, and I

did it all to the best of my ability, but the day just flew by like a flash, what with all the work and all the crazy round-and-round between my head, heart, and body.

It was after seven, almost seven thirty in the evening, before we saw Jeremy again, and he wandered the house, checking things over thoroughly—he opened every cabinet, every drawer, opened and shut every door, every window, turned on and off every light and every faucet. He checked behind doors, looked for forgotten painter's tape, peeled an errant strip of plastic off a piece of chrome trim around a mirror...he even checked the attic and basement. Turned on the heater and AC, made sure they both kicked on properly. Finally, he met us in the kitchen.

"Great job as always, Rhys," he said. "You never miss a thing do you, buddy?"

Jeremy was a huge guy, six feet four with broad shoulders and a beer belly, salt-and-blond hair, huge hairy hands, with Oakleys permanently affixed to the top of his buzzed scalp.

Rhys grinned, shrugged. "I do my best."

"Well, you do good work. The place looks great, and I get to turn over the keys a day early." He glanced at me, then. "You too, Torie. Not sure a place has ever sparkled this nice. You ever need work, you call me, I'll have something for you."

He handed me his card, and shook my hand.

Withdrawing a white envelope from his back pocket, he glanced at Rhys. "You guys got here at, what, one, and it's just about seven thirty?" He glanced at the ceiling, counting, then pulled out a battered cell phone from a hip pocket and did some quick math—counted out two piles of cash with the rapid, practiced movements of someone who counts out cash regularly, and handed one stack to me, and one to Rhys.

I was just as quick with cash, being a server, and noted that he paid Rhys an even hundred and fifty—which came out to just under twenty-five an hour. I got an even hundred, which meant he'd actually overpaid me by three dollars.

The nights I made a hundred as a server were golden days, and it was far more stressful work than this had been. I was definitely in the wrong business.

Rhys and Jeremy discussed the next job and shot the shit as guys do, and then Jeremy's phone rang and he waved at us as he vanished to do whatever guys like him do.

Rhys stretched, yawned, and glanced at me. "Well. That was a day's work, huh?"

"You do this every day? Work on cars and then build houses?"

He nodded. "And usually I go home and work on my realtor classes while I eat dinner, and then do some work on my restoration project."

"You work yourself to the bone."

He shrugged. "Used to it. It's how life has always been. I'd be up by six and at school by seven to do homework, go to school till three, work till at least nine most nights, sometimes even ten. Been my schedule since I was twelve years old."

I flapped my stack of twenties. "Thank you for this."

He snorted. "You did the work, you earned it."

"I mean the opportunity."

"Nah." Another wave of his hand, and then he eyed me with a grin. "You hungry?" My stomach growled in response, and he waved for me to follow. "Come on. I know a place that makes killer burgers. And I know the owner, so he may even accidentally give me an extra beer and then have work to do in the back, if you know what I mean."

And so we ended up in a tiny little dive bar, a hole-in-the-wall with unironic decor from the seventies. The owner, a short, stooped, gruff old guy with a voice that pegged him as being Jewish and from Brooklyn, greeted Rhys with a hug and a clap on the back.

"Rhys my boy, good to see you, son, good to see you. Been too long you're away, I miss you. Sit down, sit down already. You work your fingers to the nub, I tell you. I'll make you a burger, a big one, the juiciest

I got, extra fries too, of course. Gotta put some meat on those skinny ribs of yours, son." He looked over at me and addressed me with brown eyes sparkling with humor and zest for life. "And you bring a friend, too! Such a pretty friend, at that. Look at the eyes on this one, would you? I'm Marty, and you are?"

I shook his warm, strong, wrinkled hand. "Torie. Nice to meet you, Marty."

"Well, I don't have a menu because I only make one thing, but I make it better than anyone in four states, and that's a fact. So you're getting the biggest, juiciest cheeseburger you've ever had, you'll call me Pops like my good friends do. You're with Rhys, and that makes you good friend indeed. Rhys is a good man, I'll have you know. Not that I have to tell you, if you're here with him. But he's the finest, the best. Got my Fairlane working again and that old car is a piece of my heart. Wouldn't take a penny over cost, this boy, even though I know he spent hours of hard work figuring it out. But he's just that kind of person, and I hope you know it."

Rhys laughed, playfully socked Marty on the shoulder. "Ah shut up, Pops, you're embarrassing me."

Marty just waved him off and ambled off with a bad hip behind the bar, pulled two foamy dark beers and slid them over with a practiced flourish. "I only got two kinds'a beer, too, light and dark, local stuff a friend of mine brews. Rhys drinks it dark, and you look like you do, too. You're old enough, I take it? Of course you are. Now, you drink those and I'll have you kids fed in a jiffy."

I laughed as he vanished behind two double doors into the kitchen, and I heard the familiar rattle and clang of a spatula on a grill. "Wow, he's...a lot."

Rhys nodded, a grin on his face. "Yeah, he's even more high strung than me. He's gotta be at least eighty, but he's here at ten every morning and closes at two, and he does brisk business. All the local folks know him. We all call him Pops, and he treats us all like family. His car quit a while back, just quit working. It was...what, a '67 Fairlane? He couldn't afford to fix it, and he was riding the bus partway here and then walking a handful of miles. I saw him on the bus one day, followed him here, and asked why he wasn't driving. So, I fixed his car. Had to replace half the engine, but it was worth it to see how happy he was to have the car back. And now he only lets me pay half the time."

A comically short amount of time later, Marty brought out two plates, and he hadn't been lying— the burgers were colossal, dripping juice and cheese, and shoestring fries were piled high on the side. We thanked him, and he just waved and went to serve another local who came in at that moment—and he too was greeted with an effusive, familiar, mile-a-minute welcome.

Rhys finished half his burger in, like, three bites, and then leaned back and munched a few fries, his gaze speculative. "I had an idea."

I paused in the act of taking a bite. "Okay?"

"Now that the Nova is done and the Setters Road place is done, I actually have a little time. Usually, my jobs don't line up like that, so if I'm done with a rebuild, I'm only halfway through a house, or vice versa. So, this is a rare time for me, with both of them done. That being said, I can take some time off salvaging, and the realtor license classes are on my own time frame, no rush."

My heart leapt, and I tried to not hope he was saying what it seemed like he was saying. "Okay?"

"I was thinking, if you wanted, I could drive you part of the way. We could take turns driving, I mean. I haven't taken any time off in…shit, like, forever. So, yeah, it'd be fun, I think. I don't know that I'll be able to go all the way to Alaska, but I could get you started." He shrugged, glanced at his fries and played nonchalant. "Just thinking, you know. We get along pretty well, and…a road trip would be fun. If you wanted." He was nervous.

It was cute, and it made my heart pitter-patter.

And made other parts do...less familiar leaps and twists.

I tried to rein in my excitement. "Yeah. That'd be cool." Too reined in. "I mean, I...that sounds amazing, actually."

"It wouldn't be weird?" he asked. "I mean, we just met yesterday."

I shrugged. "I dunno. Yeah, we just met yesterday, but...maybe this sounds weird but...I feel like I know you. You know?"

"Like we're old friends," he said.

Old friends.

Old friends!

HOLY SHIT.

"Crap!" I dug my cell phone out of my pocket and glanced at it for the first time since yesterday. "I was supposed to check in with Leighton and Jillie yesterday."

"Roommates?"

I nodded as I called them both in a group FaceTime. "Yeah, roommates and best friends. They made me promise I'd check in every night at nine, and I forgot. The first night, and I forgot. God, I hope they didn't call the police."

Rhys chuckled. "Call the police? You've been gone less than forty-eight hours. Why would they call the police?"

I sighed as the line rang and rang. "Well, they both think this whole thing I'm doing is pretty stupid. They feel I should swallow my pride and just ask my sister to fly me up. They're both relatively certain I'm going to end up, as Leighton keeps saying, getting raped and murdered. So they made me swear I'd call them and check in every night at nine, or they'd call the police."

Just then, the line blurped and Leighton and Jillie appeared—clearly both at home, in their own rooms.

"I'm sorry!" I blurted. "I forgot. I was...I forgot. But I'm fine."

"You forgot...the very first night?" Leighton frowned, peering at her screen. "Wait. Where ARE you?"

"Um, well?" I winced. "I'm actually still in Connecticut."

Silence.

"You...what?" Jillie asked, blinking in confusion. "How? Why? Where?"

"Well, um. See, when I checked the bus times I was, you know, a little stoned. And I got the times mixed up. I thought there was a six thirty *p.m* bus, but it was actually six thirty *a.m.*"

"Oh my *god*, Torie, you dumbass." Leighton was laughing so hard she was snorting. "So what happened?"

"Well, I didn't exactly discover my mix-up right away. I walked to the bus station from work, which was…pretty far. And it started raining. Like, a torrential downpour."

"Oh no, you poor thing!" Jillie said. "That sucks."

"Yeah, it did. So then this, umm…Good Samaritan picked me up, and brought me to the bus station, and *that's* when I discovered that I'd mixed up the bus times." I was debating whether or not I should introduce Rhys to my friends.

"So then…?" Leighton prompted. "Why didn't you just come home?"

"Well, I was going to try the bus thing again the next morning. But I sort of overslept."

"Overslept *where*?" Leighton demanded. "You're leaving out something major, I can tell."

I eyed Rhys. He just grinned, and reached for the phone. Reluctantly, with an apologetic wince for him at the apoplectic, disbelieving interrogation he was about to receive, I handed it over.

He let out a breath, and turned on a charming smile that had my heart going pitter-patter a mile a minute. "Hi, Leighton and Jillie. My name is Rhys Frost. I'm Torie's new friend. She stayed at my place last night—*alone*. I live less than fifteen minutes from the bus station, and I was going to drive her there this morning, but we both kind of overslept, so she helped me out with some work today and made some cash. I'm twenty-six, single, I own my own engine repair and auto salvage company, I have an older sister who lives in Dallas and both parents are living and married and live in Kentucky. I have no record, criminal or traffic, and I think everyone should be so lucky as to have friends as awesome as you guys are to Torie." He paused. "Any other questions?"

There was stunned silence from both of them.

"I...do you have any plans to rape and murder my friend?" Leighton asked.

Rhys burst out laughing. "God, you found me out. Damn it. If only you hadn't guessed my nefarious plan." He laughed again.

I took the phone back. "There. That's my friend who I'm with, and now you know." I made a face of significant meaning—*shut up, don't ask any embarrassing questions, DON'T YOU FUCKING DARE*. "I really will be heading out for Alaska tomorrow, though. And I will check in tomorrow night."

"I just have one question," Leighton began.

"Ley, no. Do *not*." I glared at her. "The answer is no, and not another word out of you."

"How do you know what I'm going to ask?" she said, pretending to sound wounded.

"Because I know you."

"I was just going to ask—"

"LEIGHTON."

"—why a guy as hot as Rhys is still single," she finished.

Argh. "Dammit, Leighton, do you have to be so embarrassing?"

Rhys laughed, sounding a little self-conscious. "Well, I'm really busy. I work a lot, and I have goals I want to accomplish by a certain time, and that doesn't really leave time for…romance, I guess."

"What are those goals?" Leighton asked.

"Rhys and I have to finish eating our lunches, now," I cut in. "So question and answer hour is officially over. I've checked in, you got the story, you know I'm fine, I'll talk to you both tomorrow…"

"Torie, wait," Leighton started. "I have so many questions—"

Jillie just rolled her eyes and laughed. "Let it be, Ley. Bye, Torie! Be safe, love you."

"Bye, girls. Love you both." I ended the call, powered the phone off, and stuffed it back into my pocket. I glanced at Rhys. "Sorry to ambush you like that."

He just laughed. "Leighton isn't shy, is she?"

I cackled. "Um, no. If I hadn't shut it down, she'd probably have asked you for a dick measurement and if you have any illegitimate children out there."

"I don't have any idea, never measured, and absolutely not."

I blushed, not expecting him to answer either. "That was meant to be rhetorical, but…" I tilted my head to one side. "I guess I figured with guys being as obsessed as they are with dick size, that every guy has measured his dick at some point."

He rolled his eyes, shrugged. "Nah. Not all guys are *obsessed*. If a chick has made a guy feel insecure, maybe. If he feels like he's insufficient, maybe." An awkward pause, as he tried to figure out how say what he meant without sounding arrogant. "I guess I've never gotten any complaints, so no, I've never felt compelled to measure. And, I mean, everybody is different. So what would knowing do for me? I'd have to know the average size so I would know where I fall within that range and, depending on the answer, either end up feeling like I'm Mr. Big Dick, or feel shitty about myself because I'm below average. No thanks. I've got what I've got, and I'm happy with it. As long as my partner is happy with my performance with what I've got, then that's all that matters to me."

I felt my blush deepening from pink to as crimson as the thong he'd picked up off the floor this morning. "Oh, I'm definitely no expert, but I'd say you're well above average. Just…based purely on my limited observation."

"Thanks," he murmured. "I'll try not to let it go to my head."

"Because you've already got a big head?" I heard myself say, and then, gobsmacked at myself for saying such a thing, I clapped a hand over my mouth. "I can't believe I said that."

Rhys scraped his hat backward off his head and scratched his scalp. "So, anyway." He was grinning, somewhere between flattered and embarrassed. "The road trip idea."

"If you really want to do it, because you want to and not because you're trying to just be nice to me, then I'm down." I leveled a look at him. "No charity, or any of that garbage."

He frowned. "Doing something nice for someone doesn't have to be charity or pity. It can just be a matter of that person being…a decent human being." He grinned at me, then. "That being said, I've never taken any time off. I've worked every spare moment of my day, seven days a week, since as long as I can remember. And there's no telling when, if ever, I'll have a moment between jobs like this again, so I'm gonna take it. And, in the interest of being up front, I'm choosing to spend this rare free time with you, because you're cool, and I like you, and also you're hot and a road trip with a hot chick is always a great idea. Not that I would know from experience, but it sounds like a great time." He paused, cleared his throat. "And I'm gonna shut up now."

I bit my lip to stop myself from laughing. "So we're going on a road trip." I was excited. More excited than I should be. "Just promise me one thing—you won't go any farther than you're comfortable with." I laughed awkwardly, realizing how that could be taken. "Farther on the road, meaning you don't have to take me all the way to Alaska. That would be ridiculous. Just…tell me when you're ready to turn around and I'll go the rest of the way on my own. That's what I meant by not going farther." I covered my face. "This is getting awkward. I mean, you're not awkward, I'm awkward. You're gorgeous. Wait, what?'"

He laughed. "We're both awkward. It's cool."

I sighed. "That last part was a quote from *Frozen*. But also true."

Marty ambled up to us, then. Snagged our empty beer glasses. "You kids want another one?"

Rhys shook his head. "Nah, I'm good, Pops. Gotta drive."

"Such a responsible boy you are." Marty tossed the glasses into a sink behind the bar. "You have an extra few minutes for me, sometime? The Fairlane is making a funny noise when I turn, and I was hoping you could look at it."

Rhys nodded. "Yeah, I can take a look. Is it clicking when you turn? Louder when you go faster or turn more sharply?"

Marty nodded. "Exactly what it's doing. See? You know without even having to look at it."

"Well, noises when you turn can only be a handful of things. But it's not too serious." He glanced at me. "You got anywhere to be right now?"

I laughed. "You're my ride, so no."

"True," he said. "I guess I was asking if you'd be okay with me looking at his car now. I don't want to drag you around town on my bullshit, though."

I smiled, shrugged and shook my head. "Helping a dear like Marty isn't bullshit, Rhys. I'm down."

Marty patted me on the hand, winking at Rhys. "She's a keeper, this one."

Neither Rhys nor I knew how to respond to that one, so both of us kept quiet. Rhys fished cash out of his hip pocket, peeled off two twenties, and handed them to Marty. "You wouldn't take anything last time, so now it's my turn. You're taking that and no arguments." He glanced at an old analog clock on the wall. "You're here till close, Marty?"

Marty crumpled the bills in his fist, nodding. "Till I kick Jimmy and O'Hearn out, and they'll be here till I stop giving 'em beer."

"Well, since I've got Torie with me, we could drive the Fairlane to the shop, and I could fix it, or at least know what the issue is, and have it back to you before close. With that old Fairlane, though, just as a warning, you may need a whole new front-end suspension. I remember noting it being pretty well aged when I poked around last time."

Marty sighed, waved a hand, dug his keys out of his pocket and handed them to Rhys. "Just do what you gotta do to keep the old girl running, and we'll figure something out about payment."

Rhys nodded. "All right. I'll call you and let you know."

We left the little dive through the back door, waving to Marty as we passed through the kitchen. The Fairlane was parked in a tiny alley—it was white, beautifully painted, clean, no rust.

Rhys ran a hand over the hood. "Gorgeous car. Wonder of it is, it's original. He's kept it in this condition since he's owned it, and he's owned it since it was new. He and his wife bought it together—it was their first car. He had it repainted a few years ago, and I did the engine work, but it's just a miracle of a car. If he let me pull the engine, clean it, tighten the tranny up, and reupholster the interior? He could sell it for thirty, forty grand. He would never do it, but he *could*. Maybe get even more than that since it's all original and not a refurb."

I knew it was dumb of me, but every time he started talking cars, I just got all giddy and my belly tightened and my thighs pressed together and I just wanted to climb on him and kiss him until he…well, did things to me I'd promised myself we wouldn't do.

Until Rhys, I hadn't known I was so turned on by car talk.

Or maybe it was just Rhys.

I wasn't sure, but it was a very real thing.

"What?" He glanced at me quizzically. "You're looking at me funny."

I was looking at him like I wanted to do things with him that I'd only ever done with Max, and only in the dark, and only under the inhibition-loosening effects of pot.

"Nothing." I shrugged.

"Okay. I don't believe you, but okay." He indicated the Fairlane. "Hop in and I'll drop you off at my Jeep."

The inside of the Fairlane smelled like peppermint candy and cologne and old car. The seats were that velvety cloth they used to use, and there was a small gold oval photo frame dangling by a thin chain from the rearview mirror—inside the frame was a black and white photo of a beautiful young woman. Stuck into a seam of the dashboard was another photo, this one of a much younger Marty and the same woman, holding each other in what the internet now called "the prom pose." Rhys pulled down the visor and carefully let a stack of photos slide out into his hand—he showed them to me: Marty and his wife in their thirties, then in their forties…a photo from each decade together, until the last one, Marty and his wife together as an old couple, a few years ago.

"They were married for sixty-three years. Jenny passed four years ago, and I think Marty is just biding his time until he's ready to go, too." He stuffed the photos gently back where they'd been, and started the car. It chugged over into a rumble, the kind of throaty, belly-buzzing rumble only a classic with a big block can make. "I don't think he realized I tuned him some extra horsepower when I rebuilt his engine and replaced the exhaust. I couldn't resist. He could beat just about anything off the line, if he wanted, but he drives as slow and careful as you could imagine."

"You just…casually tuned his engine."

Rhys laughed. "Well, I had the whole top half apart, so I was already into the damn thing. Might as well bore out the cylinders a little while I'm there, right? Upgrade the intake manifold, put a better four barrel carb on there, and bam, he's turning out almost four hundred horses."

"None of that is stuff you just…*do*, just because. I don't know much, but I know those are all difficult, expensive upgrades."

He shrugged. "I had the thing out and taken apart anyway. His exhaust system was corroded through in several places, his carburetor was shot, and the intake manifold was rusted to shit. It all had to be replaced. So yeah, I may've put in parts that were technically more performance-grade than he strictly needed, but I had them on hand because a guy had me order them and then backed out on the job, so gave 'em to Marty for cost."

I patted his arm. "You sound almost defensive about doing something nice for him. I was just pointing out that you made it sound easier than it was."

"Well, I did sorta go negative on that job, helping him. And you can't really run a business on acts of generosity. I know that. But what I lost in labor costs, I've gained back and then some, in the amount of food and beer he's comped me since then."

"You shouldn't feel defensive about being a good person."

He laughed. "I know. And thanks. Not everybody understands, though."

"Yeah, well, altruism seems to be as much of a dying art as driving a manual, huh?"

He eyed me. "You think I'm altruistic?"

"Sure. You go out of your way to help people, no matter what it costs you."

He rubbed the back of his neck as he pulled up to the curb behind his Jeep. "I gained a friend, and a friend who gives me free beer and fuckin' great burgers. So I've gained as much as it cost me to comp the labor."

"And everything you've done to help me? Where's the benefit for you?" I had my hand on the latch, ready to get out.

He paused over his response. "I've done nothing. I picked you up. Spent, what, a few bucks in gas? Food I already had, some hot water? You helped me finish the Nova in half the usual time, and I got a great dinner companion."

I felt a heat in my belly, warmth on my cheeks, something powerful swirling between my thighs. "Should we get going?" I asked.

He nodded, dug his keys out of his pocket. "Third gear sticks a little, gotta put some oomph into it when you shift into and out of it."

"Got it." I took the keys, and hesitated, meeting his eyes.

It felt like there was more to say, but I wasn't sure what it was. Just...something, unsaid, something percolating under the surface.

I knew what was unsaid for me, but it wasn't something I was ready to tell him just yet.

Telling a guy you're a virgin tends to have...deleterious effects on the relationship. And I liked Rhys. Best to keep that little nugget to myself for now.

No point, right? It wasn't going to go there. Besides, I'd promised myself.

Plus, once he found out, it may not go there anyway. Guys were weird like that.

I got behind the wheel of his big old red Jeep, and started it up. I followed him back to his place and wondered if it felt a little too much like going home.

# SIX

## Rhys

Torie driving my Jeep gave me a hell of a hard-on. Now, granted, there wasn't much about the girl that didn't, but a sexy girl driving a lifted Jeep, yanking the shifter through the gears? Almost as hot as when she'd done the burnout. God, I think my cock had nearly exploded. And the ache hadn't lessened in the intervening time. And the more time I spent around her, the harder—sorry, more *difficult*—it became to control the damn thing. And when she made jokes about how big my cock was? Gaaaah.

How the hell was a guy supposed to keep his shit contained under such circumstances?

Especially when I'd seen her tits bare, and she'd seen me jerking my turkey to thoughts of *her*.

I growled. I'd have to find a few minutes alone at some point, or I *would* have a mess on my hands. Or rather, in my pants.

Probably at an inopportune moment.

For now, I just had to keep things under some kind of control, keep my eyes, hands, and overactive imagination to myself. Get Marty's car fixed. Get it back to him. Get some sleep. Figure out why the in the blue fuck I'd offered to go on a road trip with a girl I wanted like hell, but with whom I knew nothing could happen, because she'd said she couldn't.

I wasn't one to play games or push. If she said she couldn't start nothin', I wasn't going to force it. If she wanted to change her mind, I'd be there waiting to see what we could get into.

We got Marty's car into my garage and up on the lift, and I pulled the tire off the suspect side—I'd heard the noise myself and knew exactly what the issue was. And, yep, as suspected, his front suspension was no good. Fortunately for Marty, I'd salvaged a '68 Galaxie that had been rear-ended and then vandalized—the back end was toast, smashed glass, it was missing both back wheels, and the interior was rotten through, but the whole front end was basically perfect. And the Galaxie was essentially the same car, with the same suspension as the Fairlane.

It took a couple hours to get the Galaxie where I could get at it, lift the front end, and get the suspension free, and another hour or so to put it onto Marty's car. Torie was essential, able to get into places and do things I couldn't or at least not easily, willing to learn, eager to help. We got it done together in less than half the time it'd have taken me alone, and we had the Fairlane back to Marty in record time.

We got back to my place again, and by this time it was past midnight. Torie yawned prodigiously, which made me yawn.

"God, I'm gonna sleep like the dead," she said. "What a day."

"No kidding." I was trying to figure out how I could get a shower in without asking her to sit alone in the garage.

She eyed me. "What?"

I arched an eyebrow. "What, what?"

"You're thinking about something."

I laughed. "How can you tell?"

"You always scratch the back of your head when you're thinking about what to say."

I blinked at her. "I...do?"

"Yeah, you do."

"Oh. Never realized that." I rolled a shoulder. "Well, I need a shower. But you're about to fall asleep."

She nodded. "And you don't want to inconvenience me."

"Well, I don't want to keep you up any longer."

She patted my forearm, and somehow how her hand ended up just...staying there, on my forearm. "I'll sit on the outside steps and call my sister."

When we got back inside, she went right for the side exit. "Just let me know when you're done. No accidentally walking in on you, this time."

I choked on a laugh—mainly because I was planning on doing exactly what she'd walked in on me doing the last time.

I couldn't help it. I wanted what I couldn't have, but that didn't mean I couldn't imagine it.

So, once she was out on the steps and I heard her talking to her sister, I turned on the shower to let the water heat up, stripped and tossed my dirty clothes in the hamper, and then stepped into the shower. Adjusted the water. Contemplated grabbing my phone and finding visual stimulation.

Didn't need it. The moment I was naked and soaking in the hot water, my mind went right to Torie. She'd been in this shower less than twenty-four hours ago. Naked. Scrubbing her skin. Water sluicing down between her tight, pert breasts and plump nipples. Maybe she'd played with herself a little. I wondered if she liked to do it in bed, or in the shower?

Maybe both.

She'd admitted she'd thought about me...I wondered what she'd imagined, or if we'd fantasized about the same thing. Probably not.

She probably didn't imagine herself sliding over my body, laying on top of me, reaching for me, mouth open, ready to taste me.

She probably didn't imagine herself spread out on the cherry-red hood of a muscle car, taking me deep as we moved together...

Shit.

On second thought, she may very well be all about that second scenario. I noticed the way she shifted and hid a grin when I started spewing technical jargon.

It turned her on, for some reason. I should be so lucky to find a chick who was a gearhead and got off on gearhead shit like talking about Holley carburetors and Edelbrock air cleaners and boring out piston cylinders for extra horsepower.

The image of Torie splayed out on her back on the hood of a red muscle car wouldn't go away. There'd be classic rock playing the background, sun shining through the open bay door. I'd be all greasy, and she'd be all white and clean and perfect. She'd strip for me, sultry and slow. Lie back on the hood and reach for me. I'd slide up the sculpted sheet metal, and my hands would leave dark smears on her pale fresh skin. Her legs would wrap around me, her lips would touch mine and whisper to me, maybe my name, or maybe a plea to take her right then, right now...just like this.

My fist was a blur on my cock, and I was aching, pulsating with pent-up need, picturing Torie beneath me and her skin against mine, writhing with me, begging me for more...

I spurted all over the shower, and the water rinsed it away, and I finished the rest of my shower hoping I'd be able to get through this road trip with my sanity and my self-administered standards of morality intact.

I knew she was attracted to me.

I knew she knew I was attracted to her.

I wanted her more with every passing day, and it would take only the smallest spark for the churning fuel of my desire for her to combust into something explosive. A touch, a look, a hint that she'd changed her mind. That she wanted me, for whatever I could give her, for however long we had together.

It'd be temporary. It could only be temporary. Maybe that was why she was resistant to starting anything—she wasn't a fling type of chick. Shit, I knew she deserved more.

I just couldn't give her that.

I had goals. Plans.

And they didn't involve getting tied down with a woman, even one as amazing as Torie.

No, it was best to keep my fantasies of Torie just that—fantasies. For her sake and my own.

Because something told me if I got my hands on her, I'd have a hell of a hard time letting go.

I got dressed in clean gym shorts and a cut-off Pennzoil T-shirt. Poked my head out the side door and glanced at Torie, who was still on the phone. She smiled and nodded at me, held up a finger.

"Yeah, no, he's here now." She pulled the phone away from her ear, glanced at me. "Lexie wants to talk to you. You don't have to, if you don't want to."

I reached for the phone. "It's cool, I'll say hi."

"She's worse than Leighton, so just…be warned."

That gave him pause. "Worse…how?"

*"Exactly how am I worse than Leighton?"* We both heard Lexie's tinny voice over the phone—she'd clearly heard me.

"She'll ask you ridiculously inappropriate and personal questions simply for having any association with me at all."

*"Just give him the phone, you silly twat."* Lexie was audible even from a distance.

Torie took the phone back. "What the hell did you just call me?"

*"I mean it with love, Tor, you know that."*

"Well, coming from someone who was majoring in women's lit, and was all about liberation and equality and whatever, it's kind of a gross thing to call me."

Lexie's response was garbled, too muffled for me to make out, but it seemed to mollify Torie, and she handed me the phone again.

"Hi, this is Rhys," I said.

"Rhys, buddy, hi, how are you?" Lexie's voice, which I recognized from YouTube and other social media, was deceptively friendly and breezy.

Which made me distinctly wary, considering Torie's warning.

"I'm good, how are you? It's nice to meet you, sort of."

A pause. "Is my sister sitting right next to you?"

"Yeah."

"Can she hear me?"

I glanced at Torie, who was watching but didn't give any indication that she'd heard the question.

"I don't know, maybe?"

Another pause. "Have you had sex with my sister, and if not, do you plan to have sex with my sister at any point in the near future?"

I coughed. "Well...right out with it, huh? All right, I can respect that." I stood up, paced down the steps a ways. "If I had or hadn't, I wouldn't feel comfortable telling you. I haven't met you face to face, number one, number two, that would be between Torie and me, and number three, if Torie wants you to know the answer to that, she'll tell you. I've got no issue with her telling you the answer to that question, but it's not my place to do so."

"Huh," she mused. "Damn good answer. Not the one I was hoping for, but a good one."

"Anything else you want to know?"

"I mean, yeah. A ton of stuff I doubt you'll answer. What are your intentions? What do you want from her? Why are you going so far out of your way to help her? What's going to happen between you two when she's out here in Alaska and you're not?"

I barked a laugh. "Honestly, I can't answer any of that, because I don't really know." I moved further down the steps, out of earshot of Torie. "Mainly because it's not like that. It may not ever be like that. I can't say part of me doesn't *want* it to be like that because she's cool as hell and gorgeous. But…Alaska?"

"But Alaska, right." She sighed. "All right, well…I can't argue with that answer. Just…be careful with her, okay? Don't hurt her."

I laughed. "She's not delicate, Lexie. She's strong, and she's smart. She can take care of herself. I have no intentions of hurting her, of course, but telling me to be careful with her seems like you're a little…unaware of her strength as a person."

"Damn, okay, tell me how it is."

"Just saying."

"Game respects game, Rhys. All right, give me my sister back."

"Yeah. Bye. Good talking to you, Lexie."

"You too, Rhys."

I went up and gave the phone back to a wary and bemused Torie. I just shrugged, grinned, and headed back inside.

Torie was out there a few more minutes and then came in, phone in hand. "What did she ask you?"

I debated what to say and what to not say. And in the end figured I had nothing to lose by telling the whole truth and nothing but the truth. "She asked if we'd had sex, if I planned to have sex with you, what my intentions for you are, why I'm helping you, and what's going to happen between us when you're in Alaska and I'm here."

Her eyes widened, and a flush crept up into her cheeks. "And? What'd you say? About the first two questions specifically."

"I said it wasn't my place to answer that, and if you wanted her to know you'd tell her. And that I had no problem with you and her talking about what you and I have and have not done together."

"I'm sorry she asked you that—" Torie started.

I interrupted. "Don't be. You're lucky as hell to have the kind of family and friends that check in on you like this, that are willing to ask those kinds of questions. I don't mind. I'm not going to answer questions I don't think are my place to answer, but I respect the fact that they love you enough to ask."

"Your family doesn't do that? What about friends?"

I shrugged. I was acting more nonchalant than I perhaps felt. "Well, my family isn't...we're not like that. I wasn't beat up and they weren't alcoholics—which put me way better off than most of the kids I knew. I mean, they drank plenty and probably more than they should, but Shania's parents were...god, they were downright evil, and drunk from wake up to pass out." I sighed. "Anyway, no, we're not like that. They don't really call and check on me except maybe once a month or every other, and honestly they only call then to see if I can send 'em money. And my sister...? Well, like I said, we try to check in with one another a couple times a month. As for friends? I got some guys I'd call friends. From the jobsite, mainly. Some old clients will sometimes swing by to shoot the shit and talk cars. There's Marty. But, honestly, no I don't really have anyone who would check on me. I'm on my own, more or less." I laughed bitterly. "Kinda pathetic, now that I put it in so many words."

"Are you a loner by nature?"

I rolled a shoulder. "I guess so? I've never been the guy who has a whole, like, herd of friends. I had a buddy in middle school and high school, Dougy. We were pretty close. He'd help me salvage, and I'd give him some cash, which he'd use on booze and firecrackers."

"Firecrackers?"

I laughed. "Yeah, he had a thing for blowin' shit up. Firecrackers in middle school. But by high school he was tossing sticks of dynamite down rabbit holes."

She stared at me. "He'd...what?"

I laughed. "Not with anything in 'em—he'd shove a stick down the hole first, make sure nothin' came out. He just liked the big explosions. Never lost any fingers or anything, so he sort of knew what he was doing."

"Where is he now?"

"Joined the Army, went to Iraq, and stepped on an IED." I picked at my shorts. "Went out the way he'd have wanted, though—in an explosion." I glanced upward. "That joke was for you, Dougy."

She was quiet. "Wow. I'm sorry."

I shrugged. "The day he shipped out overseas, he called me. Said, 'well, buddy, I'm off to get myself killed. You be good, now, hear?' So, I think he knew, somehow."

She was quiet a long time. "My dad...the week before he died, we were working on the MG. He stopped, looked at me, and said, 'Torie, I hope you know I love you, more than anything. And that I'm sorry.'" She sniffled. "I asked what he meant, but he wouldn't say another word. One week later to the day, he died of a heart attack."

"God, Torie. I'm so sorry."

She swallowed. "I've never told anyone that— what he said to me. It just...it's always freaked me out. Like, did he know? Why would he say that? I don't think he really knew why he said what he said, because he seemed...confused. I don't know."

"Death is a weird thing," I said.

"Sure is."

A silence. Long, and profound.

"I think I'm going to go to bed," she said. "I'm so tired."

I shook my head. "Go to sleep. I'll putz around downstairs for a while."

She blinked, swallowed, eyed me. "You don't have to. I can usually fall asleep pretty easily."

Wish I could say the same. I had trouble falling asleep under normal circumstances—but with Torie only feet away, it'd be damn near impossible.

But, I was tired too, and I didn't feel like dicking around in the shop.

What I felt like doing was climbing in with Torie and getting her naked and kissing every inch of her...

I had to look away from her. Nodded. "Yeah, all right."

And so we went to our separate places.

Sleep was a long time coming. I heard every sound she made—I was hyperaware of her. Her sniffles and snorts, each time she rustled and rolled. I fought my imagination tooth and nail, trying to keep my mind off her, to keep her clothed in my mind.

I failed.

Miserably.

I kept seeing her, again and again, standing there with her shirt in her hands, looking at me, breasts bare and pale and plump and upturned and perfect and begging to be kissed and touched.

I tossed and turned, trying to blank out my mind.

Hours passed.

Eventually, I gave up. I heard Torie doing her soft light snore, not really even a snore, just a loud breathing. I went downstairs and grabbed a socket wrench and attacked the front bench seat of my F-100, freeing it and hauling it out, dragging it outside to the salvage yard. I stood out there in the late night or early morning cool—I wasn't even sure what time it was. I looked up, missing the wash and spray of stars I used to be able to see back in Kentucky. Here, there was too much light pollution. I could only really see Venus and few brighter stars.

Lost in memory, in thought, I didn't register the sound of the door opening and closing. Or of Torie's presence until she was beside me. "Not many stars to see," she said.

I jumped. "Oh, hey. Sorry, I hope I didn't wake you up." I gestured up at the sky. "Nah, not too many, not around here."

"I've never been out of Connecticut."

I eyed her. "So you've never seen the stars, like for real? Out in the country, where there ain't no lights, you can see just about every damn star there is in the galaxy."

She shook her head. "Nope. Suburbanite born and raised."

"Damn, girl." I shook my head. "This road trip, we'll do a section at night and stop somewhere out in the middle of nowhere. Ain't nothin' like it."

She smiled. "I'd like that." She glanced at me. "Sometimes you sound more country than other times."

I laughed. "Yeah, it comes and goes. Been up here long enough I'm starting to lose the accent, and honestly I get less shit from folks if I don't sound like a backwoods Kentucky hillbilly. Clients question me less, and take me more seriously. Fewer dumb questions. So I guess I'm working at losing it. But if I'm tired or whatever, sometimes it just…comes out."

"I don't mind. I kind of like it, actually."

"You do?" I smirked at her, bemused.

"Yeah. It's cute."

"You don't think it makes me sound like a mouth-breathing yokel?"

She cackled. "No, Rhys. You're smart, and there's no mistaking that, no matter what you sound like."

"Why're you up?" I asked.

She shrugged. "Woke up to pee and you weren't there. Wondered where you'd got off to."

"I…couldn't sleep."

Her eyes bored into me. "Because of me?"

I tipped my head side to side. "Not in the sense that you did anything. Just…I'm used to being alone."

"Don't bullshit me."

"What do you want to hear, Torie?"

"The real reason you couldn't sleep."

I turned to face her, leaned back against the rusted hulk of an '89 LeSabre. "The real reason? Sure you want that? I don't think you do."

"Why wouldn't I?"

"Because it's you. You're the reason I can't sleep. I get stuck thinking about you." I held her gaze.

"About you in that fucking wet T-shirt." I swallowed hard. "You without any shirt at all. I didn't mean for any of that to happen, and I mean that as true as my own name. But now I can't sleep for thinking about you, like that."

She was blushing, I was sure, though I couldn't really tell in the middle-of-the-night gloom of shadows, and the dull waning crescent moon glow. "Rhys…"

"Told you." I turned away. Peeled at a chunk of paint on the LeSabre's hood. "It ain't your fault, nor mine. And I know, you don't want to start anything, because of your trip to Alaska. And I get it. I respect it. But you wanted the truth? There it is. I can't sleep for thinking about how goddamn sexy you are, whether you're in clothes or topless, and damn if I don't want to see more of you—every damn inch of you bare. I won't push it. I'll keep my shit contained. But yeah, Torie…I'm thinking about you naked. And picturing doing things to you that'd make you blush so hard you'd start a fire."

She didn't say anything. Her eyes didn't leave me for a long, long time. Her mouth opened, closed. Her fingers twisted at the bottom of her T-shirt. Eventually, her gaze dropped, and she reached into the pocket of her shorts—tiny little things that only just covered her butt.

I couldn't make out much, but I knew what she

was doing—lifting the little tube to her mouth, lighting, inhaling. Holding.

She passed it to me, and I gratefully took it, lit it, and dragged on it; I'd slept like a baby last time, and maybe this would help me get some sleep tonight. I handed it back. "Thanks."

"I lied," she said, barely audible.

"About?"

"I woke up because I had a dream about you."

"Good dream?"

"A confusing dream. Because I...I want things. But...I'm afraid if I get involved with you, even just...just temporarily, I'll get...messed up. Attached. Involved. Wanting more than what it is. You've got your life here, and mine is...I don't even know. Leighton and Jillie don't think I'm coming back. And part of me thinks they're right. So, I...I want things, but I'm scared. And...there's other stuff that I...that I can't really talk about."

I had a dozen different responses to that, and no idea which to say. "Torie, I..."

"You don't have to say anything, Rhys. It's just safest for my heart if I don't let anything start. But don't think I don't want to. That I don't feel...*this*."

"Is this road trip a bad idea?" I asked, keeping my voice low, because if I was too loud, she might hear things I was feeling that I didn't want her hear.

"Probably," she laughed. "But smoking pot is the only interesting thing I've ever done in my life. I've never gotten a speeding ticket. Never gone anywhere. Never had a boyfriend. A lot of nevers—my whole fucking life is a list of 'I've never.' So…a bad idea, yeah, but I want to go on a road trip with a guy I just met. I guy I like—a superhot guy who's attracted to me, who's seen me half-naked, who wants to do things to me that I'm probably better off not knowing about. A guy who, in the interests of self-preservation, I shouldn't let anything happen with. A guy I like more than I've ever liked anyone. It's crazy, and maybe irresponsible. But I want to do it, just to say I've done at least one crazy, possibly irresponsible thing in my life."

"You got a bucket list, Torie?" I asked.

"A bucket list?" she repeated.

"Yeah, like a list of things you haven't ever done that you really want to do before you die."

She mused thoughtfully. "I mean, yeah. Sure. A lot of stuff."

"Like what?"

She laughed. "Some of them are embarrassing."

"So?"

She eyed me. "You can't laugh at me."

I laughed anyway. "How about I promise if I do laugh, it won't be out of meanness, and I won't make fun of you."

"Fair enough." She took a deep breath; held it, let it out; her words coming out in a rush, toppling over each other. "I want to go skinny-dipping. I want to drive a car more than a hundred miles per hour. I want to be kissed in the rain like Noah and Ally from *The Notebook*." She hesitated. "I want…I want to have sex in the bed of a pickup truck under the stars. I want to give a man a blowjob for no reason at all, surprise him with it. Maybe in a car while he's driving, I haven't decided. I want a guy to…to go down on me for no reason, and want nothing in return. I want to get a mani-pedi and a massage and a facial all in the same day. I want to go to a fancy steakhouse and order the most expensive thing on the menu. I want to stay in bed all day, watching movies and having crazy hot monkey sex and smoking copious amounts of marijuana. I want…I want to fall in love and have the man I love tell me I'm his everything. Because I've never felt like anyone's everything and I want to know what that feels like." She exhaled sharply, glanced at me. "There. The list, which no one else on the planet, even Jillie and Leighton, has ever heard. Now you tell me yours."

I hesitated. "I gotta be honest, then, since you were." I spent a moment in silence, considering. "I want to restore a classic pickup, one of the really valuable ones, like a '48 Dodge Power Wagon, and do it without sparing any expense, and I want to sell it at

Mecum. I want to make a million dollars before I'm forty. I want a big family, someday. Like, way in the future someday, but I do. I was lonely as a kid, and I just…yeah. I want a big family. I want…I want to be with someone, someday, who I can wake up with and have lazy morning sex with. I want to sell a car I've restored to someone famous. Stupid, I know, but whatever. I want to be woken up by a blowjob. I want to see the Grand Canyon. I want to fly an airplane. I want to see a whale. Stupidest one yet, but I want a big surprise birthday party. I've never had a birthday party. Folks were too poor. Mom'd make me a cupcake and put one candle in it, and Dad would give me whatever cash he had left from paying bills that month."

We looked at one another and a million things passed unsaid between us. "Seems like some of those things sorta match mine," she said.

I cleared my throat. "I noticed that, too." I laughed. "Never thought I'd tell anyone any of that."

"Me either."

Silence.

"I'm gonna try to sleep, now," I said, eventually.

"Me too."

I finally managed to fall asleep, but my dreams were of Torie.

Of doing the things on our lists…together.

# SEVEN

## Torie

WHEN I WOKE UP, RHYS HAD ALREADY MADE COFFEE, and had bacon frying. Good lord, I could get used to waking up to the smell of coffee and bacon.

He was shirtless, in nothing but a pair of gym shorts. They were a little too big for him, hanging low on his hips. Facing away from me, he had his phone in his pocket and earbuds trailing by the cord, and he was dancing. God, it was freaking adorable. He was shaking his hips, waving his hands around, a pair of tongs in one hand. Head bobbing side to side.

The shorts revealed just a hint of his buttocks, the dip of the crack and upper swell of each firm cheek. His back was broad yet lean, rippling with muscle.

I pretended I was sleeping so I could watch him.

He did a spin, faced me and, holy shitballs, his abs were absurd. Ripped. Hard. The baggy shorts hung down past his hips, revealed those sharp lines leading in a V down to his groin, and as he shook his hips to whatever music he was listening to, I could see his cock swaying against the front of the shorts, pushing and pressing.

My thighs pressed together, and my belly tightened, and my core heated. Liquid heat pooled in my center, and my nipples ached. My breasts felt heavy, tight. The way he moved, the way he danced...god, I wanted to move with him. Press up against him, slide against his hard body, touch his bare skin, feel the muscles of his back shifting under his skin, slide my hand under the waist of his shorts and cup that hard ass, feel it move under my palm. Slide my touch around and grasp him...

I closed my eyes and turned over, as if rolling over in my sleep.

Need pounded in me.

He was right there.

I couldn't.

NO.

But my fingers slid down and dipped into the front of my sleep shorts. I touched my clit. I lay on my side, knees drawn up, feigning sleep, keeping my breathing steady. Hoping his earbuds would block out whatever sounds I made. Hoping he was cooking bacon and not watching me.

Because I was feeling just reckless and careless and achy enough to do this. Now. No matter what.

I desperately needed the release.

I moved my upper leg away, just enough to allow my fingers access. As I touched myself I had that image of Rhys down at his desk, his huge thick cock in his hand, hunched over himself, head bowed, fist moving hard and fast.

I'd wanted to go to him and take care of things for him. Show him how it should be—soft and slow and gentle. Not rough and hard and almost angry.

I let my mind wander, to a fantasy of being in bed with him. Waking up to a slow warm yellow dawn. Feeling his erection, taking it in my hand. Stroking him. Making him come. Or, maybe taking him inside me. Making love to him. Holding him as I came. I'd come every time with him, and each time would be more incredible than the last. He'd probably be eager to taste me. I fantasized about that, him kneeling between my thighs, his tongue lashing me, tasting me, and that, oh god that made me wild. I had to hold my breath and grit my teeth to keep from crying out, and the very thought of his tongue on my clit was enough to send me reeling over the edge, and I tensed all over, my breath caught in my teeth, the orgasm pounding through me.

I couldn't believe I was doing this—masturbating with Rhys mere feet away, possibly even watching me. It made me come all the harder, for some reason.

I wondered if he knew. If he was watching.

I dared not look.

I felt the waves crash through me, my finger slipping in quick deft circles, coming and coming, needing to cry out, to gasp, to whimper, and not daring to make a single sound, and I came so hard I was seeing stars.

I had to let out my breath, and then tried like hell to slow my panting breath.

When it finally faded, I was limp and delirious, yet still fraught with a need for Rhys as hot and wild and deep as it had ever been.

Dammit.

Even so, I waited a couple more minutes, and then rolled over. Yawned, stretched. Glanced at Rhys—who was facing the stove, flipping bacon and wiggling his butt.

Maybe I'd gotten away with it. I hoped so.

He turned, the plate of bacon in his hand, tongs in the other, and glanced at me. "Oh, hey. You're awake. Just in time—I made bacon."

"The smell is what woke me up." I inhaled deeply. "That, and the coffee."

He held up a finger, set the plate and tongs down. Grabbed a mug, poured coffee into it, and brought it over to me.

I sat up and inhaled the glorious scent. "I think you just fulfilled an item on my bucket list I forgot to include: have someone bring me coffee in bed."

He grinned at me. "Well, I'm at your service."

His eyes flicked over me—met my gaze, explored my face, slid down my throat to the front of my shirt. I had a serious case of headlights going: still being turned on and flushed from the orgasm, my always-prominent nipples were standing on end and hard as points of a diamond; Leighton said I had a case of permanent pokies, since I almost never wore a bra. His eyes remained there a beat too long—just long enough for him to be obviously and blatantly checking me out, but not quite long enough to be a come-on.

"I also, uh…made some scrambled eggs." He seemed distracted. He stood up, turned away abruptly. "So, whenever you're ready, we can eat."

I took a sip of coffee—scalding hot, strong as hell, and black as night, the way I liked it. "I'm coming now."

Was it me, or did his shoulders tense at the word "coming?"

Probably just me. Maybe it meant he'd heard or seen me.

I slid out of bed and moved to the table, wondering how I felt about the idea of him having seen or heard me masturbating. Would I be upset? Freaked out? Embarrassed? Turned on?

I mean, I'd seen him doing the same thing. I'd stood on the bottom step of the stairs, door propped open against my shoulder, and I'd watched him jerking off, watched his fist roughly pump his cock. I'd watched him hunch over himself, growling curses under his breath…and I'd watched him come. Watched him catch his cum into a wad of toilet paper. And my only thought, in the moment? Wishing he'd just let his cum spurt all over the place. That'd have been hotter. Wayyy hotter.

So, the point being…if he had seen me, did I care? Did it…turn me on even more? Seemed that way, if I was any judge of my own emotions.

I was blushing, I knew it. God, I had to get it under control. What was wrong with me?

I'd never been like this. Even when weeks went by without Max and I meeting to fool around, and I was pent up from having only had my own fingers and vibrators to get me off, I was never *this* horny. Not this desperate. Rhys had done something to me. Ignited something, and it wouldn't be doused or quenched.

"So, you sleep well?" he asked.

I nodded. "Sure did. You?"

He shrugged, nodded. "Eventually, yeah." Rhys sat down with me, pointing to the plate of bacon and a big ceramic bowl full of scrambled eggs, and gestured. "You're a lady and a guest, so you first."

"Such manners," I said, smirking at him.

He laughed. "Had it drilled into me by Mom. She'd take me grocery shopping with her when I was a little tyke, and she'd make me open the door for her, carry the bags, let her go in or out first. 'Treat a woman right,' she'd tell me. 'You treat a woman right, she'll appreciate it, and be more likely to treat you just as good in turn. Plus, it's just the right thing to do.'" He sighed. "I don't even know how many times I heard her say those words."

"Well, you have retained the lessons. You're very polite."

A shrug. "It's easy enough to be polite. Doesn't cost nothin', doesn't take nothin' extra from me. And it makes the world a better place. Plus, like Mama said, being polite does serve me pretty well, too, I've noticed."

"Well, I do appreciate it." We ate in silence a while, and then I asked a question that had been percolating since last night. "Can I ask you something?"

He nodded. "Sure."

"Why do you want to make a million dollars by forty? Why that number? Why that age?"

A sigh, and then a long silence—he ate, washed it down with coffee, and then sat back, one hand on the mug, fingers wrapped through the handle and around the mug itself. "I've told you, I grew up pretty damn poor. Don't mean to overstate things, but...we were well below the poverty line. Never had nothin' growing up. What I had, I worked for. I've been struggling to make ends meet since I was a preteen. I'm carrying a pretty sizeable amount of debt from the loan to buy this place, plus the loan to help front the overhead to get the business itself going. I want to be debt free. More than that, I want to be...it's not about being rich, exactly. Just...not having to worry. Knowing the bills will get paid and I'll have plenty of money left over. My whole life, I've always had way too much month left at the end of my money. I'm sick of it. I want to get ahead. I'm working my ass to the bone, twelve-hour days most days and sometimes more. And I put eighty percent of my income, after taxes and bills, into paying down my debt. Save maybe a grand or so each month, and that's about it, usually less. That's why I want to get into real estate. I've got enough saved that I could invest in some kind of property. Flip it, maybe. That's what I'm thinking. Get my license to sell real estate, buy a house, fix it up, and sell it. It's why I'm working the construction job, so I can learn how to do all that shit."

"Wow, you've really got this all thought out, huh?"

He nodded. "I'm a planner."

We'd finished all the food, and were now working on our second cup of coffee.

"So," I said. "The road trip."

He grinned. "You're packed already." He gestured to a big duffel bag near the stairs. "I am too. I just gotta lock up and we can head out. I've got a route planned out. Figure I'll take first shot at the wheel, and then when we stop for lunch you can drive a bit, if you like."

I sat forward, leveled a look at him. "Rhys, I want to reiterate that I can make my own way to Alaska. If you're doing this for any reason other than simply wanting to go on a fun road trip with me, please just opt out. I'll be fine. I don't *need* your help. Not anymore. You've done more than I could ever have asked, and then some, and I'll be forever grateful to you. So just—"

"Torie, I've explained it more than once. I don't do charity. I'm not doing anything out of some weird sense of obligation or chivalry. I need a break. I need to get out of this town for a bit, see some country. Take the top off the CJ and get some wind in my hair and miles behind me. And I mean this with every last ounce of honesty I've got—Torie, I would like nothing more than to do it with you." He blinked, stammered. "I mean, it, meaning the road trip."

I felt a flush creep over me yet again. God, he made me blush faster and more easily than I ever had in my life. It was stupid, and embarrassing.

"I knew what you meant," I said, my voice low.

"Yeah, I...yeah." He laughed, rubbed the back of his neck. "Although that's true enough any way you want to mean it."

I choked on a surprised laugh. "Rhys!"

He shrugged. "Ain't gonna pull no punches, Torie."

I finished my coffee, stood up, took Rhys's empty mug from him, and all the plates. Brought the pile of dishes to the sink and washed them all—it felt way too familiar and comfortable and easy and...domestic, eating and doing dishes with Rhys.

Like we'd always done things together. Like we always would.

I think he sensed it, too: he stood up abruptly and headed for the stairs. "Gonna lock up down there. We can go out the side door. Just double check you've got everything. You don't want to leave anything behind, you know?"

And then he was gone.

Thank god...I'd had to pee since before break-fast but couldn't think of a good way to ask him to leave his own home so I could. I put the dishes on the drying rack and used the bathroom, dressed in clean jeans and a T-shirt, put on my socks and boots. Checked through my bag, made sure I had every-thing. I stripped the pull-out and gave the bathroom a quick going-over.

Time to go.

It was weird how fast I'd come to feel like this loft was home. What, two days? With a guy I'd known for the same length of time?

Was I absolutely insane for doing this?

Yeah. I was.

I took my bag and outside and, sitting on the steps, I called Leighton.

It rang twice and she answered. "It's not nine yet, dingus."

"I know. But I need you to give me a bad idea rating. Rhys has some time off, and he's going to drive me part of the way to Alaska. Like a road trip. How far, I don't know."

She hummed a low, musing note. "Wow, that's a tough one, actually. On the face of it, it's a ten out of ten horrible idea. You barely know the guy. If he de-cides to show his wacko in the middle of BFE, you're seriously screwed." She paused, thinking. "But you've slept in his bed, alone, for two nights. He hasn't made any inappropriate moves on you that felt creepy, or you'd have said so. You'd have booked it, more to the point. He's respected your space and hasn't tried to get into your pants. So, if he's hiding secret serial killer slash rapist wacko tendencies, he's hiding them pretty damn well."

"Yeah, I don't get any feelings like that from him at all. He seems to be a genuinely good person. A good man. He's polite. He's kind. He's caring." I swallowed. "He's hot as hell. He likes me."

"He likes you, huh?"

I sighed. "Yeah, there's chemistry there. A lot of it, actually."

"Which makes this road trip an even better idea. Takes it more to the other end of the good idea bad idea rating scale—into the good idea territory. He likes you, you like him. He's hot, he's good, what do you have to lose?"

I was silent a moment. I heard him inside, reached up, opened the door, peeked in at him, gestured at the phone and held up a finger. He nodded, shooting me a thumbs up.

"Well, what I have to lose is getting hurt. Because…Ley, I *really* like him." I dropped my voice to a whisper. "He turns me on like nobody else ever has. I…I freaking *want* him, Ley. But…I'm scared to let anything happen. Because I'm going to Alaska, and the more time goes by, the more I feel like you and Jillie were right, that I'm probably not coming back to Connecticut. Which sucks because I love you guys and I'll miss you like crazy. And...I just know myself well enough to know that for my first time, I'm just not capable of making it a one-time thing. A hookup. It doesn't have to be, like, *love*, just...somewhere in the realm of meaningful."

"I know, hon," Leighton said, her voice uncharacteristically tender. "My advice, and this is advice I don't give lightly, is to just take things as they happen with him. I got a good feeling from talking to him. I agree, I think he's a good guy, and you for sure lucked out in him being the dude who picked you up. So, you could do a hell of a lot worse for your first time than him, if he's genuinely as good and decent as he seems." She hesitated. "Has anything...happened... with the two of you?"

I sighed. Laughed. "Sort of. His place is a loft, all open. Even the bathroom. Totally a bachelor pad for one guy. Which is cool for him, being a single guy. But anyway. I was changing, had my shirt off, about to put it on, and he walked in. And I just...froze. Totally topless. And he...he wasn't in a hurry to look away."

"Well, who would be? You've got fantastic tits."

I laughed. "Why thank you, Leighton. Coming

from someone with epic boobs herself, that means a lot."

"I wouldn't call them epic. They hang almost to my damn belly, and I'm not even twenty-one."

"Because they're freaking enormous, hon."

She laughed. "Why are we talking about our boobs? To the point—what happened then?"

"Not much. He apologized, and left. Apologized again later, and it was kind of awkward."

"And that was it? He saw you topless, nothing else?"

I laughed hesitantly. "Well? Not quite. He washed my clothes, right? Put them in the dryer later that night and went to bed. I woke up early, thought he'd still be asleep. The washer and dryer are downstairs, the loft is upstairs. So I went down, thinking I'd grab my clothes and change before he woke up."

"And you saw something you weren't supposed to."

"Um, yeah, you could say that. I walked in on him jerking off."

"No. No! You did *not*."

"Wait, it gets better. Or worse, not sure which." I giggled. Caught my breath and finished the story. "I literally watched him finish. And...he was watching this video of a girl in a wet T-shirt. Who was kinda thin, with long black hair."

"Um."

"And guess what? The day he picked me up, we came back to his place and I took off my hoodie. And being soaked to the bone as I was, my shirt was see-through soaked. So that clearly must have turned him on, because he was watching a video of a girl who looked a hell of a lot like me in a wet T-shirt." I paused for effect. "Ready for the most OMG part? He admitted he'd been thinking about me. Trying not to, he said, thus the video, but the video was as close to me as you could get."

"You caught him jerking off while thinking about *you*?"

"Yeah."

"Torie. How the hell are you still a virgin? You're alone in the home of a ridiculously hot man who clearly wants you seriously fucking bad. He's seen your tits. You've seen his cock. All that's left is to just get it on already." A pause. "Wait. What's his cock like?"

"Horrifyingly, beautifully, incredibly enormous. I mean, just *massive*."

"Porn star big?"

"Porn star big."

"Bigger than Max?"

Max, my best friend with sort of benefits, possessed an improbably large member, considering he was a skinny goth anime nerd and computer programmer.

"Way, way, *way* bigger." I whispered, then. "Like, I'm a little scared of it. And he's not the biggest guy either. He's ripped, but not, like, huge."

"Honestly, those are the guys who seem to have the biggest packages. I never go for the big beefy body builders, because for one thing I don't like that look, but also because in my experience, it's the guys who don't look it that have big dicks." She laughed. "And they tend to be freaky, too."

"Well, you have way more experience than me, so I'll take your word for it."

"My word is that you should just sort of see what happens. Don't rush things or force them with him, but don't fight it either." A brief pause. "But you *have* to tell him, and *before* anything happens."

"Yeah, I know," I said. "That's part of what worries me. What if we sleep together and it's amazing and I fall for him, and then he goes back to Connecticut and I go to Alaska? I've never had my heart broken, and I don't want my first time to be what breaks my heart."

"If you get your heart broken, we'll be there for you. Your sisters and mom will be there for you. You'll survive it. Getting your heart broken fucking blows chunks, not gonna lie. But you'll get over it. It's part of life. And you can't go around avoiding what could be amazing experiences because you're afraid of getting hurt. You'll never do anything, never experience anything that way."

"That sounds like me: a virgin at almost twenty-one, never left Connecticut, no career, no hobby, no passion. Because I've never dared to try anything."

"I know I was against this trip of yours, but this is a different situation now, babe. I'd say go for it. Be careful. Be alert. Trust your gut if something feels wrong. Call us every night. But go for it. And if things happen, go with it. And call me right after!"

"Yeah, I will. The moment he finishes, I'll call you."

"Not what I meant, but if you want to, sure." She laughed. "I wouldn't mind a look at his peepee."

"Leighton. Come on."

"I'm your inappropriate best friend. Gotta live up to the name." A laugh. "Oh! Did you ever talk to Max?"

I hissed. "Crap. No. I feel awful. I never even told him I was leaving."

"Well, technically, you haven't. You're still in Connecticut."

"True." I sighed. "We're leaving soon, though, so I'll call him later. He'll understand."

"Be gentle with him, Torie. He likes you. He

knows you'll never fall for him, but he still has feelings for you. And he's a cute little guy."

"That's demeaning."

"Because messing around with him but refusing to have sex with him isn't? That's the ultimate tease!"

"I told him if it was too hard for him to live with that, we should stop messing around. He said no, he'd take what he could get with me, and he understood."

"Because he was hoping you'd change your mind."

"Shit." I slapped my forehead. "You're probably right. Well, in that case, this is for the best. But I'll be gentle."

"I'm at work, so I gotta go."

"Yeah, me too. Thanks, Ley."

"It's what best friends are for. And for real, fill me in if anything hot happens. You know I'm a dirty voyeur."

"Yeah, yeah. Talk to you later."

I wanted to put off talking to Max, which was all the more reason to call him now. As usual, he let it ring for a long time before answering, and when he did, it was distracted, because he was either playing a game or coding, or both.

"Hey, T," he said. "I was gonna call you. I'm almost done with a big project and I'll have some free time, if you wanna come over. I kinda want to watch *Akira* again, if you're interested."

I laughed, because we'd watched that so many times I could quote it. "Actually, I'm calling for a different reason. Um…can I get your full attention for a minute?"

I knew if I didn't ask, he'd be only partially focused on what I was saying and would miss some, if not all of what I was saying.

A pause, buttons clicking, and then a clatter as he tossed his controller down on his coffee table—I knew him so well I could see it in my mind's eye. In three, two, one…

"Okay, I'm focused," he said, on cue, with a sigh as he flopped to his couch—he played standing up, bouncing from foot to foot, full agitated energy.

"No way to ease into this, so I'm just gonna say it. I'm leaving Connecticut."

A silence.

"Um…like, for good? You're moving? When? Where? Why?"

"Well, it's more of a trip right now—Lexie is getting married up in Alaska, and I have to go up for the wedding. And, honestly, I have a feeling I'll end up staying there. Everyone but me and Poppy live there, and…I miss Mom and my sisters, and to be brutally honest, my life here is going nowhere fast. So I'm not like one hundred percent certain I'm moving, but it's a good likelihood."

"Wow." He needed a moment or two to process and figure out how to express himself. "Will I get to see you before you go?"

I felt a lump in my throat. "Um, no, actually. I'm about to leave right now."

"Oh."

"Max, I..."

He cleared his throat. "It's cool. I understand. I'm not very good with emotions or goodbyes, so emotional goodbyes are the worst." He was silent a moment. "But then, fuck that. We've been friends since second grade and I get a phone call when you move away forever? Harsh, T."

"Max—"

"Be honest, Torie."

I gulped. "Fine. I'm avoiding you. I'm avoiding the goodbye. You and me—what we do, it's...I...I've enjoyed it. It's been fun. But...you want the truth? The truth is I know you have feelings for me and I won't ever share them, Max. You've been my best friend, and I love you as friends, and yes, there's a level of physical attraction to you. But...Max, it had to end. We couldn't keep messing around like we were. It had to either be more, or less. And it was never going to be more. And that's not—it's not because of anything you are or aren't as a person. You're amazing, and I—"

"I've been in love with you since the day we met, Victoria. I've taken your scraps of affection and attention. I've waited. I've hoped. I've taken what I can get. And I've always known it would never be anything more, but I guess I've always held out hope that...I don't know, honestly."

"That I'd never find anyone and get desperate enough to settle for you?"

He huffed, somewhere between bitter and hurt. "Yeah, basically."

"You deserve better, Max. Better than waiting for some dumb girl to get desperate enough to *settle* for you. I'm sorry if I've hurt you. I never wanted to hurt you."

"But I was convenient and safe."

"Yeah."

"Dunno how I feel about that."

"Can I give you my honest opinion as your best friend and as a woman?"

He sighed. "Yeah, please do."

"Don't wait. When a girl comes along that you like, that you're hot for, don't wait. Don't hope. Don't take what you can get with the lowest hanging fruit, which is what I was, for you. You're better looking than you know. You're a good person. You're sweet and funny, and you deserve someone who really likes you and wants to be with you, not just someone who was using you because you were safe and convenient."

He laughed. "You say that, now. But I get your meaning." He let out a slow sigh. "I let it happen, Torie. I knew what the score was between us, and I stuck around for it. So don't, like, get all 'I'm such a villain for using Max,' okay? I let you. I knew you'd never love me. And honestly, it was sort of the same for me. You were safe. I knew you didn't love me, but you *liked* me, and you liked hanging out with me and you put up with my stupid anime shows. So...you were a safe, convenient way for me to get to touch some boobies and get my penis touched without having to deal with yucky, awkward garbage emotions, because I knew as long as I could ignore the fact that I'm in love with you, it would just be cheap, convenient quasisexual fun. And, being a guy skilled at ignoring and suppressing inconvenient emotions, I was easily able to just go along with what you were offering for as long as things went on."

"So, what you're saying is I shouldn't feel bad for using you because you were using me too?"

"'All right, we'll call it a draw,'" he said, and I recognized the quote from his second-favorite movie, *Monty Python and the Holy Grail*.

"I will miss you, Max. And I'm sorry for avoiding

you and saying goodbye to my oldest friend over the phone."

"You *should* feel a little bad about that," he said. "But it's okay. I get it. And I was serious when I said it's probably for the best because I'm not good with good-byes or emotions, much less emotional goodbyes."

"So…" The lump was hot and hard to swallow, harder to talk around. "This is harder than I thought it would be."

"Which is why you were avoiding doing it."

"Right," I whispered. "I'll miss you, Maximillian. Goodbye."

"I'll miss you too, Victoria. Send me a postcard from Alaska."

Silence.

"You sure I can't convince you to swing by for one last bowl and a handie?"

I laughed. "Max."

"Had to try." He sighed. "I'm hanging up now. Bye, T. Be safe."

"Bye, Max," I whispered, but he'd already hung up.

I sat in silence for a bit, absorbing the reality of that whole situation.

I went inside, after a few minutes, leaving my bag on the step. Rhys was pouring coffee into a pair of beat-up travel mugs.

He grinned at me, a quick, easy, familiar grin. "Hey. Good talk?"

"Yeah, it was Leighton. Wanted to run a few things by her." I decided to keep my talk with Max private, for now.

"Like if this road trip with me is a terrible idea?"

I frowned. "Were you eavesdropping?"

"No!" he laughed, holding up both hands. "I wasn't, I swear."

"Because that's exactly what we talked about."

"And? What was her advice?"

"Well, honestly, she said to go for it. You seem like a good and decent guy, so she said just be careful and listen to my gut if anything feels off."

"So, I have her somewhat conditional blessing?"

"Yeah. Just don't rape and murder me."

"Not sure how I'm supposed to answer that. Nothing could be further from my mind."

I smiled at him. "I wouldn't be going with you if I didn't know you were such a good person. And, I wouldn't have slept here if I'd had any reservations about you."

"I'm glad you feel that way, because you *are* safe with me." He hesitated. Swallowed. "You're safe with me, Torie. I may make stupid and inappropriate comments sometimes, but…I heard what you said about not starting anything, and I respect that. So…you're safe in that sense, too. We're just two friends on a road trip."

"I…" I trailed off, unsure what I wanted to say.

I was so confused. I didn't want to be *that* safe with him, not in that sense. Maybe I'd overstated my case.

Maybe I wanted him to take a chance. To push me a little.

Maybe my fear was getting in my way. Maybe I was holding on to my virginity a little too tightly. Maybe…maybe I had built it up into this…*THING*. The right person, the right time, the right situation. Not to mention that word I used so much: MEANINGFUL.

Maybe I should loosen up a bit. Let myself explore my own desires and just see what happens.

"I don't mind the inappropriate comments so much," I whispered. "And I'm…I don't know. I'm just doing a lot of thinking."

"Anything you want to share?"

I shook my head. "Not yet." What a lie that was—I wanted to share a lot of things with Rhys.

Like, for example, the fact that I really wanted him.

Like, the fact that I was very much reconsidering my vow to not let anything happen with him.

What I was *not* so sure about was sharing the issue of my virginity.

I bet that would send him running for the hills.

I AM SO CONFUSED.

What do I want?

What should I do?

I had no clue.

Rhys and I took one final look around the loft then went downstairs and tossed our bags into the back of his Jeep. He locked up his shop, and we headed out on our road trip.

And I, for the first time in my life, left Connecticut.

With a man I'd met two days ago…

To whom I was seriously considering giving my virginity.

# EIGHT

## Rhys

I WONDER IF I SHOULD TELL H ER I'D SEEN HER AND HEARD her this morning?

I'm hyperaware of Torie. At all times. Every moment, even asleep, I know where she is. I can just… feel her.

So, this morning, I knew when she was sleeping, and I knew the moment she woke up. I felt her watching me.

I felt her desire. It was palpable.

For her sake, I pretended to be unaware of her attention. I also pretended to be grooving to my music when, in fact, I had it turned down low.

I heard her roll over and thought okay, fine, she's going back to sleep. Right?

Maybe she thought she was being super quiet, I don't know. Maybe I'm just extra observant. I don't know that either. I just know I turned around to grab a plate for the bacon, and I saw her. She was laying on her side, knees drawn up, and the blanket was moving slightly. Rhythmically. And her breathing was... hitched. Tensed. Suppressed. Quickening, tightening. I watched her shoulders round, heard the tiniest, high-pitched whimper—Torie orgasming.

Mere feet away from me.

Thinking I was oblivious.

She'd have gotten away with it too, if I enjoyed loud music. I just have sensitive ears, and being around roaring engines all day every day, my hearing is already somewhat lessened, which means I just keep the music low to preserve my hearing. So, I heard her.

And now I know what she sounds like when she comes, and I want to be the one to make her come.

I heard the doubt in her voice, earlier, when she said she didn't mind my comments. She wasn't sure about her commitment to us not hooking up. Her desire for me was obvious, but her reluctance, nerves, even fear, was just as obvious. And I wasn't about to mess with that fear, that reluctance. If her sexual desire overcame whatever was holding her back, great. I'd be all over that, and ready to make her feel better than she's ever felt. But I'm not pushing her into something she's not ready for, or doesn't fully want.

It made for big emotional, mental stress. Because *damn*, I wanted that girl. And everything about her made me want her more—her body, her tumultuous sexuality and the innocence which was at odds with it…her intelligence, her humor, the way she waffled between sometimes being unfiltered and opinionated, and other times shy and reluctant to open up.

Everything she was as a person, not just her body, made me crazy with desire. And shit yeah, I wanted that too. In the worst way. Now, having had such tantalizing glimpses of her body and her sexuality, that desire went to another level.

The fact that she was willing and daring enough to masturbate in the same room with me? It spoke of a potent libido. Possibly an underserved one—and by possibly, I mean definitely. What that meant, I wasn't sure. She was a gorgeous single young girl, with an incredible body, an active, agile mind, a sharp sense of humor, and a healthy dose of independence. Why should she be under-sexed?

It made no sense to me: she should have men lining up to please her.

The first few minutes of our drive were in companionable silence, the radio off, the windows down.

It was still a fairly cool morning, so I'd left the top up for now, figuring we'd put it down after lunch. One of the upgrades I'd done to this Jeep was replacing the old, worn factory soft top with a new aftermarket one that folded back simply and easily.

As we left the area outside New Haven where I lived, we faced a choice of routes. I glanced at Torie. "So, there's two ways we can go from here to get you on the way to Alaska. Either go south and through the States, under the Great Lakes and then north, or we go up through Canada. Choice is yours."

She frowned at me. "I've never been anywhere, so I don't know which is better? I've never seen anything but New Haven, and New York City a couple times, but that's it. For all intents and purposes, I've never left Connecticut. So it makes more sense to me for you to pick which route to take."

I nodded. "A good point." I thought it over. "I was planning on taking the route through the States, but I wanted to give you the option. Canada *is* a different country, but that may be an experience for another time."

"Makes sense to me." She glanced at me, but then away again. "Plus, when it's time for you to turn around and go back home, it might be better for me to be in the States to find a means of transportation the rest of the way."

A niggling worm of discomfort sat in my belly at the idea of just…leaving Torie at a bus stop somewhere in the middle of, like, North Dakota or somewhere. It's not like I could go all the way to fuckin' Alaska.

Right?

Of course not.

"States route it is, then," was all I said, and guided us toward the freeway. I had the route pulled up on my phone, but it was pretty simple once we were on the freeway, so I didn't use it to actively navigate us. I'd probably turn it on when it was Torie's turn to drive, since she'd never driven any real distance on a freeway.

Another long period of silence as we took I-95 south toward New York. I was fine with the silence, and I think she was, too. We went past Stamford and Greenwich, and then New Rochelle, and then we were making the transition through the Bronx and over the river to I-80.

By this time, it was obvious Torie had something on her mind. I waited it out a bit longer, though. Maybe she just needed some time to think.

She didn't say a word until the "WELCOME TO PENNSYLVANIA" sign was in sight. She looked over at me, then, and a small smile spread across her face.

"'If I take one more step, I'll be the farthest from home

*I've ever been.'"* She said this with a tone of voice that made it sound like a quotation.

"Is that a quote?"

*"The Fellowship of the Ring,"* she said. *"Lord of the Rings."*

"Oh, seen the movies, but I've never had much time for reading for pleasure."

She smiled at me. *"'Come on, Sam. Remember what Bilbo used to say: 'It's a dangerous business, Frodo, going out your door. You step onto the road, and if you don't keep your feet, there's no telling where you might be swept off to.'"*

"You have the whole book memorized?" I said, laughing.

"Not hardly. I just love that quote. Always have. Having never been anywhere, I've always been sort of obsessed with their whole adventure. Adventures and travel in general, really. I guess I'm pretty excited to be actually *going* somewhere."

"I mean, it's Pennsylvania, not all that exciting," I said, smirking at her. "No offense meant to all the fine folks who live here."

She snorted. "Every single person in Pennsylvania just heard your comment, took it personally, and now they're mad at you. Better watch behind us for the angry mob with pitchforks and torches."

I cackled. "Seems like you're in good spirits,

now. Thought for a while there you were upset or something."

She shook her head. "Nah, just…thinking."

I put on a thick Kentucky twang. "Well, now, I may not be the sharpest crayon in the tool shed, but if you feel like talkin', I could listen."

"Not the sharpest crayon in the tool shed?"

I shrugged. "I may have mixed a few metaphors, there."

She was quiet another moment. "I guess I'm just…thinking about what I want."

"Okay—and what do you want?"

"A lot of things. We went over our bucket lists, but this is different. I want…a future."

I didn't respond right away—that deserved a more thoughtful response. "Well, the smartass thing to say is that you've got a future, still being, you know, alive and all. But you mean something more specific. Like, a career type of thing."

She nodded. "Yeah. I just…I feel like I never really launched. Charlie, Cassie, Poppy, they all launched like rockets. Lexie not as much, but she still had an angle and a direction. I just…sort of sputtered into a holding pattern. If I'd grown up somewhere like your hometown, I'd probably never leave. I'd just be stuck there forever. And I want more than that; I just…don't know *what* I want. I know I hate school.

I hated high school, like with a passion. I was bored stupid in all my classes, except math, which can burn in hell. Then I tried a semester of community college the fall after graduation, and I hated that even more than high school. Honestly, it was all just... on me. Like, no one cared if I showed up, or what grade I got, or if I was struggling or having a shit day. It was just...impersonal. I was just another face out of thousands. And that was a tiny local community college. Expand that by about a hundredfold and a university seems like it'd be even worse. And I just didn't see the point anyway, if I had no idea what to study, or what to major in."

I nodded. "College was never an option for me. I make jokes about being a redneck or a hillbilly or whatever, but it's all just jokes, mostly. I'm smart enough, but not in a books type of way. Never had time for homework, or for studying. None of it ever seemed to matter much. I had goals, and knowing about the War of 1812, or how cells divide, or how to multiply an integer or whatever the hell, none of that was relevant to what I wanted out of life, which was to work on cars, to make money, and to get the hell out of Kentucky." I laughed. "Meaning, I barely graduated. My GPA was...embarrassing. I could've done better if I had bothered to try, but I just barely saw the point of even showing up. I did the bare minimum to get my fuckin' diploma. In high school, if I got a hot tip on a good salvage, I'd skip faster'n you could say boo. School was just never a thing for me."

"Well, things clearly worked for you," she said, scraping a line up and down her thigh, creating a *zzzzhp-zzzzhp-zzzzhp* sound, "considering you own your own company at twenty-six."

"But the question is, what do *you* want?"

"That's the problem, I don't *know!* I don't want to go to school, so that kinda cuts out a lot of options. I'm not really artistic, not like Poppy, Lexie, or Cassie. So I just…don't know."

"Well, what do you like? What are you passionate about?"

She seemed embarrassed. "I like reading. If given the opportunity, I'd rather sit and smoke a bowl and read a book. But no one's gonna pay me to read and smoke pot."

I eyed her. "Question, which you're not at all obligated to answer."

"Okay?"

"Why do you smoke pot?"

A long sigh. "I've avoided asking myself that question for a while." She watched the scenery pass by for a bit, and I gave her space to think. "I guess because I like being able to get out of my head. I can relax. Not think. Just be…happy. It's not, like, *joy*, because there is a big difference between joy and happiness. But it's something. Since I graduated high school I've been just working as a server, making ends meet. Paying rent, buying food. Hanging with Jillie and Leighton, messing around with Max. We'll see a movie now and then, and Leighton is a hostess at a place that has live music on the weekends, so we'll sometimes go see a show if the band is good—we're all underage, but her manager lets us in as long as we don't drink. I guess I just…don't really have a purpose. I feel like I'm just drifting. And that's uncomfortable."

Another silence.

"I don't see anything wrong with it," she continued. "I'm not, like, self-medicating. It's not a gateway to meth or whatever. I have zero interest in anything but pot. I worked with a dishwasher who was a meth-head and, hoooo boy, did that cure me of any curiosity."

"I bet." I grimaced. "More than a few of my friends got hooked on it—well, not really friends, just people I went to school with. It's ugly shit." I glanced her way. "So it's just something to…pass the time, sort of?"

"More to distract me from my lack of purpose. Also, it's just a nice way to relax at the end of the day, because I'm not really a huge fan of getting drunk. Tried it a couple times with my roommates, and the hangover is *so* not worth the feeling of being out of control. Weird, maybe, but alcohol just is not my thing."

"You're very self-aware," I said. "Most people would just be like, 'I dunno, I just like it.'"

"You asked me why, I'm not gonna pass the question off with a blah answer." She looked at me. "You have any vices?"

I shrugged. "Honestly? No. Work, maybe. I'm a workaholic. This is the first break or vacation I've ever taken, and I'm fighting feeling guilty about it. Time away from work is time I'm not making money, and I have this fear, irrational maybe, that I'll go broke and have to move back with my parents, and there is no way in motherfucking *hell* that'll ever happen. I'd be homeless first."

Her expression was confused and speculative. "You have a complicated relationship with your parents, I think."

I laughed. "Yeah, I do."

She chewed on the lower right corner of her lip. "You don't have to talk about it, but I am curious."

"Well." I sighed. "There ain't much in my life I don't like talking about. Most shit, I'm an open book about. Grew up poor white trash, lived in a single-wide trailer, wore my dad's old clothes half my life even when they were eight sizes too big because we were too poor to afford anything else, even from the thrift store."

She blinked in shock. "Wow. That's...that's..."

"It sucked. I think I mentioned there were times we couldn't afford both groceries and electricity, or electricity and water, so we had to choose, which meant no plumbing for a couple weeks, or no electricity, or no food."

"So you've gone hungry, not had lights..."

"Had to carry buckets a couple miles to the shop where Dad worked to fill 'em up with water, so we could flush the toilets and make Mac 'N Cheese and hot dogs, which, most of the time, we made over a fire in the backyard because it was free."

"Wow."

"Yeah. So you asked before why I want to make a million? That's why. I won't ever feel that way again. Not ever." I let out a breath. "But my relationship with my parents is something that's hard for me to talk about."

"You don't have to."

"It's cool. I trust you." I waffled, trying to get started. "So. Mom...I told you she worked at a bar. Little dive bar, piece of shit place that served watery beer, dollar store whiskey, and literal backwoods, homemade moonshine, which, by the way, is illegal."

"Yikes."

"Yeah. She worked at a gas station as a cashier in the day, and at the bar at night. The bar was our main income, actually. Dad got paid shit, but it was steady, whereas Mom might make fifty bucks one night and a hundred another."

She nodded. "I know about that all too well."

"Right." I rubbed the back of my neck. "So, um. Yeah. I've never told anyone this." A long, long pause. "Sometimes, if things were really, really tight. Like not enough to pay *any* of the bills, Mom would, uh… go home with guys from the bar. For money."

She was silent a long, tense moment. "Like… prostitution?"

I blew out a breath. "Yeah. I don't really remember how I found out. I think…it woulda been in middle school. Or ninth grade, maybe. I had been out late with buddies, blowing off firecrackers and racing dirt bikes back in the hollers. We'd passed behind some houses—trailers way out there, you know? The places you gotta know are there to know how to get there. And I think I saw her. It'd have been late, like two, three in the morning. I saw her leaving some guy's house. Standing on the step, shoes in hand, barely half dressed, and he gave her money."

"You were allowed out at three in the morning in middle school?"

I laughed. "That's what you fix on? Yeah, I

mean, not *allowed*. But Dad worked early and slept like a dead man, and Mom worked late, so I just did whatever the hell I wanted. If I wanted to hang out with buddies till dawn drinking and cutting up, they wouldn't know. Didn't really care, either. Just making ends meet and making sure I had a roof and food was all they had time for. They cared about me, but keeping me fed, housed, and clothed was their only real concern. What I did otherwise was up to me. *'Just don't get killed, don't end up in the hospital 'cause we don't got money for no stitches, y'hear? And for god's sake, don't get your dumb ass arrested.'"* I said that last few sentences in my dad's backwoods drawl.

She frowned. "So your mom would sell herself to make ends meet, sometimes. And your dad...*knew?*"

I shrugged. "I dunno how that worked. I think it was something they just didn't talk about. Mom would do what she had to do, and if she brought home extra money, great. He wouldn't ask how."

"Did they love each other?"

I wanted to laugh at that, but it was an honest question. "Love is a luxury they couldn't afford, I think. They respected each other. Liked each other. Didn't fight much and got over it quick. They rarely saw each other, really. Dad worked six in the morning till six at night most days. Sometimes later. And Mom worked from eight till four at the gas station, and five thirty to past close at the bar. So they might see each other in passing, or on the weekends. Sunday mornings, mostly, was their time together." I winced, and she caught it.

"What?" she asked.

"Well, I learned real early on to get the hell out of the house on Sunday mornings. Those walls weren't much but two-by-fours and shitty fake wood paneling. Didn't baffle the sound at all."

She widened her eyes. "Ohhh. So, they still had that together, at least? Trying to find the good."

I laughed. "Bless your heart for that, Torie. Yeah, they had that. Loudly. Every Sunday morning at nine. You coulda set a clock by it. So I'd get up early and go fishing, most Sundays. Once I could drive, I'd go salvaging."

She was quiet, thoughtful, her eyes on me.

"What?" I asked. "You got somethin' to say, I can tell."

"When you talk about your parents or Kentucky or your past, you sound more southern again." She shrugged. "That's not what I was gonna say, though. I guess…I'm just wondering how you feel, about… your mom. And what she did."

I scratched the back of my head. "I dunno. Try not to think about it much, honestly. I guess I don't like it, as you might guess. Everybody knew. It was a tiny place, where I grew up. Not on most maps. Not really even a name to it. No mayor, just a few old retired folks who called themselves the city council made sure there was a stop light and all that municipal shit. So, everybody knew my mom was, literally, the town whore. She wasn't on the street corner, maybe, but it was common knowledge. You needed your rocks off and had some cash to burn, Della Frost down at the Crooked Barstool on the county line would go home with you." I gripped the shifter with white knuckles, barely feeling it. "Got teased some for it. But hey, knock a few teeth out and the comments stopped. To my face, at least."

"God, Rhys."

"She's a good woman. Took care of me and Saoirse. Of Dad. Made dinner. Kept the place clean on top of two jobs. I got respect for her, for how hard she worked. But it's...it's a complicated thing. I know she didn't want to. But it was that or we starve, or don't take a shower for a month 'cause the water bill was so damn expensive. As it was I'd go to school early and take showers in the locker room 'cause it was free there."

And, of course, at that exact moment, my phone rang.

And who was it?

My dad.

Dammit.

I hesitated and then glanced at Torie.

She shrugged. "Don't mind me. I'll just be over here minding my own business.

I chuckled. "Yeah, well, you're about to get an earful." I accepted the call and turned it onto speaker and tossed the phone up onto the dash so I could drive hands-free. "Hey, Dad."

"RJ, how are you son?" Dad's deep, pack-and-a-half-a-day voice.

I hated that nickname. "I'm all right, but I'd be better if you called me Rhys. How are you?"

"Fuck that, boy. Been callin' you RJ since you were a day old. You think I'm gonna stop now, you best think again."

I half sighed, half laughed. "Yeah, yeah. I know how you are, you stubborn old sonofabitch."

"Sounds like you're far away."

"You're on speaker, I'm in the car."

"Where ya headed?"

I had no intention of bringing Torie into this conversation, for her sake rather than mine; I winked at her and held a finger to my lips to shush her. She nodded.

"Oh, just on a road trip. Had some time between projects, so I thought I'd get the hell outta Dodge for a few days. What are you and Mom up to?"

"You know, nothin' different. Danny Brower blew his transmission on his old Ford, so I'm fixing that, because his daddy gave him that truck back in the seventies and he said he'd be damned to hell before he got a new one. Costin' him an arm and just about half a leg, but it's worth it to him, but I don't gotta tell you that."

"No, folks get attached to their trucks, especially family pieces like Dan Brower's." I chewed on my lip for a moment. "How's Mom?"

"Oh, she's all right. At the Corner Mart where she's been every mornin' for nigh on thirty years now. We're havin' roast tonight."

"She still at the Crooked Barstool?"

"Ehh, you know your momma. They'll have to drag her to the nursing home and pry that apron and order pad outta her old hands." I hated the question, but had to ask. "She been…working late, lately?"

A gruff, frustrated sigh. "Nah. Home ten after two most nights, now. Kinda gettin' past the age where those extra hours are worth it to her, you know?" He hated that question as much as I did.

Reading between the lines of Dad's answer, the message was that Mom was getting too old to be able to get anyone to pay for her anymore.

Which meant the reason for Dad's call would be coming the next time he opened his mouth.

"Means things are awful tight, though. Been taking some simple jobs on the side here in the driveway, just for extra cash, but it's tricky since I don't got all the tools myself. I been just using what's at the shop all these years."

I had no patience for his edging around the ask. "I'll send you what I can when I get home, Dad."

"Awful good of you, son. Hate askin', but times are tighter than ever."

"I know it."

A long silence. "I appreciate you, RJ."

"Tell Mom I said hi."

"Will do."

"Love you, son."

"You too, Dad. See ya."

"See ya."

I reached up, touched the red phone icon to end the call, and shoved the phone under my thigh. Waited for the questions.

None came. I glanced at Torie. "I know you got about dozen things to say to that."

She shrugged. "It was a private conversation I just happened to be unable to avoid overhearing."

I sighed. "I've been running away from that damn nickname my whole life. It chases me."

She grinned. "RJ, huh?"

"Rhys Jonathan Frost. Dad, as you heard, has

called me RJ my whole life, and I've been tellin' him to stop since I was sixteen. But everyone from my hometown just calls me RJ, and if anyone hears it, I'm RJ to them from then on. It's a sticky sonafabitch nickname."

She just gazed levelly at me. "If you don't like it, then I'll call you Rhys."

I just sighed, grinned ruefully. "You'll try, but now that you've heard it, you'll use it. It's inevitable."

She tipped her head to one side. "I don't know. You seem more like Rhys to me. It's...an elegant, strong name. RJ is..."

"Country?"

"Something like that. And there's nothing wrong with that."

"Nope. I just don't like it. I like Rhys. It's my name. It's a good name, and it's what I prefer. Dad's just an ornery old goat who's been set in his ways since he was born."

"You send money to your parents?"

I nodded, watched the road, not wanting to see her expression. "They're my folks. I send 'em a couple hundred dollars every month. Sometimes more, if they need it."

"Rhys, that's—"

I interrupted. "What kind of a person would I be if my folks asked for help and I didn't give it when I had it to give? They're decent people. It wasn't their fault we were poor. They were just...products of... of a particular system. Dad never went to school past sixth grade, had to help on the farm, and then he started driving a tow truck for the gas station the day he got his license, took some auto mechanic courses at a trade school near Lexington, but ran outta money to get certified. So he's been at that gas station doing simple repairs and oil changes and brake jobs since he was, shit, twenty? That's where he met Mom. There's two gas stations in town. He works at one, she works at the other. Mom never went to any school past high school. She was pregnant with Saoirse at eighteen, and me by twenty, then got sick and lost the ability to have any more. And that debt was what sunk 'em— the hospital bill for Mom getting ovarian cancer at twenty-four. She survived it, but...it just ruined them. Been fighting to keep their heads above water ever since." I let out a sigh. "My feelings about what Mom did are complicated, but my feelings about my dad are even more so. I guess...I guess I feel like he oughta stepped up and done something, anything, so Mom didn't have to do that. I know he worked twelve-hour days. But...I'd work twenty hours a day to keep some-one I care about from having to do that. So I guess I resent Dad for letting her whore herself out. And I know Saoirse does, too, maybe more than I even do."

I scrubbed my face again. "It just sucks and is complicated as fuck, that's all."

"Damn," she breathed. "That's rough."

"So yeah, I send 'em money."

She frowned at me. "You sound defensive again about doing a good thing."

I laughed bitterly. "Most people don't understand, and think I'm stupid for sending them money. But they use it on bills, not booze or drugs. And I guess I just...I don't want people to think I'm someone I'm not."

"Like a good person who takes care of his parents?"

I snorted. "You make it sound so simple."

"Isn't it?"

"I'm not a Carebear. I just feel responsible for doing what I can."

She laughed gently, touched my hand as it rested on the gear shifter. "You want to, what? Be seen as some macho asshole tough guy?"

I rolled my eyes at her. "No, but I ain't no saint."

"I don't know, Saint Rhys has a nice ring to it."

I faked a glare at her, but couldn't hold it for long. "Ha ha. You're hilarious."

"I try." She ran a hand over the dash. "You did this one, I take it?"

I nodded. "My first shot at a restoration. My

real area of expertise is engine repair. I can muddle through transmissions and I can do simple things like brakes and whatever, but a lot of stuff requires special equipment and tools, especially with newer cars. I don't do wiring and computer stuff for the new models. I just like the old engines—classic internal combustion, baby. Diesel is a whole other game, and I'm slowly teaching myself that."

She laughed. "You were telling me about the Jeep."

"I was rambling again, wasn't I?"

She held her forefinger and thumb an inch apart. "A little."

"So, yeah. Anyway. I got this on salvage. Engine was seized, tranny was blown. Rust in the quarter panels and rocker panels and both bumpers, but the interior was nearly mint. It was weird. Like, the headliner is tight, all the gauges work, the stock radio works, floors and upholstery were all in great shape. The interior was pretty much as you see it now. I replaced the seats with new racing buckets because they're more comfortable, and I replaced the soft top because it was aging and a tricky piece of shit. I did all the bodywork myself, got rid of the rust where I could, replaced the panels where I couldn't, welded on new steel in other places. Put in a beefy old V8 from an '89 Suburban totaled in a T-bone accident, a five-speed manual from another CJ. New suspension with a three-inch lift, new tires and wheels, and a new coat of paint." I laughed. "I overdid it. I could sell it for twenty, maybe twenty-five, but what I spent on parts and my labor time and paint? Eesh."

She frowned. "Wait, you pay yourself labor?"

"It's one of those business things. I have an LLC, which just means the shop's income goes through the LLC, and I pay myself after I've paid all the overhead bills and taxes and all that."

"Oh, right."

"And how do you like doing restorations?"

"Eh, well? I'd like them better if I could hire an auto body guy to do the welding and rust mitigation and shit. I don't like that part all that much—I can do it, and do it well, but it ain't fun for me. I like the vision, and the final product, and getting into the engine. Tinkering with welders and grinding or torching away rust is work I just don't like. But I'll do it because the final product is cool." I patted the dashboard. "I think this turned out pretty well. Which is why I've kept it to drive myself."

"But you're working on that truck."

"Because I needed a new personal project. And I guess I have a short attention span when it comes to what I'm driving. I like to change it up."

She grinned. "I love this thing, personally. I like

being up high, I like how powerful the engine is. I like the manual transmission. I like the soft top, and I just think it's cool, but I've always loved Jeeps."

"You have?"

She nodded. "Oh yeah. Ever since I was a kid, I always wanted my first car to be a Wrangler. I wanted a red one, with a soft top, and big wheels. I just thought they were the coolest thing on the road, and whenever I saw a girl driving a cool Jeep, I'd get, like, a little girl crush. Like, *she's cool*. I dunno." A self-conscious shrug.

We'd been on the road for a while now, and it was well past lunchtime. We passed a sign announcing an upcoming exit with lots of good food options, and I pulled onto the exit ramp.

"Hey, Jeeps are cool. And chicks driving pimped-out Jeeps are hot." We pulled into the parking lot of a Sonic; I parked in one of the car service spots, and grinned at her. "Lunch time, and then I hope you're up for driving."

She clapped her hands, grinning joyfully. "Yay! Sonic for lunch *and* I get to drive the Jeep again." We both jumped out and switched seats, and then we ordered food. While we waited, she eyed me. "So, when you said chicks driving pimped-out Jeeps are hot, was that a general statement? Or was it angled at anyone in particular."

I snickered. "It was a segue to you driving. You, a hot girl, driving a pimped-out Jeep? Double dose of hotness." I shrugged. "It's not really pimped out, though. Just a lift kit and bigger tires."

"I personally think it's just right. When you put, like, LED light bars and winches and snorkels and all that, it's a little much, just to me personally. Unless you're a serious off-roader and actually use all that gear."

"Which I don't, so I went more minimal."

She wiggled in the seat as the food arrived, and then we dug into our meals. Once we were done eating, had used the restrooms and stretched our legs, ready to set out again, I put the top back, and took the passenger seat. Plugging my phone into the cigarette lighter adapter, I brought up the GPS directions. There was nowhere to really put the phone—I'd forgone the aftermarket console between the seats in favor of a more minimalist look, and once it was plugged in the phone wouldn't reach the dashboard. Which meant it had to be balanced on Torie's thigh.

So, I placed the phone on her thigh, but it wobbled off, and I grabbed it.

She was, at that moment, navigating onto the freeway, and needed both hands to switch gears and steer. "Maybe just hold it and tell me when I need to exit or whatever?" The wind noise was loud, and she had to shout.

The next several hours were total fun. Honestly, it was the easiest conversation I'd ever had. We talked about our favorite movies, favorite music, most embarrassing childhood stories, dumbest teachers, coolest teachers...everything under the sun. And, sometimes, in between threads of conversation, we were just comfortably quiet.

Like me, she tended to leave her hand on the shifter while she was driving; a bad habit, technically, I know. Third gear tended to stick, a little—not a major problem and not worth pulling the thing out to fix, so I just left it sticky. But sometimes, every once in a while, it just...stuck real good and needed a nice hard whack.

This happened as we were finally coming through a slow-down in the traffic. Vehicles were piling up behind us, horns going off, and the damn shifter wouldn't go out of third gear no matter how hard she pushed.

With horns blaring and impatient drivers behind us, Torie was getting a little flustered.

I put my hand on top of hers on the shifter knob, and we both gave it nice hard shove, and it finally snarled out of third into fourth—she let out the clutch abruptly with the gas pedal putting the RPMs nice and high...we jolted forward, the burly V8 belching a roar and our rear tires squealed, and Torie cackled as we zipped up to speed and rejoined the flow of traffic.

My hand stayed there, on top of hers, for several minutes.

Her hand was small and soft and warm. Touching her made my whole arm tingle.

She noticed, too.

She shot a look sideways at me, and then at our hands.

A beat.

I tingled. She smiled, her cheeks turning pink.

Could she hear my heart thundering? What was I? Fourteen again?

Stupid.

But there it was, me, twenty-six and by no means innocent, with tingles and a pounding heart at the idea of touching Torie's hand.

I left it there, now that we were both aware of it.

What would she do?

I watched her out of the corner of my eye—she swallowed, glanced at me, at our hands, and let out a sharp sigh.

She flipped her hand over so it was underneath mine, and now we were palm-to-palm. Naturally, our fingers twined.

Our eyes met.

I risked a small, hopeful smile.

Torie moved our hands to rest on her thigh, mine on bottom, facing up. I felt her thigh muscles bunch as she let off the accelerator as we slid up behind a semi, and then she sped up to pass.

Finally, the sun started sinking in the western sky—we'd left early, stopped for a short lunch; we'd put more than eight hours behind us already, and I was ready to stop for dinner and the night.

We reached the outskirts of Cleveland as the sun was nearly down, and I used the "search along the route" option to find a hotel and diner in close proximity to each other and not far off the freeway. Dinner first, at a small local diner with retro plastic booths and neon lighting—and great chicken strips and fries.

Then the hotel, a Best Western. The clerk behind the counter checked his computer and clicked his tongue.

"Sorry, we're full. There's a huge convention or something going on in Cleveland, so all the hotels are really full. You might have better luck if you go a bit farther down the freeway."

Crap.

So, we hit the freeway again. We drove past a few more exits, but by that point we were past the suburban area outside Cleveland, and the exits were getting fewer and farther between.

Torie yawned and eyed me. "We have to stop soon. I've never driven this long before and I'm getting fried."

The next exit advertised a motel of some kind, so we pulled off and into the parking lot outside the motel office.

It was…not great. Small, local place, a freeway-exit motel that had seen better days, and those better days were, oh, thirty years ago.

I checked my phone, but the signal was shitty and things took forever to load. I sighed and grimaced at Torie. "It's this or keep going to Toledo, and I think that's nearly another two hours, maybe an hour and a half from here. I can drive, if you want."

But, at that moment, I yawned too.

I hadn't slept well for the past couple of nights—too aware of Torie, and too worked up from wanting her to sleep.

I shouldn't drive now either.

She rubbed her face, shook her head. "It won't be the Ritz, or even Best Western, but it's somewhere to sleep."

"Fine by me." I swallowed, hesitated. "I'll ask for two beds."

She didn't say anything to that suggestion. We just grabbed our bags and headed into the office.

It smelled like cigarettes and burned coffee. The lady behind the counter looked bored as she read a paperback bodice ripper, a small TV in one corner playing one of those vote for your favorite singer reality shows.

"Hi," she said, in a voice almost as rough as my dad's. "Room?"

"Yeah, two beds, please."

She shook her head, lighting a cigarette from the butt of another. "Sorry, only got singles. Not really a double beds kinda place, if you catch my drift."

"Really?" I asked, frustrated.

She shrugged. "Hey, the next place with any beds at all is another twenty minutes east on I-90. I got a single for seventy-five a night. I got nobody else, so do whatever the hell you want, just don't trash the place."

I slid her a hundred dollar bill, got twenty-five back and a key. "Thanks."

"It's room three. Not that hard to find. It's the nicest room. Just had the bathroom redid."

"Great, thanks." I gave her what I hoped was a grateful smile, and Torie and I headed out to find room three.

The space between the queen bed and the dresser, which was topped with an old TV, was barely wide enough for me to slide through sideways. The window faced the parking lot, an ancient window AC unit jammed in the bottom. The bathroom, which, true to her word, had recently had a touchup of paint and a new vanity and toilet. The shower, I think, had just been scrubbed until the white subway tiles were something like white again, with a new showerhead.

I stood with my back to the door and slapped my thighs. "Well. No roaches, and I don't see any used condoms, so…win?"

Torie laughed. "Yeah, win." She tossed her backpack to the floor and sat on the bed. "So. The elephant in the room—we're sharing a bed."

"Yep."

"It's hot in here."

"Yep." I tried the window AC, and it blew a meager blast of lukewarm air. "This has seen better days, too."

She shrugged. Smiled. "It's fine."

"Totally fine." I set my bag near hers. Tossed my wallet and phone onto the dresser in front of the TV. "We're adults. We can share a bed without it being weird."

"We totally can," she agreed.

Except neither of us believed that.

At the thought of sharing a bed with Torie, my cock went on high alert, and nothing I thought about or told myself would lessen that.

Problem one.

Problem two, I hated sleeping in jeans. I'd brought a pair of shorts, but that wasn't going to do much to hide my problem.

Torie, however, was yawning. "I'm honestly too tired to care." She blinked at me. "We agreed we're adults, and this doesn't have to be weird. Right?"

"Right."

"I'm too tired to change into shorts. So..." She kept her eyes on me as she unbuttoned her jeans, and lowered the zipper.

Baby blue underwear.

Shit.

She kicked the jeans off, and I had no choice but to notice that her underwear was a thong. I think that was all she wore.

God, her legs were long. Smooth. Strong. Shapely legs. I mean, guys used to talk about a woman's legs, but these days most guys are only concerned with tits and ass. But Torie, man...she made me a believer in legs. So fucking sexy.

She wore a tight yellow T-shirt with some weird graphic on it, and it highlighted the fact that she wasn't wearing a bra. And yeah, I'd been stealing glimpses at those perky, upturned tits all damn day.

Just the T-shirt and the thong.

Fuck.

I swallowed hard. "Yeah, we're adults. It's cool."

Control my cock, I told myself. Two adults sharing a bed out of necessity.

We'd held hands for hours.

She'd seen my cock, seen me jerk off.

I'd seen her topless. Watched her masturbate under the covers, heard her orgasm.

But we were just friends, just two people sharing a bed.

She glanced at me as she slid into bed, under the covers, and then gazed sleepily at me. "What do you usually sleep in, Rhys?"

I rubbed the back of my neck. "When it's just me? Usually nothing."

"Not sure that will work in this situation," she murmured, but her eyes slid over my shoulders, down my torso, to my zipper.

Which was still strained somewhat.

"No," I bit out. "Probably not."

Her eyes lingered. "Rhys..."

"I'll change into shorts."

She blinked at me owlishly. "Underwear would be fine. I don't mind."

"Torie, I..." I knew she knew what I was fighting, right now. "Not sure that's a good idea."

"You need to use the bathroom?" she asked, smirking deviously. "I'll try not to walk in this time."

"No, Torie. No. I'm not...I wouldn't..." I laughed nervously. "You know what? Fine. You can plainly see what's going on. It's an issue, because yeah, I like you. I'm attracted to you, and god*damn* your legs are sexy. And the T-shirt, no bra? That is *not* helping. But I'm an adult. I can handle myself. So just...I'll keep to my side of the bed."

She didn't look away, and I chewed on the inside of my cheek before mentally saying *fuck it*.

Grabbed a handful of T-shirt at the back of my neck, I ripped the shirt off over my head, and tossed it aside. Oddly, coincidentally, totally accidentally, it landed on Torie's jeans. I was hesitant about dropping my jeans in front of her while sporting an enormous erection I could not even begin to hope to control. But it was that or sleep in jeans, and that was a hard pass.

I slid the button free, lowered the zipper, and stepped out of the jeans. And...my cock sprang out into the opening, pressing with a thick bulge against the confines of my underwear. I heard a sound from Torie, I wasn't sure exactly what, though. A gulp? A snort of laughter? A soft, quickly suppressed sound. I glanced at her, and she wasn't even pretending not to stare.

"You sure you're okay?" she asked, her eyes wide and her voice tight, muffled because she had the blanket up over her mouth and nose, hiding her face except for her eyes. "That's...um...that looks problematic for you."

"Yeah, it kind of is." My mouth ran off with my sense again. "You offering to help?"

She ducked all the way under the blanket. "Nope," came the muffled reply.

I hissed in frustration. "This is stupid. I'll be back. I just…I need a minute." I headed for the bathroom, wincing as walking set the damned engorged problem to swaying.

"Where ya goin'?" she drawled. "Taking care of things?"

I glanced at her over my shoulder. "No. The opposite."

"What's the opposite of jerking off?"

"Thinking about old nuns and dead puppies."

"Oh."

"Why, you wanna watch again?" I smirked.

She had just come out from under the covers again. "Nope."

I hesitated in the doorway of the bathroom, and then turned to face her. "You gonna take care of issues yourself?"

She lowered the blanket a touch, and narrowed her eyes at me. "Nope." Should I reveal my little secret? Her eyes met mine and they narrowed even further. Blush reddened her cheeks to flaming pink. "I saw you this morning. You're a good dancer." The blanket was still at her eyes. They twinkled, mischief sparkling in them.

"Am not. I just move my hips a little."

"You wiggle your butt. It's…I was gonna say cute but that's not really the right word."

"And what is the right word?"

"Sexy," she whispered. "Like the rest of you."

"Whisper at me like that while you're half-dressed in the bed, and I'm already fighting this little issue, and we're gonna have an issue."

"What issue?"

"Where I do something I never do—break a promise."

"What promise?" That whisper, low, sultry, seductive without trying.

"That I wouldn't touch you unless you made it clear you wanted me to."

"What's wrong with the way I whisper?"

I swallowed hard. Clutched the doorpost until it creaked—she'd tugged the blanket down to her throat, and her smile was...hesitant yet bold, seductive yet shy. Complicated. Intriguing.

"Nothing wrong with it." I let out a breath. "It's just...one more thing to make it superhard for me to resist you."

"Resist me?"

"Been down this conversation with you, Torie." I had turn around, away from those eyes, those lips. That throat, the delicate butterfly rhythm of her pulse. "You know I want you like crazy. I know you don't want to start nothin'. And I don't have the ability to go partway with you."

"It's dumb to have this conversation from across the room," she whispered. "Just come get in bed."

Get in bed...with her?

God, that was a terrible idea...but a great idea.

I got in bed.

Stiffly—no pun intended. I lay down, arrow straight, arms at my sides, like a corpse. I stared at the ceiling.

Torie rolled to face me, on her side. She poked the side of my bicep. "Hey."

I sighed and tugged the blanket up to hide my erection. I couldn't see any of her but her face and throat and a hand. Yet, the erection remained, like I'd taken Viagra. The erection wouldn't go away.

I rolled over to face her. "Hey."

Inches separated us.

The blanket was molded to the curve of her hip. It was tempting to rest my hand there.

"I'm having trouble resisting you, too," she whispered. And damn that whisper. It did me in.

"I thought you didn't want to start anything."

"I don't. But you make it fucking impossible. You're too...good. Too hot, too sexy. Too capable. Too nice, too funny. Too easy to be with. And I...I've never felt this way about anyone, and it scares me. And I have to go Alaska, and you have your life in New Haven."

"And you don't do hookups."

She laughed, a sharp bark. "No, it's safe to say I do not do hookups."

That was an oddly sharp reaction. Was she hiding something, perhaps?

There was silence, then. I had no idea what to say, what to do. Touch her? She was acting like...like she'd changed her mind about me, about us. Or...that wasn't exactly right. It's not that she'd changed her mind about *us* or *me*, but about what there could be between us, and what that was.

She'd just said she was having trouble resisting me, and god knew I was finding it fucking impossible to do the same.

So, fuck it.

A gentle approach, just to see what she did. If she showed even the least sign of resistance, I'd back off again.

I slid toward her, only an inch or two. But it was enough to close the distance between us, to make the space and the moment go from close, but still mostly platonic, to definitely, unmistakably intimate.

I reached out, slowly, telegraphing my movement, and rested my hand on the swell of her hip.

A moment fraught with boiling sexual tension followed.

She said nothing, and neither did I. But our eyes,

and the unexpressed feelings boiling between us...it said everything.

She wanted more. To be touched. To touch me.

But there was still the reticence, the fear, and the worry. The "but what if" lingering within her.

I was about to remove my hand when she hissed, a catlike sound. "Fuck it," she murmured.

Her palm touched my cheek, scratching and smoothing and caressing my stubble. And then her lips touched mine. Soft at first. Gently questing. Testing. Tasting.

She broke away—mere centimeters—her beautiful pale brown eyes searching my face.

"Oh thank fuck," I breathed.

And then I kissed her.

# NINE

## Torie

Lordy, but the man was a good kisser.

He legitimately took my breath away, stole it, demanded it, devoured it. His tongue was all over my mouth, searching and delving, and his lips were soft, pliant, and strong. His hand cupped the side of my face, and he brought me closer to him. His stubble was scratchy against my upper lip, tickling, sort of rough, but in a delicious, intoxicating kind of way.

I was under the covers, he on top of them. He'd tugged the blanket up to hide his hard-on, and I found myself wishing he hadn't. I wanted to see it.

To touch it. To hold it.

To wrap my lips around it. To feel him surge, throb, and explode.

I'd done that once, with Max, and I'd enjoyed his reactions. That had also been the last time I'd seen him, over a month ago. And that, coincidentally, had been the last time someone other than me had given me an orgasm.

And I wanted one, from Rhys. Because it just wasn't the same taking care of yourself.

But Rhys had said he couldn't stop partway.

Oh god, my brain. Why wouldn't my brain stop?

He was still kissing me, and I was delirious from it. Completely breathless. He pulled me toward him, rolled to his back, and I went with it. I slid over top of him and straddled him. God, he was big. Lean, hard. So strong, so powerfully built, like a wolf. His hand brushed my cheek and cupped my jaw, still kissing me, still devouring me like he'd never kissed anyone before, and would die immediately if we stopped kissing. His other hand grazed over my back. My T-shirt had hiked up which meant, considering I was wearing a teeny little string thong, my ass was bare. And his hands were headed that way.

Yes, oh yes. Please, please put your hands on my ass. I wanted his touch in the worst way. Ever since I'd seen those big strong hands wrapped around the steering wheel the first moment we met, I'd wanted him touch me. Then I'd seen those hands covered in grease, and the need to have his hands on me had only gotten stronger.

His palms slid down my spine, teasing each knob of vertebrae, dancing, scratching, smoothing. My ability to remain focused on the kiss caught a hitch as his hands neared my tailbone.

And then, god, oh glory; he was cradling my ass in his hands like it was the Holy Grail. He growled, a wolfish noise low in his throat—raw male appreciation. My body showed its appreciation for his touch by flexing my hips into his.

Holy shit, oh my god, dear lord, was that his *cock*?

I'd seen it, sure, but only from a distance, and wrapped in his fist.

I'd known it was big, but…

I shivered, breaking the kiss, touching my forehead to his.

"Okay?" he whispered.

I nodded. I pulled back enough to be able to look him in the eye again. But I had no clue what to say.

I needn't have worried. My body did the talking.

My hips flexed, and when he kneaded my ass again, I whimpered. My mouth dropped to his and my lips slashed across his, but I need to sate a curiosity: what would his stubble taste like, what would it feel like as I kissed it? So, I set about finding out. I kissed his upper lip, his cheek where the stubble ran in a curved line down to his lip and up to his temple. I kissed his jaw, where his ear met his jawline. His breath caught and his hands clawed into my ass, and he held on tight—he liked me kissing his face. So I kept going. Down the sharp hard edge of his jawline. He tilted his head, and I kissed the tender, almost delicate spot under his jawline, where I tasted the *bum-BUHbum* of his pulse. He hissed, and I needed to taste more, to elicit more hisses and more reactions.

What would he do if I kissed him…there? Right under his chin.

He groaned softly, and that was a sound which shot straight to my core.

The groan made me throb and pulsate, and it created liquid heat between my thighs.

I was dripping with arousal.

I kissed his throat, and his grip on my buttocks became almost painful—he seemed to realize that, and immediately relinquished his death grip, and began gently stroking my butt. I liked that, a lot.

I meowed as he petted me, and he laughed, lifting my shirt and caressing my bare back. I arched my back and pressed my core into him. I felt something the size of my wrist pressed against me. I also felt the little dot of wetness on his underwear that told me exactly how he was feeling about this.

This was so hot I could barely think.

Then we were rolling over, and I was under him, and I just belonged here, beneath his broad shoulders, pinned beautifully against the bed by his bulk, his hard abs and round shoulders and lean hips my entire world. Then Rhys returned to the glorious torture of a thousand kisses. Everywhere I'd kissed him, he kissed me.

And then he delved lower, to the circle of my shirt's neck. He tugged it lower. And god, the stupid thing was in the way. I ripped it off, or meant to, but I accidentally whacked him on the chin.

"Graceful I am not," I murmured, now tangled half in my shirt and half out.

He laughed, and rescued me from my shirt by pulling it off and tossing it aside. And now I was all but naked under him, the only article of clothing left was a miniscule scrap of blue fabric covering the slit of my sex. Rhys lifted up on an elbow and gazed down at me, his eyes raking over me, absorbing and soaking up every line and curve of my body.

"Fuckin' beautiful," he breathed, awed. "You are so perfect."

My heart melted and began hammering at the same time. "I'm not."

"You are to me," he said. "And that's what counts."

I laughed at that, but then all laughter ceased as he dipped down to resume his kissing exploration of me; my throat, breastbone, left shoulder, then the right. Finally to the space between my breasts.

Yes, there. Please.

I wanted his mouth there, in the worst way.

I cupped my breasts and offered them to him.

He started to laugh, but it turned into a growl. "Know how bad I've wanted to get my mouth on these beauties?"

"Show me," I breathed, need racing through me and erasing all sense, all control. I was lost to this, to him. This was all I wanted.

He showed me.

God, did he show me. His mouth was ravenous, and if I'd thought he kissed the shit out of my mouth, what he did to my tits was...pure worship. He kissed them all over, licked, suckled, caressed. One in both hands, taking it from me, laving his tongue over it, suckling the nipple into his mouth and flicking it with his tongue until I was whimpering, and aching and trembling.

"God, Rhys," I whispered. "I don't know what the hell you're doing, but it feels so good I could almost come just from that."

"Yeah?" he breathed, barely pausing to remove his mouth from my breast. "Let's find out, shall we?"

I mean, I'd known I had sensitive breasts, but this was ridiculous.

The more he played with and kissed and worshipped my breasts, the more worked up I got. I was shaking, trembling, clutching the back of his head with my right hand, his shoulder with my left, hips flexing, and I knew, I *knew* if I even touched my clit, I'd explode.

And I *needed* to explode.

This morning had been…a precursor. Sometimes, my orgasms didn't feel quite…finished. Like, I'd come, but not all the way. So I'd have to wait awhile, and then try again. Sometimes, it took three attempts to get an orgasm that felt like it was the whole thing, all the way, and when that last one finally hit me, *ohhh shit*—it'd blow through me like an atom bomb and leave me limp and senseless for a good ten minutes.

If he made me come right now, it'd be that kind of an O.

I was a little scared of it.

Oh god, my stupid brain. Taking over.

I pushed the orgasm away, along with my need, because I was afraid of how needy and desperate I was.

His mouth seizing my left breast took over my consciousness, and I whimpered again, because Miss Righty was way more sensitive than Miss Lefty. Like, tons more. So sensitive, in fact, that even an accidental

touch would make me wince, and this kind of eroge-
nous sexual touching was nearly too much.

Nearly.

Just too much to be exactly enough.

The whimper became a whine, and then a gasp,
and he was following my sounds, doing whatever drew
the most desperate sound, and now he was sliding his
body lower on the bed, keeping his mouth on my right
breast and one hand on my left, tweaking and toying
with my nipple, and his right hand was sliding teas-
ingly over my stomach, over my hipbone.

Yes, touch me.

Make me come.

Ohh shit, oh god, he was running a finger under
the string around my hip, telling me what he was doing, letting me push his hand away.

God, it felt good, doing this with Rhys. Right,
and good, and perfect, and everything I'd imagined it
would be and more.

I didn't want it to stop.

That triggered a niggling thought in the back of
my head, but his finger was following the string of my
thong over my navel, stopping, and going back, to my
hipbone. Under again, and this time his fingertip slid
along the outer skin of my labia, and I shook like a
leaf at that touch, my hips pushing upward. Needing
more, asking for more.

Ohh god. He drew his finger over the seam, then. Teasing. I gasped, and he dragged his finger down the seam parting the lips. I sang a note of pleading, hips lifting.

He was leaning into me, on his side, while I was on my back. And my hands decided to acquire a mind of their own, and I reached for him.

I did it on purpose. I'm not going to hide behind "oh, I was so lost in need I didn't know what I was doing." I knew what I wanted: to feel him in my hand.

To know if the improbable girth I'd felt would be as fat and hard in my fist as it felt against my core and belly.

He was wearing tight black briefs. And god, they were brief. I felt his belly, the planes and bulges of his abs. The elastic band of his underwear, at his hip-bone. As he'd done, I teased a finger under the elastic and ran it over toward the middle. And met…him. Springy and warm and soft, yet firm. I tugged down, and took his cock into my fist.

And yeah, oh yeah, it was everything I'd felt and more. So…fucking…*thick*. Long, too. God, what a dick. I caressed it, marveling.

He groaned. "Ohh Jesus, Torie. You can't do that too much," he breathed against my breast. "Been so worked up for so long I'll go in a second if you don't stop."

"Don't wanna," I gasped. "Love how you feel."

He flexed his hips. "Gonna pop off like I'm fuckin' fourteen again."

"Don't care." I grabbed his wrist and guided his hand closer to my core. "More of this, please."

He rumbled a laugh and delved his finger into me.

I reached up, clasped the back of his head and drew him down to my breasts. "More of this, too."

He laughed, but it was a wild, nervous, tense laugh, because I was caressing him, and I felt him flex his abs, pull his belly in as I slid my fist around him, up the glorious length of him, fingers barely able to circle the huge thickness of his shaft. I focused on feeling him in my hand—both hands, and still there was so much cock left to caress. Ridges of veins, closely trimmed thatch of dark hair, the grooved ring around the top where my fingers fit perfectly. I rubbed my thumb over the tiny hole in the top, exploring the broad roundness of the head. Smearing his seeping pre-cum along the head.

He groaned, his hips flexed.

With his fingers inside me, his lips on my nipples, I was his for the taking.

I was right there. Trembling. On the edge.

Aching.

Shaking.

My hips flexed up, and he slid two fingers into me, curled them and drew them out and smeared my juices over my clit, and I cried out, feeling it hit me, letting myself fly over the edge. I curled upward, into him, gripping hard him in my fist as I came with the force of a thousand hurricanes, screaming, my spine arched in an upward bow, hips flying against his fingers as they circled my clit with blinding speed, as if he just knew how to touch me, how to make me come, and what I liked and needed.

He was there, on the edge, too. I knew he was close.

I moved my hands along his length.

"Torie, I—shit, I don't want to come like this."

"I just did," I breathed.

"But I want *you*." He couldn't help pushing into my touch, even as he tried to pull away. "I want more than just your hands. I need you."

No, no, no.

Now the niggling worm in the back of my head erupted into an evil dragon.

I didn't want to heed it.

It was roaring two words: *TELL HIM!*

NO.

He'd freak.

He wouldn't want me anymore.

He'd get scared off.

I let my hands do the convincing.

For someone who'd said he'd pop off like a four-teen-year-old, he sure had lasting power.

A growl, frustrated and wild. "Torie…"

"Rhys, just let me…"

He flopped to his back and I followed him, rolling into him, on my side now. My breasts on his chest and my mouth on his, he was too far gone to kiss, and that was okay. I stroked him, felt him pump his hips. Heard the groan.

"Tor—wait, god, oh god…your hands are magical." He was flexing into my hand now, fast.

"Just let me have it, Rhys," I whispered.

"Oh fuck, I can't stop it, now." His eyes met mine, and I saw the questions, and I knew he knew something was up. "Fuck, Torie. I gotta…shit, shit you feel so good. Love your hands, love how this feels. Shit, shit, shit, don't stop, please…ohhhhhh…"

I didn't hurry, I went slow. In fact, as he begged me to not stop, I went slower, twisting my fist around him, caressing lazily, my touch firm yet gentle. And then he was arching up off the bed and growling, roaring, hips pumping into my fist.

His eyes on mine, hazed with orgasm, he did not look away.

"Oh fuck, there—*now.*" He snarled it, eyes locked on mine. "Gonna come now, Torie. Oh fuck, there it is. Ohhh—*fuck…*"

I loved how he talked through the beginning of his orgasm; the helpless guttural tone of his voice, the power, and the desperation, even as he gave in to what I wanted.

And that was for him to come.

I rolled my fist over the top of him, twisted around the plump head one last time. He made a single soft sound, a breath. And then he came.

A spouting fountain of cum burst through my fingers. I let it coat my fingers, gripped him and smeared it all over him and used it as lubrication to pump him faster and harder, and now he was wordlessly crying out, flexed taut, every muscle straining as I drew more and more out of him. My fist was a blur on his cock, I felt the vein on the underside pulsate as he spurted again and again, all over his belly, shooting up to his diaphragm—I cupped his balls and slid them through my palm on my way to stroking him again, and again, through another jet of thick white cum, until he was dripping it on my hand, on his belly, groaning with intense pleasure.

"Torie," he groaned. "Holy…holy shit." His eyes met mine, his delirious, and wild. "You need another one."

He didn't wait for an answer, and neither did I. He pulled me upward, and I went to where he could reach me, keeping my messy hand out of the way.

His fingers found me, and I brought my breasts to his mouth, and he teased me, but only for a moment.

He found the nub of my clit and touched me, teasing me until I moaned, and then when I gasped at a certain touch, a specific pressure, he stayed there, repeating it, while his mouth was on my nipples. He knew the sensitive one already, focused there, playing with the other one with his hand.

Before Rhys, my orgasms had been like riding a steamship across the ocean, and now I was on a rocket ship to the stars. Maybe it was what we'd just shared, touching him, feeling his sticky warm wet cum on my hands and him still shaking from the orgasm… but this was like nothing I'd ever experienced.

He got me there faster than I'd thought possible. Swift circles, the perfect pressure, flicking my sensitive left nipple with his tongue, tweaking my right with pinches until it almost hurt…

"Rhys, oh god, Rhys…" I breathed.

"Like this?" he growled.

"Yeah, oh yeah, just like this."

"Nope."

"Wh—what?"

He lifted me, picked me up seemingly without effort and suddenly I was straddling him, sitting on his face and holding on to the headboard for dear life because *holy shit* he was devouring me, and with such passionate ravenous insatiable hunger that it eclipsed the way he'd kissed my mouth, or the worship he'd paid my breasts…

This was something beyond.

What Rhys Frost did to my pussy over the next sixty seconds was out of this fucking world.

I screamed. A literal, legitimate scream. And he devoured me through the scream, holding me up with one hand and he had two more fingers inside me plunging in and out as he slathered his tongue over my clit. I couldn't stop coming, the whole universe was this orgasm, this mind-altering detonation, and I wanted to live here forever with his mouth and fingers doing exactly this to me, taking me to this new and unexplored nadir of orgasmic perfection.

Fuck.

I came so hard I started crying, and not a cute little tear down my cheek but actual sobs of climactic release, hips gyrating, grinding on his mouth as he pushed and pushed until I was just…gone.

I fell over, completely limp, flopping onto the bed.

"Fucking…hell," I gasped. "Rhys…you win."

"I dunno," he murmured. "I still can't feel my face or move my toes."

A long, weird silence.

"Torie?"

"Yeah, Rhys?"

"Look at me."

I flopped my head to the side, to look at him. "Yeah?"

I knew what was coming.

"Why did we do that?"

"Do what?"

"Not have sex."

"I…"

Shit, shit, shit.

"I have condoms in my bag."

"Rhys…"

"Torie."

"I'm a virgin."

He blinked at me. "You…you're…a *virgin?*"

"Yes."

He took my hand, the one he'd come all over, which was still messy. "You knew what you were doing. That was not your first time doing that."

I closed my eyes. "It's…complicated."

"Not really."

I sighed. "No, not really. I've done other stuff. Just not…intercourse."

"Is that why you didn't want to start anything? Because it'd be your first time."

"And I don't do hookups."

He barked a laugh. "You certainly don't." He rolled out of bed, went to the bathroom.

I heard the sink going and turned to watch. It was a small bathroom and the mirror was placed so there was no privacy if the door was open. So I got to watch as he used a washcloth to clean himself. His cock, his belly, his chest. Then, he wet a new washcloth in steaming water and came over to me, and stood beside me. He took my hand, and gently cleaned each finger, and in between, and my palm and the back, the wrist.

It had the feeling of…an act of tender service.

And then he yanked open his bag, jerked on a pair of shorts, shoved his feet bare into his sneakers, and went for the exit. He opened the door, flipped the deadbolt so the door wouldn't latch, and left.

"Need a minute to think," he shot over his shoulder.

Yep, see?

Tell a guy you're a virgin, and *zhooom*, off he goes, like a scared little rabbit.

Of course, I did spring it on him moments after we'd given each other earth-shattering orgasms. So maybe it was warranted.

Some time to think about the fact that I, the girl he was clearly very, *very* turned on by, was a virgin.

I just had to hope he'd come back and say…

What?

What did I want?

I was more confused than ever.

Because pretty much every fiber of my being was screaming and begging for me to have sex with him. Again, and again, and again.

It'd be...*everything*.

And therein lay the problem: It would be too much everything and I'd never want to stop, and our lives were headed in literally opposite geographical directions.

I collapsed backward onto the bed, naked, confused, glutted from a concussive, mind-melting orgasm, which somehow managed to leave me hornier and needier than ever.

# TEN

## Rhys

S HE WAS A VIRGIN?

What—the—hell?

How?

That handjob she gave me was…fucking incredible.

What we'd done had been, to her, not a means to an end, but the entire experience. Touching each other for the sake of touching, to make the other person orgasm, but *not* via sex.

Bizarre, to my way of thinking.

Of course, it made sense if I thought about it from the perspective of her being a virgin who had still done other things.

Gah, what a confusing situation.

I was even more fucked up in the head about this girl. Because, *fuck*, she was gorgeous. To get her naked like that? Glorious. Every damned inch of her was perfect. Her skin was soft and pale, warm and pliant. I wanted to keep touching her for the rest of my life, to kiss her everywhere and never stop. I had already wanted that before I got to see her bare all over, before I got those sweet, plump, upturned tits in my hands, in my mouth. Before I got that tight, delicate, sensitive pussy against my lips.

Fuck, I was hard again just thinking about her.

But she was a virgin, and I was wary, at best.

I just didn't know what to think.

I wanted her.

I wanted to feel her come again, to make her scream again. To keep her naked and orgasming until she begged me to let her stop coming. I wanted her mouth on my cock. I wanted her pussy on my tongue. I wanted her to ride me until my cock refused to get hard again.

I wanted to make her *mine*.

The potency of that possessiveness scared the hell out of me.

The virulent, scorching, all-consuming *need* I felt for Torie Goode was terrifyingly intense.

And she was a virgin.

She'd never felt a man penetrate her.

Never been held in the afterglow, sated and replete and aching and full of satisfaction.

Shit, this was bad.

I had to talk to her.

I'd paced the parking lot about a dozen times thinking this over, and gotten nowhere but I was hard as a rock and confused as hell.

I went back inside, locking the door behind me.

The lights were off, because we'd never turned them on—the only light was a sliver of dim orange glow from the parking lot lights through the curtains. Torie was naked on the bed, splayed diagonally across it.

Asleep.

On her back, her head turned to the side, one hand resting low on her belly, the other curled up against her cheek. One knee drawn up, foot flat against the inside of her calf. She was displayed for me, and I soaked up the sight of her. Considering what we'd just done, I didn't feel guilty for staring at her, for memorizing her features. She had a mole on her left hip, and a small red birthmark under her right breast, near the outside, close enough underneath that it would likely be hidden by her breast when she was standing up. A spray of freckles dotted her belly. A small thin white scar ran at an angle over her right hipbone.

God, her curves were absurd. How could she be so slender and svelte, yet still have hips that wouldn't quit? Thin, slender waist, flat stomach, and a curve to her hips and ass and thighs that was just…too much for my poor male brain to handle without walking around erect all the time.

Those tits.

All that hair? God, so much thick black hair. She'd had it braided, but as we'd driven with the top back, it had slowly begun to come free of the braid, and now, in her sleep, it was more undone than it was braided. I wanted to see it loose, to run my fingers through the shimmery raven-black tresses and feel it draped in a waterfall around my face as she rode me…

I clenched a fist and turned away from her, forcing my breathing to slow, trying to force my libido to slow down.

God, I was tired.

I wasn't a guy to pass out the moment I blew my load, but it did make me tired, and I'd already been tired from barely sleeping for two days and then spending the day in the car. So now I was deliriously exhausted.

And Torie was taking up the entire bed.

I didn't want to disturb her.

Dared not touch her. Because I was so horny that even exhausted, my hands would likely do something inappropriate.

But I *had* to lie down.

I had to just move her, or wake her up enough to get her to slide over, just a little.

I sat on the edge of the bed, slid my hands under her shoulders, lifted gently, and moved her over.

She stirred, snuffled, shifted. Eyes fluttered. "Hmmm?" It was more of a sound than a word.

"Sorry. Just getting into bed."

She nodded sleepily, gave a little half smile that about melted my heart straight to liquid. "Mmmmhmmm."

She fell back asleep. Without making room.

I sighed. Nudged her a little more firmly. "Torie, scoot over a little."

She blinked her eyes open at me. "Wha?"

I brushed her cheek with the back of my hand. "You're across the whole bed. Make a little room for me, would you?"

She blinked again. "You came back."

I frowned. "Of course. I just needed a minute to process and think."

"Sleepy." She wriggled with awkward adorableness so she was properly oriented in the bed. "Cold."

I slid in, pulled up the covers, and tucked them in around her chin. "Better?"

"Mmmhmmm. Thank you." Her eyes were unfocused but gazing at me. "Sorry I'm a virgin."

I laughed softly. "Don't be sorry."

"Will you still be here when I wake up?"

She had issues about this virginity thing, it was obvious. "Yes, Torie. I'm not going anywhere."

"Okay." Another of those tiny, sleepy, heart-melting smiles. "Good."

I was a side sleeper, so I rolled toward her, watched her tumble into drowsiness, twitching as she fell asleep.

I almost laughed out loud when she twitched so hard that it was almost a full body jerk, which brought her semi-awake again.

"Huh?" she mumbled.

I shook my head. Cupped her cheek. "You're just twitching. It's okay. Sleep."

"I'm a twitcher when I'm sleepy. Watch your shins."

I snorted a laugh. "I will."

Another twitch, her eyelids fluttered open and closed. "Rhys?"

"Mmm?"

"You have the most beautiful penis I've ever seen."

I choked on a laugh. "I…thanks?"

"I've only seen two, including yours. But yours is just…it has to be the prettiest penis there is."

Was she sleep-talking? Or did she just get weirdly unfiltered when she was half asleep?

She seemed to fall fully asleep after that, taking away the need of a response, which was good since I wasn't sure how to respond.

I dozed, and then the dozing turned to deep sleep.

My dreams, of course, were of Torie. Namely, her mouth, doing delightful things to me.

I woke up disoriented, confused. Entangled. Something was tickling my nose; something else was weighing on my chest. And why did my dick hurt?

I struggled to make sense of my existence.

Where was I?

I forced my eyes open, and saw a world blurred and distorted by a snarl of black strands.

Hair?

Something—some*one* was on my chest. So, so disoriented. More than half asleep.

Not ready to wake up.

A vague awareness filtered into my brain—I was in a hotel, and it was Torie sleeping on me, splayed entirely across me, her face on my chest, one hand on my stomach, and one leg tossed over mine. My dick hurt because it was morning wood hard, meaning so hard it ached painfully, and I had to pee. Which was always a tricky combination.

And I was pinned under Torie.

But my bladder felt like it was bulging against my insides, pounding with the need to pee.

Reluctantly, I wiggled out from under Torie, who murmured a small soft whimper of protest as I left the bed. Stumbling, eyes not quite all the way open, I made it to the bathroom and tried to figure out how the hell to pee with a monster erection. I was way too sleepy to do the trigonometry of arcing it while standing up, so I just sat down and bent way, way forward. Pressed my fat, throbbing dick down and cut loose.

I must have peed for, god, at least a full minute.

When I was finally done, my bladder sighed in relief, but my cock was still standing up like a flagpole.

This erection was not going away anytime soon, dammit.

I slid back into bed, for the first time in memory not even caring what time it was—I had nowhere to be, nothing to do, and it was the greatest feeling in the world.

Especially because, as I slid into bed, Torie peered at me through one slitted eyelid, and wriggled toward me, clawed at me clumsily, and tucked herself against me. She rested her head back on my chest, in the crook of my arm, and mewled like a contented kitten.

I wasn't sure whether to melt from pure

overwhelmed heart-blossom joy, be scared of how right and natural this felt, or just relax and enjoy it for what it was.

She wiggled again, as if trying to get closer.

She threw a leg over mine, and I felt the scratch of her trimmed pubic hair against my leg, the silk of her inner thigh on mine. Her breast pressed against my ribcage.

She fell back asleep.

I, as sleepy as I was, couldn't quite fall back asleep right away—I wasn't sure what to do with my hands. One arm was naturally curled against her hip, cupping the indent where her hipbone and pubic bone met, a delicate, porcelain patch of skin that my fingers just wanted to trace and caress as I drowsed. My other hand rested on her knee, near her thigh.

None of this was helping my erection.

Yet, eventually, despite the unfamiliar yet perfect feel of Torie wrapped around me, I did fall asleep again.

The next time I woke up, I came fully awake as I normally did. Torie was still draped over me, but even without looking at her, and with my eyes still closed, I knew she was awake.

I blinked my eyes open, and there she was. Her light brown eyes gazing at me. One hand on my chest, her chin on my shoulder.

"Hi," she whispered.

I smiled. "Hey."

A blush crept over her cheeks. "I fell asleep naked."

"Yes, you did." I let my hand explore the warm curve of her buttock, and I cupped it. "And I am certainly not complaining—at *all*."

Her eyes closed, and I was pretty sure she was relishing the way my hand felt, caressing her. "I've… never slept in the same bed as anyone before. I mean, not a male. I have with Jillie and Leighton plenty of times, but they're my girls, and it's not a weird or sexual thing, obviously, we're just comfortable with each other. And I've certainly never slept naked with anyone."

"Would you believe I've never slept naked with anyone?"

"But you have slept, like actual sleep-slept—with a woman?"

I swallowed. "A little early for probing questions, isn't it?"

She snorted. "It's eleven."

I blinked in shock. "It is? I've never slept till eleven in my entire life."

"Well, you needed it. You were sleeping hard there for a while."

"How long have you been awake?" I asked.

A little shrug. "Half an hour? Forty-five minutes at the most."

"Just watching me sleep?"

A nod. "Yeah." Demure eyes, looking at me and away. "Is that okay?"

"To wake up with you naked, laying all over me? Fuck yes, it's okay."

I was getting hard again, and my shorts, thin and stretchy and loose, would do zero to hide that. Mainly because her leg, thrown over me, would feel it as I engorged. I wasn't sure how to proceed, though. We had to talk about her being a virgin. And what it meant for what we did next.

But *god*, I wanted to get freaky with her. Not, like, kinky freaky, just...sex. I wanted whatever she was willing to do. Weird to say, but I honestly just wanted to feel her hand on me again. I'd never have thought I'd be eager for a handjob, but the way she'd touched me was...pure magic. Raw, sizzling erotic magic.

And I wanted it again.

Her eyes met mine, and I knew she was feeling my arousal grow. "Whatcha thinking about, Rhys?" she murmured, a small, playful smile on her face.

"That I'm horny as fuck, that you're naked and

sexy, that I want to taste your pussy again and make you come, that I want you to jerk me off again, that I want your mouth on my cock, that I want you to ride me, that I'm confused about how you're a virgin yet so sexy and sultry and seductive."

"That's a lot."

"Yeah, it is."

"I'm confused too." She pressed a kiss to my chest. "And just as horny, and I wish you were naked too, and I want…all of that."

"All of it?" I met her eyes.

Conflict in those seductive eyes. "Do I *want* all of it? Hell yes. Am I sure I'm ready for it? If I'm ready to climb on and ride you right this moment? Not exactly."

"We need to talk about that, Torie."

"I know." Her hand slithered down my belly, skittered under my shorts. Brushed my cock. "Can the conversation happen *after* we do nice things to each other?"

"Nice things?" I said, my belly tightening as she teased her hands inside my shorts without actually grasping me yet. "What nice things did you have in mind?"

"I dunno," she murmured. "Last night was pretty…*nice.*"

"Yeah, it was. Very…*nice.*"

Her eyes fixed on mine as she took me in her hand. "I really just want to touch you some more. But…I don't—I don't want to confuse you, or make things hard for you."

"Too late." I hissed in pleasure as her small strong warm hand slid down my shaft, stuttering slowly to my base. "Already confused as hell, but shit, the way you touch me, Torie? I couldn't stop you if I wanted to, and I don't want to. And obviously, I'm plenty hard."

"You don't even have to do anything," she murmured. "Just…let me enjoy touching you."

"Oh, I'll do something." I felt my brain turning sideways, felt my reason abandoning me. "I'm gonna make you…make you feel so good."

Her laugh was low and sultry. "God, you made me feel incredible last night. I've never come that hard in my life."

"You came, like, three times, but not boom-boom-boom."

"Weird, huh?"

"Not weird, just…unique." It was so difficult right now to put two words together, to make sense, to carry on a conversation.

Her hand was moving with glacial slowness up and down my shaft, and her thumb would slide over my tip at the top, and she'd twist her fist on the way down.

"I have this...thing, with orgasms. Not sure how to explain it. The first time, it's like...it's a real orgasm, but when I'm done I feel like...like I'm not done coming. So, if I can get another one, it's even better. But still, usually, that's not it, like—I'm not all the way orgasmed. Usually it takes three before I feel like I've really come all the way."

"So...um." I had to close my eyes and focus on what I wanted to say. "You...when you come—I mean, when you jerk off." I groaned as she did something that involved a twist and a pump at the same time. "You're a girl."

"You noticed," she laughed.

"I mean, you don't jerk off. But when you do your girl thing." I laughed at myself. "You make it hard to make sense because what you're doing right now feels so fucking good. "When you masturbate, you do it three times?"

She sighed, sounding irritated. "Well, that's the tricky part. I'm not normally super fast to get there. Like, it's kinda hard for me to reach orgasm. So, no, not usually. Usually, I have to break it up into sessions, like in the morning, and then that night, then the next morning. And most of the time, it's hard to find the privacy to do so, living with two other girls, and until recently it was four other girls. Bathroom time, every-one up, doors slamming open, music going, someone banging pans in the kitchen, it's just hard to get in the right mood when you live with a bunch of people."

"Well, you came pretty fast and pretty close together last night," I pointed out.

She bit her lower lip, and pushed my shorts down over my cock. "These need to go. I want to see you. I need to watch when you come."

I lifted my hips and she let go of me long enough to pull my shorts down past my butt, and I kicked them off. She immediately grasped me in her hand again. Stroked me. Then let go, and moved to a sitting position—I spread my legs wide and she nestled between them, reached and tucked each of my legs over her crossed legs, so now she was sitting cross-legged in the enclosure of my legs, facing me. Her hands slid up my thighs, caressing my legs, petting them, feeling the muscles of my thighs, then grazing her palms up to my hipbones, over my belly, sliding her hands down either side of my cock before gathering it in both hands.

I had no clue what to do with my hands—she was out of reach, and it felt weird to just let them rest idly at my sides, so I tucked them behind my head.

"I think you had something to do with how fast and how hard I came last night," she said. "And by something, I mean everything."

"I want nothing more than to make you come as

many times and as hard as you can, for as long as I can keep you coming."

She twisted both hands up my cock, stroked them down, one atop the other, and didn't stop at the base of me but slid her hands down to cradle my balls and proceeded to caress and play with them as erotically and lovingly as she did my cock. I groaned at that, because holy hell—how had I not known it could feel so good? No one had ever touched me the way she did. No one, not ever. Her tongue was sticking out, a smile on her face, that little tip of her cute pink tongue running over her lower lip again and again as she plied me with her hands.

"You making me come was the best thing that's ever happened to me," she whispered. "And I mean that very literally. So please, I beg of you, *please*, use any and every opportunity to do so again, as frequently and as creatively as you can."

"Is that an invitation to touch you whenever I want?"

"For now?" a hesitation in her voice, as we both skirted around several major issues. "Yes. It is. Free rein to touch me, to make me come, however, whenever. Just…don't embarrass me in front of people, or get me arrested for indecent exposure."

I could only shake my head, because what she was doing now was too incredible to allow something as complicated as speech. What the hell *was* she doing? I had to remember how to open my eyes, and when I did, the sight of Torie, naked between my legs, my cock in her hands? It was too much. I nearly came just from that, but held it back, because I wanted this to go on forever. I didn't need food or oxygen or anything, just this. Torie's hands on my cock, her tits shifting and swaying and jiggling as she touched me.

"You're lasting a *long* time," she murmured. "Last night, too."

"I don't want it to end," I growled. "Sorry if it's—"

"You better not apologize for that." She smirked. "What if I made it last as long as possible?"

"I might die from how incredible it is?"

"Well, don't die, because I need you to make me orgasm."

"Oh, I will. I may need a few minutes to remember how to be a people, but I'll make you come so hard you'll see stars."

She had that tongue out again, and my heart wanted to explode, for some reason. It expanded with some kind of blossoming, sun-hot emotion, something about the way she stuck that tongue out, a joyful, aroused little smile gracing the corners of her mouth…it did something to my whole being. Shifted me, twisted me into a braided pretzel of confused, overwhelmed emotion. Something like joy, but bigger, deeper, hotter.

It was a feeling that screamed in a universe-sized voice *THIS WOMAN IS MINE!*

It scared me shitless, but it had me in its grip and I was powerless to fight it.

She never did the same exact sequence of touches twice in a row, stroking, twisting, thumb over the tip, cradle and squeeze and caress my balls, pump my shaft with both hands, then one, then just around the base, then just around the tip.

It was as if she was making a game out of touching me, learning how I felt, watching how I reacted. If I groaned at something, she'd do it again. If I tipped my hips up, she did that again. Then, she'd do both of those things one after the other and I'd let out a gasping breathless snarl, hips rocking.

Her tongue. I wanted to tell her to stop doing that, I couldn't handle her tongue sticking out. It was too much for my poor overwhelmed heart, and my poor pounding throbbing cock.

Then she drew it in and bit her lower lip, chewing on the corner as if contemplating something. I saw the decision in her eyes. I had no clue what that decision was, but I had no capacity to speak, or to ask her what she was thinking. I could only ride along with whatever she was deciding on.

Whatever it was, I was pretty sure I would like it.

She held me in both hands, pulled me away so my cock was standing perpendicular to my body. She hesitated and then leaned over me, and I realized what she was about to do the moment she did it. Her mouth slid around me, and I let out a disbelieving, guttural groan as her hot wet tight mouth took me.

"Oh *fuck*, Torie," I snarled, the words torn out of me.

She pumped me with her hands and drew her mouth up toward the tip, stroked her fists down and suckled around me, and I made a sound somewhere between a laugh and a sigh and a groan of ecstasy. My hands drifted out and I tangled her hair in my hands, drew the shimmering black mass up and ran my fingers through it, teasing the tangles out, gathering it in my hands and running my fingers though the seemingly endless silken locks.

I was lost, then. There was no me, only her hair in my hands and my cock in her mouth and her hands. That was everything. The whole universe.

After a moment, she pulled away and I popped out of her mouth and the world beyond the confines of her mouth was a wet cold place and I didn't like it at all. She made up for it, though. And then some. She did that thing where she twisted her fists around the head and then caressed downward in a

hand-over-hand movement that left me aching, gasping, and made my hips thrust up helplessly.

Then her mouth was on me again, this time just
around the very tip, sucking, her tongue flicking and
rolling around as if tasting the seeping essence. She
kept doing that, I think, because of the way I reacted.
Then she added to it with one hand cupping and
squeezing my balls and another pumping the center
of my shaft, and that combination was all I could take.

I cried out, an embarrassing and unmanly whimper of absolutely gone from this world rapture. She
didn't stop. She kept her mouth on me, her fist pumping, caressing my sac with the same speed and rhythm
as my shaft.

My hips left the bed and she moved with me, and
I had to thrust, had no choice. She accepted it, moved
with it, and my fists were knotted in her hair, holding
on for dear life, just holding, gripping the thick mass
of her lush hair and hanging on as she took me to
heaven.

"Torie, oh fuck, oh fuck, Torie, I'm gonna come.
God, oh god—Ohhhhh…Torie, oh *Torie*…" I gasped.

Her mouth left me and she clutched my balls in a
rhythmic squeeze and pumped me and I roared wordlessly as I came, and came, and came.

My eyes flew open and watched as she watched
me come, her fist unhurriedly pulsing down, and up,

twisting, down, and up, and my cum spurted in stream after stream onto my belly; she had my cum all over her fingers, and she was watching avidly, aroused, as she drew more and more cum from me.

It was the most intense, unending orgasm I'd ever felt, and the way her palm and fingers cradled my balls and kneaded them as they pulsed was delirium-inducing, and then as I was nearing the end of the climax she finally began stroking me hard and fast—I'd thought I'd come already and couldn't again for a few minutes at least, but oh god and holy shit she proved me wrong.

I felt it rising in me again, impossibly, and I made a strangled sound of blissed-out disbelief. "Holy fuck, Torie, what are you *doing* to me?"

Her eyes smiled, and she just shrugged, and kept going. Then, as I was about to erupt a second time, she slid that tight wet mouth on me and I felt myself convulse uncontrollably, and she moaned, and I was awash in a sea of white light, blinded by the force of what she was doing to me, something beyond an orgasm, something more. And she didn't stop until I was panting as if I'd sprinted a hundred meters uphill.

Finally, when I was unable to move, choking on my own gasping breath, she backed away and just sat, watching me.

How long I lay there, wallowing in the throes of

ecstasy and delirium, I don't even know. But when I regained consciousness, she was still there, watching me.

"Hi," she murmured, a pleased, thrilled grin on her beautiful face.

"I think I just…I think I died and went to heaven," I mumbled.

She was blushing. Touched her lips, wiped at them. "I like how you taste." Her smile brightened. "I wasn't expecting that."

"Was that…your first time doing that?" I asked.

She nodded. "Yeah." A thoughtful frown. "Well, sort of."

"Sort of?" That baffled me.

"I'll explain later." She dragged her fingers through the mess on my belly. "Don't move. I'll clean you up."

I couldn't move if I wanted to, and by the time I remembered how to move, she was off the bed and traipsing into the bathroom—and *god*, what a view. Her ass was taut, tight and round, shaking just slightly with each step, and then she washed her hands and rinsed out the washcloth and was coming back; the view as she returned was just as good, if not better, with the extra jiggle of her tits.

She saw me looking, stopped near the bed, weight on one foot, hipped popped. "Whatcha looking at?"

"You," I said, "and enjoying the hell out of the view."

I reached for the washcloth, but she shook her head. "No, let me."

She wiped me clean with the warm damp washcloth, even lifting my now-flaccid cock and wiping the tip and the sides, tilting it this way and that, which definitely threatened its flaccidity.

I was roused, now. I could tell by the hesitant look in her eye that she was trying to figure what was next—she wanted hers, but wasn't quite able to ask for it.

And she didn't have to.

I snagged the washcloth from her, sat up and flung it into the bathroom. Grinning at her, a hungry, feral baring of my teeth, I snatched her waist and hauled her to me, onto the bed, and threw her down onto her back. She gasped at the sudden aggression, eyes wide, not quite fearful and definitely eager.

"Your turn," I whispered, kneeling over her prone, lush figure. Stared down at her, palms scouring her belly, up to her breasts. "Gonna make you scream, darlin'."

"Oh god, Rhys," she whimpered, the rough scratch of my hands over her sensitive nipples making them stand on end, making her thighs whisper against each other. "I want to come so bad. Watching you come all over my hands made me so hot."

"You're gonna come till you can't come anymore, baby." I don't know where that word came from; her eyes met mine as I said it, but I didn't take it back and she didn't question it.

I cupped her tits in my hand and worshipped their perfection with my mouth, and I kissed my way to her belly, dipped my tongue into her belly button and licked her left hipbone. She whimpered as my tongue slid across her sex, just above the very keyhole of the top, to kiss her other hip.

"Rhys, I want your mouth on me," she whispered. "Please."

"You'll get it," I promised. "Right...now."

I delved into her, plunging my stiffened tongue into her slit and gathering her essence and tasting it and licking upward to her clit, which was prominent and thick and begging.

I gave her what she wanted, my mouth all over her, taking her clit into my mouth and suckling until she whimpered, and then flicking my tongue over it, going all in, unrelenting, until her hips were bucking against my mouth.

"Fingers," she whimpered, breathless. "Fingers too...please. Put them—put them inside me."

God, her telling me exactly what she wanted was the hottest fucking thing. I gave that to her, too. One finger at first, and even with just my index finger she was tight, clamping hard. Then I added a second finger, my palm facing up, index and middle fingers curling in and slicking out and pumping until she was bucking all over again, and I let her rise, let her gasp and whimper and pump against my mouth and fingers, and then when her moans told me she was close, I slowed with my fingers and went after her clit with my tongue. Two fingers slowly driving in, curling in a come-here motion on the way out, my tongue lashing her. She was wild, then, and I tongued her to the cusp, until she was groaning and grasping at my head and her heels were scrabbling—

And I slowed again, and now added a third finger, and she was so tight around those three fingers I had to keep them bunched together, and she was clamping down hard, spasming around my fingers so hard I could barely move inside her. So I slid them deeper and curled them and rocked my hand like that, finding that spot inside her that made her...

"RHYS!" she screamed. "Ohhhh *fuck*, Rhys, yes, yes, yes!"

She wasn't even coming yet. She thought she was. And I think I understood her confusion over her partial orgasms—she was stopping too soon. Mistaking the preliminary wave of orgasmic power for the main show. Time to demonstrate the difference.

I kept rocking those three fingers inside her, my palm against her seam, tongue now wild on her clit, thrashing in circles, and she arched up off the bed, bucking against me and crying out, a hoarse scream, and I reached up and pinched her more sensitive nipple *hard*, and her scream ratcheted up into a howl and I kept going, kept building speed with my fingers until my wrist ached and my jaw protested.

She was coming, now. Really, truly orgasming. Screaming wordlessly, arched, tensed, trying to pump against me but too caught up in the mad frenzy of climax to have any control. And I did not relent. Not even when she began sobbing and her hips finally started to buck. I rode her thrashing with my mouth and fingers, and she was a wild thing under me, voicing her ecstasy with utter abandon, screaming my name—*"Rhys! Rhys! Rhys!"* Chanting it, again and again as she came and came, and the taste of her orgasm and the sound of her voice and the rapture on her face and the sweat beading on her glorious body took me to arousal and into a state of bliss so that I could have orgasmed with her.

I didn't, though. This was hers.

I kept her there as she thrashed, tensed, arched. She started to come down, slowly, but still quaking, bucking; I tweaked her nipple again and curled my fingers...

And she cried out, a broken sound, and a flood of wetness gushed over my fingers, and she was whimpering, shaking. "Stop, god, oh god, I can't take any more. I can't—I can't take any more—oh fuck, Rhys, it's too much…"

I let her down, then, pulled away and slowly slid my fingers out of her. I crawled up to the head of the bed and gathered her in my arms, because I just *had* to. She went willingly, gratefully, trembling all over.

And then…

We experienced the most awkward silence that had ever existed between us.

She was panting, and I could feel her heart beating like a drum.

"I didn't know," she whispered. "I didn't know it could be like that."

"I didn't know it was possible for a handjob to feel that way."

"I didn't know a mouth could do that."

"I didn't know not having sex could be this good."

And that was it—the elephant in the room.

"Rhys…" she trailed off.

Her hand was low on my belly. And my desire for the woman in my arms was *not* abating. The reverse. She saw the evidence of that.

"Already?" she whispered, and twisted on my chest to look up at my eyes. "Seriously?"

"I just…need you." I closed my eyes and spoke the truth. "More than I've ever wanted anyone, I want you. It's…a little scary."

Silence. There was no clock ticking. No refrigerator humming. No faucet dripping. No traffic. No animal or insect sounds. It was strange, how loud the silence was.

"I know you have questions," Torie said, eventually.

"Yeah," I admitted. "Not sure I want to ask them, or if I want the answers, though."

"Not sure I want to answer them."

"We don't have to," I said. "It could just be… this."

She shook her head, her cheek moving against my chest. "Once or twice is fine. But you wouldn't be content with just…this."

"No, I wouldn't," I agreed with a sigh. "As incredible as you made me feel with just your hands, and for a few minutes, your mouth, no, I would want more. I already *do* want more."

She sat up, crossed her legs, and sat naked facing me, her hands covering her sex. "So. Fire away, Mr. Frost."

# ELEVEN

## Torie

After a brief silence, he scratched his jaw and said, "I guess the place to start for me is, how is it you're a virgin at almost twenty-one?"

I'd been thinking about the answer to this question for some time, so I figured I would just try to explain everything as best I could. "I was shy as a kid. Bookish. Spent most of my time reading, not really socializing. I was also…what you might call a late bloomer." I sighed, remembering the painful years. "I was shy and antisocial because I was skinny, flat, and boring."

"I cannot believe you were ever any of those things."

I smiled at him. "That's sweet of you to say, but it's just the truth. I started puberty around the same time as most of the other girls, you know, got my first period at twelve, moods, all that fun stuff. But… my body didn't change. Nothing happened. None. Zero. Not even little, like, buds. By eighth grade, I still barely even needed a sports bra for gym class. No butt. No hips. Just…stick legs, spaghetti noodle arms. I had the body of a boy. Plus, I was hungry all the time. I could out-eat most guys I knew, and would. So that was extremely uncool. And I read lots of books, but not just any books. I was reading *Anna Karenina* in eighth grade, and Jane Austen, and the Brontë sisters, Tolkien, C.S. Lewis, all the classics I could get my hands on at the library. And to make matters worse, my favorite hobby other than reading was working on cars with my dad. I'd arrive at school on Monday with my hands stained with the grease I couldn't get off. And was the only girl in Mr. Moody's auto shop during the four years I went." I sighed. "I was made fun of by *everyone*. Even the kids who everyone else made fun of, made fun of me."

He made a face of pained commiseration. "God, that sucks. High school is the worst."

I made a *what can you do* face. "So, yeah, I didn't exactly have anyone lined up to relieve me of my virginity in high school. Never went to a single high school or middle school dance. Not one." I laughed. "The night of prom, Dad and I were putting in a new flywheel. We had pizza and listened to most of Led Zeppelin's entire discography."

"Did you ever have a crush on anyone?"

I snorted. "Sure. I had the worst crush on Jeff Ringold. He was the coolest kid in school, drove a Mercedes G-Wagen, captain of the soccer and lacrosse teams. Hot as hell. Big shoulders, blond hair that was just like Brad Pitt's—that perfect. I told him I liked him, and I thought he was cute. I did it after school one day. He laughed in my face, told everyone what I'd said, and they all made fun of me so bad I ran home crying."

"Jesus. What a prick."

"Yeah, he was. I just...I'd had a crush on him since he was a pimply violin dork in fifth grade. Wasn't my fault he'd blossomed into a teenage heart-throb. And a major jackass." I closed my eyes, remembering. "Every time he saw me, he'd laugh, and shake his head, like he couldn't believe I'd even talk to him. So that kind of soured me on boys for the rest of high school."

He frowned. "So..."

I could tell he was figuring out how to phrase his question. "Just ask, Rhys. I won't be offended."

"What we did? None of that was your first time.

You said you'd done other stuff. So…how'd you get from boys are pathetic to…that?"

I laughed. "I graduated high school at just barely seventeen—I skipped a grade, which also didn't help my unpopularity. And that year, the year I graduated, was when I finally got these." I cupped my breasts and shook them. And his eyes followed them for a comically long time. And the sheet he'd covered his erection with tented even more. "I filled out, and without the pressure of high school, I just…was a little happier. I think the stress and pressure of high school literally kept me from developing all the way. I dunno."

"You didn't answer the question," he said. "You also said, maybe you don't remember saying it, but last night or this morning you said you'd only seen two penises, but mine was your favorite, or something like that."

"What I said was, yours has to be the prettiest penis there is." I laughed. "I get weird when I'm half asleep."

He snorted, grinning at me. "I know, I noticed. I like it."

"Because I compliment your penis?"

"Because it's adorable."

I rolled my eyes. "Adorable. Not sure how I feel about being adorable."

"In an arousing kind of way?"

I laughed. "Better." I twisted my hair in my hands, a nervous habit. "You really want to know?"

He laughed ruefully. "Yeah, and no. But yeah."

"My saving grace, ever since sixth grade, has been Max Horowitz. The only kid more unpopular than me. Chess genius, computer genius, and the literal Hollywood personification of nerd. Thick-rimmed glasses, dressed like a college professor, was getting college credit by tenth grade, played the bassoon."

"The what?"

I laughed. "It's a wind instrument."

"Oh. Never heard of it."

"They're weird." I sighed. "Max and I would sit together at lunch. He'd read his programming or chess books, and I'd read my classic literature. He's the kind of chess genius who knows how to play chess with moves that have names like 'Harkov's Gambit' or something. He used to go to Manhattan on the weekend and play speed chess for money. Actually, I think he still does."

"Now we're getting somewhere."

I nodded, laughing. "So, yeah. Max, being just as unpopular as me, was just as lonely as me. We both graduated high school and were like, now what. He's insanely smart, and he could do just about anything, but for whatever reason, he decided what he wanted to do was be a freelance programmer. He could, like, be in the NSA, if he wanted, but he's happy designing websites and playing speed chess." I sighed again, not wanting to get into this. "We hung out a lot. We both tried pot together for the first time. He had this roommate, his first roommate in his first apartment on his own; we were both just barely eighteen. His roommate was like, dude you have zero vices, it's annoying, try some pot. But he was scared to try it alone, so we did it together. And that's how it started between us. We'd hang out at his apartment, smoke pot, and watch movies. Talk."

I paused, because it was weird to talk about this. Jillie and Leighton knew, because they'd been there for most of it, but even they didn't really *know*.

I needed to tell him. So I continued. "Then, one day, we were sitting there on his couch, stoned, watching some movie. It had a sex scene in it, and I noticed Max was getting a little…excited. And I was like, that looks like it's a problem. It was awkward. And he looked at me, and he was like, I'm a virgin. Never kissed anyone, never done anything sexual. And I told him I was the same. And he said, so, what if we…did stuff together. Maybe not sex, but…stuff. So…we did. We've never talked about it since, and it's just a thing we do…did. Once in a while, I'd go over to Max's, and we'd smoke a bowl and watch porn, and mess around. Just hands, usually."

He frowned. "And it never went to sex?"

"No. Because pretty early on, I realized I really enjoyed the sensations, the physical stuff we did, but I knew I had no feelings for Max beyond friendship, and that wouldn't change—for me anyway. Just messing around, getting handsy, hasn't changed my feelings. He's my friend. My best friend, in a lot of ways. And if I never touched him again, he'd still be my best friend. If we had sex, I couldn't be his friend. And I couldn't—haven't, and won't—have sex with him because I don't have feelings for him." I swallowed hard. "By the time I was seventeen and the only person I knew other than Max who was still a virgin, I knew having sex needed to be something meaningful. With someone I had something with. I've never been like…" I put on a faint, breathy voice. *"I'm waiting for Prince Charming to sweep me off my feet and live happily ever after'."* I resumed my normal voice. "But it wasn't going to be—and it *won't* be—just a hookup, just to get rid of my virginity. So, I'm not, like, saving myself for marriage or true love, I'm just not going to give it away cheaply."

Rhys nodded. "I admire that a lot."

I frowned at him. "You do?"

"Hell yeah. You have a conviction. It means something to you, and you've stuck with it. It's awesome." He shrugged. "So you and Max. You literally just…get stoned and give each other handjobs? And that's *all* you've ever done with him?"

I nodded, then tilted my head to the side. "Yeah… well, sort of. One time, he tried going down on me, but it…tickled. I dunno. I wasn't feeling it and neither was he, and he stopped. And the last time we hung out, about a month and a half ago, I tried going down on him, with similar results. I was scared of him coming in my mouth, and it just…was weird. So I stopped."

He eyed me. "You did it to me, though."

I blushed. "Yeah. I wanted to try it again."

"And?"

I blushed harder. Whispered. "I liked doing it to you." I met his yes. "A fucking *lot*."

He grinned. "It was incredible."

"Maybe sometime I could do it again. You know. For practice."

His eyes darkened. "I'd be okay with that."

"You have something going on under there," I said, pointing at the sheet. "Now might be a good time."

He hissed. "In a shock to myself, I'm going to say we should finish this talk. Because there's still things to talk about."

I let out a breath. "Yeah." I let my hair go, and untwisted it. "Such as, where does this leave us?"

"I guess that's up to you."

"Don't make it all on me. Dear god, I can't handle that kind of pressure." I pointed at him. "Is me being a virgin a problem for you? Because it seems like you're conflicted about it."

"It's not a problem. I just—"

"Because Rhys, if I were to decide I wanted to go there with you, it wouldn't come with, like, expectations. I do mean that."

He shook his head. "It's not that." Rhys rubbed the back of his neck, which meant it was story time. "After I left home, I told you I worked my way north and east. I'd stay somewhere long enough to make enough to cash to keep moving. And, you know, being an unattached and horny eighteen-year-old, I'd find local girls willing to have some fun. I was always forthcoming about the fact that I was just going through and would be moving on soon, so there were never any hurt feelings. Which more than a few times cost me the fun for the night. But I'd always rather that than have a girl with a broken heart on my hands, because broken hearts mean angry dads and brothers." He sighed. "So, I think I was in…New Jersey, somewhere. The countryside. Working on this guy's C-10 Fleetside for fresh eggs, a place to sleep in his hayloft, and a hundred bucks cash. And, at nights, I'd go up to the little town square, hang out with the local kids.

And there was this girl. We hit it off, the usual banter, whatever. We decide to go for a drive out to the little spur-line, a little road that dead-ended at a small pond. Private, right? Things start happening. I always made sure they were okay with how things were going, and it was no different with this girl, Emily. You all right? You want to keep going? Things like that. She was like, yeah, yeah. But something kept feeling a little... off. She was...clumsy, I guess. Hesitant. I dunno how to put it. Like she wasn't sure of herself, or me, or what was happening. And I was getting weirded out, but she kept telling me she was fine, she wanted to keep going.

"And I just gotta make this clear, I asked like half a dozen times if she wanted to keep going. Because of how weird she was being. So finally, we, you know. Did it. And she was...just dead silent. She didn't move. Didn't make a damn sound. I was like, you okay? She was like yeah, I'm good, keep going. So I did. It was dark in the truck, so I couldn't see all that well, but it seemed like she was wincing or something, and I even asked if it felt okay, and she faked this giggle, like, yeah, it's great."

I sighed. "Oh dear."

"Yeah. So I finish, and she never really, like, got into it. She clearly did *not* enjoy it. So I cleaned up and I was finally like, what was that? I admit I was a little angry, or annoyed, or whatever. She said forget it, it was great, can we go? Fine, whatever, I took her home. But it left a sour taste in my mouth, you know? I couldn't figure it out." He let out a long breath. "So, I spent another week finishing Smith's truck, and I thought I'd hang another day or two, say goodbye to the kids I'd been friends with. And there I was, in the town square where everyone hung out at night, and here comes Emily. With her dad. And her brother. And her uncle. And they all had shotguns."

"She did *not* cry rape."

He barked a laugh. "No, thank god. But she told her sister she'd had sex with me, and her sister told her mom, and somehow it got twisted, and suddenly I was this evil seducer who defiled their precious daughter—they used the word 'deflowered.'" He growled. "It had been her first time, and she'd been using me to, as you put it, *get rid of* her virginity. As a way of getting at her parents. She used me, the vagrant who didn't belong, the rough kid from Kentucky who was on his own at eighteen when most of them barely knew how to even tie their own shoes much less survive on their own. I got run out of town that night— at gun point. They followed me to Smith's house and made me pack up and leave."

"Wow."

"So, since then, I've just been wary, I guess. Her

first time should have been a lot different. If she'd told me, if I'd known, I'd have been…I dunno. Different. It's not like I was…I don't know, railing her doggy style as hard as I could. But if she'd just told me I'd have made it different. But she didn't seem to want to fool around. I kept trying to get her in the mood, and she was just like, no, let's just do it. And then we did and she obviously wasn't into it, if not actively hurt by it. I don't know. Never got the chance to ask, obviously. But, I guess I'm not exactly a small guy, and I didn't know she was a virgin, so the first time I…I went in, I wasn't…I wasn't as gentle as I would've been, had I known." He looked at me, assessing my reaction.

I could see how me being a virgin would mess with him, considering that story. "Rhys, that was not your fault."

He shook his head, shrugged. "No, I know. But I still feel bad. I just remember having the impression she was wincing the whole time, and I can't help but wonder if she'd ever actually enjoy sex, if that was her first experience. I just feel bad."

"You shouldn't. She used you. Being a virgin is an important thing not to disclose."

"Yeah, no kidding."

Another silence.

I swallowed hard. "So, where does this leave us?"

"I…don't know." He scratched his jaw. "Maybe we should hit the road, and each of us can spend some time thinking."

"Yeah," I whispered. "Probably smart."

He touched my thigh. "Torie, I'm not saying I don't…that how I feel about you has changed. It hasn't. But the reasons you didn't want to start anything haven't changed either."

"But what you want and what I want might be different. Where I want us to go from here may not look the same as what you want it to look like."

"Right." His voice was quiet, perhaps a little distant.

I looked away, shifted away from him. "So, we'll just get dressed and head out, maybe stop for breakfast somewhere along the way."

I shifted off the bed, gathered my clothes from the floor. I contemplated taking my things into the bathroom to change but didn't see a point. He'd seen all of me there was to see at this point, so why bother with modesty or privacy? I stepped into a clean thong, and then the same jeans I'd been wearing, tugged on a clean plain green V-neck T-shirt, and my sandals, shoving the boots into the bag along with the dirty underwear and T-shirt.

Rhys watched me dress with fascination.

I glanced at him, smirking a question. "What? Never watched a girl get dressed?"

"I mean, yeah, sure. But it never loses its sexiness. And watching you dress is almost as hot as seeing you naked."

I bit my lip around a flattered grin. "You're sweet. If I'd known you thought it was that hot, I may have made more of a show of it."

His eyes flicked over my chest, my braless breasts poking against the thin T-shirt, as if he hadn't just had his hands and mouth all over them. "Maybe good you didn't. If you'd put on a show, we'd never leave."

I slung my bag over one shoulder. "Don't tempt me, Rhys. We're supposed to be taking time to think about things."

He sighed. "I know. But I can't help wanting to get you naked and screaming every time I look at you."

I had to get out of here before I tore off my clothes and threw caution and prudence to wind. "Dammit, Rhys. You and your dirty, sexy mouth." I turned away, headed for the door. "Get dressed before anything else happens."

He just let out a dry, amused chuckle as I made my escape outside.

Within a couple minutes, Rhys joined me outside and we jumped into the Jeep and headed out—it looked like he'd done the same thing as me: clean underwear and a T-shirt, but same jeans as yesterday.

Once we hit the highway, top back, wind blowing and sun shining, it was easier for me to sink into my complicated, twisted, chaotic thoughts and feelings regarding Rhys, my attraction to him, and my virginity.

I didn't know what I wanted the future to look like. Time to think was definitely necessary. But he was…cooled off toward me. Maybe cooled off wasn't the right phrase. I'd instigated things last night and this morning. And, honestly, if nothing else happened between us, I wouldn't regret anything. If anything, I was glad I'd gone for it. He'd made me feel things I hadn't known were possible. I hadn't known I could come like that—once, hard, and all the way.

And god knows I'd learned a delightful lesson in making him feel good. In fact, I was fighting a seething desire to get my mouth on him again. I'd never imagined I'd *want* to do that. But I did. Badly. The short time I'd had my mouth on him, he'd gone wild, clearly enjoying it so much he couldn't seem to cope with it. I'd had a momentary impulse to finish him that way, in my mouth, but I'd chickened out. I was scared of the cum in my mouth, afraid of swallowing it. Did I spit it out? Where would I spit it? I hadn't known what it tasted like. He'd come, this morning, and then I'd wanted him in my mouth and had second-guessed not having him come in my mouth—he'd…I don't think it was a real second orgasm, because nothing had come out except a few little drips, but the taste of *that* had been enough to make me want more.

What that said about me, I wasn't sure. I wanted to talk to my girls about it, how they felt about blowjobs, and maybe get some tips. I knew Leighton was a bit of a dick aficionado, and talked about going down quite frequently, Jillie not so much.

Was it weird that I *wanted* to suck him off and swallow every drop of his cum?

I didn't care.

I wanted to.

I wanted him to go absolutely crazy. Lose all control. Gasp and pant and cry out my name as I made him come so hard he saw heaven. Or, as he'd said, make him die and go to heaven.

He wanted sex. Actual, real sex. He wouldn't be content with handjobs and blowjobs. I mean, sure, he'd take them and he'd give as good as he got, and then some. But he wanted to fuck me. He wanted things I knew for a fact I had no clue about. I was fairly confident in my handjob skills as I'd pretty much perfected them on Max, with the help of plenty of porn, because how else is a girl supposed to learn new techniques?

And I knew Rhys had appreciated the techniques I'd learned, because he'd made sounds that had told me so. I mean, at first, with Max, I'd just done plain old up and down jerking. Then I'd watched a video where the lady had done all sorts of things with her hands, twisting and using both hands and cupping and playing with his balls, and I'd realized there was a hell of a lot more to giving a guy a great handjob than just jerking up and down. If that was what he wanted, he could do that to himself. I wanted to do things he couldn't and wouldn't do to himself, which meant technique. I'd watched enough porn to know about blowjobs and figured I could do those pretty well, and definitely planned on trying it on Rhys at least once before whatever this was between us ended.

But did I want to have actual sex? Was I ready to give my virginity away? Did I want to give it to Rhys?

The complicating factor was that I was certain there were real feelings developing. For him as well as me. I *liked* him. And now that I'd gotten a little freaky with him, I liked him even more. Whereas with Max things had been fun, and I'd enjoyed the things we did, but there was nothing more. I would never *want* or *need* Max. He was convenient, and he was safe— we'd both agreed on that. I had risked nothing with him. I could jerk him off as many times as either of us wanted, I could get fingered by him as many times as either of us wanted, and I'd never feel for him the way I already did for Rhys.

That was a problem.

Feelings were a big problem in this scenario; I knew enough about sex to know that if I slept with Rhys, things would change. Shit, we'd only messed around in familiar territory and things had already changed. If I gave him my virginity it would mega change. Whatever I felt for him would be intensified by an untold amount.

I'd fall in love with him.

Truthfully, I was already falling in love with him.

Dammit.

I choked, my eyes misting as the realization hit me. Thank god for the wind and the noise, because they covered for me.

I was falling for everything Rhys was. His thoughtfulness and kindness. His hint of roughness, the hard edges around his soft, giving center. The way he spoke, the twang that came and went. His humor. His love for cars, and the way he'd start rambling passionately about them.

I wanted to get into an engine with him. Hand him tools, wedge my little hand into places he couldn't. Fix cars with him. Build things with him. Ride along on salvage runs. I wanted to be his partner.

I was falling for his body. His jawline and the stubble, his sharp cheekbones and puppy dog eyes that could shift from humor to intelligence to boiling with sexual heat. I was falling for his lean frame, his hard shoulders and shredded abs, his sharp hips and taut ass. His huge, long, fat cock with the round pink head and the tan wrinkled flesh of the shaft and the purple veins, and the bulging, heavy, swaying balls which he went crazy for when I played with them. I was falling for the way he kissed me, like I was the last woman on earth and he'd die if he didn't kiss me.

I was falling for the way he seemed to literally and absolutely love my breasts—which I'd always been self-conscious about. They were small, sloped, with upturned tips, plumper at the base than the peaks. They weren't anything like the tits on the girls in the locker room of high school gym class, much less those of the women on the porn I watched. Just more reasons to be insecure or, at the very least, self-conscious.

Jillie and Leighton thought it made no sense that I was self-conscious about what my boobs looked like.

But…Rhys seemed obsessed with my breasts, seemed to go bonkers to look at them, and even crazier to get his hands on them, and his mouth. He made me feel beautiful. Sexy. He made me feel confident in my body, like I was a curvy, desirable woman instead of the skinny, flat-chested, no ass, boyish girl I'd always felt like. He changed that, just by the way he looked at me, the way he touched me, the things he said.

And I was falling in love with that.

How could I not?

But…how could I let it happen? The farther from Connecticut I got, the more I knew I wasn't going back.

But he had to return. He owned a business there. He had a life there. He'd fought like hell to build what he had, and there was no way I'd ever ask him to give that up for me, and nor did I expect him to, or think he would. And going back to my dead-end life in Connecticut was no longer an option for me. I needed a change, and a drastic one—spending time in Alaska with Mom and my sisters was just what I needed. Whether I moved there or not, I was sure the change would be good. I knew I was going to be there for a while, figuring out my next step in life.

Being in love with a man who lived in Connecticut was not a convenient or realistic part of that. It was impossible. Alaska and Connecticut were about as far apart as you could get, and starting a long-distance relationship with a man I'd known only a matter of days, with no end goal in sight in terms of ever being together was probably not the best idea I'd ever had.

It was stupid, that's what it was.

So why the hell would I risk the integrity of my heart by sleeping with him? I'd just fall all the harder, and when he went back to Connecticut, I'd be devastated.

On the other hand…

If we did sleep together, there was no doubt whatsoever that it would be…beyond amazing. More than merely magical. It would be profound. Wild. Heart-altering, mind-bending, and body-shifting.

How could I pass that up?

Would it be worth the inevitable heartbreak?

That was what I had to decide, and I had less than zero clue how to make that decision.

# TWELVE

## Rhys

SHE WAS WORKING THROUGH SOMETHING IN HER MIND, I could tell. We spent a very, very long time in silence, both of us thinking. We stopped for drive-through breakfast sandwiches and coffee and were back on the road in minutes.

I, meanwhile, was completely fucked up over Torie Goode.

Last night and this morning had easily been the hottest, most pleasurable, most intense sexual experiences of my life, and we hadn't even had sex.

I was desperate for her. Even now, I was aching with suppressed sexual need. I needed her. I needed to kiss her. To have her naked body in my hands, her hot smooth flesh pressed up against me. I needed her on top of me, writhing as she came. I needed her under me, legs around my waist, crying into my shoulder as she came apart.

I needed to be inside her.

It was a biological, emotional, and mental imperative. If I didn't get to sink inside Torie's slick wet sex very soon, I might just explode, and not in a sexy way.

But I *couldn't*. I couldn't take that from her. I couldn't demand it of her. I wasn't even sure I was ready to be her—or anyone's—first. I hadn't wanted to be Emily's first. I felt...violated, in a way, by what she'd done. She had taken advantage of me, certainly.

Torie had stopped us before we got there, and she had told me. She'd respected me by telling me and letting me decide what I wanted, what I was capable of.

I knew I was developing feelings for her—strong feelings—but I didn't feel I could tell her. Not when she was planning on staying in Alaska, and not returning to Connecticut. And that was where my life was.

What a mess.

I was falling for a girl I couldn't have. I finally find a girl who understands me, who shares my passion for cars, who gets it...and I can't have her. I can't be with her.

If she wasn't a virgin, I'd be more likely to sleep

with her and accept the consequential heartache when it was time to say goodbye. But not with Torie. I couldn't do that to her.

I felt something powerful enough for her that I knew it was unique and special. And I also knew it wouldn't be easy to get over her, even if I never got to sleep with her.

I didn't want to think about how I'd feel when we parted ways.

Shit, just thinking about driving away from her made my heart squeeze.

But the fact was, it was getting close to the time for me to turn around. We were almost halfway between New Haven and Alaska by now, and the farther I got from my shop, the longer it'd take to get home. In the back of my mind I had figured that my little "vacation" would mean being away from the shop for less than a week. I could be gone that long without income. I had savings, but I categorically refused to touch that money under any circumstances except the most dire of emergencies. Getting that call from Dad reminded me that Mom and Dad depended on the money I was able to send them every month. I couldn't afford not to be working much longer.

Shit.

But...where did I leave her? Chicago? Minneapolis? And how would I do that? Just take her to a bus station or airport and be like, bye? Drop her off and peace out like nothing had ever happened?

No fucking way.

It would be like leaving her on the side of the road.

But where did I stop? Where did I draw the line?

A bigger issue was our physical and emotional connection. The longer we were in this car, the deeper our connection would become. And the nights... would be impossible. How could I sleep in the same room, much less the same bed, as Torie and not end up having sex with her? And that would happen, I had no doubt. She wanted it as much as I did, I could tell. Maybe even more. Or...differently. I had a point of reference for what it would be, for how it would feel, for the connection, the deepened sense of intimacy. She didn't. She couldn't know how it would affect her, or me, let alone us together.

I wasn't one of those guys who saw sex as just getting my rocks off, just a physical thing. I was fine with a temporary, one-time thing with a willing girl, but it was always a little more than just a purely phys-ical thing. We'd lie there afterward and talk, and there would be a connection between us, a camaraderie of sharing the moment, the sex, the one-time rush of sleeping with a stranger.

I'd already felt that emotional component with

Torie, intensely so…and we hadn't really even had sex. We just fooled around in a way I hadn't done since I was a kid. And damn, was it fun. The lack of expectations, the sense of not having a destination in mind, so to speak, just touching and giving and receiving pleasure for the sake of pleasure itself, for the sake of enjoying each other's body…god, how addictive.

And dammitall, it wasn't the sexuality itself that was addicting, it was *her*.

Torie.

All that she was. The mix of innocent and sultry, sweet and dirty, nervous and bold, confident yet insecure at times. Slender, yet curvy. Tight, but soft. Strong, but tender.

I glanced over at the girl in question—the woman, I mean. She was all woman. A virgin, perhaps, but not entirely innocent, and all woman.

She was sleeping. Her head rested against the pillar near the seat belt, the end of her braid laying on her shoulder. Mouth slightly open. Hands tucked between her thighs.

This was sweet, innocent Torie. Looking at her like this made my heart do melting flips, which was confusing because I'd never felt this way about anyone before.

*How can I leave her?* That thought ran through my head, back and forth, again and again, as I drove, putting miles behind us, trying in vain to forget that little motel room where I'd gotten my first taste of the most magical woman I'd ever encountered.

Scenes from the night before and this morning ran through my head.

Torie, sleepy, erotic hunger blazing in her eyes. Reaching under the waistband of my underwear, grasping me. Taking me in her mouth, taking me to heights of ecstasy I'd never experienced before. Writhing under my mouth, her spine arched to press her slit into my tongue.

I wondered if she realized she'd squirted. I'd heard about that, of course, seen it on the internet, but I always figured it was some exaggerated, scripted porn thing.

But, no.

She'd squirted all over my hands. Not enough that there'd been a wet spot on the bed, and she may not have even noticed with how far gone into orgasmic bliss she'd been.

Fuck, so hot.

I needed to stop thinking about this shit or I'd get myself all worked up again. I needed to get my shit together and really figure things out.

But then…what was there to figure out?

I wanted her.

I wanted to sleep with her.

I wanted to be with her.

I wanted to bend her over the bed and fuck her until she lost her damned mind. I wanted to make slow sweet gentle love to her, something I'd never wanted or done with anyone.

I wanted it all, with her. And only her. I wanted to dive into everything she was as a person and never come back up.

That scared me shitless, absolutely shitless.

We passed by Chicago, hitting a brief slowdown in traffic right outside the city, and Torie kept sleeping.

And I kept waffling.

*How can I leave her?*

What right did I have to take her virginity, and then just casually go back to my life in Connecticut? She said she didn't want her first experience of sexual intercourse to be casual, one-time. And maybe if we did have sex, it wouldn't be casual, and definitely not just once, because I knew once I got inside her, I'd need her as many times as I could get her. But still, it was not what she wanted.

Which begged the question, what *did* she want? She said she didn't expect it to be love, but what was there that was less than love and more than casual?

It made me think maybe she was avoiding what she really did want, which *was* love, and she was just scared of actually allowing herself to want it.

And if that was the case, sleeping with her would be a massive mistake for both of us. I probably shouldn't have let anything happen at all. But it was done and I had no regrets. But shit, I wanted more. So much more.

And if I let it happen, I risked breaking her heart.

And mine.

Yeah, mine too.

"Deep in thought, there, are you?" Torie's voice was sleepy and amused, startling me.

I jumped, laughing. "Holy shit, you scared me."

"I've been awake and watching you for like, ten or fifteen minutes. I think you're driving on autopilot."

I chuckled, rubbed the back of my neck. "Yeah, I guess. Just thinking."

She sat up, rubbed her eyes. Stretched—and damn, the sight of her stretching was distracting enough that I had to force my eyes away or risk a wreck. "Feel like talking about it?"

I shrugged, sighed. "I dunno. You?"

She glanced away. "Honestly? No, not yet."

I laughed and sighed. "Good, me either."

Torie was looking out the window and she said, "Where are we?"

"Just outside Chicago."

She looked back at me. "You want to switch?"

I nodded. "Yeah, actually."

We ended up driving to the next exit with food. This time we went in—another fast food joint with burgers and milkshakes. With the topic at hand weighing heavily, we were pretty quiet, suppressing any idle chitchat.

We finished our lunch, used the restrooms, gassed up and rolled back onto the freeway, and I let myself doze off.

Dozing turned to actually sleeping, and when I woke up I realized I'd missed most of Wisconsin. We pulled onto the shoulder and put the top up since it was actually getting hot, and then continued on. I put on some classic rock, which was what I'd been raised on, and which Torie had said she and her dad listened to in their garage.

She shot me a look when "Paint it Black" was the first song on queue. "Are you playing classic rock for me?"

I laughed. "Yes I am. Growing up, it was what pretty much everyone listened to. Zeppelin, the Stones, ZZ Top, Pink Floyd, The Who. The only local radio station we got was a classic rock station, so my truck was just tuned it all the time, and so was everyone else's."

She grinned, drumming a beat on the steering wheel. "Jillie and Leighton make fun of me for liking classic rock. Like, could you be any more of a typical stoner? But it's just…comfortable. Familiar for me. Dad loved it and he used to be in a classic rock band, back in the day."

The taut, weighty silence was broken and our natural conversational flow returned, a wide-ranging discussion of classic rock bands, rating them, talking about individual players, guitar styles, and that conversation took us into Minnesota. We stopped in Minneapolis for dinner, and the conversation wandered into random rabbit trails of endless, easy talk.

As we left the diner, I shot a look at her. "You wanna switch, keep driving, or call it a night here in Minneapolis?"

She leaned her butt against the hood, considering. "Honestly, I'm not tired at all. That nap was like power fuel or something. I'm good to keep going, if you are."

"Sounds good to me. Let me know when you get sleepy."

"I will."

Onward, then. Silences alternated with conversation and we played a game with the songs on queue, trying to pick the next song based on ever-changing criteria—number one hit that same year, or bands that ended up sharing a member, or words that appeared in both song titles, until we'd covered almost all of classic rock and moved into southern rock and country.

By the time we reached North Dakota I could tell she was getting tired, but I figured I'd wait for her to call it.

I was about to suggest a switch, but then she seemed to get a second wind, perking up, finding new energy that took us through half of North Dakota before we had to stop and pee and refuel. She let me take over, then, well past midnight. We'd agreed to keep going until we were both too tired to drive anymore. We both got coffees and snacks and, somehow, despite the seemingly endless hours and miles, we always had something else to talk about.

We reached the border at Raymond, Montana, and drove over to Regway, Saskatchewan where we talked to the Canadian border agent. We answered a few questions and crossed without issue, but not before Torie got her first stamp in her passport. And just for fun I got one, too. I'd driven up to New Brunswick a few times to get car parts, but I'd never got a stamp in my passport, so it was fun to share a first with Torie.

Despite the coffee, Torie eventually fell asleep, leaving me to the music and the miles and my thoughts.

I was glad we'd kept going. I knew we were putting off the inevitable, but neither of us wanted to address the elephant in the Jeep.

About six a.m., I started yawning uncontrollably, and I needed to stretch my legs and get some air, so I pulled over on the side of the deserted highway just before dawn—when the sky wasn't quite gray, but not quite light. It was cool, with a sweet smell to the air. The land was very flat where we were, just beyond Regina, a stand of trees here and there, but mostly flat farmland.

I tried to open the door quietly, but Torie stirred and woke up, smiling sleepily at me—the smile that got my heart every time. It was a smile that said she was just so happy to see me, even though she'd been right next to me in that passenger seat for hours at this point. It just got me, that sleepy little grin.

She got out of the car and stretched, up onto her toes, arms overhead, shirt lifting to bare her belly and the undersides of her breasts, which trembled as she shook with the force of the stretch.

"Where are we?" she asked, yawning, her voice muzzy, and something about it felt like the most familiar sound in all the world, somehow.

"Regina, Saskatchewan, or just past it." I yawned, then, catching it from her. "We're more than halfway to Alaska, now."

"Rhys…" she started, and then trailed off. She strode out into the grass beyond the shoulder. I followed. "When are you going to turn around?"

Good question. I picked a long stalk of grass and twisted it in my fingers. "I dunno. Been trying to figure that out, but…"

Her pale brown eyes searched me. "But what?"

"It's complicated," I said, avoiding the meaning behind her question.

"No, it's not. You have to get back to New Haven. You have jobs lined up. Yet here you are in Regina motherfucking Saskatchewan with me. So again, I ask you—how far are you willing to go?"

I swallowed. Dropped my eyes to the grass—watched a big green grasshopper struggle up a stalk of grass. "I don't *know*, Torie. I've been thinking about it for hours and I don't fuckin' know, okay?" I felt honesty rising in my throat like bile. "The thought of just…leaving you outside a bus station makes my stomach hurt. I just don't know that I can do that."

"I'd be fine if you did, Rhys. I'm a big girl, I can take care of myself."

"Maybe *I* wouldn't be fine," I muttered, more to the grass than her. "I know you're capable—it's not about that."

She was rocked back by that answer. "Then what's it about?"

"It's about a whole big, deep, hard conversation we've been avoiding since fuckin' Ohio."

"Oh." She kicked at the tall grass, walking away a little bit. "Maybe…maybe we should agree to not…to not *do* anything for right now. Until we do figure that out."

"Yeah, probably a good plan," I said. "I'm for sure too tired to talk about it right now." I yawned again. "We should just go back to Regina and crash."

She shook her head. "I'm good to go—I'll stop for gas and coffee at the next stop, but I want to keep going, if you're okay sleeping in the car again."

I nodded. "Fine by me. I'll put the seat back and crash."

She laughed. "Since we're driving, maybe don't use the term 'crash.'"

"Yeah, good point. Get some sleep, is all I mean."

We went back to the Jeep, and continued to the next stop, where I refueled and bought coffees and more snacks. I saved my coffee for after I woke up; it'd be cold by then, but I was accustomed to drinking cold coffee in the shop when I was too busy to make more or reheat it.

Once we were well on the way, I fell asleep within minutes to the hum of the tires and the low jangle of the classic rock playlist.

I woke up just outside Saskatoon, drank some coffee and looked over at my driving partner. I could see that Torie was lost in thought, as I'd been when she startled me the day before. We'd been driving without stop for over twenty-four hours.

"How you doing?" I asked.

She started, laughed self-consciously. "Got me back," she breathed, shaking her head. "I'm about ready to hand it over."

"You thinking we should keep going? Or grab a motel and rest for the day?"

She shrugged. "I'm tired, but I'm wired, and I don't think I'll be able to sleep anytime soon, so I guess if you're game to drive a while, we could keep going and stop early."

I didn't ask the question. Thought it, but didn't ask it.

It was another long day on the Canadian prairies. The silence was a little awkward, and it seemed impossible to break. What to say? Where to start?

So we did the ostrich thing, burying our heads in the metaphorical sand and refusing to address the issue—thus, we didn't talk much at all. Between the elephant and the ostrich, the Jeep was beginning to look like a zoo.

Despite her claim, Torie fell asleep. It was better that way.

She slept through my pit stop for gas and coffee and the restroom.

She was still sleeping when we drove past Edmonton.

I was now in the zone, a captive of highway hypnotism. I had the radio off, my window down, arm out. I forgot about being hungry, tired, horny and the issues between us—I was focused on nothing but the drive.

And Torie slept on. Longer than she'd ever slept since I'd known her—through an entire tank of gas, another cup of coffee and emptied bladder. She was still sleeping when night fell.

She snored. Real, actual snores. Loud enough to make me laugh every time, because it was so damned cute.

In the middle of the night, she finally stirred. Blinked awake. "Shit. I slept. Where are we?"

"You were out for damn near twelve hours." I pointed out the window at the darkness.

She blinked again. *"Twelve hours?"*

I nodded. "Yep."

She bit her lip and sat upright. "I, um…have to pee."

I glanced at the GPS. "Don't think we're all that near a stop. How bad?"

She winced. "Like, pull over right the fuck now."

I pointed at the windshield—which was wet, wipers going. "Uh, it's pouring out."

"Well, I'm about to go in my big girl panties in about ten seconds. I'll just have to get a little hardcore."

I glanced at her, and she had her knees pinched hard together and was bouncing in her seat. "Shit, all right. Here we go."

I pulled over onto the shoulder and put on the flashers—fortunately, we were in an area with an actual shoulder, a place where the hills approached the mountains, and there wasn't a car in sight. As soon as we were fully stopped, she threw open the door and leaped out.

"Shit, it's really fucking raining!" she yelled, then glanced at me. "This is gonna be an eyeful for you, Rhys."

And right there in the relative lee of the open door, rain spattering the seat and the door and the inside of the Jeep, she dropped her jeans and kicked off one leg, moving with desperate, jerky speed, held them out of the way, and squatted.

"Don't watch," she muttered. "It's embarrassing."

"No it ain't," I said, even as I looked out the other side.

I heard her peeing, though, and it *was* a little weird. Intensely personal, hearing her pee hit the grass in a very, very long stream.

Finally, she stood up and leapt into the Jeep and shut the door, her jeans and underwear half on and half off. She was dripping wet and soaked through from spending mere moments outside. She just sat on the seat, half-dressed, a blank expression on her face.

And then she started laughing, hysterical and unhinged. "I really just have the worst luck with rain, don't I?" The laughter died, and she started putting her jeans and thong back on, but they were wet from being in the rain. She glanced at me. "I'm guessing you wouldn't be super mad if I just...didn't put my pants back on?"

I couldn't help but look at her—we were still stopped, flashers on, so I took my time looking her over. Nothing on but a wet T-shirt, and that was sticking to her, highlighting her curves.

I swallowed hard. "Uh, no. Nope. Wouldn't be upset if you didn't put pants back on." In the interest of keeping to our agreement of not touching each other, I turned off the flashers and checked over my shoulder for traffic before accelerating onto the highway again. "I mean, shit, you wanna just take off your shirt too, I'd be all right with that."

She kicked her jeans off with her toes and then tugged her thong off and tossed both behind her onto the back seat. "Just...buck naked in the car?" she asked, an eyebrow quirked, a smirk at the corner of her mouth.

I nodded, shrugged. "Middle of the night, middle of nowhere, got three-quarters of a tank of gas." I gestured at her. "Strip down if you want. Can't guarantee I won't be stealing looks at you, but I'll do my damnedest to keep my hands to myself and keep driving."

"If I'm naked, you're allowed to look." She swallowed hard, ducked her head. "I like the way you look at me." A long hesitation. "I like the way you touch me."

I gripped the steering wheel hard, yanking the shifter down into fourth and then slamming it up into fifth as I reached the speed limit. "We agreed we wouldn't touch each other until we had a chance to figure things out."

She peeled her shirt off, setting her tits free with a bounce and a sway, and then I had myself a naked Torie in my Jeep—and a hell of a hard-on.

I clutched the shifter so hard I heard the plastic creak in protest.

I had to focus on the road, dammit. But there she was, naked. Thighs splayed just enough to give me a teasing glimpse at her core, thin pink outer lips and protruding delicate clitoris, just fucking begging for me to pull over, lean my seat back, and sit her on my face so I could make her scream.

Never been attracted to a vagina itself, before.

The woman attached to it, sure, but—perhaps oddly—I've never really spent too much time examining a girl's hoo-ha in detail. More focused on getting inside it, touching it to make her feel good.

But Torie? Even her pussy was a delicate, pink blossom of sensual beauty.

God, I was in trouble.

I had to turn the music up in an attempt to distract myself. Telling her she could be naked had been a mistake. I was not strong-willed enough, not by a long damn shot.

"You all right?" I heard her ask, turning the music back down.

I gritted my teeth and nodded. "Yep."

"Why do I not believe you?"

I sighed, laughed ruefully. "I'm an idiot, that's why."

She frowned at me. "Why do you say that?"

"Because I clearly overestimated my willpower."

"Meaning what?"

"Meaning you sitting there naked is more of a problem for me than I thought. Which is on me, not you. I just…" I hissed. "Resisting you was hard enough when I didn't know what you looked like naked, how you feel, how you taste, what you sound like when you come. Now that I've had that taste, it's damn near impossible."

She chewed on that a moment. "Why…why do you have to resist me?"

"Because I can't have you."

"You already have, though."

I shook my head. "What we did in that hotel room? That was…shit, that was like getting one little bite of fresh-made key lime pie and being told I can't have a whole piece. It was a tease."

She frowned at me, hard. "Rhys, I wasn't teasing you."

I rubbed my face with one hand. "I know that, dammit. I wasn't saying you're a tease. You ain't. Not at all. Far from. I'm saying, I want so much fuckin' more with you, and knowin' I can't have it? It's a tease. And it ain't your fault."

"What is it you want, then, Rhys?"

"I don't think I oughta say. I'm not trying to get you to do anything you're not ready for."

"Maybe I am ready, though."

I hesitated. "You say that, but *are* you? How do you know you are?"

"Wait, wait. You're not even saying what it is you want that you think I'm not ready for." She tugged her hair out of the braid and ran her fingers through it, letting the long black tresses hang over her shoulders, so it nearly covered the tips of her breasts. "This conversation isn't fair and doesn't make sense if we're not clear and on the same page about it."

"It's about sex, Torie," I snapped, unfairly. "It's about the difference in what you're willing and ready to do, and what you aren't. It's about how I want you, all of you. Mind, heart, soul, and body, I just fuckin' *want* you, Torie Goode. And I want...I want to have sex with you."

I shook my head. Hissed in frustration as I hunted for a way to put it strongly enough that she'd *get* it.

"I want to *fuck* you," I said, my voice low, growling. "That clear enough for you? I want you to ride me in that passenger seat, my cock buried to the hilt inside your soaking wet pussy. I want to pull over, drag you into the grass, put you on your hands and knees and fuck you from behind until your ass shakes. I want you in a hotel bed, on your back with your legs around my waist while I fuck you and fuck you and fuck you until you beg me for a break from being fucked."

I looked at her, gave her the full, unfiltered intensity of my gaze. "You know, when I slept in that seat there, earlier, I had a wet dream about you. Legit, I woke up with my cock hard and seconds from coming. You know what I was dreaming about? You, straddling me. Taking my cock and riding me as hard as you could. Tits bouncing, screaming my name.

That's what I dreamed about. That's what I want."
I was worked up, emotional, hands shaking; I pulled
over onto the shoulder again. "I want more than that,
though. More than sex. More than fucking. I want to
*make love* to you, Torie. I want all the emotions that
go with it. I want to make love to you and never stop.
That's what I want."

I leveled a hard, open stare at her. "And as you've
pointed out, I got my life back in New Haven, and it's
a near-certainty you're never coming back there. So
I don't know where the hell that leaves us, because
maybe you're content fooling around, but I'm not.
Don't get me wrong, I enjoyed what we did more
than I've ever enjoyed anything in my whole damn
life, and I could die tomorrow a happy fuckin' man,
because I got to experience that with you. The problem, Torie, is that the next time I get my hands on
you, I don't know that I'll be able to stop at just eating
your pussy, just getting a handjob or even a blowjob
from you. I want more. Need more. And if I were to
get a little of you, I'd take all of you."

I swallowed hard. Looked away. Returned to the
freeway, tires skidding on the rain-slicked pavement
as I nailed the gas a little too hard.

"The problem, Torie, is that *that* ain't mine to
take."

"It is if I give it to you."

"Did you hear everything I said?" I asked. "What I said I want?"

She nodded. "Every single syllable. And yes, I've never experienced that so I can't say I want those things specifically. Some of it sounds a little scary, honestly. But being with you at all is scary. You make me want things that scare me. You make me feel things that scare me. But part of all that, being scared of the things you make me feel and want is that I've never felt so *alive* as when I'm with you." Naked, bold, eyes fiery and on mine. "So, yes, Rhys. I want those things. I want it all. I'm scared of it, yes. But I want it." She swallowed, blinking. "What scares me the most is what you said—that you never want to stop. Because I never want to stop either. I didn't want to stop the other morning, in that motel. I wanted to keep going. I didn't want to tell you I'm a virgin because I knew it would scare you. Guys see virginity as this... this precious thing. They see taking it as a responsibility. As if my entire future of sexuality hinges on their performance during my first time. And I'm like, get over yourself! You're giving yourself too much credit. Not you specifically, just men in general, guys who I've had experiences with that could have led to sex."

"Other than Max?" I asked.

"Other than Max, yes. A few guys." She looked away. "There was a cook at the restaurant. We flirted, went on a date. We kissed. That was it. Went on another date. I went home with him and we made out, and it was obvious he was assuming, naturally enough, it was leading towards sex. So I told him I'm a virgin, and he noped out of that, didn't want any part of taking my V-card, as he called it. That's happened two other times. No discussion, no option for me to decide what I wanted, if I was even offering, no respect for my autonomy, my will, my desires."

"That ain't what's happening here, though," I said.

"No, it's not," she agreed. "But you're still scared of my virginity."

"Yeah, I guess maybe I am, a little."

She nodded. "I know. But I told you. I've given you plenty of time to think about it. And, you'll notice, I'm still not exactly saying let's do it right now. If I offer you my virginity, you'll know. It won't be in a car. It won't be an accident. It'll be me telling you what I want, that I want it, that I'm ready. If we get there—*if,* say, *if*—you'll know because I'll say it in so many words, that I want to have sex with you, that I want to go there. Your role, at that point, is to decide one thing—if you want that with me. Your responsibility, and your *only* responsibility, is to decide if you want to have sex with me. The consequences of it, how I feel about it, how it affects my future sexuality, that's on me. Not you. You don't decide that for me. If I were to offer it to you, it would be because I've decided you're the man I want to experience the full totality of sex with. I'll have chosen you.

"I *trust* you, because I know you'll treat me right and make my experience a good one. And that's all you have to do. That's your *only* responsibility—do your best to make my experience the best it can be. I don't expect fireworks and a parade and a twenty-one gun salute. I know there may be some discomfort. I also know once that initial moment is over, it'll be amazing. Or, that it *can* be. And I know with you, it would be. I don't need you to assume you're *taking* anything from me." She held my gaze, long and hard and direct. "If we were in a room, in a bed, and I told you I want to have sex with you, that wouldn't be you *taking* anything. It'd be me giving it to you. So keep that in mind. And, by the way, if we were to do anything else in between, I hope you understand that I trust you to control yourself. To take what I'm offering and no more. I *trust* you, Rhys. I know you're a good man. I know that no matter what you say right now, all worked up and horny and emotional about it, mixed up maybe, upset, confused—when push came to shove and we were messing around and you wanted to fuck me and I said no, I *know*, without a doubt, that you'd stop in a heartbeat. Because that's the kind of man you are. And that's why I'm even in this car with you. Why I'm so strongly considering giving you my virginity no matter what the future may or may not hold for us."

She paused and sucked in a shaky breath.

I was just about to reply when I realized she had something else to say, so I held my tongue.

"I don't know that we have a future together. If you even want that, if *I* want that. How we'd get there, considering the logistical issues standing in the way. And, yes, I have feelings for you that make me wonder if we could have a future together, and a damned good one. And that scares me. A lot. Because if I gave you my virginity, I know those feelings would multiply by like, infinity. Make it *so* much harder to say goodbye when that time comes. But I also think that maybe…maybe it'd be worth it anyway."

"Torie—"

She held up a hand. "Don't. Just think about it. Take some time and think on all that."

Even though she was naked, I did exactly that—I thought about all that she'd said.

At some indeterminate amount of time later, she pulled her sleep shorts and a tank top out of her bag, slipped into them, not bothering with anything else.

I yawned, hard enough that I swerved, and Torie frowned at me. "My turn. I'm wide awake, now."

"Should we stop?"

She shook her head. "Why? I got twelve hours of sleep. Don't even need coffee, although I may stop at the next good exit and get some. We've got to be getting close to almost being there."

"Our major destination is Prince Rupert. That's where we take the car ferry to Ketchikan itself."

She eyed me. "We."

I nodded. "I've decided I'm just gonna see you all the way to your family. I'm most of the way there, so I might as well see Alaska while I'm at it."

In an instant her face lit up. Her eyes sparkled and she smiled, and I knew I'd just made the best decision of my life.

I pulled off onto the next exit that had a gas station, and I practically ran to the men's room and emptied my own bladder, which had been turning my eyes yellow at that point. I filled up the gas tank and then we switched places. Torie took us through a 24-hour Tim Hortons, where we got real food and a big box of Timbits. We hit the highway and headed for the northern coast of British Columbia. After eating, I realized I really was tired; the hours of driving had taken their toll. I leaned my seat back, left the lap belt buckled, tucked a spare T-shirt between my face and the door, and fell asleep.

# THIRTEEN

## Torie

I'D THOUGHT THAT ONCE WE GOT THAT HARD conversation out of the way, things would loosen up. But they didn't, not really. When both of us were awake, unspoken feelings simmered between us in the car. Chemistry and sexual tension churned in the silence.

Hours and miles passed. We traded again somewhere in the mountains of British Columbia. Drove through the day, into the next evening, living on coffee and naps and fast food.

It felt like we'd always lived this life—me and Rhys, alone in the car, hours on end. Days, and days. This was life. This was all there was.

Wanting him, not having him.

Watching him stretch in the passenger seat, arms straining the sleeves of his T-shirt, the hem lifting as he yawned, baring those abs. Seeing the bulge of his cock behind the zipper. Wanting him so much I ached. I wanted him so bad. It was more than a sexual need, more than the heavy, burning, turgid ache of needing an orgasm. This was more. This was...a need that rifled through my mere physicality and speared into my soul, into my heart, into my psyche.

I knew, after hours of driving and thinking, that I was going to sleep with Rhys.

I *had* to.

When he'd been telling me all the things he wanted to do to me, I'd nearly jumped him then and there. Even now, thinking about his words, the dirty promises of fucking me doggy style in the grass, the image of riding him, having him inside me as I fucked him? I needed that.

I needed to *know*. Him. Myself. Us, together. How it felt. I needed to know what it felt like to be filled, to be penetrated and taken...by *him*.

I finally saw the first sign for Prince Rupert. It had been in kilometers, though, and I wasn't sure how that translated into miles and travel time. I mean, his Jeep had a speedometer that also showed kilometers per hour, so if I was going the posted limit of 100/kph, and the sign said 280 km to Prince Rupert, then it should take us...fuck, math was hard...two point eight hours? What was point-eight of an hour, though? Eighty minutes? Duh, no, moron. Forty minutes? Something like that. I figured it was a little under three hours to Prince Rupert.

Then we'd get a ferry, and that would end the driving for a while.

Which would be weird.

Prince Rupert was beautiful—moody, misty, surrounded by snow-capped mountains and the cleanest, freshest air I had ever smelled. The ferry was mind-bogglingly expensive, and Rhys paid the whole fare for both us and his Jeep, ignoring my offer to help pay.

We parked the Jeep on the ferry and took our cabin—a one-bed. We tossed our bags on the floor and sat on opposite sides of the bed, facing away from each other.

I lay down, first.

For a moment it was as stiff and awkward as the first moment I'd lain in a bed with him.

He finally snorted. "This is dumb." He slid his

arm under my neck, and I rolled into him, and snuggled against him. "Let's just rest and enjoy not driving, okay?"

I nodded. "Okay."

We slept all the way to Ketchikan, and not a single thing happened between us but sleep.

Rhys took the wheel in Ketchikan which was, easily, the most breathtakingly beautiful place I'd ever seen. I plugged Mom's address into his phone and we ended up at a condo complex outside the downtown area of Ketchikan.

Rhys pulled into a parking spot outside the building, put the Jeep into neutral and set the parking brake. He shut off the motor. It ticked as it cooled, and the sudden silence was, somehow, deafening and oddly final.

"Well." Rhys rubbed the back of his head. "Here you are."

"Here *we* are," I said. "That was quite a taxi ride," I joked. "I can't believe you've driven me all the way to Alaska. Well, shall we go in and meet my family?"

"Okay."

"I'm just going to introduce you as Rhys. No commentary on the status or non-status of whatever we are or aren't. But be prepared, Lexie will corner you, or me, or both of us, for sure, and ask prying, personal, inappropriate questions."

He nodded. "I'd expect nothing less, after our talk on the phone."

I let out a breath. "Okay, let's go in."

I grabbed my backpack and stepped out of the Jeep, and felt oddly sad that the road trip was actually, finally over.

I went to the door, pressed the button marked *O. Goode.* It buzzed.

A silence.

"Yes?" came Mom's voice.

"Uh, hi, Mom. It's Torie."

A stunned silence. "Torie? Torie! You're here, oh my gosh! Okay, okay, I'm coming down."

I laughed. "Or just, you know, buzz us in and we'll come up?"

"Us?" Another pause. "Well, I guess I'll find out. Yes, yes, come up, Torie and unknown person."

The door buzzed and I pulled it open. We went up and found Mom's door, which was already open and she was standing right there.

And that was when I realized I hadn't seen my mother in more than two years. Almost three.

I started to cry, unexpectedly.

Mom made a mom-noise, a whimper and a sigh,

pulled me close and brought us into the condo. "Oh, oh, oh, come here, baby girl."

Just like that, I was in my mom's arms, smelling her scent, feeling her familiar arms and the enveloping comfort of her embrace.

"I guess…" I said, and then hiccupped, the sounds muffled in her shoulder. "I guess I didn't realize how much I missed you until I got here."

She kissed my temple, and just held me. I heard her sniffle. "Torie makes four. Just need one more, and my family is all here." She kissed the top of my head. "You're here, now, Tor. I've got you."

The weight of being on my own suddenly felt like it had been too much, it had been much harder than I'd realized. A weight I hadn't known I was carrying until I was back in Mom's arms, feeling her, smelling her, hearing her. I knew, right then, that I wasn't going anywhere. I'd made it to Ketchikan, and I wasn't leaving.

But there was a man behind me, standing patiently, who'd gotten me here. With whom I had an unwritten story.

I pulled away from Mom. Cupped her cheek. "I'm so glad to be here. You have no idea."

She sniffled, wiped a tear away from underneath her eyelid, with her middle finger, glancing up at the ceiling and blinking. "I do, Tor, I really, really do. Of all my daughters, I've worried about you the most. And now you're here."

I turned and gestured to Rhys. "Mom, this is Rhys Frost. We drove here together." I found myself holding his hand, drawing him forward, not letting go. "Rhys, this is my mom, Olivia Goode."

She shook his hand. "You can call me Liv."

Rhys gave her that grin of his, bright, eager, warm, welcoming, charming. "It sure is a pleasure to meet you, Liv."

She was assessing him, both as a woman and as my mother. Letting him have the full force of the Mom-looking-INTO-you stare, that left you feeling like she'd seen just about everything there was to see and was weighing it all.

"Thank you for helping my daughter get here, Rhys. We've all been worried about her, knowing she was too stubborn and independent to let us help her."

Rhys just held the smile, not at all discomfited by her assessment, confident in who he was. "She's a remarkable human being, Mrs. Goode, which, from where I'm standing, means you must be a hell of a woman yourself."

Mom grinned at me. "He's a charmer, Torie."

"Don't I know it," I said.

And that, for some reason, was when I realized

I'd entirely stopped checking in with Leighton and Jillie. They were going to be so mad.

Later. All of it, later.

Mom laughed. "So you two crazy kids drove all the way here from New Haven?"

I nodded. "Almost nonstop, too. Once we started, we just...kept going, trading off when one of us got tired. We only stopped the first night, in...Ohio, I think it was?"

Rhys nodded. "Just outside Cleveland."

Mom shook her head. "That's crazy. But you're here, you're safe, and there's plenty of time before the wedding to find you a dress." She looked me up and down. "And, no offense, but a bra."

I rolled my eyes at her. "Oh, don't start that up, Mom. I brought one. I just don't like to wear them. But I will for Lexie's wedding." I frowned. "Not thrilled at the idea of a dress, though."

Mom laughed, glanced at Rhys. "Not sure if you've picked up on this, but my dear Victoria is not exactly the type to wear dresses."

I shook my head. "I've worn a dress exactly twice in my life. And I've hated it both times."

"I've picked up on it, yes." Rhys grinned. "What were the two times?"

I winced. "Um. Grandma and Grandpa, Mom's parents, died within days of each other, when I was...

nine? I wore a dress to their joint funeral. And then to…um. To Dad's funeral."

Rhys closed his eyes briefly. "Shit, I should've known. I'm sorry."

I shook my head. "No, it's okay." I brightened, with a bit of effort. "I'm glad to be wearing a dress for a happy occasion."

"Amen to that," Mom said, then clapped her hands. "So, kids. Where are you two staying?"

We glanced at each other.

"Oh…I…we—" I stammered. "Um."

I glanced at Rhys, but he was no help.

"Um." I sighed. "I hadn't thought that far, and Rhys and I are…we're not…we haven't quite figured out…"

Mom's eyes widened. "Oh, shoot. I guess I assumed the wrong thing, huh?" A pause, as she sorted through the situation. "Well, Rhys, you're staying for the wedding, yes? You drove all the way here, so you may as well stay. It's going to be a big old party, and we'd love to have you."

He stammered. "I…I…" He glanced at me. "I mean…"

I was still holding his hand. "He's staying for the wedding. As for who's staying where, we'll have to figure that out."

"You're both welcome to stay here, but if you're

not staying *together*, then Rhys can hang with Myles and the guys. The week leading up the wedding itself has sort of turned into this weird, crazy bonanza bachelor-bachelorette…thing. The guys hang out by themselves all day, the girls with the girls, and then at night we all get together and just…" she sighed. "Well, you'll see for yourself. Point is, Rhys, if you're comfortable getting acquainted with a bunch of loud, vulgar, rough, wild, Alaskan men, then I guarantee you'll have a great time, and they'll make sure you're taken care of."

"Ma'am," he drawled, "I grew up in no-name holler in the backwoods of Kentucky. Loud, vulgar, rough, and wild sounds like home to me."

She laughed. "You'll do just fine, in that case."

I looked around. "Where is everyone else?"

"Well, I'm just here for a quick change of clothes. I had a client meeting this morning and then I showed a house we just finished remodeling, and now I'm getting changed and I'm gonna go find the crew."

I laughed. "The *crew?*"

She shook her head. "Torie, my love, you have no idea what you're about to be introduced to. We use a lot of words to describe ourselves—crew, tribe, clan, those are the most common. But, in the end, they all mean the same thing—family." She squeezed my arm, giddy and excited. "And now you're here! Holy hell, I'm so happy."

I blinked in shock. "Mom...you just...*swore*."

She cackled. "Oh my, wait until you meet my Lucas. He's changed me, and for the better, but if you're not used to the new me, he can be a bit of a shock to the system."

That was an odd statement that I had no way of understanding, so I didn't bother trying.

I stepped back and looked Mom over—she'd put on weight, and it suited her, filling out her hips and bust, the way a little extra would on me. She was... lighter, brighter, happier. A spark of joy burned in her eyes, and I realized that for years leading up to Dad's death, and in the months after, that spark had faded and died. It was back now, and brighter than ever.

"You look *amazing*, Mom," I said.

She curtsied, which looked funny as she was wearing a power pantsuit. "Thank you, my dear. It's amazing what healthy eating, an active lifestyle, someone to love you, and a whole hell of a lot of great sex can do for a person."

You could have knocked me over with a feather. "*MOM!*"

She just cackled. "I told you, baby girl, I'm not the Momma you knew when I left New Haven."

"I don't think I've ever heard you refer to sex and

yourself in the same sentence in my life," I said, still reeling.

She patted me on the shoulder. "You'll get used to it. Now, you two just set your bags here while I get changed. There's a shower in the guest room, if you want to rinse off real quick.

"God, honestly, a shower sounds incredible," I said. "I haven't had one since Connecticut."

And, considering some of the things that had gone on since then, I felt a little...crusty.

Rhys nodded. "I wouldn't mind one myself, if there's time."

Mom eyed us. "Well, there's certainly no rush." She chewed on her lip a moment, her eyes going between Rhys and me. "Do I, uh, need to turn on music?"

I realized what she was getting at, and boggled yet again. "Mom! Oh my god, no. We're taking *separate* showers. It's not like that." I sighed. "I mean, it is, but it's not. You know what? It's fucking complicated, okay? But no, we're not...no."

She shrugged, and didn't even address my F-bomb. "You're adults. But regardless, take your time. I'll get changed and then I have a few emails to take care of before I go play hooky for the day." She led the way down the hall and gestured into the guest room. "There's shampoo, conditioner, body wash, lotion, all the good stuff. Take your time, and make yourself at home, honey. And if you need anything, just let me know. I bet you're famished, but there'll be plenty of everything at the party."

She kissed me on the cheek again, and then went into her room and closed the door. And despite the conversation, music started playing—Lexie and Myles, it sounded like. Loud enough to drown out just about anything.

I went into the guest room and looked around, Rhys with me.

Our hands were still joined, fingers twined, like we'd always been this way. No wonder Mom assumed we were together.

"Your mom is the fuckin' coolest," he said. "For real."

I laughed. "You know, I always loved Mom, I mean, she's my mom and she's great, but I never really saw her as…cool, or uncool. She was just…*Mom*. I wasn't embarrassed by her, but I didn't think I had, like, a cool mom." I gestured in the direction of her room. "That? That's someone I've never met before, in Mom's body. She's cool, she's…casual, confident, funny. I don't know. It's weird, seeing her like that, after so long apart." I sighed. "She seems happier than I've ever seen her, though."

"That's a good thing, right?" Rhys asked.

I sat down on the end of the bed, and Rhys sat beside me. "Yes. But…god, it's weird. It's bringing up a lot of other stuff. Like, if she's this happy now, how unhappy was she before? With Dad? She's a whole new person."

He squeezed my leg. "I think, maybe, that's a conversation you and her should have together. I don't think you need to try and figure it out right now." He smiled, comforting, easy. "Why don't you take a shower? I'll go hang out in the living room."

I snorted. "Rhys, at this point, regardless of what happens between us, I don't see any point in shyness."

"I mean, I don't want to assume anything."

"I appreciate that." I had so much to say, so much I wanted.

I wanted him in the shower with me.

Yeah, even in my mother's condo, with her only a few feet away.

I said nothing. Just got up, walked toward the shower. Peeled my shirt off, tossed it aside. Stepped out of my shorts, tossed them the other way. Naked, then. I felt his eyes. His desire.

I turned, pausing in the doorway of the bathroom. I stared at Rhys. Saw the evidence of his desire bulging against the zipper of his jeans. "Rhys…"

He shook his head. "Not here, not like this,

Torie. If nothing else, out of respect for your mother and my own qualms…and as much as I want to get in that shower with you, I can't."

I bit my lip. "I'll be thinking about you, then."

"What are you trying to do to me, goddamit?" he hissed. "I'm trying to be the good guy, here."

I felt something reaching a full, rolling boil inside me. "Maybe all good all the time is overrated."

I went to the bedroom door and locked it. I felt that boiling place inside me bubble over. Spill over. Like a steam engine exploding under too much pressure.

Rhys was just watching me. Sitting on the end of the bed, hands on his thighs, gripping hard.

I had to…*do*…something. Anything to alleviate the need I felt for him. "This is for me, Rhys."

"What's for you?" he asked, his voice a ragged whisper.

I knelt in front of him and held his eyes. I saw the moment he understood, and I saw the resistance, his innate goodness trying to win over his own natural need and desire.

I took my hair of the loose, sloppy braid and let it fall around my shoulders. I did not take my eyes off him.

"This is me checking something off my bucket list." I unbuttoned his jeans. "It's me doing something

I want to do, for my own reasons. Which I might share with you…later, if you want to know them."

"Tell me now."

I shook my head. "No."

I lowered his zipper. Pulled at the jeans and, despite his obvious misgivings, he lifted his ass—I yanked them off, all the way. He sat in tight gray briefs, the front bulging, tented. He wasn't all the way there, yet. Good. I wanted to take him from limp to coming.

"Take your shirt off," I told him. "I like looking at you. You're a beautiful man, Rhys. You have an incredible body."

"It's mostly genetics."

"Don't be modest."

He laughed. "Fine. I haven't had time to work out since I met you, but I do, a lot. And I often go long periods without eating. It results in a decent body."

I watched him peel his shirt off, baring those delicious abs. "No, it results in a glorious, divine, absolutely wicked body."

"If you say so," he murmured.

I tugged at his briefs, and he lifted to let me slip them off. And then he was naked, and his cock was curled like a comma against his thigh, not quite completely flaccid—which meant the giant bulge I'd seen before was just…him, flaccid. God, he had an amazing dick.

I ran my hands up his thighs and watched him tense. "Don't say anything, Rhys." I kissed his leg, just outside and above his knee. "Unless it's my name, or to tell me how good it feels."

"Shit," he muttered. "Why, Torie?"

I held on to the outsides of his thighs and kissed up near his right hipbone. "I told you. I want to. This has nothing to do with our conversation; that whole are we/aren't we, will we/ won't we thing. I know what I want, and I know the time for it is not this moment. This is…just me being horny, and you being here."

"Shit, shit, shit," he hissed, as I kissed his belly, above his navel. "I want—"

"I don't care what you want," I interrupted. "Not right now. Right now, I'm doing something *I* want to do. And what I want to do is suck your cock until you don't know who the fuck you are."

I kissed his other hipbone, and I felt his cock against my cheek, felt it firming.

"Oh-shit-oh-fuck," he breathed.

I laughed. "I haven't done anything yet." I pulled away, looked up at him. "By the way, yes, this will be the first time I'll have done this, from start to finish. So…I hope I do okay."

His laugh was a hoarse bark of disbelief. "Oh, something tells me you'll do fucking amazing. Everything you do is fucking amazing."

I smiled at him. "Good answer, Rhys."

His hands lifted, fluttered, as if he didn't know what to do with them. Kneeling between his thighs, I took his hands in mine. Lifted them to my face, guided his fingers to slide into my hair. Smiled at him.

"Just enjoy it, Rhys. And if you're so inclined, repay me in kind, at a later date. Maybe surprise me with it. I give you permission, right now, open-ended permission to do that to me, whenever you want. Without question."

He just nodded, swallowing hard. "Oh—okay." He shifted, moving his hips, digging his fingers deeper into my hair. "Not in my nature to just sit back and enjoy things."

"Then this will be a lesson." I bit my lip around a heated grin. "Now, I'm done talking. I have other uses for my mouth."

"I like you a little bossy," he murmured. "It's fuckin' hot."

I shifted closer. His cock was mostly straight now, but still more limp than erect. I palmed his thighs, ran my hands up and over his hips to cup the upper portion of his ass. I kept my eyes open, on his member, slowly bringing my mouth to it. Tilted my head to the side, opened my mouth…and took him between my lips. Flesh, salt, heat. He let out a breath, soft and slow.

I moved my face to bring him away from his thigh, and took all of him into my mouth—he was still small and soft enough that it was possible. I touched my tongue to his balls, licked up to his tip. Used my tongue to gather him back into my mouth. Felt him hardening in my mouth, engorging against my lips.

His hands snarled in my hair, and then loosened, and he gathered my long thick hair away from my face, taking the mass of it in one fist—I had enough hair that he could and did wrap the glossy black sheaf around his fist so his grip against my scalp was tight and firm.

God, that was hot.

His other hand cupped the back of my neck, encouraging but not applying any pressure.

Oh god, he was growing *fast*. Inches of cock expanded between my lips. My hands slid back to his thighs, and then I cupped his thickening length in one hand, stroking it as I licked and suckled the tip.

More, then. Harder. God, so much cock. I backed away and stroked him slowly, my other hand curling under his balls and massaging them—I knew he particularly liked that. In fact...

I took them into my mouth, tickled by the small dark hairs but not turned off by them. He groaned, long and low, as I mouthed his heavy sac and stroked his length.

"Fuck, Torie. So good."

He was completely hard, then, too many inches to fit in my mouth, but damn me if I wasn't going to try. I held the base of his cock and angled him away, licking over the tip, tasting his leaking pre-cum. I wrapped my lips around him, flicked my tongue against him, and then slowly accepted more and more of him into my mouth, toward the back of my throat. He groaned again, a deep, guttural sound that shot straight to my core. His pleasure was my pleasure. And he *really* liked this. The more of him I took, the more his ass lifted involuntarily, the harder his stomach tensed.

So, I took more. Leaning over him, I let the fat springy head press against the back of my throat. He hissed, his hands tightening in my hair, as if resisting the urge to push me lower. I opened my throat and accepted more of him, and his involuntary growl was enough to make me back away, take a breath, and try again. I glanced up at him as I slowly pushed him back into my mouth—his eyes were closed in absolute rapture, head thrown back, jaw open, disbelief written on his features.

His eyes snapped open as I took more of him this time, my eyes widening as I felt him in my mouth, my throat, swallowing around him. There was a little panic for a moment as I swallowed and felt nothing but him, as if I couldn't breathe, couldn't swallow, audibly gagging a little. But my nostrils flared and I sucked in oxygen, and he groaned loud, ragged, watching me as my lips slid over him, as his cock slowly vanished into my mouth...

There were a couple of inches between my lips and his body...

Then one inch...

Then I felt my nose against his belly, and I had all of him...*all* of him, every last incredible, jaw-stretching inch. My jaw was, indeed, cracked far apart, and I had to swallow and swallow around him, and then I had to let him out of my mouth and, somewhat gratefully, wiggle my jaw and take a breath. I smiled up at him.

"Holy fucking hell, Torie," he breathed, absolutely gutted, awed. "You took all of it."

I kissed the tip, licked it, ran my tongue down the base. Paused with him in my fist, bulbous head against my lips like a microphone. "I didn't know I could do that."

"First for you, first for me."

"No one has ever deepthroated you before?" I asked, and then wrapped my lips around the head.

He shook his head, brow wrinkled, huffing as I circled him with my tongue. "Hell no. No one has ever tried." A gasp of laughter mixed with a groan of pleasure. "Un-fucking-believable. Incredible."

I smiled, loving his disbelief, the rapture of his pleasure. I went deeper, and he groaned all over again, hips flexing. I grasped him by the root, cupped his balls, and decided it was time to quit playing around and make him come.

Not fast, but *hard*.

I stroked him, cradled his balls, and used my lip and tongue on his head, slowly, lovingly. He groaned, growled, and now his hips were lifting off the bed, flexing up, touching down, only to lift again, needing a rhythm, wanting more, aching to come. I felt his balls tighten. Felt his belly go rock hard. Heard his breathing hitch.

"F-fuck," he snarled. "I'm...god, I'm so close, Torie."

I knew that. I felt it.

Wanted it.

All of it.

Wanted him to lose his mind. Lose all control.

"Don't hold back," I whispered.

"I...I don't think I'm capable of it," he growled, his voice hoarse and ragged.

I kept doing what I was doing, alternating speed and the way I used my mouth, keeping it slow. I made love to his cock with my mouth, is what I did. Kissed it, tongued it, made it mine.

I would never have anticipated liking this. I'd

always sort of assumed I wouldn't, that I'd probably do it if asked, but that was about it.

No.

This was...power. He was *mine*. His pleasure was *mine*.

I loved every second of it. Especially as his hips lifted, and began to pump.

"Mmm," I hummed, as he started involuntarily flexing, pumping his cock into my throat. "Mmmhmmm," I moaned, and then gulped around him.

"Oh *fuck*, Torie, oh fuck, holy fuck...what are you *doing* to me?" he gasped.

I moaned again, and he snarled as my throat humming tightened around him, and now he was thrusting, helpless and wild, and I let him, pulled away far enough that his thrusting brought the head of his cock to the back of my throat and no farther. I moved my hands around him in time with his manic pumping, stroking him hard now, with one hand around his root and the other cupping and squeezing his balls the way I knew he liked so much.

"I'm gonna come ohgodTorieoh*FUCK*ohgod..."

I felt the way his sac tensed, throbbed, felt the vein running under his balls and up the back of his length as it pulsed. I knew the explosion was imminent.

His hands jerked in my hair, twice. "I'm gonna come, Torie," he gasped, warning me at the last possible moment.

"Mmmm," I hummed, eager for him to let go.

He was writhing, hips pivoted as far up as they would go, heels braced on the floor, lying back on the bed, not really thrusting so much as trying to push deeper into my mouth, into my plunging fist.

Another ragged groan, and then Rhys broke.

I tasted a flood of tangy, smoky salt on the back of my tongue and then I had to gulp. I pulled away so only the plump head of him was in my mouth and I squeezed his balls and stroked him fast, and tasted his orgasm in rush after rush.

He was arched, hands in my hair and on the back of my head, holding me against his cock, pushing me deeper, so I went deeper. His cum filled my mouth and I swallowed, but not fast enough, and it trickled out of the corners of my lips around his massive throbbing shaft, down my chin.

Again, he spasmed, and dear God how much cum did the man have? More of it filled my mouth, overloading me, and I swallowed some but couldn't take it all at once and he was still groaning, gasping, ragged and raw, and the wild bliss on his face and in his voice and in every line of his body was beautiful, the desperate ecstasy was glorious, the fact that I'd brought this man to this state of helplessness and powerlessness was…intoxicating.

Finally, it felt like he was done coming, and I backed away, let him out of my mouth, kept my lips sealed against the hot thick mouthful of his essence I hadn't swallowed yet. I kept stroking him, milking his climax for all he had, and was rewarded with another tiny pulse of liquid seeping out of him, a broken gasp from Rhys accompanying it.

He was panting raggedly, as if he'd just done a hundred-yard dash, uphill, carrying weights. Sweating. Eyes closed, his face somewhere between heaven and earth.

I was regaining my breath.

His eyes opened, fixed on me. "Holy shit, Torie." He blinked. Let out a breath. "Holy shit, I think I love you."

I gulped, coughed, and wiped at my lips and chin. Coughed again. "Wh—what?"

He struggled to sit up, weak as a kitten. He latched onto my wrist, pulled me toward him—it was a weak tug, and I climbed up onto the bed. He pulled me closer, onto his lap. I hadn't meant to engage emotional intimacy, only to alleviate my own physical desire for Rhys and his god body.

He held me close, my head tucked against his chest, under his chin. His arms around me. Holding me tight, as if to never let go.

My eyes stung and I told myself it was just because of the coughing fit I'd just gotten over.

"I don't take it back," he murmured.

"It was just heat of the moment, right?" I asked. "Like, holy shit I think I love you for doing that."

He shook his head. "I mean, sure, that's one meaning."

"Rhys."

"Not taking it back. Not apologizing. Not pretending I don't know what I meant."

"It was a blowjob, Rhys. Just a blowjob. You've gotten blowjobs before."

"Sure. Never like that, though." He let out a sharp, disbelieving breath. "Whenever you touch me, it's always just...*more*. More intense, more pleasurable, more...meaningful."

"You're just using that word because I used it."

"No."

"Rhys. You can't tell me you love me because I sucked you off."

"I didn't tell you I loved you. I told you I *think* I love you. And not because you sucked me off. It was an admission of the truth, and it happened because you made me lose control over my filter." He pulled me away, held my face in both hands, stared me down so I wanted to look away from his intense gaze, but couldn't. "It may have been an involuntary verbal ejaculation, but I meant it and I don't take it back. Do with it what you will."

I was trembling. My heart was pounding. My brain was spinning. "I…"

He sighed, long and slow. Held my face. Kissed me, tenderly, briefly. Pushed me off of him, off the bed. "Go. Take a shower."

I went, not bothering to close the bathroom door. I turned on the shower, letting it get hot while I rummaged in the drawer of the vanity—as long as I'd been alive, Mom kept a stash of new toothbrushes and tubes of toothpaste in the drawer of each bathroom. And, sure enough, there they were. I brushed my teeth. Rinsed. Brushed again.

Still tasted Rhys's cum.

Salty, musky. Smoky, pungent. Felt it in my mouth, coating my lips and tongue, teeth and inside of my cheeks.

I liked the taste.

Liked the feel of it.

Liked knowing I'd done something to him that no one ever had. Liked thinking maybe I'd done it to him so well that no one, in the future, would ever be able to compare. But that thought was gross—the idea of another woman, after me, putting her mouth on his cock. Touching him. Kissing him. Another woman's hands where mine had been?

NO.

He was *mine*.

Fuck, that thought was potent, like lightning striking my gut, lancing through my soul, piercing my heart.

I felt his eyes on me as I brushed my teeth a third time and then washed my hands.

It wasn't that I wanted the taste of him out of my mouth. On the contrary. I wanted *more* of him. I wanted him more than ever. I wanted to sit on his lap and play with his limp cock until it got hard again so I could suck it dry all over again. See if I could make him even crazier.

I wanted to climb on his lap and take that big hard pulsing cock inside me.

That's what I *really* wanted, more than anything I'd ever wanted.

I wanted to know what that felt like. Needed it. Needed to be filled by him. Taken by him. Owned, possessed, penetrated.

Fucked.

Loved.

*Holy shit, Torie. I think I love you.*

I got in the shower and scrubbed obsessively, as if I could scrub away the feel of his hands on my skin, and yet I couldn't scrub away the fantasy that filled my suddenly sex-obsessed mind: him, kneeling over me as I lie on my back on the bed, him with his cock in my hands, jerking him hard and fast, him, exploding with a shout to let loose a thick flood of hot wet cum all over my belly and breasts and face.

I shook my head to clear it of the image.

Too much porn, clearly.

Gross, right?

No, no way.

Even if I'd liked him in my mouth, liked feeling him down my throat, liked the way he'd overfilled my mouth and leaked out, had liked the feel of it trickling down my chin, I didn't want him to come *on* me. No way. I'd clearly lost my damn mind.

I put it out of my head, or tried. Shut off the water, toweled off, wrapped the towel around my torso and knotted it at my chest. I flipped my sopping wet hair upside down and wrapped a towel around it in a turban, glanced back into the bedroom at Rhys.

"It'll take for freaking ever for my hair to dry. You should jump in now."

"I can wait till you're done."

I laughed. "You don't understand. I only wash my hair a couple times a week because it's so long and thick it takes literally hours for it to dry. Go ahead and shower. At this point, we may as well just share the space, right?"

He nodded. Troubled, I think. His eyes were conflicted. "Tor, I…"

He was standing in front of me. Naked. Limp cock hanging down to the floor. Hard body tense and lined with conflict.

I touched his lips with my tongue. Gazed up at him. "It's okay, Rhys. I just…I need to process what you said and how I feel about it."

His eyes burned. "I want to return the favor." He made to drop to his knees.

I grabbed his elbows to stop him. "You have no fucking clue how much I want to let you. But…" I let out a breath. "One, I want what I did to stand alone. To not be part of more. To be something I did for you, because I wanted to. Two, if I let you do that, go down on me, we won't stop. And it's not the right time. We don't have the time or the privacy for what that will be, when it happens."

He nodded, and then tilted his head. "Okay, I get it. I'll wait. But you said to surprise you with it—and I'm going to. When you least expect it."

I felt a frisson of excitement. "That's exactly what I'm hoping for."

He sighed heavily. "I better get in the shower before I decide to ignore what you want and take what I want."

I shivered. I kind of wanted that. Like, a lot.

He reached into the shower, twisted on the water, held his hand under the spray to test the temperature.

Still breathing hard, it seemed as if holding back his desires was taking all of his effort.

"Fuck it," he breathed.

And turned on me, erotic ferocity burning in his eyes.

# FOURTEEN

## Rhys

I HAD NO POWER TO HOLD BACK. SHE'D DRAINED IT OUT OF me.

I slammed my body against hers, ripped the towel off her and let it drop to the floor. We stood skin to skin with her breasts smashed against my chest, her taut, soft core nestled against my cock, our bodies lined up perfectly. I tilted my face down, took her lips and devoured her. Demanded more. Tongues on tongues, lips moving, tangling, sliding wet and slick and warm. Her skin was so soft, so hot. I palmed her shoulders, ran my hands down her waist. Cupped her beautiful round ass in my hands.

I lifted her up and held her around my waist. Her

legs scissored around my hips, her responses natural and immediate. With one arm under her ass I held her up, and I caressed her breasts with the other, kissing, kissing.

I left the water running, but I didn't care.

I carried her to the bed.

Hard already, I could move just so, tilt, thrust, and I'd inside her.

Fuck, I needed to be there. To sink home into the woman I was falling for.

I let her fall onto the bed and hovered over her, our bodies lined up, centimeters separating my erection from her slit.

She saw the need, the impulse.

"Rhys," she breathed.

"I know," I whispered.

I'd heard the plea. To do it, to not do it.

She didn't know.

She was lost in desire, but desperately trying to hold to her decision.

I slid lower. Kissing as I went, I moved down her body. Belly, hip, slit. I took her clit into my mouth and did all the things she liked the most, all at once, no mercy, no drawing it out, no letting her down and bringing her back up.

Hard and fast, I took her there.

She fell over the edge, whimpering my name,

slapping a palm over her mouth, and then biting down on the edge of her hand to muffle the scream as she came.

I left her orgasming, stood up as she twisted and writhed, knees sliding against each other, rolling to the side and curling up as it shook her.

"Just a tease of what I'm going to do to you," I told her. "Had to. Couldn't stop myself. I've been dying to taste you again since we left Ohio."

She just whimpered, nodded, trembling all over and occasionally twitching as the climax continued to shiver through her.

"Was that all the way, or a partial?" I asked.

She gulped for air, rolled to her back, flopping to sprawl out wide as I perched on the edge of the bed. "I...I don't even know."

"You mad?"

She lolled her head to one side. "I got a miracle of an orgasm. So...no. But one of these days, I'm gonna surprise you with a BJ at a time when you can't give it back to me."

"Why is that important to you?" I asked, sliding a palm over her belly, touching her just to feel her skin, her body.

A lazy shrug of a shoulder. "I dunno. It just is. I don't want everything between us to always be a back and forth. I want to give you things, do things just because I enjoy doing it, just because I like making you feel good. Not because I know you're going to do something to me in return."

"Well the problem with that premise—if you can call it a problem—is that I feel the same way. I want to do…everything to you, for you. All the time. Whether I've gotten anything from you or not, whether I will or not." I traced a fingertip around the darker flesh of her areola. "Just because."

She rested a hand over mine, where it lay on her breast. "That's what scares me about this, Rhys—that sounds an awful lot like love to me."

"I said it, didn't I?"

"You said you think you do."

I nodded. Held her eyes. "Well, where's the line between I think, and I do?"

She closed her eyes, turned her head away to face the ceiling. Inhaled slowly, deeply—let it out shakily between pursed lips. "This wasn't supposed to happen."

"No shit," I said, somewhere between a laugh and a sigh. "But it did."

Another shaky breath. "Rhys…I…" She turned to look at me again, this time with tear-hazed eyes. "I'm way past I think."

"Dammit," I hissed. "You couldn't just not feel the same way? You couldn't just not give a shit? Just break my heart, Torie. It'd be easier than this."

A long silence. "I know. I feel the same way," she said. "If you just wanted to screw me and go your way, I'd be better off. I could give you my V-card, have some great memories, and then just get over my feelings and move on with my life."

"Yet, here we both are."

"In Alaska," she said. She rubbed her face; she still had the towel around her hair, but it was coming loose, exposing a hint of black underneath. "The place I'm staying, and you're not."

I swallowed hard. "You're staying, huh?"

She seemed barely able to summon a whisper. "The moment I hugged my mama, I knew." Her eyes met mine. "Part of me would rather go back with you after the wedding."

I held down my turbulent emotions. "Nah. Your family is here, Tor. This is where you belong."

"I'd…I'd rather belong with you."

My eyes stung. "You say that, but…I've never belonged to anyone, never had anyone belong to me. Not even a dog. I was more of a roommate with my parents once I got to middle school. I'd…selfishly, I'd love nothin' more than to belong to you, and you to me. But I don't…I don't know if I could uproot myself from New Haven and start over here. And I sure as shit ain't gonna ask you to come back to New Haven—you said it yourself, that place is a dead end for you."

"So where does that leave us?" she whispered, barely audible.

"With amazing memories and broken hearts, I guess."

"It's been, what, six or seven days? How the hell can I feel this strongly for you after less than a week? It's stupid. That shit only happens in movies and cheesy romance novels, not in real life."

"I don't know," I said.

She was quiet a while, and I let the silence breathe. After a minute or two, she pushed at me. "Go. Get cleaned up. We gotta meet my enormous new family."

"Yeah, you're right. Let's get ready."

I stood up, and she held on to my wrist, stopping me before I walked away. "Rhys? You…you can go. Like, leave. If it's easier. For…you. You don't have to stay for the wedding. Or at all. You can, you're invited, and selfishly I'd love more time with you. But if you feel like it's best to just rip the Band-Aid off, I understand." She blinked hard. "I just…you have the out. If you want it."

"Let me shower and think about that." I rubbed the back of my neck. "Truthfully, that does have a certain appeal. But so does more time with you."

I got into the shower, and when I got out, Torie was gone, and I heard a hair dryer going in her mother's bathroom, and both towels were on the bed. Me being me, I threw them over the towel rack.

I hadn't figured out if I should leave or not. Meeting her whole family sounded like fun, but maybe it would just end up being a different version of falling in love with Torie and then having to leave. Maybe it would be better if I just left.

I toweled off, dressed in clean underwear, jeans, and a T-shirt, ran my hand through my hair to get it to lie down as much as it ever would, which wasn't much. It was thick and unruly, and I rarely had patience to do anything special with it.

I couldn't just leave. I was burnt out on driving.

I'd leave tomorrow.

Early. Tell her goodbye tonight, and leave at first light.

It'd be best.

It meant not getting to sleep with her, but that was safest. If we did that, I'd fall all the way, and fixing the break in my heart would be...more than I could handle.

Besides...

I couldn't.

Selfishly, I couldn't.

And unselfishly, I couldn't take that from Torie, even if she was offering it willingly. I couldn't just get up and then leave.

Something told me if she made that move tonight and I said no, though…she'd be upset. Hurt.
Maybe angry.

But I had no other choice.

I had to.

For both of us.

Somehow the girl made jeans and a T-shirt erotic.
Maybe it was just me, and the way I saw her, but it
was just sinful the way she filled out the jeans, what
she did to a plain blue V-neck with pockets over each
breast.

Her chunky boots were left open and mostly
unlaced, the cuffs of her jeans loosely tucked into
the openings. Her hair was done in twin braids, one
hanging over each shoulder, and the very ends of
each braid twisting and curling up. A little pink on her
lips, some dark over her eyelids. Just her, natural. Her
scent. Her lovely face. Her perfect body.

And our first real date.

We drove with her mom, and ended up at a place
on the waterfront, parking in a private lot near a bar
called Badd's Bar and Grille, which faced the water.
Bobbing in the channel was a huge yacht, a truly massive thing, what I think they called a mega-yacht.

I whistled. "Damn, that's a big boat."

Liv laughed. "It belongs to Xavier and Harlow. That's actually where tonight's festivities are happening."

"What? On that giant boat?" I asked, suddenly feeling a little out of my depth.

"Yeah." She was breezy. "It'll be a great time." She glanced at me, and Liv's observant gaze caught my nerves. "Rhys, they're all just people. It'll be fine."

I laughed. "I'm just...I've never been on or in anything that expensive. That's worth, like, literally more than everything everyone in my entire home-town has ever and will ever own put together."

"And yet, it's still just a boat. Goes on the water. Runs on fuel. Has toilets where people poop and beds where people screw."

Torie snorted. "Ohmy*god*, Mom. Really?"

Liv just laughed. "Would it help or make things worse for you to know that there will be at least two famous people on the boat tonight?"

I sighed. "Torie has mentioned that this whole wedding is for Lexie and Myles, as in Myles North."

"Right." Liv gestured at the boat as we walked along the dock toward it. "And that boat belongs to Harlow Grace."

"Harlow..." I let out a breath. "Harlow Grace? Shit."

Torie eyed me. "What?"

"The first time I saw her in *Finding Diamond* I was, like, gone for her. Huge crush. I mean, I've grown out of it since, but still. Harlow Grace, huh?"

"Around us, she's just Low." Liv eyed me. "And you know that my...well, I think of them as nephews, even though they're nephews-in-law, and even then Lucas and I aren't married, but still, they're my nephews. Canaan and Corin, and their wives Aerie and Tate, they're all musicians, and successful ones at that. Canaan and Corin were in a band called Bishop's Pawn, and now Canaan and Aerie tour together as Canary."

I nodded. "Heard of all of them. I was a fan of Bishop's Pawn, but I'm typically more of a classic rock guy. It's the one kind of music you can put on in a shop that just about no one will ever complain about."

"What kind of shop?" Liv asked.

"Auto. I repair and rebuild big block engines."

"And Rhys restores cars, and builds houses, and is getting his realtor license," Torie put in. "He's being modest."

Liv smiled at me. "Well, you'll fit right in. We have builders, realtors, designers, marketers, computer hackers, musicians, painters, photographers, bartenders and bar owners...let's see, what else?

Pilots, ex-Navy SEALs, ex-football players turned personal trainers. Someone in the family can do just about everything. And oh, don't forget Xavier, our resident robotics genius inventor."

"And actors, and dancers turned trainer and teacher, and women's lit majors turned world famous musicians, and…me, who does nothing." Torie said, laughing and sighing.

Liv shook her by the shoulders, gentle and playful. "And *that* is why you're here. You'll find your place and your purpose. Just give it time."

*You'll fit right in.* I've never fit in anywhere. I didn't fit in back home, didn't fit in any of the towns I stayed in on the way to New Haven. And even in New Haven I only really settled in because I got a good deal on a property and I was tired of being itinerant.

We were crossing a fancy gangway thing, a bridge between the dock and the boat, with chrome handrails and nonslip footing, which shifted with the bobbing of the boat. There were already people on board, gathered in a living room-type area on the main level—the walls slid aside entirely so the whole main floor of the boat was open on both sides. Music was playing from invisible speakers, and I saw a line of restaurant buffet-style food service trays with the little cans of flammable gel underneath. There were people on the top deck, too, gathered in groups. So many people. All laughing, and everyone knew everyone else. Family.

A big, big family.

Nerves rifled through me.

I've never been great with big parties. I'm fine in small groups, and among people I know, but big parties full of strangers? Nah. I get jittery and don't know how to be.

Torie noticed. "You okay?"

I grinned at her. "Yeah, sure, I'm good."

She rolled her eyes at me. "Don't bullshit me, Rhys. I can tell you're about to shit your pants."

"I don't know about that, but this is a lot of people. And I only know you."

Torie laughed. "Well, if it makes you feel any better, I only know my mom and sisters. Everyone else is just as much a stranger to me as they are you."

Liv slid between us as we stood on the boat, and slid an arm around each of us. "Strangers are just friends you haven't met yet. Trust me, everyone is wonderful. I know it can be intimidating at first, but by the end of the night, I promise you, you'll be one of the clan." She pulled us toward the living room. "Now come on. Put on your big girl and big boy panties and make friends."

I gave in. "All right, all right."

Liv wasn't lying. I spent the first hour being

introduced to roughly two dozen people. Now, make no mistake, I'm strictly hetero, and not a perv either. But the men were all hot, jacked, intimidating, scary, and entirely too cool, and the women were all fucking gorgeous, each one with a body to kill for, perfect hair, cool clothes, amazing stories, musical laughs.

At one point, I pulled Torie aside. "Are we being punked?" I hissed to her.

Her eyes were wide, scanning over the crowd. "I feel like we are. Did you meet Bax yet? That is the most muscular human being I've ever seen. His muscles have muscles, and those muscles have veins. But he's also, like, sweet and hilarious."

"Right?" I shook my head. "Myles is, literally, the coolest dude I've ever met. He's the actual walking definition of a rock star."

Torie sighed. "I know. But he's perfect for Lex. They're crazy together, but it works." She indicated a cluster of women all standing together not far away, each with a glass of wine. "I know you've noticed the women, who are all not exactly lacking in the beauty department."

I shook my head, eyes wide. "Uh, yeah, I've noticed."

Torie grinned. "If you had to pick, who's the hottest?"

"Of everyone on the boat?"

She nodded. "Yeah. Honest answer. Quick, no thinking," she said, snapping her fingers.

I pretended to scan the living room, which I'd learned was called *the saloon*, because the living room of a fancy boat has to have a fancy name. "Well, it's a tough competition to call one person over the other but..." I brought my gaze back to her. "That's easy—you."

She rolled her eyes, dripping vitriolic sarcasm. "Yeeeaaahhh, right."

"For real. I'm not kidding"

She snorted as she gestured at the group of women. "Look at them, Rhys. D-cups and size nothing waists, each of them. Big juicy butts, perfect hair, perfect makeup. And you're gonna try and tell me *I'm* even in the same universe as women like them?"

"Whose butt is juicy?" I heard a female voice ask.

"Whose butt is big?" asked another.

"D-cup? Please. I'm double D, thank you *very* fucking much. Triple D, if I'm nursing."

"Size nothing waist? Try size seven, sweetheart. I haven't been below a five since I had the baby."

We were surrounded by the group of women we'd been talking about.

Torie was frozen, blushing. "I...I..."

There was a burst of cackling laughter from a pixie blond with small tits and a fairly sizeable butt for a woman who was barely five feet tall. She wrapped an arm around Torie. "Honey, you're comparing apples to oranges to kumquats."

"Yeah, and you're the kum-twat, I mean, kumquat." This from a short woman with longer hair and ridiculously huge boobs.

As Torie had pointed out, there wasn't a plain woman among them.

"Shut up, Mara." She said this straight-faced and turned back to Torie. "Ignore her, she's a slut. My point is—I'm Claire by the way—I've decided to be your fairy goddessmother, and I hereby vow to make sure you feel at home and that everyone is nice, and to make sure you have at least eight shots of whiskey before the night is over."

"I'm twenty." Torie lifted an eyebrow.

Claire blinked. Turned, cupped her hands around her mouth, and bellowed. "MAMA LIVVIE!"

Torie gaped. "Mama Livvie?"

Claire winked at Torie. "Oh yeah. She's our honorary Mama Bear. You have the best mother in the whole wide motherfuckin' world, by the way. Hope you know that."

Liv came over with a can of light beer in her hand, and a gargantuan grizzly bear turned human at her side. "You bellowed, my love?"

The man was six-six at least, and built like a bear,

with massive arms that were solid muscle, wearing a cut-off T-shirt and sporting tattoos and a salt and pepper goatee.

"Yeah. Can I get Torie naked wasted even though she's not twenty-one yet?"

Liv snickered. "I dunno about naked wasted, but she's lived on her own since she was seventeen, and I'm under no misapprehensions that she hasn't indulged in that time. So I would say that Torie is entirely capable of making her own decisions on that score." She shrugged. "Beware, though, of all my daughters, Torie is the most unpredictable. You never know what you're gonna get with her, so I'm guessing her tolerance might surprise you."

I blinked at Mom. "Unpredictable?"

Mom just smiled at me. "Yes, my dear. You're a 'still waters run deep' sort. Somewhere between Cassie and Charlie. Not a livewire like Lex, but not a goody-goody like Charlie."

"I'm *not* a goody-goody," came a voice from one side, and a woman who was clearly a Goode sister pushed into the circle, which widened to accommodate her. "I just don't find it fun to flaunt the rules. Usually."

Beside her was a tall, angular man with messy black hair and mirrored sunglasses on his head. Just going by appearances, he looked like he was Native

American. He was wearing black jeans, big black shit-kicker biker boots, and a black leather vest with motorcycle club patches all over it.

I was just listening, watching the banter.

"So, by the by, how did this mini gathering come about?" Liv asked.

Claire jerked a thumb at Torie. "This one was expressing how she has a major girl crush on all of us."

The other blond, Mara, I think her name was, whacked Claire across the shoulder. "Oh shut up, bitch-face. She was not. She was…well…"

"I was being insecure," Torie finished. "Everyone here is beautiful and voluptuous, and I've always had a bit of a thing about being flat."

Claire turned to face Torie and, brazen as you please, cupped Torie's boobs over her shirt, giving them a heft and a squeeze. She shook her head, pressed her hands to her shirt to highlight a whole of, well, admittedly not much. "Nope. You're not flat—*this* is flat." She cut a look at me. "Avert your eyes, new guy to whom I've not been introduced, you too Papa Lucas."

I blinked, hesitated a moment, and turned around, found myself next to the bear-man, who was also facing away.

"*These* are itty bitty titties," I heard Claire say. "Barely mosquito bites. *You* have magnificent mammaries, and you're being ridiculous, and if you don't stop it we're going to be fighting and trust me, you don't want to get on my bad side. I can be a major bitch. You're sexy as fuck, and your boy toy is a lucky, lucky man."

"Hear hear," I said, pumping my fist in the air.

That got a round of laughter, and Torie span me back around. "This is Rhys."

Claire shook my hand. "I'm Claire. Welcome to the clan, Rhys. You scared yet?"

I laughed. "A little. But only of all the giant men."

The bear-man reached out a massive paw. "I'm Lucas."

"Nice to meet you, Lucas."

He grinned. "Come on. I'll get you acquainted. Let's let these ladies talk girl talk. And by girl talk, I mean dicks and periods."

"Women talk about dicks?" I asked. "I didn't figure that."

"Women are nasty, kid. Get 'em alone, and they'll be cackling about cock and comparing boobs in no time. And this crew? They don't even need to be in a girls-only crowd, as you just witnessed."

"I don't believe you, sorry," I laughed.

Lucas snagged a nearby woman—this one with fiery red hair. "Dru. When it's just you girls, what do you talk about?"

"Our periods and, honestly, penises. How silly they are, and how obsessed you men are with them. And, after a few drinks, maybe some more complimentary things, and a few jokes." She laughed, and reached out to shake my hand. "I'm Dru."

"Rhys."

"This is Torie's boyfriend, or something like that," Lucas said.

I laughed. "More something like that, I think."

"Ah, the old *it's complicated*," Dru said. "Let me uncomplicate it for you—if you try to leave her, and it feels wrong, it is. Simple as that. You can fight it, but in the end, you won't be right until you're with her. On the flip side, if you leave and it hurts but it's fine, you'll get over it."

I rubbed the back of my neck, laughing. "I guess we'll have to see, huh?"

Lucas whacked my back, and I think it was meant to be a playful, affectionate thing, but it made my teeth rattle. "Come on. Most of the guys are up top shooting whiskey like fools."

"Rhys!" I heard Torie's voice behind me.

I stopped, turned. "Miss me already, huh?"

"Of course," she said, deadpan enough that I don't think it was a joke. "I just wanted to say go for it."

"Go for what?"

She gestured at the stairs to the roof. "Have fun. Be a little irresponsible."

I held her gaze. Nodded. "You too. This is your family."

Lucas was watching this exchange; after Torie hesitated, then waved awkwardly and went back to the circle of women, he nudged me to the stairs.

"That's a lot of complicated you two got going on," he noted.

I laughed, a somewhat bitter sound. "Yeah. You're telling me."

He directed me across the top deck to where the men, a good dozen or more of them, were all gathered in a circle, some standing, some sitting on chairs, others leaning against railings.

"Well, you'll sort it out. For now, just relax." Another of those teeth-jarring back pats. "Cut loose if you want. I'm the self-assigned sober daddy, so I'll be here to pick you up if you get sloppy."

Like I was one of the crew already.

And, as the night wore on, I found myself welcomed as I'd never been in my life. Despite being intimidatingly good-looking, muscular, successful, and cool, the guys were all warm and friendly. There were as many F-bombs dropped as if I was back home, and the triplets—Lucas's sons, I came to discover—each had a faint southern twang that kept bringing mine out.

They were all, as Liv had claimed, rough, wild, a little crazy, fun, vulgar, and just all-around great people. And without even trying, I found myself feeling like one of them. Telling rowdy stories of growing up in the holler, which were always matched by someone else's story. I was handed a glass with a few ice cubes and roughly six fingers of whiskey. I could tell just from smelling it that it was super high-end old stuff. And when I tasted it, it went down like spicy silk, fiery in my gut.

I sipped at it, not wanting to get hammered my first time around these guys. But no matter how much I sipped at it, my glass was always full. I'd be talking to someone, gesturing, and someone would just…top it off. I lost count of the number of bottles that got emptied, and even though there was a lot of slurring as the night went on, and a lot of raucous, too-loud laughter, there was never a moment of conflict. No one ever got pissy and lost their temper. No one said anything to offend anyone else, or insulted anyone's girlfriend or mama.

I tapped the beefy, rock-hard shoulder of…uh… Bast? I think his name was Bast. By that point I'd had enough to drink that things were fuzzy and loose, and names were getting hard to keep straight. "Hey, so."

He peered at me, and I could tell he was as far gone as I was. "So…Rhys. You're with Torie, right? Mama Livvie's second-to-youngest."

I shrugged, tipped my head. "Sort of. I'm here with her, yes."

He laughed. "You're here, you're with her, so you're here with her." He clapped me on the back, and the teeth-jarring power of it was clearly a family trait. "Bro, just get one thing straight, a'ight? Once you're in, you don't leave. Not for good. It's a thing. Nobody gets into this group and then just vanishes. Doesn't happen. If Torie brought you, and Mama Livvie approves, you're in. So, it may be complicated, but shit, dude, it ain't *that* complicated."

"What I was going to ask was, is it always like this?" I gestured at the men.

He frowned, eyeing the bunch—there was an arm-wrestling match going on, with a lot of cheering by the onlookers. "Ehh? This is pretty chill. We're going easy because this wedding thing is turning into a two-week ordeal, so we gotta pace ourselves."

"This is chill?"

He nodded. "It gets pretty rowdy sometimes."

I nodded. "It's just weird. Nobody has gotten feisty, yet. Where I come from, a party ain't a party till someone's got a black eye."

Bast shook his head, blowing a raspberry. "Hell, no, dude. We're tight. Plus, there are some dangerous dudes in this group, and none of us want to risk that kind of damage on drunk-ass bullshit." He gestured at one of the guys—shorter than Bast, resembling him, but with a razor-sharp, lethal air to him. "That's my brother Zane, an ex-SEAL. He knows more ways to kill you bare-handed than I can count. Bax, the one with the wannabe mohawk, used to be a bare-knuckle prize brawler, and he never lost. So no, we never get like that. And me? Well…look at me. Been a few fellas that have seen the wrong end of my big ol' fists." He shook his head. "Nah, fightin' ain't our family ethos, if you get me."

Not in their family ethos.

My heart twinged.

I shoved that down, savagely.

By the time the party started dwindling, and the guys began saying their goodbyes and leaving with their women, I was clobbered. I was able to walk, but I was drunk. I ambled carefully downstairs and found Torie on the couch, her legs across Charlie's thighs, her head on Lexie's lap, passed out, with Claire sitting on the other side of Lexie, braiding Torie's hair into a billion tiny braids.

I felt my heart twinge again, this time it was the sight of Torie with her family. "Looks like somebody overdindulged." I shook my head. "Thass not the right word. Over*indulged*."

Claire snickered, held her cell phone to her mouth and pretended to be talking into a walkie-talkie. "Hello, Pot? This is Kettle. Come in, Pot, over."

I nodded and leaned heavily against a wall. "Yep. I have a not very good tolerance. Not a drinker-er of heavy alcohols." I shook my head. "Fuck, I sound stupid even to myself."

"Don't worry, you sound plenty stupid to us, too," Claire said, her voice bright and chipper. "It's all good, bro. We got your back."

"Sweet of you to say, but you don't know me. I got my own back. I've had my own back since I was fuckin'...fuckin' twelve. Ain't nobody never had my back but me."

Lexie's gaze upon me was speculative, sorrowful. "Speaking from experience here, buddy—that is a toxic as fuck way of thinking. Keeps you isolated and lonely, and keeps you from opening yourself to people who can, will, and want to bring you into their lives." She gestured at the saloon, which was now occupied by Liv and Lucas, Lexie, Charlie, Cassie, Ink, Myles, Crow, Harlow, and Xavier—and shit but I was proud of myself for remembering all those names and faces. "Case in point."

The twinge in my heart was suddenly like a crack, the way a chip in a windshield turns into a spider web of breaks.

"I'm leavin' in the mornin'," I said. "First light."

Myles laughed. "Yeah, okay, killer. You can barely stand upright, and it's already damn near first light now."

Ink, who was even more bearlike than Lucas with his long black hair and thick beard, put a paw on my shoulder—he managed to actually be gentle enough that my teeth didn't rattle. "Listen up, man. We all, every single one of us, knows where you're at, right now. None of us got much by way of family outside this group. It's why we're as tight as we are. And the thing that binds us is that we chose this as our place, as our home, and chose this group as our family. Every single motherfuckin' one of us had to decide if we had the balls to make the choice between the lonely road we'd been going down, and a new, scary road full of new people. Trust me, I fuckin' get it. And I get you can't just drop your whole life and stay here."

"It's more than that," I said. "It's…her. Us. It's tricky."

"Tricky meanin' you scared, bro," Crow said, a small smirk on his lips.

"Yeah, I am," I admitted. "Known her less'n a week. And suddenly it's like…it's like someone else is walkin' around the world with my actual physical heart in her fuckin' hands. How the fuck does it happen so fast?"

Crow nodded. "All of us wondered the same thing. And funny part is, a relationship like this?" He gestured at Charlie and then himself. "It's just a question of getting used to that feeling. Trusting her to carry your heart around."

"The real funny part of it is," Lucas put in, "you come to realize she takes a hell of a lot better care of it than you do."

"I dunno if I'm too drunk to be having this conversation, or just drunk enough that it's making more sense than I'm comfortable with," I said.

"Bit of both, I'd guess," Lucas rumbled. "Come on."

"Where'm I going?" I slurred.

"Harlow has offered one of her extra berths down below for you to crash in. Be easier than tryin' to get your butt back across town to Liv's."

"What about her?" I asked, gesturing at Torie.

"We've got her," Lexie said, flicking a thumb at herself, Charlie, and Cassie. "You'll see her in the morning."

I shook my head. "I gotta go home. Gotta rip the Band-Aid off."

"If you leave without saying goodbye to her, you'd best not even think about coming back," Cassie said, hard eyes scrutinizing me. "Because that'd be it for you."

I shook my head. "Couldn't. Couldn't not say good-bye. 'I may be an asshole,'" I quoted, "'but I'm not a hundred percent a dick.'"

"*Guardians of the Galaxy*," Lexie said. "Anyone who can quote great movies can't be all bad."

"Come on, guardian of the galaxy," Lucas said, his huge paw nudging me toward a steep staircase. "Time for bed."

I stared at the stairs, which were more ladder than stairs. "I can't go down that."

Lucas laughed. "Sure you can. Take it like a ladder. Plus, it ain't that far. You fall, you're drunk enough you won't feel it."

I nodded. Tried it, and made it down without issue. Lucas showed me the berth, which was a luxury one-room apartment nicer than anything I'd ever stayed in. Big bed, a round window showing the waterline not far below, a bureau built into the wall. I collapsed onto the bed, half asleep by the time I hit the mattress.

"Thanks, Lucas," I mumbled.

"No problem, kiddo," he growled. "You're all right, Rhys. You're a good kid."

"Someone's gonna find out," I heard myself say, "So it may as well be you."

"Find out what?"

"Torie knows. She's been good about it so far, but it's just a matter of time."

"The hell are you talking about, kid?"

"RJ. It's gonna happen, somebody is gonna hear it. Been RJ my whole life. Rhys Jonathan—RJ to everybody."

"RJ, huh?" He laughed. "I'll keep your secret for now."

I felt myself spinning.

I heard the floor creak under Lucas's bulk.

"Lucas?" I said.

"Yeah, kid."

"How d'you know it's real, and worth it? Love, I mean. When it's only been four or five days. Or six, or however many it's been. How do you know?"

"You don't. You jump outta the airplane and hope the parachute opens. Ain't any other way of doing it."

"Love is like parachuting?"

"Well, all three of my boys jumped outta airplanes for a living, and all three of 'em have made the comparison, so I guess it's probably pretty accurate."

"I'm not a risk taker," I mumbled, my face smashed into the mattress. "I make plans and I stick to them, and I don't deviate."

"And then life comes along and fucks your plans right up the pooper. And that's when you realize sometimes you gotta leave the plans behind and just...go off road."

"You got a lot of metaphors."

He chuckled. "Yeah, I guess so."

"Okay," I said. "Night night time."

I fell asleep, and for the first time in days, I didn't dream about Torie. But only because I was too wasted to dream about anything.

# FIFTEEN

## Torie

I WOKE UP WITH A POUNDING HEADACHE AND A DRY MOUTH. I felt bodies on both sides of me—Lexie on my left, Charlie on my right. I was pinned between them, and I had to pee so bad it hurt.

I struggled out from under the blankets and army crawled across the bed to the foot, flopped ungracefully to the floor in a pile of moaning drunk girl, stumbled to my feet using the wall and door post. Where was I? I didn't recognize the room. The door was weird, too. I opened it, stumbled out, and wondered if I was still more drunk than I thought, or if the floor was moving. A glance out a nearby round window showed the world tipping up and down—and I remembered I was on a boat.

I found a bathroom and spent a very, very long time relieving myself, washed up, and followed my nose topside to coffee. Harlow was sitting at a tiny bistro table in the bow of the boat, wearing a bikini and sunglasses and a big floppy hat, with a pour-over coffee set on the table and a tray of upside-down white porcelain mugs beside it.

She heard me, twisted, and smiled at me. "Hi, there! Surprised to see you upright this early. You're the first one up."

I followed the railing and hesitated, squinting in the bright post-dawn sunlight—this was her boat, her coffee, and I didn't want to just assume or invite myself into her quiet moment alone. "Yeah, my bladder woke me up."

"No matter how drunk I get, my bladder wakes me up every time," she said, laughing. "So I commiserate with that." She tugged her sunglasses off, and patted the open chair. "Here, sit. Put these on."

And just like that, I had Harlow Grace's personal sunglasses on my face and she was pouring me coffee. Thick, black, strong coffee.

"This is amazing coffee," I said.

Harlow sighed, a smile hidden behind her mug. "Isn't it? Xavier makes it. He has this whole process he insists on, and I don't know what it all includes but it ends up with this truly amazing coffee."

"Where is Xavier?"

"Oh, he made me coffee and then went back to sleep."

"Jealous of that ability. Once I'm up, I'm up."

"Same," she said. Glanced at me. "We don't have to talk. I'm fine sitting here and drinking coffee 'til you're sober enough to function."

I groaned in gratitude. "Thank fuck. Talking is hard."

She laughed, and we sat together in surprisingly companionable silence, the boat gently rocking, the sun shining, the seagulls screeing.

I heard steps, twisted, and saw Rhys approaching, his eyes squinted, shirtless, wearing his jeans but unbuttoned and unzipped, barefoot, T-shirt in one hand and shoes and socks in the other. Harlow noticed him too, and her eyes shot to mine.

"You need a minute with him?"

I shrugged. "I dunno."

She poured a coffee, and handed it to Rhys as he leaned against the bow railing. "Here, have some life juice. You look like you need it."

He accepted it, shielding his eyes with one hand. "This is why I don't get drunk. I hate hangovers." A sip. "Fuckin' hell, this coffee was made by Jesus hisownself."

"Or my dear husband, but he's pretty close, if you ask me."

"You guys are married?" I asked. "It's hard to tell who's actually married and who's not."

Harlow laughed. "We all look at marriage pretty loosely. Have we been joined in legal matrimony? No, not yet. We will, someday. Maybe once we feel like we're ready to have kids, which I'm not, yet, and neither is he. But he's my husband in every way that matters."

Harlow's eyes bounced between Rhys and me. "Well. The tension between you two is thick as mud, so I think I'll go, now. Help yourself to the coffee, and if you're hungry, there's plenty of food in the kitchen."

"Thank you, Harlow," I said. "For the coffee, and the hospitality."

She smiled at me. "You're more than welcome. And please, call me Low."

And with that, she vanished back inside, and I was alone with Rhys. He sat in the chair recently vacated by Low.

"You have fun last night?" he asked me.

I nodded. "Yeah. Maybe a little too much. And yeah, this is why I tend to smoke rather than drink. No matter how stoned I get, by the time I wake up I'm fine."

"I feel like you may be onto something, there," he said.

"How about you?" I asked him. "Have a good time with the guys?"

He nodded. "Coolest dudes I've ever met." He was quiet a moment. "You're walking into a pretty amazing situation here, Tor."

I swallowed hard at the implication. "It's too early for hard conversations, Rhys."

He sipped. "I think I gotta rip the Band-Aid off."

I hid behind my coffee, and hoped the sunglasses hid the haze of tears. "I know." A thick pause. "When?"

"Today."

"So soon?"

He turned away, probably for the same reason I was hiding behind a coffee mug and Harlow's bug-eyes sunglasses. "The longer I stay, the harder it is. I don't want to leave. I like it here. I like all the people. You, most of all. But…"

"You have a life back down in New Haven."

He shrugged. "Been thinking about that, too." He turned back to me. "If…if I got to a point where I could…cut some ties loose down there, would… would I be welcome, here? With you?"

I shook all over, holding back the tears, but only by virtue of extreme effort. "If you're asking if I'll wait for you, then yes. I'll be here, and it'll be…just me. I won't be with anyone else. Not in any way. And if you come back up here, yes, there'd be…there'd be an us to figure out."

He nodded. "I'm not trying to, like, get away but still leave myself an in just in case. I just…I can't just stay here, no matter what I want or how I feel. I have clients and a boss and financial stuff I have to figure out."

I swallowed around a hot lump. "I'm not asking you to give up your life in New Haven for me, Rhys. I'm not saying you have to choose between me and your life there. I just…I need to be here. And you need to be there, and it just sucks because…because I'm in love with you."

A big, deep, pounding silence. He sucked in a breath, let it out slowly, shakily. "I'm in love with you too, Tor. I am. I have been. I will be."

He wiped at his face.

"And I know you're not asking me to choose, Torie," he continued. "I just…I can't offer you anything more concrete than I know how I feel about you, and it's making my life back in New Haven seem a lot less attractive than it used to be. I just don't know how I'd go about transferring my life here. I own property there, I have clientele there, and I'm almost done getting my realtor license. I'm about to be promoted to Jeremy's framing crew, which I've been working toward for months. I just don't know how or even *if* I can cut all that loose and come up here. It's all off-plan. I just…I need time, I guess. To figure out a new plan."

"I don't know how to say what I'm feeling," I whispered. "I'm in love with you. I want to be in your life. But I need my own future. I need to figure it out—what I want my life to look like. Who I want to be besides a stoner and a waitress." I sighed, soft and quiet and tremulous. "But it's hard to even think about that when everything inside me is screaming at me to not let you go."

"So…so maybe this isn't *it*, like goodbye. Maybe it's just…both of us need some time to figure out how and when our lives can intersect again so we can be together."

"I hate it," I whispered, tears now on my cheeks. "I wish you were an asshole."

"I wish you were a bitch." He laughed. "I guess there's just one thing left, then."

"What's that?"

He reached over, picked me up, set me on his lap. Held my face. "This."

He kissed me. Soft and slow at first, then hungrily and with building passion. It wasn't sexual, though. It was him telling me nonverbally that he was past the I think phase. It was a declaration of love.

"Dammit, Rhys," I breathed, a tear-wet sigh.

"I'll come back. I don't know how or when, but I will."

"You better. You have to."

"I have to, huh?"

"Yeah. Because I can't give you my virginity until you do."

He held me against him in a long hard embrace, then. "I know."

Eventually, I had to climb off his lap before I started something we couldn't finish. "I'll call Mom, she can come get us so you can get your bag and your Jeep."

He shook his head. "Been thinking about that, too." He pointed at the road, beyond the dock, where the truck I recognized as belonging to Lucas waited. "He has my bag. He's gonna take me to the airport."

"The airport?" I echoed, confused. "Why the airport?"

"Because." He showed me his phone, which had a digital boarding pass on the screen. "I have a one-way ticket back home. There's a number of layovers, but it'll get me to New Haven."

"I'm not following."

He dug into his pocket. Pulled out his keyring. Removed the key to the Jeep and handed it to me. "It's yours."

I shook my head. "No."

He laughed. "Yes. I'm giving it to you. I can't face the sixty-some hour drive home alone, for one thing. For another, I'll never make any progress on my truck if I have the Jeep. And also…" He tucked the key into my hand. "I just want you to have it. She's meant for you. I guess I just have a thing for hot girls in pimped-out Jeeps."

"Rhys…"

"When I get back home, I'll mail you the title signed over to you. Then you just have to sign it and take it to the DMV and make it official." He waved a hand. "Gifting a car has a few other steps to it, I guess, but between you, me, your mom, and Lucas, we'll figure it out. Point is, the Jeep is yours and I'm not discussing it. It's a done deal, sweetheart."

I held the key. "I don't know what to say. Thank you seems insufficient."

"I never meant to keep it forever. And I can't think of anyone else who could love that Jeep as much as I do but you."

"Well, for lack of anything better to say…thank you." I sniffled.

He stood up. "I…I better go before I start something we can't finish."

I laughed. "I literally just thought that exact thing. Why do you think I got off your lap?" I stood up, and we faced each other, holding hands. "I don't want you to go."

"I don't want to."

"But you have to." I had to suck it up. Try to make it easier for him. I touched his jaw, leaned in for one last kiss. "Until we meet again, Rhys Frost."

"Until we meet again, Torie Goode."

He touched my lips with two fingers, and then turned away. Strode to the gangway, carrying his shirt and shoes. Stopped on the dock, shrugged into his shirt, stuffed his feet bare into the shoes, stuck his socks into his pocket, and kept going. He didn't look back until he was at the truck. A wave. Blew a kiss. And then he was gone.

I sat in lonely, saddened silence for a long, long time.

Eventually, Lexie came out. "Hey, you," she said, kissing the top of my head as she sat down. There was a little coffee left, and she pointed to it. "Can I have some of this?"

I nodded. "It was Harlow's, but I'm sure she'd be okay with that."

"Oh." She poured the rest into a mug. "Where is she?"

"Back upstairs, I think."

"Ooh, it's a little cold. But still coffee." She looked around, then back at me. "You're just sitting here alone?"

"Harlow was here, then Rhys. But now Rhys is gone."

"Oh? Where'd he go?"

"Home."

That got her full attention. "Oh. I'm sorry to hear that. I liked him."

"Me too," I whispered. "But like isn't the right L-word."

She sighed. "I guess I thought he felt the same way."

"He does."

She blinked into a silence. "Then I'm confused."

"He has to go back to sort out his life. He owns a company and property back in New Haven. He can't just…say fuck it and stay here."

"Oh. So…he's coming back?"

"Someday, hopefully."

"Do you have plans to stay in touch?"

I sniffled. "I dunno. We didn't discuss that. Maybe. Probably. Maybe not. I don't fucking know. Talking to him may be harder than just…not." I held up the Jeep key. "He gave me the Jeep."

"No shit. The big red pimped-out classic in Mom's lot?"

I nodded. "That one."

"No shit. That thing is cool as hell. He just…*gave* it to you?"

"He sure did."

Lexie set her mug down and twisted to face me. "Are you okay? You don't seem okay."

"I'm not. But I will be. I miss him. But he has things to figure out, and so do I." I tried to brighten. "Plus, you're getting married!"

She grinned. "When you said you'd find your own way here, I had no clue it would lead to all this."

"Me either," I said, laughing. "So. Where are you and Myles going on your honeymoon?"

"We're not. We spent like two months in a hut on a remote Indonesian island owned by a billionaire friend of one of Myles's friends. So now we're getting married. We just did the honeymoon part first, is all."

I snickered. "I wonder what you two did for two months alone in a hut in the middle of nowhere."

"A lot of that. I mean, a *lot* a lot." A pause. "We also talked. About...um. Some things in my past that...that kept me messed up for a long, long time."

I held her eyes. "I see. And is this why you got so worked about my virginity?"

She nodded. "The short, simple version of a very long, painful story is that I was sexually abused by my voice teacher for several years." She shrugged, clear-eyed, but still obviously affected by the telling. "He, uhhh...he was my first and my only sexual experience until I moved away for college. So...yeah. I just...I wanted your first time to be a different experience than mine."

"It will be," I said.

She stared at me. "Wait. You and Rhys didn't fuck?"

I bobbed my head side to side. "No. Not really. We did other things, and I was going to, but then it was obvious we were falling for each other and if I'd slept with him and he had to leave I'd be even more upset. I'm still technically a virgin, in that I haven't had sexual intercourse yet. And I won't, not until I can share that with Rhys."

"What if—"

"I'm not entertaining any negative what-if scenarios, Lex. I'm a virgin. I'm in love with Rhys. I can't be with him right now. All that being true, I have no interest in thinking about what I would do in some fictional or hypothetical future that doesn't involve Rhys. For right now, I just want to figure out what my life looks like."

She nodded. "I respect that." A silence, and then she smirked at me. "How do you feel about going dress shopping?"

I sighed. "I hate wearing dresses. Are you going to make me wear some stupid frilly bullshit that makes me look like I'm wearing a tea cozy?"

Lexie leaned toward me, fake angry disbelief on her face. "Have you *ever* fucking met me?"

I laughed. "Good point."

She wiggled her eyebrows. "Now that you're

here, and you got here on your own, you have no choice but let me spoil you with Myles's money."

I stared at her. "I'm afraid to ask what that means."

"It means you, Mom, Cassie, Charlie, Poppy—if she ever gets her ass here—and all the other women of the Badd clan, are boarding a jet Myles has chartered for us, and we're flying to LA where he's hired an A-list glam squad to give us all makeovers, followed by forty-eight hours at an exclusive spa resort for massages and all that spa shit, then a designer with an Italian name I can't pronounce is going to put us each in dresses that cost more than some houses. And then, once we're all done getting the ever-loving hell pampered out of us, we fly back here for the wedding."

"Really?"

"Would I make up something like that?"

"It sounds like a fairy tale."

"Don't get me wrong, I love Myles for who he is, and I'd love him if he was broke and homeless. But him being who he is *does* have its perks. Which includes him dropping a couple hundred grand like it's nothing so all my girls can get pampered in style."

"He's that rich?"

She snorted. "Babe. He invests eighty percent of his earnings and lives exclusively off of a single endorsement stream. He owns entire buildings in Dallas, Nashville, and Manhattan, has stock in several super successful companies, and owns the rights and royalties to all his music, which he publishes himself under his own record company." She snapped her fingers. "Oh yeah, it's like that. My man is *set.*"

I laughed. "Your man. Never thought I'd hear you say that."

She didn't laugh. "Wanna hear something even more shocking? I'm his woman. There's not a single thing he could ask of me that I wouldn't do for him—except be with anyone else or share him."

"Wow. It's like that?"

She nodded. "Just like that. For life."

"How does it feel?"

"To be in a relationship like that? To be his, and him be mine?"

"Yeah. That," I whispered.

"Awesome. Scary as hell, but worth it." She blinked hard, and my tough as nails, never-cries sister was crying. "He saved me. Rescued me from me. From a destructive, toxic, dead-end life. I'm in therapy, Tor. Every week, for an hour, I video conference with a therapist in San Francisco about being the victim of long-term sexual abuse, and it's the best thing I've ever done." She tilted her head. "Well, the best-best thing I've ever done was jerk off Myles backstage at that festival. Because I've not spent a day apart from him since, and I never will, but therapy is making me a better person, helping me finally and truly heal from years of trauma."

"Years?" I asked.

"Yes, years. But it's over, and there's no point rehashing it. If you have specific questions, I'll answer them, but I'd honestly just as soon let it lie. You know about it now, and you know I'm getting treated for it."

I touched her arm. "Thank you for sharing. There's nothing I need to know that you've not told me. I'm just glad you're finding your way to okay."

She hugged me. "Awesome. Now let's go have Papa Lucas make us breakfast. He makes the best spinach and cream cheese omelets I've ever had."

"Papa Lucas? Mama Livvie? It's weird."

"It's not weird, it's family." She laughed. "Okay, it's a little weird. But it's family, and families are weird."

The next twenty-four hours were a whirlwind. The guys were in frenzy of macho packing—apparently they were going on some hunting, whiskey drinking, gun shooting, manly-man version of our girls' trip, and thus everyone in the entire clan was running around like crazy people, trading clothes and gear, making arrangements, figuring out where kids were going and who was watching whom and when, and figuring who was managing the bars and…I was exhausted just watching it all.

And, in the middle of it all, Poppy showed up.

With a boyfriend.

Poppy…god, I'd missed her. She was more amazing than ever—she'd reached her full height by tenth grade, and had spent the past few years flowering into her adult body…which, unfairly, meant her boobs got bigger, her ass rounder yet somehow tighter, her waist narrower, her cheekbones even more perfect. And, of course, living in New York had given her a distinctly Bohemian fashion sense that just fit her perfectly.

Case in point: she and her boyfriend—whose name, I shit you not, was Errol, because even her boyfriend was over-the-top cool—showed up in a vintage VW Westfalia camper van. Poppy descended from the driver's seat wearing a long, loose, flowy, bohemian skirt, a peasant blouse showing a nearly-but-not-quite obscene amount of cleavage, a thick black leather belt, and knee-high black boots. Her hair was nearly as long as mine, but thick and feathered in natural waves and layers, worn loose under a floppy fedora-type hat. Huge gold hoop earrings, a diamond stud in her left nostril, and, ohhh shit, Mom was gonna freak—nipple piercings, obvious through the front of her shirt, because apparently she didn't believe in bras either, even though her tatas were *way* too big for that to be practical or comfortable.

Oh my god, Poppy, you freak.

I was the first to see her, being the only one with nothing to do but sit outside Badd's Bar and Grille and sip soda water and watch various members of the clan fly in and out looking for something or someone—Badd's was ground zero, apparently, where all the luggage for those of us going to LA, and the guys going up into the bush, was being held.

Poppy saw me, and burst into a run, pawing her hat off her head and slamming into me for a hug. "God, Torie, I don't know how I've lived without you these last couple years," she whispered in my ear.

I clung as tightly to her as she was me. "I know, right? Why did we think it was a good idea to be apart?"

"I had this whole stupid *I'm gonna go to an Ivy League university like Charlie* thing going on." She sounded so derisive, self-deprecating. "What an idiot I was."

"So now you're…what?"

She laughed. "I don't know! Not going to Columbia anymore, at least. I officially withdrew a couple months ago." She pulled away, held me by the shoulders at arm's length. "Let me look at you."

She did just that, looked me up and down. Then, with a giddy grin, she tapped the underside of my boobs.

"Torie, you have titties!"

I rolled my eyes and whacked her hands away. "Shut up. I just grew them, like, last year and I'm very sensitive about them, so be nice." I reached out and flicked the bead of her nipple piercing. "Yours got even bigger…and *pierced*. You know Mom is going to shit puppies, right?"

"They did get bigger, didn't they? It's because I put on the freshman fifteen, except it was more freshman twenty, and most of it went to my tits and ass."

"Right, because life isn't fair and you suck."

She rolled her eyes. "Yeah, well, you try lugging these monstrosities around all day," she drawled, cupping the objects in question. "Why are we still talking about our boobs? Come on, let me introduce you to Errol."

"I'd gladly lug those around for a day, just to see what it's like," I said, following her back toward the VW van, which was parked down the street.

"Save you the trouble—tie a pair of sandbags to your chest, fill them with ten pounds of Jell-O each, and make them freakishly sensitive to everything."

"And you pierced them…why?"

She leaned close to me. "I was lit, and it sounded

like a good idea at the time." Her voice dropped to a whisper. "And then I met Errol, and it turns out it was a *great* idea." She shivered, a meaningful expression on her face. "The things he can do with his mouth? Oh man."

"Poppy!"

She laughed. "What? I'm an adult."

"Barely."

"I'm over the age of consent, I'm legally an adult, and I've been on my own as long as you have." She gestured, and the passenger side door opened, and a veritable angel of the Lord himself appeared.

If angels had colorful tattoos, blond hair in a surfer man-bun, scruffy stubble, and the most piercing blue eyes known to mankind, that is.

God, he was hot. I mean, I'm in love with Rhys and all, but *damn*. The eyes, the stubble, the man-bun, the stubble, the tattoos? He wore board shorts like he'd been born in them, flip flops, a tank-top, and what looked like a necklace made of shark teeth.

He had an air of confidence, like he'd seen the worst life could throw at him, handled it, and then said *let's go chill at the beach*.

Poppy took his hand, twined her fingers in his. "Errol, this is my next oldest and possibly favorite sister, Torie. Torie, this is Errol."

When he grinned at me and shook my hand, the

charming brilliance of grin threatened the integrity of the sun itself. Clearly, Poppy did not mess around with her choice in men.

"Hey," he said, in a thick Australian or New Zealand accent. "Nice to meet ya, finally. Pop's talked my ear off about her four cool-as-hell sisters."

Pop? That was cozy.

I widened my eyes at Poppy, because he had a sexy accent, too? I mean, come on.

"Well, it's nice to meet you," I said to Errol, "although I can't say I've heard anything about you other than that you were coming with Poppy to the wedding."

"Yeah, we're kind of new at whatever this is, so she's playing it kinda close to the vest, if you know what I mean."

I nodded. "I do. My own we're-not-sure-what-we-are situation just went back to Connecticut yesterday, so I'm still sort of reeling from that myself."

Poppy rubbed my arm. "I talked to Mom yesterday to fill her in on our ETA, and she said your…whatever… Rhys? Is that right? Went back to New Haven and you're sort of broken up over it, so be gentle."

I laughed. "Being gentle would have been her letting me fill you on it myself, but it's good to know Mom hasn't changed *that* much. She wouldn't be Mom if she didn't meddle and interfere with the best possible motives."

Poppy tilted her head. "What do you mean, Mom hasn't changed *that* much? How much has she changed, and how?"

I laughed. "Oh, just wait. You'll see."

"That's ominous."

I shook my head, still laughing. "It's not ominous. She's just…a new and improved Mom, shall we say. Different, but good. It just takes some getting used to."

"What do you mean?"

"It wouldn't do any good to tell you. Just brace yourself. Things here in Alaska are…pretty crazy."

Poppy, Errol, and I walked together back to the bar.

"Mom said something about a trip somewhere?" Poppy said, as we entered the bar.

"Yeah, to LA, on a private jet. Lexie's fiancé is springing for us to get makeovers by a Hollywood A-list glam squad, two days at a spa resort, and dresses by some Italian designer, tailored for each of us."

Poppy's eyes widened. "I know he's, like, Myles North, but…really?"

"Apparently."

"Have you met him? What's he like?"

Before I could answer that question I saw a man behind the bar—one of the Badd men, although I was still figuring out who was who; what with all the testosterone and badassery and insane looks, it was hard keeping them straight. I think this one was the former SEAL. His name started with a Z, I think.

He smiled at us as we sat at the bar. "Hey, all. Torie, you I know. You two are new, which means you're Mama Livvie's youngest, Poppy, and her friend." He extended his hand, and they both shook it. "I'm Zane, one of the owners."

"I'm Poppy," my sister affirmed. "And this is Errol."

Errol greeted Zane, and then the burly bartender slapped his palms on the bar. "Well, we're closed to the public for the day, which means I'm allowed to assume you're all twenty-one."

Errol raised his hand. "I mean, I'm actually twenty-four."

Poppy assumed an innocent expression. "I have a license *saying* I'm twenty-one."

I glared at her. "You do not."

She shrugged. "A friend of friend is a professional forger for some mysterious organization. It's all very hush-hush, and I had to pose in some rather risqué outfits for his personal collection."

I stared at her. "I feel like I may have missed some things about your life in New York."

"Our girl is quite the adventurous type, Pop is," Errol said. "When I met her, she was hitchhiking on the highway in the middle of Missouri."

I frowned at her. "You're a beautiful eighteen-year-old girl hitchhiking down a rural freeway?" Kettle, meet Pot, I know, but still.

She had a large purse made from quilt patchwork stitched together with pieces of leather, canvas, flannel, and a dozen other materials, with a drawstring opening and handles repurposed from what looked like an old timey medical bag or carpet bag.

She fiddled with the handles. "I can handle myself. And I like to think the world isn't as horrible and scary as the news makes it out to be." A bright grin. "There are good people out there. Kind, wonderful people." She reached into the bag and pulled out a beautiful antique camera. "And I've taken photographs of quite a lot of them, on the way up here from Manhattan." She replaced the camera. "I'll take my chances out in the world. How else am I supposed to find all the art I'm meant to make?"

My little sister Poppy had grown up in more ways than one.

LA was everything I expected it to be, and more. There were thousand-dollar bottles of champagne on the flight from Ketchikan to LA, and a pair of limousines waiting for us on the tarmac. The glam squad—who saw us in a salon on Rodeo Drive, included a whole team of people. They trimmed my hair back several inches, tutting over the dead ends, did some sort of treatment to it, and I don't even know what else. Then it was off to the resort where we got massages and manicures and pedicures, all the while sipping drinks and talking nonstop.

I got to know all the other women, and they were all, as Mom said, warm and welcoming and funny and inappropriate. And the wonder of it all was that Mom was just as hysterically inappropriate.

It was amazing, and *almost* took my mind off of Rhys.

Poppy got hell from Mom over the nipple piercings, and when it threatened to boil over into a real fight, Poppy yanked off her shirt in the hotel room in front of all of the gathered girls and removed both piercings.

"There. If you care that much, I'll take them out, just for you. But I'll put them back in the moment this trip is over. It's my body and I like them." Poppy stood topless in front of Mom, bold, unapologetic. "I don't see the big deal, but I don't want to fight with you, so there, they're out."

Mom stared her down. "I've never been a fan of body piercings, you know that. My friend in college got a belly button ring and it got super infected and she was very sick. But, if you feel that strongly about it, I won't say another word. It *is* your body, and it *is* your choice. I just don't agree with it."

Poppy put her shirt back on. "You just don't like it because it means I'm an adult and you're just now really realizing it."

Mom laughed. "Actually, if you want the truth, it's more because I'm of a certain age and I have hold-over ideas about body piercings."

"Fair enough." Poppy grinned. "You *are* old."

Mom laughed. "Oh shut up, I'm not *that* old."

Mara, once the silence threatened to go on too long, raised her hand. "Does anyone else share a sense of extreme inferiority, after seeing Poppy's ridiculously amazing eighteen-year-old titties?"

"Ooh, ooh," Claire said. "Me, me! But I feel inferior to all of you in that department, so it's not new. It's just not fair that she has melons the size of my goddamn head that are *that* fucking perky *and* that high *and* that tight."

Poppy shook her head, snorting. "God, would you all stop about my boobs? I didn't *do* anything, they just grew like that and I had nothing to do with it."

"And grew, and grew, and grew, and now it's a wonder you don't fall over like a Weeble-Wobble," Dru said, laughing.

"You realize women pay tens of thousands of dollars to get what you have naturally," Eva said. "My mother, for example."

Poppy shrugged. "I've thought about a reduction, actually. I had a friend who was a senior last year, and she got one and said it made her life a lot easier. But then, she had, like, double E's or something."

Dru winced. "Yikes."

"Yeah, she *reduced* to a triple D."

Claire snorted. "That's bullshit." She cupped herself. "I barely have an A-cup."

Once upon a time, Mom wouldn't have let that go so easily. Liberated and open minded, indeed.

A lot of the conversation revolved around men, and sex, and babies, and love...and that made it impossible not to think about Rhys.

And then, once we were back in Ketchikan, three days later, Lexie and Myles got married.

The wedding took place on the roof of Badd Kitty, and the officiant was a monster of a man with the body of an Olympian god who was, apparently, Myles's drummer, and who had gotten his license online just so he could perform this ceremony.

The wedding march was played acoustically by Canaan, Corin, Aerie, Tate, and Crow, a quintet of two guitars, a ukulele, a cello, and a mandolin.

There were white twinkling lights strung by the thousands overhead in a brilliant lacework of golden light. The space was decorated with white orchids and lilies and daisies and roses—hundreds of flowers.

There were children all over the place, laughing, playing, making noise, and if anyone tried to shush them Lexie just told them to let the kids play, it was not a formal event but a celebration so they should have all the fun in the world.

Lexie read a poem she'd written for her vows, and there wasn't a dry eye in the place when she was done.

And then, because he was that guy, Myles played a song he'd written for *his* vows, and people were sobbing. Mom, loudly so.

When Jupiter, the appropriately named drummer and officiant, announced they were legally married and would you please kiss the bride already you dumb knucklehead, Myles lifted the veil—an actual, over-the-face veil—and kissed Lexie until people started whistling and clapping.

And *that* was the beginning of a week-long reception. Party after party, endless amounts of food, and even though neither Poppy nor I were of drinking age, no one really asked and we didn't make a big deal of it.

It was an amazing wedding and an incredible celebration. I just wished Rhys had been here. I really missed him, and I only thought about him once or twice…every hour.

The receptions eventually ended, and things in Ketchikan settled down somewhat. Although, it quickly became clear that this clan made regular get togethers a quasi-religious thing. Every Sunday, they all gathered somewhere. And during the week, someone was always doing something. I found myself painting a house that Zane was remodeling, and the next day I was filling in as a waitress at one of the bars, and then I was spending a day with Eva, being taught how to paint, and then Poppy and I were borrowing Mom's car for a trip down to Seattle. I got roped into posing for Poppy, who turned the black-and-white photo of me into a stunning and ethereal piece; I spent a lot of time helping Zane with the remodel, and it turned out getting dirty and building things was quickly becoming my favorite thing to do, and I gradually spent more and more time working with, and eventually for, Zane, working on houses.

And that, of course, made me think of Rhys.

Then I got a letter from him, an actual snail-mail letter—a little over two months after he left:

*Torie,*

*I disconnected my cell phone, and I'm too chicken to call you from the shop landline because hearing your voice would make me miss you even more than I already do. I'm making arrangements. I can't really say much more so I don't jinx anything, but just be watching out your window. One of these days, you just might see me.*

*You know how they say absence makes the heart grow fonder? It's true. I just wish that phrase could express how much it hurts to miss someone this bad.*

*Love hurts.*

*I'm on my way, Victoria.*

*~RJ*

RJ. He signed it RJ.

He was coming? He was on his way?

Victoria? No one called me that unless it was Mom when she was either angry or joking.

But I liked it, from him.

The moment I read those words, I rushed to the window of Mom's guest room where I'd been living...but there was no one out there in the parking lot.

My heart was pounding, though.

He was on his way.

The palpitations became butterflies, and then I was soaring on the wings of hope.

# SIXTEEN

## Rhys

IT WAS UNEXPECTED, WHEN IT ALL CAME TOGETHER.

One of my competitors, one of the only other guys in two counties who specialized in engines the way I did, came to my shop one evening. We'd had beers together a few times, but it was always a bit tense, because every job I got was one he didn't, and vice versa. He was older than me by about ten or twelve years, a guy named Rog—just that, Rog, soft G sound.

He ambled in the open bay door late one evening while I was under my Ford F-100, putting the new exhaust in. I saw his boots, and knew it was him. I finished the bolt I was working on, and then slid the creeper out from under it.

"Hey, Rog. What's up?"

He had a six-pack of local beer and two cigars. "I was hopin' I'd find you in a good mood."

I wiped my hands on a rag. "Eh. Honestly? Struggling with some things."

He eyed the exhaust parts strewn on the floor. "Havin' issues with the catback?"

"Nah. More personal stuff."

Rog—same height as me but beefy, burly, and black, with an easy smile and thick, scarred hands—nodded. "Well, what I got to say may help, may not."

I moved to sit on a tire, wiped at my forehead with the back of my wrist. "What's on your mind?"

"I've had good business lately, real good. And I'm findin' myself thinking about expanding."

My heart did a weird flip. "Yeah, I've been…streamlining a bit, taking on fewer clients, I guess."

"Well, I can't really expand my current setup. And I was wonderin', maybe it's a long shot, but I was wonderin' if you were willin' to sell."

"Sell?" I gazed around. "I…"

I stood up. I'd taken on no long-term jobs since I'd left Alaska. I'd reduced my hours on Jeremy's crew, and stayed on the finishing end of things. I had completed my realtor classes, but hadn't applied for a license in the state of Connecticut. I could, without this place and this business, pick up and start over…in Ketchikan.

It would be heading off into the unknown. Off plan. No assurance that I could start my business over, up there. No assurance that things with Torie and me would pan out as I hoped. No assurances, period. But maybe it was time to go off plan.

Out of the blue, I had an offer on this place.

"I'd give you what you paid for it, plus ten percent."

Shit—that was a sweet offer.

"I can't sell everything," I said. "I'd need the tools and some of the equipment, some select parts from the salvage."

Rog got up off the tire he was sitting on, leaving his beer on the floor. "Tell you what—I got an old enclosed hauler I don't need no more. It'd hook up to your old Ford there nice and easy. I'll give you that as part of the sale. Pack up whatever you need, leave what you can't take, or don't want to haul. If you got clients on the hook, I'll take 'em—we both know I'm pretty well-known around here."

"So you're offering what I paid plus ten percent, the trailer, all my tools, and my pick of salvage?" I hesitated. "Is the trailer gonna fall apart before I get where I'm going?"

He laughed. "Nah, man, it's good. I've taken care of it. I brought my shop up here from Virginia in that thing. It's got some miles on it all right, but it'll hold."

I sighed. "It's a sweet deal, man, that's for sure. I

just…I've put so fuckin' much work into building this business."

He nodded. "I don't offer lightly. You do good work, and I got a lot of respect for you." He eyed me. "You goin' after a woman?"

I nodded. "How'd you know?"

"You got the look." He grinned. "A man says personal problems, that means it's a woman, and you look lovesick, my friend."

I nodded again. "You got it in one." I sighed, because it was not really even a decision. I held out my hand. "Deal."

He grinned wider, handed me a cigar and a clipper, and we lit up. Cracked open the beers, and clinked. "To big engines and good women."

I laughed, feeling lighter, now. "Big engines and *amazing* women."

We sipped, and he jerked his chin at me. "So. Where you headed?"

"Ketchikan, Alaska."

"What's her name?"

"Torie. Victoria Goode."

"So when I said good women, I was more right than I knew?"

I cackled at that. "Damn, dude, I hadn't thought about that, but yeah." I sighed. "Man, now that we've got a deal, I feel better. I been trying to figure it out for two damn months, and you come along and fix it for me in one evening."

"Part of me wishes we could go into business together. I'd love to get into a big ol' V-8 with you, sometime. But, my old lady and I got a kid in middle school and another in elementary, and this deal is gonna help me put 'em in new school clothes. I got more jobs lined up than I can take on my own, and my cousin is gonna move up and start workin' for me."

"Well, good luck to you," I said.

"You too, man."

We sipped beer and smoked the stogies, and talked about women and trucks until the wee hours, and then I crashed.

The next morning I wrote a letter to Torie, stuck it in the mailbox, and started packing.

A month later, I had my engine hoist, creeper, all the tool crates and tool boxes and rolling carts and everything else all loaded in the trailer, along with various other things like compression testers and spare parts, and a few of the best of the salvaged parts, plus all my personal belongings. Most of that fit in the bed of the truck, which wasn't a hundred percent restored, but good enough to make the trip.

I'd signed the contract for the building and all the agreed upon property, got paid, and hit the road—but not before stopping by a certain old diner to say goodbye to Marty. He gave me a big bear hug, told me to love her like he'd loved his Jenny, and gave me a big old burger for the road. God, I would miss that man.

Here I was, driving to Alaska, again. This time, I was on my own, and I had my whole life with me.

I stopped at the post office on the way to check my P.O. Box, and arrange to have all my mail forwarded to Ketchikan. And there was a letter for me.

From Torie.

*RJ—*

*Or should I still call you Rhys? You signed your letter RJ, so I wasn't sure. I like you calling me Victoria.*

*I've missed you more than I can say, and I understand about you not calling me.*

*When I say I'll be standing at the window watching and waiting, I'm not kidding. If I'm home, I'll be watching for your arrival.*

*I hope it's not too forward to sign this letter this way…*

*I love you,*

*Your Victoria*

Holy hell. My heart leapt like a trout in a river. She loved me.

I mean, hearing it when I was with her was one thing, but to read it in a letter after three months apart? That was something else entirely.

I left New Haven with that letter in my back pocket and a grin on my face.

I made it to Ketchikan in record time, considering I was hauling a trailer and driving a '49 F-1. I stopped to sleep in my truck in a truck stop twice, and only for a few hours at a time, preferring to keep driving, needing to be with Torie as soon as possible.

I arrived in Ketchikan at two in the morning. I parked in the back of her mom's condo lot. Locked everything, grabbed my backpack and went for the door.

I buzzed her mom's unit. "H'lo?" Lucas's deep rumble, sleepy and annoyed.

"Sorry to wake you, Lucas. It's Rhys."

"RJ." It was said with a laugh. "She ain't here."

"Oh." My heart sank.

"Don't sound s'down hearted, son. She's got her own place. I'll come down and tell you how to get there."

A few minutes later, a sleepy Lucas emerged from the front door wearing a pair of shorts and nothing else. He gave me directions to her place across town, and another one of those claps on the back that shook my teeth.

"She's been workin' her tail off, that girl," he said.

"Oh? Doin' what?" I asked.

"Working for Zane, helping him and Liv flip houses. She's right handy with a circular saw, that girl, and knows her way around a paint roller like nobody I seen. Got a real eye for colors and such."

"And she's got her own apartment?"

"Apartment, hell. She's got a rent-to-own house from her ma and Zane. One of the ones they flipped—part of her wages is payment on it, and her mom did her right by it, Liv bein' Liv. Cute little place." He nodded, grinned. "She's got a fire under her ass, shows up early, stays late, learns everything she can. Walks around with her own tool belt and hardhat. Three months, and she's already Zane's top employee, and he don't favor her none."

"Wow." I was impressed, but not surprised. "Construction, huh?"

He nodded. "Yep. I figure she'll have her own work in time. She's got a real eye for remodels, takin' what's there and makin' it better. Loves the work." He clapped me on the back again. "Go. She's missed you like hell."

I got back in the truck and headed across town.

Her house was a little white ranch with a gray roof and red shutters, squared-off box shrubs under the bay windows, flowers along the little path to the front door, a detached garage and a small fenced-in backyard. Fuckin' adorable.

I pulled into her driveway, and the trailer barely cleared the sidewalk.

By the time I had the engine turned off, she was out the front door and pulling my door open. The night was cool, early fall in Alaska, and she was out there in a T-shirt and not a damn thing else.

She didn't say a word of hello, just climbed right into the truck and onto my lap, leaning back against the steering wheel, cupping my face in her hands and kissing me with all the words neither of us had.

I kissed her back with three months' worth of loving her from thirty-five-hundred miles away.

She pulled away enough to meet eyes with me, her hands still on my face. "Say it, Rhys."

I knew what she meant. "I love you, Torie."

"Three months apart didn't change that?"

"Three months apart made me realize I love you more than I even realized."

She kissed me again, as if she couldn't help it. She wriggled against me, and her breath was sweet and warm, her skin soft under the shirt where my hands roamed.

"I was so afraid it had all been a dream," she whispered against my lips. "It was such a whirlwind of...of everythingness, and then you were gone and it was like it never happened, but I just had you in my heart and you wouldn't get out, and I fucking—I dream about you every night, Rhys."

"I'm sorry I never called. I wanted to so many times, but I just—"

She touched my mouth to shush me. "No. It was better that way. Easier to miss you and just sort of...try to forget while holding on to hope. If we had talked every day it would have been fucking awful missing you, wanting you, hearing your voice, feeling like you were close but not..." She shook her head, the loose pigtail braids shaking. "No. It was better how it was. I understood, and it was for the best."

I just held her against me, her nose in my neck, my hands under her shirt exploring the curve and knobs of her back down to the swell of her hips and her thighs where they splayed to straddle me in the driver's seat. I just inhaled her scent.

"Missed you so fucking much, Victoria."

She shivered. "I like that."

"I signed that letter RJ as a joke."

"You're Rhys, to me."

"I told Lucas I was RJ when I was drunk, that night before I left. It's gonna happen."

"You'll always be my Rhys," she breathed. She pulled away, nose to nose with me. "Carry me inside and make love to me."

My answer was to slide out of the truck and stand up with her latched around my waist, her T-shirt hiking up to expose her bare ass. She kept her nose in the side of my neck and her arms around my shoulders and her hands in my hair as I carried her inside. I found her bedroom, a small room with a king bed taking up most of the space, a small bureau, a closet with a tri-fold door and some clothes poking out on hangers. Three candles were lit on the bedside table. Six more on the bureau. Her bed was made, pillows plumped and neatly arranged, the quilt turned back. There was an en suite bathroom with a clawfoot bathtub visible through an arched entryway, with steaming water rising and more candles around the base of the tub and on the sink and the windowsill.

My breath caught. "Tor, what...?"

She wiggled, and I let her slide down to stand up. She peeled my shirt up, caressed my abs, and gazed up at me with soft limpid passionate eyes. "Mom texted me that you were on the way over. I only had a few minutes and I wanted—I had to do something to...to welcome you. To show you that I want to be yours. I thought about getting dressed up or something, but I didn't really have time for that, and I don't really dress up anyway and I don't have any lingerie, so…"

She was rambling from nerves.

I shut her up with a kiss, and she tossed my shirt aside. Undid the button and fly of my shorts, tugged them off along with my underwear and I stepped out of them. I helped her out of her shirt.

Naked together again, finally.

And this time, there would be no stopping at fooling around.

I palmed the lush weight of her breast. "I have a bit of a fail to admit."

She pulled back to meet my eyes. "And that would be what?"

"I don't…I didn't bring any condoms. I may have some somewhere in my stuff in the back of my truck, but…"

"Have you been with anyone?"

"No. Not since a few weeks before I met you, almost four months ago."

"So you'd be clean."

"Absolutely." I swallowed hard. "But…I would be anyway, because I've always been safe, you know?" I hesitated. "What are you saying?"

"I'm saying I got on birth control not long after you left. I'm saying, I just want you." She grasped me, caressed me with a sigh as if relieved to have me in her hand again. "I don't want anything between us. I want our first time together to be...just us. Nothing else."

"Tor, even birth control ain't a hundred percent guarantee against pregnancy."

"If I got pregnant, would you leave?"

"Ain't a thing could happen that could get me to leave, now I'm here."

"Then we'll take that risk."

Her fist gliding down my length was glorious—I'd obviously been celibate since leaving her, obviously, except for frequent use of my own fist accompanied by thoughts of her and the things we'd done together. Her hand on me, then, was utter heaven.

I let her touch me for a minute, and then lifted her up and set her on the bed. She refused to let me out of her touch, and when I pulled away so I could kiss her throat and then her breasts, she palmed my head and grasped my shoulders, and as I kissed lower and lower, she gathered my head in her hands.

"Oh god, Rhys, I've dreamed of you between my thighs. Your mouth. That stubble."

I tasted her. "Been thinking about growing a beard, if I'm gonna be an Alaskan."

She laughed, and the laugh became a gasp. "I don't think it's a prerequisite for living in Alaska, but I'd love to see you with a full beard." Another gasp as I lapped at her, swirled my tongue around her clit. "I bet it would feel so good on my skin when you're going down on me."

And then there was no more talking as I brought her to the crumbling, desperate edge. She got there, but pushed me away before she fell over the edge. She pulled me up.

"I've had such trouble reaching orgasm without you," she whispered. "I've tried so many times, but I just...I'd get close, but I can't get all the way there."

"So why not let me take you all the way?"

She slid lower so she was fully under me, lined up perfectly. She spread her thighs apart, grasped me, and brought me to her slit. "Because when I finally come again, it's going to be with you inside me."

"It's been so long without you that I ain't gonna last long," I told her, growling as she writhed against me, grasping me, teasing her slit with the head my cock.

"Good," she whispered. "We have all night, all day. We have the rest of our lives together. I just want this to be...beautiful, and desperate."

"I'll try to be gentle."

"I know you will." She held my eyes, one hand on my cock, the other wrapped around the back of my neck. "You'll take care of me. You'll make me feel so good. So loved. So beautiful."

She bit her lower lip, sucked in a deep, slow breath. Held it. Nestled me between her lips. Hesitated. I wanted this part to be at her pace, her way. So I held still, let her lead, let her guide. She paused, let out her breath, shaky, emotional. Then she tilted her hips and slid more of me into her, and holy *fuck* she was so tight, so tight it was like a vise, and she was already squeezing me, I felt her walls clamping and pulsing around me.

"Oh god," she breathed.

"Okay?" I whispered.

She nodded. "It's good, it's just…a lot. Just…be patient. Okay?"

"All the time in the world, love."

She held the back of my neck in a tight grip, her other hand now possessively, affectionately on my buttock, holding, gripping. Pulling.

She held still again, and I felt her tense, and then relax, and her walls squeezed and pulsated. Fucking so tight, and it was such hot slick wet perfection that not moving and not letting go required every last shred of restraint I possessed.

And then she pulled my head down so our foreheads rested together, and she was gasping, panting. "Oh god, Rhys. I'm so glad it's you."

"Only me, always me."

I felt a…resistance within her. She pulled me

closer, cheek to cheek, panting in my ear, and then tilted her hips hard and pulled at my buttocks, and I felt our hips meet, and she was gasping, sharp, shrill, her breast heaving against my chest.

Then a slow sigh as the tense squeeze around me loosened, and she was still tight but not vise-grip tight.

"Oh god," she breathed, and this time it had a different quality. An awed tone, as if understanding had dawned. She inhaled slowly, held it again, and rolled her hips. "Oh my fucking *god*."

"Tor?" I whispered.

"Move with me," she gasped. Clutching my ass in both hands she pulled at me. "Move with me, Rhys."

I felt her hips roll, and met her movements with my own—slow, soft, gentle. Careful, and shallow. She kept it there for a while, testing the roll of her hips, pushing against me. Then, gradually, she found a rhythm, and her gasps matched it, sharp panting whispers of my name, again and again.

"Torie, you feel so good." I rested my lips on her chest, between her breasts. "So fucking good. You're mine, Tor."

"I'm yours, Rhys," she whispered. "And you're mine."

"All yours."

She gazed up at me, then. "Are you holding back?"

I nodded. "I wanted to let you get used to it. I don't want to hurt you."

She lifted to kiss me. "Don't hold back. You won't hurt me."

Still, I matched her intensity, gauged her responses. And truly, the more I met her and gave her myself in thrust after thrust, the more she gasped, cried out my name.

We moved together, then. In perfect unison. I had to hold back, couldn't let go until I felt her find her own release. As we slid together, our lips meeting clumsily in gasping kissing, hands sliding and sweat-slickening skin, she pressed her palm between our meeting bodies, and her fingers found her clit, and I moved to make room, and she touched herself to find what she needed.

Her eyes met mine, suddenly, her hand freezing. "Wait, is it okay?"

I touched her hand, set it to moving again. "Anything. Everything. This is about us." I smiled down at her. "Not just okay, Tor, it's beautiful and it's right and it's perfect."

"Oh thank fuck, I just need to…" she trailed off. "A little more…oh fuck, oh god, Rhys."

Her hips began to tilt, to pump and gyrate. Holding back became more than difficult, it became impossible. But I wanted her to come first, so I gritted my teeth and growled as I moved with her, but what I needed was to let go, to take her, to feel us driving into heaven together.

Her whimpers became desperate, shrill. Her movements erratic and thrashing. Her eyes met mine, liquid and tearful, awed. "Rhys, I love you, god this is so fucking amazing—I love you, I fucking love you. I don't want it to end, never end, but I have to come, I have to…"

"Come for me, love," I breathed, snarled. "Please come. Let me watch you come."

Her fingers flew and our hips met, and she cried out, and I felt her spasming around my cock, and that was it, that was everything I could take. I couldn't hold back anymore. Not with her crying my name, sobbing my name, sobbing that she loved me, her walls clamping around me.

"Tor, Victoria, god, my love, Victoria," I gasped, hoarse, my cock throbbing, my balls aching, pulsing, my cum boiling inside me. "Come, so I can come."

"With me, Rhys," she sobbed. "Come with me, Rhys. *Right now.*"

"Now, love. Now, Torie."

Now.

I felt her clench around me, tight hard and wild, and I felt myself unleash, and I couldn't have held it back for anything. I cried out, and I knew tears were in it, but I didn't care, she was crying too and holding me tight, pulling at my ass, and her legs were clinched around my waist and she was writhing against me and sobbing my name as I shouted hers, and I poured into her, unleashed, and felt her move with me and clench around me and it was an eternity of heaven we shared in those moments, everything, together, always.

Us.

Perfection.

Love.

# SEVENTEEN

## Torie

WE SLEPT AFTER THAT FIRST TIME.

We woke up together, and I was sore, but it was beautiful. He pulled me on top of him and filled me, and I knew then I was a cowgirl kind of girl, because that was the most intense orgasm of my life, riding him, screaming on top of him, slamming onto him so hard my tits bounced 'til they ached. And I couldn't get enough. There wasn't enough.

I collapsed sideways, passed out, and when I woke up again, he'd relit the candles and refreshed the hot water in the tub, and carried me to it. Set me in it, and got in with me, and we lazed in the tub together talking about our lives together until the water got cool, and then we got in the shower and I discovered that shower sex was, in fact, highly overrated, but at this point any sex with Rhys was amazing. I made him breakfast, and we drank coffee—in *my* house. Zane texted and told me to stay home today, and so that's what we did. We stayed home all day, talking, making plans, and making love.

Again, and again, and again, until I knew my poor hoo-ha needed a break. So we went out and I showed him a place Zane and I had been working on. We took the Jeep, and I drove into the more industrial area of town, to a small building with a For Sale sign on it. The sign had a SOLD slider on top, however.

It was a garage. Four bays, two lifts, an office, with a fenced-in yard out back and a small pole barn off to one side.

He sat in the passenger seat and stared, musing. "That's a nice place. Says it's sold, though."

I nodded. "It had like three interested parties, but Mom, Zane, and Dru snapped it up for a steal. We've been working on fixing up the office, which hadn't been cleaned since roughly 1976. We ripped everything out, stripped it all down to concrete and bare wood, and Zane and I are putting in a new built-in desk, some shelves, all the necessary auto garage office stuff. Replacing the chain link fence, cleaning the concrete in the bays, new pegboard for the tools."

He eyed me. "Tor."

"I don't want to be presumptuous, or speak for you, or make plans with your money since I'm only just getting started, but…"

He laughed. "You want me to buy it?"

"I know Mom, Zane, and Dru would give you a hell of a deal."

"Will you be my business partner?"

"I'm your partner in everything, Rhys."

"Then you're not making decisions for me, or speaking for *my* money. It's *our* money." He glanced at the building again. "I think this is a good investment, and I did make a nice profit off the sale back in New Haven."

"Mom and Dru say it's a prime location, that this area is building up."

"Let's do it," he said.

I nodded. "I still want to get into remodels, but I want to work on cars with you more than just about anything."

"You wanna know what I discovered, working for Jeremy?"

"What?"

"I don't like major construction so much as the finishing touches, taking something partway there, still a little ugly or unfinished, and making it beautiful."

I grinned at him. "Like that truck."

He nodded. "Exactly. So we can split our businesses. Remodel houses, and build vintage four-by-fours together."

"And lots and lots and lots of sex." I bit my lip and grinned at him.

"I latched onto a hurricane with you, didn't I?" he asked with a smirk.

I nodded, wide-eyed. "I feel like there's not enough time in the day to have all the sex I want to have with you. I want to try everything."

"Like what?"

I licked my lips. "Maybe you could show me something new and fun."

"I can think of a few things."

"So…let's go back home and get started."

Home. Our home. In Alaska. I was a homeowner, I had a boyfriend who loved me, a future in business with him, and I wasn't a virgin.

I think Alaska is turning out pretty good.


**THE END**

# EPILOGUE

## Poppy

*Three and a half months earlier*

"THIS JUST ISN'T FOR ME," I TOLD MY ADVISOR. "I'VE been fighting the realization for a long time, but the degree, the hoity-toity art world, it's just not what I want."

Mrs. DuPuis, my art school advisor, tutted. "You have such talent, though, Poppy. Such promise. I know the classes can be hard, but—"

"The classes aren't *hard*," I interrupted, a bit snippily, "they're *boring*. Useless. I just want to be an artist, Mrs. D. I want to do art. I want to see the world. I want to meet a boy out there and be wild and irresponsible.

I want…I want to *live*, and I'm not doing that stuck in the damn classroom." I gestured at the world beyond her office windows. "Life is out *there*."

She nodded, pushed at her mass of natural curls, touched a turquoise fingernail to her elegantly arched African-American cheekbone. "Well, I do understand. I took a gap year after high school, and the gap year turned into living in Spain for three years, teaching English and painting orange trees and flamenco dancers and cute little cafes." She pointed at a painting of a bull and a bullfighter. "I did that in Pamplona. I ran with the bulls two years in a row. I didn't settle down until I knew what I wanted to do."

"And what I want to do is live life and make art."

She nodded. "Well, I'll be sad to see you go, Poppy. You're a wonderfully bright young lady with monumental talent." Her smile was warm. "You'll do well in the world, I know. Just…make sure when you fall for the boy, he doesn't replace your art."

I sighed. "Good advice, and I know if there's a pitfall out there for me, it's that. I tend to fall hard and fast and get blinded."

She laughed, a tinkling, bell-like sound. "Oh Poppy, you're barely eighteen, how can you know that about yourself?"

"I'm an old soul, Mrs. D."

"Indeed you are."

I laughed. "Well, I'm glad you understand, because I already withdrew from classes."

She reached into a drawer and withdrew an aged leather camera case. "This is an antique Minolta camera. I bought it here in New York from a thrift store the year before I left home. I had it with me in Spain, France, Italy, Switzerland and all over Europe the years I was there. Go buy as much black-and-white and color film as you can afford, and take a million, million pictures. Take photos of everything. Send the rolls to me in bulk, and I'll have them developed for you by my friend who has one of the few remaining professional darkrooms in the city, and I'll mail them all back to your next destination."

I held the case gingerly. "Oh, Mrs. D., I…I can't take this. You've had this camera half your life. You've told stories in class about it."

She patted my hand. "I could never have children, and we never felt like adoption was right for us. And I've always had a special place in my heart for you, since the first day you showed up, more sixteen than seventeen, wide-eyed, talented, and so innocent. I want you to have it." She touched the case. "Besides, the old girl hasn't been on an adventure in a decade. She needs to see new things. Who better than with you?"

"Are you sure, Mrs. D.?"

"Absolutely. Just send me the film so I can share all the beautiful things you see—you have such a lovely and unique vision, you know." She patted my hand again. "And now that you're not a student anymore, call me Sofia."

I felt a little emotional, now, and stood up to hug her. "Thank you, Sofia. You've been a wonderful mentor."

She shook her head. "No, Poppy, dear. I've been your professor, thus far. The mentorship begins *now*. Go, Poppy. Fall in love. Make art. Make love, and find art. It's all over the world, in everything—you just have to see it, find it, capture it."

"I will."

"Send me your film, with an address where I can send it back."

I hesitated. And then wrote down Mom's address—I had to check it on my phone. "Just send it all here, to my mom's place. It's where I'll end up."

"It's good to have an eventual destination, or you just might get lost wandering and never find anywhere to just be."

Wise words, it felt like.

I said goodbye to her, and then to all my friends from Columbia, and my favorite barista at the coffee shop not far from my dorm, and the bagel guy on the corner where I got my bagels and halal street meat. And then I did the craziest thing: I set out into the world on my own, with a few thousand dollars cash in my purse, a backpack full of clothes, an antique camera and a few hundred rolls of film, and my cell phone. I had no plan whatsoever, other than end up in Alaska, someday, somehow.

Hopefully there was a cute boy on the road ahead of me somewhere—I'd had my heart broken recently, and I was antsy to meet some cute guys and do some heartbreaking of my own. Love 'em and leave 'em, that was the way. No more of this thinking the first guy to smile nice at me shit rainbows and burped unicorns. I didn't want someone who said he *loved* me just because he said so while inside me.

Oh no, no more of that. I'd learned my lesson. My heart was closed for business.

I took a bus out of Manhattan.

Another bus into Pennsylvania. And then, just because it was a nice day and I had good boots and strong legs, I started walking. I would see where the road took me, and maybe catch a ride from someone interesting.

I thought of a quote from Tolkien, as I walked down a lonely highway in the middle of Pennsylvania: "It's a dangerous business, Frodo, going out your door. You step onto the road, and if you don't keep your feet, there's no knowing where you might be swept off to."

Where would my road take me?

Who in the wide world was waiting to meet me?

I was eager to find out.

**COMING SOON...**

# GOODE VIBRATIONS
**THE VERY LAST BOOK IN THE BADD AND THE GOODE SERIES!**

# Also by
# Jasinda Wilder

Visit me at my website: **www.jasindawilder.com**
Email me: **jasindawilder@gmail.com**

If you enjoyed this book, you can help others enjoy it as well by recommending it to friends and family, or by mentioning it in reading and discussion groups and online forums. You can also review it on the site from which you purchased it. But, whether you recommend it to anyone else or not, thank you *so much* for taking the time to read my book! Your support means the world to me!

My other titles:

Preacher's Son:
*Unbound*
*Unleashed*
*Unbroken*

Delilah's Diary:
*A Sexy Journey*
*La Vita Sexy*
*A Sexy Surrender*

Big Girls Do It:
*Boxed Set*
*Married*
*On Christmas*
*Pregnant*

Rock Stars Do It:
*Harder*
*Dirty*
*Forever*

From the world of *Big Girls* and *Rock Stars*:
*Big Love Abroad*

Biker Billionaire:
*Wild Ride*

The Falling Series:
*Falling Into You*
*Falling Into Us*
*Falling Under*
*Falling Away*
*Falling For Colton*

The Ever Trilogy:
*Forever & Always*
*After Forever*
*Saving Forever*

The world of *Wounded:*
*Wounded*
*Captured*

The world of *Stripped:*
*Stripped*
*Trashed*

The world of *Alpha:*
*Alpha*
*Beta*
*Omega*
*Harris: Alpha One Security Book 1*
*Thresh: Alpha One Security Book 2*
*Duke Alpha One Security Book 3*
*Puck: Alpha One Security Book 4*
*Lear: Alpha One Security Book 5*
*Anselm: Alpha One Security Book 6*

The Houri Legends:
*Jack and Djinn*
*Djinn and Tonic*

The Madame X Series:
*Madame X*
*Exposed*
*Exiled*

Dad Bod Contracting:
*Hammered*
*Drilled*
*Nailed*
*Screwed*

Fifty States of Love:
*Pregnant in Pennsylvania*
*Cowboy in Colorado*
*Married in Michigan*

Goode Girls
*For a Goode Time Call...*
*Not So Goode*
*Goode to Be Bad*

Standalone titles:
*Yours*

Non-Fiction titles:
*You Can Do It*
*You Can Do It: Strength*
*You Can Do It: Fasting*

Jack Wilder Titles:
*The Missionary*

JJ Wilder Titles:
*Ark*

To be informed of new releases, special offers, and other Jasinda news, sign up for Jasinda's email newsletter.